Producer & International Distributor
eBookPro Publishing
www.ebook-pro.com

CHECK POINT
Maor Kohn
Copyright © 2024 Maor Kohn

All rights reserved; No parts of this book may be reproduced or transmitted in any form or by any means, electronic or mechanical, including photocopying, recording, taping, or by any information retrieval system, without the permission, in writing, of the author.

Translation: Leeor Doron
Editing: Adi Kafri

Contact: maor@maorkohn.co.il
Website: maorkohn.co.il

ISBN 9798877262485

CHECK POINT

A Thriller

*This is the third book in the Yael Lavie series.
From Maor Kohn, creator of the Emmy award-winning
thriller series "Tehran"*

MAOR KOHN

PART A

1.

12.2.2015

The village of Al Mawasi, southern Gaza strip

The freezing western wind blowing in from the sea brought a mix of salty mist, dust, and humidity. The stormy weather relentlessly battered the village for two consecutive days, leaving destruction in its wake across the Gaza Strip. Rainwater flooded the streets, waves relentlessly pounded the shores, and the piers, both wooden and concrete, disintegrated them into the sea. Fishing boats in Gaza port occasionally collided with sandbars and rocks around the shallow port, some breaking free from their ropes and drifting into the heart of the artificial bay. Throughout the city, trees were uprooted by the fierce winds, falling onto old cars that desperately needed maintenance. Power cords were ripped from the poles, hanging down to the ground, plunging some neighborhoods into darkness for days. The rural areas fared even worse, with deep sinkholes forming in the unpaved dirt roads and cracked pavement, filling with water and posing risks to pedestrians, vehicles, and travel wagons pulled by donkeys. The heavy rainfall turned the streets into raging rivers, flooding houses and stores, and sewage water and trash rose from pipes and drainage ditches, infiltrating the lower floors of buildings and leaving behind stench and filth. As always, the Gaza Strip appeared wretched, dreary, and devastated—an overlooked region without a promising future, a forgotten past, or a stable present.

Externally, the citizens pointed fingers at anyone they could blame for their miserable lives, feeling abandoned by the world and left to fend for themselves. However, deep down, the Palestinian Arabs living in Gaza understood that their tragic situation was a result of the isolating and violent dictatorial rule of the terrorist organization Hamas, which seized control of the strip in 2007. This move isolated them from their kin in Judea and Samaria, plunged them into poverty, and made them entirely reliant on the countries they vehemently despised. In their despair, the Gazans found themselves caught in a vicious cycle of conflict and siege, bound within the narratives they constructed for themselves, amid the fences and concrete walls enclosing their cities, and the mounting unemployment, hunger, and misery, living under the shadow of constant missile barrages launched by Hamas from amidst their own houses towards Israeli cities. This dangerous situation inevitably led to counter-bombings that claimed many lives. The glorification of death, known as the '*Shahadah*,' was never so glorious as it was experienced by the residents of the Gaza Strip since Hamas conquered it. But during the storm, Gaza seemed even more desolate and grim. The dark, heavy rain clouds gathered from the sea, moving northward in a menacing arc, threatening to drown everything in their path, washing away all the filth into the sea. As darkness enveloped the village, stone, tin, and wooden houses disappeared from view, leaving a sense of hopelessness in the air.

***

Malak Hamdan was just 17 when she married her husband, Yazid. He was a reserved and introverted man, who ran a small clothing store on Um Allymoun Street in the heart of Gaza city. With that modest business, he barely provided for Malak and their only son, Khalil. Malak shared her husband's liberal and secular beliefs, but she concealed them beneath the hijab she wore every day. Since childhood, she had dreamt of studying biology at university and had hoped to convince Yazid to leave Gaza before their son was born. However, Yazid was hesitant to abandon his family, especially his aging parents, and relocate to Egypt or Hungary, as Malak desired. He'd promised her a better future once they saved enough money, but as the years passed, little to nothing changed. It wasn't until Hamas took control of the strip that their circumstances were truly affected. Now, twelve years later, they continued living in the same poignant shack, in the same rundown village, their dreams and finances remaining stagnant. Despite the hardship, Malak considered herself fortunate when it came to her friends and neighbors. Her father, Aziz Shafiki, held a prominent position in the Hamas organization and led the '*Murabitat*,' Hamas's civil army, responsible for maintaining order and enforcing laws in the strip. Adequately, he had many connections and status, many feared him, and consequently, many feared her and treated her with respect. Shafiki liked his son-in-law Yazid, and in secret, her father also supported the couple, ensuring she and Yazid were not harassed by the authorities or their opponent, assuring that all their needs were met. He kept a close eye on their well-being. This support allowed the Hamdan family to create a quiet and stable haven of their own, at least since their son, Khalil, was born.

However, Malak could not shake the feeling of failure and loss, sensing she was wasting away her life. These thoughts came creeping back every moment, no matter where she was. Whenever she passed Al-Azhar University in Gaza or heard about scientific breakthroughs around the world, her heart ached with the awareness of missed opportunities. At 29 years old, Malak recognized that her dreams were slipping further away, and so was left to resign herself to a life confined within the self-imposed prison of her circumstances. The burden of household chores weighed heavily on her, leaving her feeling disgusted with herself and the men in her life. Sometimes, she entertained thoughts of escaping to a faraway European country, starting afresh under a new identity. But when her son, Khalil, would run into her arms and hug her bravely, her heart would shatter, and she would start crying uncontrollably, knowing she would not be able to take him with her on this journey, to disappear without being chased down and without being able to protect him.

***

The winds howled and relentlessly battered the window shutters of the small, weather-beaten shack, as Malak pulled out the clothes pile from the old laundry machine in the patio. Above her, a lone light bulb swayed under the plastic canopy, dancing in the ferocious gusts. Malak looked for a dry distant place where she could handle the laundry without getting wet from the rain or tossed on the floor from the strong wind blows. She cast another distracted glance at the ruins of the building that stood at the edge of their backyard, a building that was bombed by the Israelis in the last round of fighting a few months ago. A small family once lived there—a couple and their two daughters—tragically lost to the impact of a missile. In the building with them, five members of the Islamic Jihad squad were hiding. A missile launcher they had planted in the family's shared backyard had unleashed five missiles toward the Israeli city of Ashkelon just mere minutes before the counterattack. Malak, her husband Yazid, and their son Khalil, had not been present at the time. They were staying with distant relatives in Judea and Samaria. However, when she saw the news report that evening, Malak recognized their home, pleading with Yazid never to return to Gaza. She longed to shield Khalil from the grim realities of war and the relentless tragedies engulfing their community. One of the little girls that was killed was in Khalil's class in school. **How could he cope with such grief at such a tender age?** This question haunted her persistently. Yet, her pleas fell on deaf ears. Yazid firmly believed in the righteousness of the Palestinian struggle and refused to witness his people's submission to Israel or the world. To him, their resilience was a testament to their existence and a refusal to be relegated to mere footnotes in the history pages. Yazid Hamdan was a man of unwavering ideology and unyielding principles. While not a devout Muslim, he possessed immense pride in his Palestinian heritage. Never conscripted by Hamas, he nevertheless saw himself as a silent warrior, contributing to the resistance merely by remaining in Gaza.

Amidst the remnants of the bombarded building, a place not

yet renovated or claimed by another family, Khalil discovered a new playground. Clad in a camouflage uniform, with a gallabiyah wrapped around his head, he wielded a weapon he fashioned with his father from sticks and plastic remnants, imagining himself on the edge of their plot, a brave soldier in his make-believe battlefield. Malak detested this game, but in her despair, while lamenting her own fate, she looked away and let her kid do as he pleased. In the past, when Khalil was in the first grade, she devoted hours to educate him, and he thrived under her guidance. He learned to read and write ahead of his peers, solving mathematical riddles with ease. However, since the bombing, Malak's introversion took hold and she gave up. Her despair had immense power over her, and she felt she could not cope alone. She did house chores as was expected of her and wasted the rest of her day.

As she hung yet another pants and shirt on the rope, her gaze returned to the ruins of the building. How long had it been since she last heard Khalil's voice carried away by the whistling wind between those shattered walls? Was it minutes or perhaps ten? Lost in her reverie, she'd failed to notice his absence until now. She attempted to calm herself, telling herself that the boy must be pretending to ambush an imaginary enemy or silently creeping closer to her, but a sense of unease crept over her and she couldn't quite grasp its source. Glancing at her watch, a gift from her father upon her engagement to Yazid, she saw that it was nearly 6 PM. Her eyes strained to pierce the darkness, but the swinging lightbulb above cast shifting shadows, obscuring her view and preventing her from seeing further into the darkness.

She pulled a black dress from the pile, shook it, and spread it facing the wind as she called out into the night, "Khalil!" But no reply echoed back. "Khalil, where are you? I want you to come home. The rain is about to start," she implored, securing the black dress with clothespins on the line.

Silence.

"Khalil!" she shouted again toward the ruined building, her hands resting on her waist. The wind's whistle intensified, and the rain began to batter the canopy.

She stepped into the muddy yard, scanning the surroundings, but Khalil was nowhere to be seen. "Khalil!" she cried out once more, knowing deep down there would be no answer. She stood there for a moment listening to the wind, drenched by raindrops, then she turned back to the house and fetched a coat for her and her son, an umbrella, and a metal pocket torch found among the rubble, likely belonging to one of the fighters who had hidden there.With the torch illuminating her path, she ventured back into the rain, cautiously making her way toward the ruins. "Khalil!" she called again, barely hearing her own voice over the raging elements. Lightning tore through the sky, followed by a loud thunder.

Crossing a stone fence and avoiding a puddle that accumulated in the gaping pit formed by the explosion, she climbed the crumbling cement walls that remained. "Khalil? Where are you?" Her voice grew more desperate with each cry for her son. Her mind wandered off, trying to recall whether he had mentioned going elsewhere, to visit a nearby friend. She couldn't remember him saying so. A sudden sound from her right made her point the torch in that direction, only to discover it was the wooden door flapping in the wind against the cement. She descended to the lower part of the ruined building, where the iron skeleton stood exposed. There, bound by fabric ropes to the massive iron poles, unconscious and wounded in the head, she found him.

Khalil lay there, still clad in his camouflage uniform, his head tilted back, and his eyes tightly shut. Bound by fabric ropes that extended to his side, blood trickled from his head, mixing with the rain's relentless downpour. Malak, consumed by worry for her son, failed to notice the storm raging around her. Thunder roared above, lightning streaked across the sky, but she was oblivious to it all as she leaned toward her injured son Khalil. "Khalil!" she cried out, gently slapping his cheeks in an attempt to rouse him. But the child remained unconscious, his eyes refusing to open. She pressed her ear to his mouth, attempting to feel his breath amidst the commotion, but the rain drowned out any sound.

Determined to free him from the rubble, she began untying the fabric ropes, her mind racing for a solution to pull him out of the rubble and carry him back to their home by herself. She berated herself for her hastiness in leaving the house without her phone, now unable to call her husband for help. Khalil, an eight-year-old boy with a sturdy frame, was too heavy for her to carry on her own, weighing nearly 30 kilos. Suddenly, from the corner of her eye, she spotted a swift movement, darting behind the walls into the darkness. Clutching the torch again, she searched the area but found nothing. "Who is it? Who's out there?" she called out in desperation, her voice pleading for assistance, but no response came.

Her torch's beam scanned frantically in all directions, yet wherever the torch beamed, all she saw were the remnants of the house and mud. The rain obscured her vision, making it difficult to discern anything. She draped her coat over Khalil to shield him as she continued untying him. **Who could have done this?** Was it a game gone awry? Another movement caught her eye, a tall figure eluding her once more. This time she glimpsed the silhouette of a man, and as she illuminated him with her torch, he fled behind a nearby wall. She heard cement bricks collapsing as someone hopped on them. "Who is it?" she cried. "Help me!" Her gut told her this was bad news, and she knew that whoever was out there would not offer help. Her fate, and perhaps her son's fate too, felt sealed. She brandished the torch and an iron pole she had found, scanning for any potential threats.

This time, the beam of light landed on a man standing in front of her. However, before she could illuminate his face, the man swiftly turned and disappeared behind a nearby retaining wall. She continued to shine the light everywhere, in every direction, cursing herself for feeling desperate and fearful, which had momentarily paralyzed her. She turned the beam of light and the iron rod in all directions—a wall, a broken door, a ruined bath, Khalil... *Boom!*

In an instant, a heavy blow struck her head, sending her collapsing onto Khalil's body. Her left eye stopped seeing, and she flailed her hands blindly at the space that gaped in front of her, attempting to strike with the iron pole, unsure if she still held it. Her right eye searched for danger as she tried to rise, leaning against the adjacent wall. Her body trembled, breathing rapid and shallow, mouth filling with saliva and rainwater. Intense pain radiated from her head, coursing through her neck and body. She tried to call for help, but her lips remained mute.

Amid the blur, a veiled face appeared before her, she moved her head back to focus on the eyes watching her, but rainwater blurred her vision, and she could not move her hands, hindering her from wiping it away. "No," she whispered, "Please, no." The figure drew nearer, their breath brushing against her face. "Please, let the child live," she begged. Suddenly, a sharp, agonizing stab pierced the back of her neck, as if a fractured bone tore through her flesh. Darkness engulfed her, enveloping everything, carrying her desperate thoughts far away from that place, to somewhere else completely.

2.

At 6:18 PM, an old Ford vehicle parked in front of Yazid and Malak Hamdan's house. Yazid lingered in the car for a few moments, gazing at the gloomy street where faint lights glimmered from the wretched houses. In the distance, he noticed the lights of another car driving away, disappearing behind a sand hill as it merged with the traffic on Gaza's main streets. He wondered about the person braving the terrible weather to venture into town, possibly one of his neighbors. Hoping the rain might subside, he waited a bit longer but eventually gave up, locking his vehicle and hastening toward his house.

Upon reaching the front door, Yazid found it locked. As he inserted his key and tried to turn it, he felt another key jammed from the other side, preventing the door from opening. Knocking on the door, he felt the rain drenching his clothes, seeping into his pants, and chilling his skin. There was no response from inside. He wondered where Malak and Khalil were in this weather. The rain relentlessly battered the walls, adding to the tumult outside. He knocked again, but still, no one answered. Taking out his phone, covering it from the rain, contemplating whether to retreat to his car, he called Malak, listening as the phone rang from the other side of the door.

"Malak," he called out again, knocking fervently. "Khalil!" But there was no reply.

He decided to check around the house. Jumping over the low stone fence bordering the property, he entered the backyard, half-running as he almost slipped on the wet ground. There, under the canopy, he saw the red tub half-filled with wet laundry, and some clothes hung on the rope. The door leading from the patio to the living room was ajar. Yazid entered the house, pondering what might have happened. Where could they have disappeared to? Moving through the house, he checked each room. The shower room was steaming, water vapors clouding the mirror. The laundry machine's door was open, and it still radiated warmth. A deafening thunder reverberated through the entire house. Once more, he called out, "Malak?" but it became evident that his wife and son were not present. Why had Malak left the house open and her phone in the living room? Yazid pulled out his phone and began calling several parents and neighbors, friends of Khalil and Malak. Then he dialed his parents and finally, Aziz Shafiki, his father-in-law, who happened to be in a meeting. Shafiki asked purposefully, "Is this urgent?"

In three concise sentences, Yazid conveyed the situation to Shafiki. In response, Shafiki advised, "Go to the backyard, check around the house. Perhaps something happened. Maybe Khalil slipped and got hurt in the rain, and Malak is with him. Let me know in a few minutes if you find them. If not, I will come over, and we will search together." Yazid ended the call, donned his coat, and searched for the torch Malak had found in the rubble after the bombing. Regrettably, he couldn't locate it anywhere in the house. Abandoning the search, he grabbed an umbrella and ventured out into the relentless rain.

***

It had been nearly four agonizing hours since Malak disappeared. Yazid Hamdan's small house was now filled with men, young and eager, some wearing uniforms, following the commands of their leader, Aziz Shafiki. In the modest kitchen, Shafiki stood, one hand embracing Yazid while waving his other hand and throwing commands to the men in the room. The living room bore muddy footprints and small puddles. As time passed, it became apparent that this was a serious crisis. The men tirelessly knocked on every door in the neighborhood, gathering volunteers armed with torches and coats, scouring the area for any sign of the missing mother and son. But the relentless rain and powerful winds made the search incredibly challenging.

Initially, they surmised that Malak and Khalil might have sought refuge in one of the town's ruins, perhaps falling into a pit or losing their way. However, as the hours stretched on, there was still no sign of them. The house was abandoned at once, leaving it unlocked and open. Deep inside, Yazid knew that something terrible had happened, and Shafiki tried his best to offer solace, but it proved futile.

Hours ticked by with no news. Yazid scoured the entire vicinity again and again: climbing the ruins of the bombarded house, searching for any clues, but the rain had washed away any evidence that might have been left behind. Nevertheless, the ruins seemed like the most likely place to find some trace. If Malak had gone to town, she would have finished hanging the laundry, would have locked the house and took her phone with her. She could not have gone too far. A few minutes after midnight, as the storm eased, he asked two of Shafiki's soldiers to join him looking for clues in the bombarded house again. All three men sunk in the mud and fell once or twice into a deep pit filled with water. They eventually made it to the ruin. One soldier approached from the east, the other from the west, while Yazid climbed the broken walls, casting his torch's light in all directions. No signs of a struggle, bloodstains, or discarded clothing were visible in the darkness. Determined, Yazid squeezed his way between two cement beams, aware of the danger. The rain's weakening grip on the structure could cause it to collapse and entrap him. Nonetheless, he slid down to the pit where their construction had created a cavity, sinking into the water accumulation up to his knees. He made an effort to tread carefully, yet his steps kept slipping, his legs started bleeding.

Then, a voice rang out in the distance, one of the soldiers exclaiming, "I found him; he is here!"

"Where?" Yazid cried out, pulling his legs from the water.

"Behind the only standing wall. He is tied to the iron skeletal house frame," the soldier called back.

Yazid hurried toward the cement beam, but in his haste, he slipped and fell on his shoulder blade. An iron pole, narrow and long, embedded in the cement, dug into his back, and he screamed in pain. Only a few seconds later, the second soldier arrived and assisted Yazid by placing his arm under his back and pulling, removing the iron pole from his flesh, causing him so much pain he thought he was about faint at any moment. Amidst the pain, Yazid asked anxiously, "Where is he? Where is Khalil?"

With the soldier's support, he moved slowly toward the only standing cement wall. There, on the iron frame, he saw the second soldier untying a series of ropes around his son binding him to the exposed poles. "Is he okay?" Yazid asked, kneeling down. "Is he alive?"

"He is breathing, and he has a pulse," the soldier responded. "But we don't have much time." The second soldier had already called for Shafiki and the ambulance and rescue team. They carefully untied Khalil, who remained unconscious and freezing. His lips were blue, but he was alive. The soldier removed a black women's coat that had covered him—Malak's coat—and replaced it with a thick, wide, dry one. Yazid crawled towards his son and embraced him, trying to warm him up, and said, "Malak was here. That's her coat. We need to find her. Something might have happened to her."

"After we get you away from here," one of the soldiers assured, "I promise we will find her."

***

For three long days, Aziz Shafiki's soldiers tirelessly searched for his daughter, Malak Hamdan, but their efforts yielded no results. The relentless rain had washed away any traces that could have provided clues to her whereabouts. No one saw a thing, and no one had recognized her since, despite Hamas's TV channel, Al-Aqsa, broadcasting non-stop reports about her disappearance, along with her photos. Malak seemed to have vanished into thin air. Meanwhile, Yazid remained at his injured son's side in Shifa hospital, on Ibn Sina Street. Only on the evening of the third day did the eight-year-old finally open his eyes and begin to utter incomprehensible words. The trauma had left him in shock, recoiling from any touch, even from his own father and grandfather. Doctors tirelessly fought for his life throughout the night until they finally stabilized him. Yazid also had undergone a complicated surgery, suffering from broken blades and chest bones, along with several bruises.

Shafiki attempted to speak with the boy to understand what had transpired on that fateful night. He had all possible resources at his disposal, but they were useless. Neither Khalil nor anyone else knew where Malak had disappeared to. Khalil could not remember anything. After an hour and a half of trying, the grandfather nodded to the doctor standing in the corner. It was time to sedate the boy again, allowing him to rest and regain strength. The doctor rose, took a syringe from the trolley, and approached Khalil's bed, with the boy now holding onto his father's hand. But as the child turned to look at the doctor, he became frightened by the sight of the syringe and started screaming in horror. Both men attempted to calm him, but he continued to call out for his mother, trembling and sweating with fear. There was no other choice. Yazid held his son's face, trying to soothe him, while Shafiki took his hand and presented it to the doctor. The doctor found a vein near his wrist and inserted the needle. A few moments later, the room fell silent as Khalil drifted to sleep, his breathing growing faint, blending into the sound of the monitoring machines beeping rhythmically in the room.

3.
17.2.2015

The settlement of Eli, Judea and Samaria, Israel.

'Shirat Hanna' school stood proudly as one of the two `Torah study` for girls' schools in the picturesque settlement of Eli, nestled on the southern hillside of the Binyamin mountains. From the classroom windows, the view was enchanting, especially in winter when the region adorned itself with lush flora, occasionally sprinkled with snow patches, creating a European-like ambiance. The school's location, just off the 60 highway, made it easily accessible for girls from nearby villages who eagerly came to study there. Eli, as a whole, provided a range of amenities to the surrounding settlements, including healthcare, education, religious centers, youth movements, and even industrial facilities.

The school boasted small class sizes, with no more than 20 students in each class, engaging in a curriculum that blended orthodox biblical education with core subjects like Torah, history, math, and geography. Modesty was a hallmark of the girls' school uniform, featuring black dresses over white shirts and cotton stockings. Their attire covered their skin up to their necks, and their hair was neatly braided. Each age group had its own class, spanning from first grade to eighth grade, making it a close-knit, unassuming institution.

As the school day concluded, the bell rang at precisely 1:30 PM, and the classroom doors swung open in perfect harmony, releasing the girls into the schoolyard. They hurriedly made their way to the school gate, where parents awaited in their cars parked in the designated safety bay. Within moments, the school emptied, leaving the teachers to retire to the teacher's room for post-day discussions, report writing, and preparation for the next day's lessons. To an outsider, it might have been challenging to distinguish the girls from one another, as they all seemed to be cut from the same cloth, almost identical in appearance save for variations in hair color and height. However, this didn't prevent the girls from quickly getting into the pick-up vehicles and a few of them boarding the shuttle vehicle parked in its designated bay, all under the supervision of their assigned teacher. But among them was one girl, no more than a meter tall, with darkish skin and warm brown eyes, who stood alone in the safety bay, waiting anxiously for her mother.

As the minutes ticked by, her worry intensified, and she paced back and forth, scanning the winding Wadi road in the hopes of spotting her mother's vehicle. Unfortunately, no sign of her mother's arrival presented itself. With the safety bay now empty, even the transportation van having had departed, she was left feeling utterly alone and abandoned. Despondently, she turned back towards the school, seeking assistance. The schoolyard was deserted, and classrooms locked, and only the echoing sounds of Arab cleaners busy tidying up the hallways and dining room filled the air.

Suddenly, a woman's voice with a thick Arabic accent called out to her from behind; "What is your name?" Startled, she turned to find a mature, heavyset woman clad in a pale blue robe and a kerchief adorning her head, holding a squeegee in one hand.

"Tzofia," replied the little girl in a squeaky desperate voice.

"Where is your mother?" asked the cleaner, drawing closer to the girl. Feeling uneasy, Tzofia, a third-grader, stepped back and slipped on a puddle of water left by the cleaners, causing her to fall to the floor. The Arab cleaner quickly rushed to her aid, lifting her back onto her feet and helping her shoulder her heavy bag full of books.

"Where is your mother?" she asked again. Tzofia felt the horror spreading throughout her body. She was always warned to stay away from the Arab cleaners. Much like in every settlement in Judea and Samaria, the fear of contact between Arabs and Jews was felt in Eli too. "Someone can kidnap you," her mother would tell her. "Always keep a lookout. If anyone of them comes near you, make sure you are not alone and that there is an adult Jew around." Alerts about child abductions were news normal in Eli. And here she was, Tzofia, finding herself picked up by an Arab.

"I don't know," said the little girl.

"Did she not come to pick you up?"

"No, I did not see her," Tzofia replied, her voice quivering with fear.

The Arab cleaner looked around, but there was no one in the hallway. She knew that in a few moments, the school would be empty of all teachers and staff, and only her friends – the Arab cleaners – would be the only ones left behind. She grabbed the little girl's hand with determination. "Come! Quick! Before they leave," she ordered, and the two quickly walked to the teacher's room in the adjacent building.

***

The phone rang multipole times, yet it was left unanswered. Fifteen rings, time and again, until the voicemail claimed the unanswered calls. Tzofia sat with the Talmud study coordinator in the teacher's room and waited. The school systems had shut down for the day, and even the executive office was locked tight, leaving the coordinator at a loss as to who else to reach out to.

"Tell me, sweetie," the coordinator gently inquired, "what is your mother's name?"

"Dvora," the little girl replied in a hushed voice.

"And her surname?"

"Goshen."

"Where do you live?"

"In Levona."

"Ma'ale Levona?"

"I believe so."

It took several anxious minutes before the coordinator managed to obtain Dvora's phone number. However, the lack of response from her mother raised alarm bells within her heart. The principal was called back to the school, urgently unlocking the computer to retrieve the father's and family's details. Her family and the authorities were informed, along with the police and the army. In the Jewish settlements of Judea and Samaria, such a disappearance triggered a full-scale security response, akin to an abduction alert, until the missing person was located. And so, this was how the matter was handled.

Dvora Goshen had vanished without a trace, along with her phone and her handbag. Attempts to locate her phone proved futile; someone had switched it off and discarded the battery. The army was called in, and as the hours ticked by, desperation grew. The father arrived to collect his daughter, but the situation had escalated, drawing IBP (Israeli border police) and reserve duty units into the search, scouring the vast expanse between Ma'ale Levona and Eli, yet finding no sign of the missing woman.

As word spread through the local community, a group of men who were residents of the area decided to gather at the family's house. They aimed to comb the terrain, retracing Dvora's steps from her departure point to the school, hoping for any lead. At 7 AM, the woman had set off for work, planning to return by 1 PM, take her car and pick up her daughter from school, a routine followed every day. But her car remained parked near the house, and she was nowhere to be found. The search persisted through the day and well into the evening until, at 9:20 PM, when darkness enshrouded the land and the cold chilled the searchers to their bones, a report came in from a Palestinian farmer toiling amidst his olive orchard in the village of Sawia. A woman's lifeless body had been discovered, discarded amid the trees. Time stood still for a moment, the weight of the news settling heavily upon everyone present. Then, like a rushing storm, they hastened to the scene, tearing through the countryside with the colossal tires of their military jeeps, all while a haunting question lingered in their minds: Could the deceased woman be Dvora Goshen?

***

Chief Superintendent Uri Amit had just celebrated his 51st birthday. Six years ago, when he assumed command of the tumultuous Judea and Samaria district within the blue police force, little did he foresee that he would remain in this demanding position for so long. His age and status brought swift promotions and commanding roles, yet Uri Amit had sensed that this district would mark the culmination of his professional journey, leading him to an early retirement from the police force.

The Judea and Samaria district proved to be the most intricate and perplexing of all police territories. Countless enforcement agencies, including the military, ISA (Israel Security Agency), IBP, and regular blue police, shared authority within the area, often stepping on each other's toes in the process. Historical decisions and a convoluted geopolitical landscape, with a divided sovereignty between Israel and Palestine, added to the complexity. Numerous organizations, both local and international, like the UN, EU, and NGO's, closely monitored the district, rendering jurisdictional boundaries unclear and causing many incidents of terror and crime to fall through the cracks.

Uri Amit tirelessly endeavored to resolve the myriad challenges that arose, primarily for the sake of the hundred thousand Jews who resided in the numerous settlements across Judea and Samaria. Yet, he found himself frequently entangled in clashes with other enforcement agencies instead of solely battling criminal organizations.

Nevertheless, it was not the disapproval of his superiors that kept Uri Amit in his post; on the contrary, he excelled in his role. Through the building of strong relationships with senior members of the Palestinian enforcement agencies, Amit possessed an intimate knowledge of the region and its diverse Arab and Jewish inhabitants. His affable demeanor earned him respect and admiration from all corners. Years prior, the leaders of the settlements had accepted him, granting him access to valuable intelligence information and acknowledging his unparalleled experience. Under his guidance, numerous life-saving operations were carried out, terrorist attacks were prevented, and he managed to quell the simmering tensions in this volatile region. The complicated district was a constant battleground, a simmering cauldron of tensions between Jews and Arabs, Israelis and Palestinians, human rights groups and settler leaders. It was as if a spark was ever ready to ignite the turbulent atmosphere, plunging the region into chaos. Everyone seemed infused with an unwavering battle spirit, steadfastly convinced that their way was the right one. And amidst this fiery conflict, Uri Amit's task was not only to carry out his myriad responsibilities but also to neutralize the very elements that could ignite a full-blown war, preventing needless bloodshed and ensuring that peace prevailed.

But as soon as he arrived at the crime scene, Amit sensed that this murder would ignite a firestorm. The crime scene would quickly be declared a terror attack, leaving little time for a thorough investigation. The military and ISA would plunge into an intense manhunt for the killer, sparing no effort until he was found. And in the meantime, what would unfold? Most likely, the area would become a focal point for riots, with rocks hurled and violence erupting between the Jewish settlers and the Palestinians. Amit knew that tough days lay ahead. He had already warned the officers under his command to brace for the worst. But now, together with a police investigator of the assassination cases, he arrived at the scene to examine the findings and send the body for examination at the Institute of Forensic Medicine in Abu Kabir, Tel Aviv.

From the first moment of standing at the crime scene Amit felt a growing unease. It was evident to him that this was no ordinary case; it demanded profound contemplation, especially regarding the motive behind the murder. No, Amit didn't believe it was a simple nationalistic motive at play here. The killer had gone to great lengths, positioning the body in an impossible manner that must have required significant time and risk of exposure. He approached the body, standing about 30 meters away, when one of the officers approached him and spoke, "This is Dvora Goshen, the woman who disappeared this afternoon."

"Are you sure?" Amit inquired.

"We'll need the family to come and identify her officially, but her face matches the photo in her ID."

"Did you manage to salvage any evidence before the military stormed the scene?"

"Nothing. Everything was destroyed. But they left the body untouched, leaving us to handle the mess."

Amit nodded, lightly patting the officer's back, and then proceeded towards the body. As he approached, an investigator from the IBP approached him, talking to him in such passion as if they had been converting for a while.

"A Palestinian farmer found her and alerted the Palestinian authority. We received the report, contacted the military, and rushed here. We scoured the surroundings for evidence, interrogated the farmer and his family, and even searched for any signs of a vehicle that may have entered the orchard. But we found nothing. No one saw or heard a suspicious vehicle, no one noticed any strange activity in the area. The killer moved through the orchard like a shadow, leaving the body as you see it."

They were now just a few meters from the body, which was seated, leaning against the trunk of an olive tree in its shade. The ground was muddy and heavy, clinging to the soles of their shoes, and the woman, fully clothed, appeared as if she had merely sought a moment's respite, leaning against the tree to rest. "The farmer said he thought she was sleeping until he approached to wake her up."

"Where is he now?" Amit inquired.

"Under investigation at the station, but I don't think he has anything to do with it. I'm almost certain he's telling the truth. He didn't kill her."

"We'll look into it," Amit assured him, then knelt down beside the body. Everything seemed strangely natural, except for one detail that gnawed at him, defying rational explanation: Dvora Goshen's legs were buried up to her knees in the muddy ground. Amit had never seen anything like it, and he wondered why the killer would invest so much time and effort to dig and conceal only her legs in this terrain, while it would have been easier to leave her as she was or bury her entirely to ensure she was never found.

***

Three officers painstakingly dug Dvora Goshen's legs out of the muddy earth. Fear lingered in the air, as they dreaded the possibility of the killer having attached a bomb to her legs that might hurt the officers. Chief Superintendent Uri Amit called upon the canine unit to detect any traces of explosives. However, the relentless rain washed away any scent, rendering the effort futile.

Gradually, her legs were revealed, yet they showed no signs of physical abuse. They seemed unharmed, like the rest of her body. As they carefully cleared away the sand and laid it aside for mapping next to the body, they noticed her left foot bare of any shoe, and her footwear was nowhere in sight. With cautious hands, one of the officers gently tugged and freed her from the clinging mud. Only her right leg remained buried.

The atmosphere weighed heavily on everyone at the crime scene. The rain had stopped, yet the cold gusts of wind intensified. Amit knelt down, his fingers delicately uncovering millimeter after millimeter. Then, his hand encountered something peculiar—a thin string tied around Dvora's ankle. Though at first, he thought it might be a simple bracelet, he quickly discerned that this was a plain string, stretching deeper into the ground, attached to something concealed beneath the earth's surface.

Amit contemplated tugging the string, fearing it might activate an underground bomb, a mine, or even a grenade safety latch. He was expecting the worst. Gathering everyone at a safe distance, Amit tied the string to his shoelace and retreated behind a protective rock. Only after making sure everyone was safe, did he pull the string lightly.

Nothing happened. Amit pulled again, with more force, but still, there was no explosion. Finally, mustering all his bravery, he approached the pit and began digging with his bare hands, uncovering Dvora Goshen's legs entirely. The ambulance team arrived, and they transported the woman's body to the Institute of Forensic Medicine.

Amit knew the mission was far from over. With two other officers, he continued digging, finding the ground easier to penetrate as they went deeper, trying to figure out what was tied on the other side of the string. Centimeter by centimeter, the strange string was unveiled, but what they encountered on the other end was beyond anyone's expectations. At a depth of 80 centimeters, they found the string connected to another woman's wrist.

***

Throughout the long and harrowing night, the relentless digging continued until, around 5 AM, the second body emerged from the ground. It lay in a state of decomposition, barefoot and completely naked besides her undergarments, curled up in a fetal position, with no clues to who she was. Her skin got darker and was covered with purple bruises, parts of her flesh decomposed and absorbed into the earth. The forensic unit worked diligently, but the evidence revealed one stark truth that night—the location of the women's burial was not the place of their murder. No traces of blood or struggle were found at the scene, suggesting that this was merely a random spot where the killer had chosen to discard the bodies. Canines and small bulldozers were dispatched to scour the area for potential graves, but by 11 AM, their search had yielded no further discoveries.

At 7:30 AM, a swarm of reporters descended upon the scene, now surrounded by fences and yellow-red tape. They clamored for information—details about the victims, potential sexual assault, the motive, and any leads on the elusive murderer. Chief Superintendent Uri Amit, standing alone amidst the relentless barrage of questions, pondered whether the murder scene or the reporters were more difficult to handle. Exhaustion weighed heavily on him after the long, cold night at the crime scene. His hands and uniform were caked in filth, and all he longed for was a cup of hot coffee and a few hours of rest. Uri Amit was no longer young.

Finally, when the reporters realized that the investigation was still in its infancy and none of their questions would be answered yet, they reluctantly allowed him some respite. At 8:05 AM, however, a group of protesters arrived, and the media had now placed its focal point there. After hearing the news that morning, the Israelis came there expressing their shock and frustration at the perceived helplessness of the security services. How could two women be murdered under their very noses? Calls for justice and vengeance rang out from all sides. The general officer of the central command and the minister of defense soon arrived at the scene to assess the situation and display their commitment to the investigation.

In the midst of this exhausting day, Uri Amit sought brief solace in his car while waiting for the ambulance to transport the unnamed woman's body to the Institute of Forensic Medicine. Upon hearing the arrival of the central command's vehicle, Amit emerged from his car, washed his face with freezing water from his canteen, and braced himself for the demanding day ahead.

"Amit, you look terrible," said the general officer of the central command, Aharon Shaked.

"Thank you, Commander," Amit responded, his weariness palpable as he stole a glance at the vehicle's side mirror.

"I'm sending you a company of reserve duties to secure the place in case of any disorderly conduct," Shaked said with determination. The two men shook hands firmly and exchanged a brief hug.

"I'm leaving in five minutes, run the scene as you see fit," Amit stated, his hand offering a reassuring pat on Shaked's back. Although Shaked, at 48, was younger and a higher-ranking military officer, he had never displayed arrogance towards Amit. Their friendship had only grown stronger over the years, bolstered by mutual appreciation and trust. As Shaked peered into Amit's bleary eyes, a silent question hung in the air. He wondered if he should challenge Amit's decision. But Amit understood the unspoken concern and promptly clarified, "I need to go to Abu Kabir. This is going to be a long day. You take care of this."

Agreeing with a nod, Shaked called his deputy to join him as the ambulance finally arrived. Covered in military canvas, the body was carefully lifted and carried away, even as the distant cries of protesters reverberated through the scene. Shaked approached the reporters with purpose, assuring them that the army would spare no effort to bring the murderers to justice; "Even if it takes a few days, we will not rest until we find them." Their words laced with clichéd promises. Once the media spectacle concluded, Shaked retraced his steps towards the commanding vehicle.

Unexpectedly, a rock suddenly soared through the air and struck Shaked's jeep. Without hesitation, he halted, raised his hand, and issued swift orders to his soldiers to regain control of the area. The scene was soon evacuated, and soldiers pursued protesters who scattered in every direction. From a distance, Amit observed the scene unfold, a faint smile curling on his lips.

Minutes later, seated in his car making his way back to the police station, Amit's thoughts were consumed by the enigmatic mystery of the woman found tied to Dvora Goshen.

***

"This woman has been dead for at least a week," Superintendent Yael Lavie informed her commander, Chief Superintendent Uri Amit, as she entered his office at 3:30 PM. "We received the first autopsy report from the pathological institute. I asked them to prioritize identifying the second body before proceeding with Dvora Goshen's case."

"Why?" questioned Amit.

"Because we have an unidentified woman. Someone has been sitting at home for many days now, unaware of what happened to his wife, the mother of his children. I believe this should be our first priority."

"Have there been any missing persons cases reported in the past week?"

"We haven't received any new missing persons reports. I checked all the country's districts, including Judea and Samaria, and the Palestinian authority. No one has reported a missing woman from a week ago or even in the last few months. There are no open investigations about missing women her age. It's as if she fell from the sky."

"Has any terrorist group claimed responsibility for the murder?" asked Amit.

"No group has taken responsibility."

"I can't recall anything like this in all my years working for the police."

"What are your instructions?" Yael asked, taking a seat in front of him with an open notebook and a pen. "Shall we issue a formal press release with her photo?"

"Have you tried running the face scanner on the computer?"

"I tried, but I couldn't find her. She doesn't resemble anyone in the system. Her face was also badly swollen, and her eyes... not much remained of them. I believe the photo is distorted, making it difficult for the algorithm to recognize her easily. I suggest we fix her up a bit and then send the photo."

"I assume it will be hard publishing a photo of her face in this state."

"We can digitally enhance the photo, making it as similar as possible to the victim's original face. However, we both know this restoration may be problematic."

"Very well. Proceed with it. I'll send a formal message to the spokesperson, and we'll release the photo so she can appear in the news tonight."

"Done," Yael replied, rising from her chair. She took a few steps toward the door, then paused, turned around, and looked at Amit. "You know that whoever murdered them wanted us to find the bodies, don't you?"

"Yes," Amit straightened his back.

"So why do you think he bothered tying them together? Why did he hide only Dvora's legs in the mud, but completely bury the woman who was murdered first?"

"I have no clue," admitted Amit. "What do you think?"

"I believe our killer is seeking attention. He orchestrated an artistic performance and wants the entire world to know of its existence. There might be other reasons, too."

"Perhaps it's the psychological state of the killer, seeking vengeance..."

"And maybe something else," added Yael.

"What?"

"Consider this—he didn't rape or violently attack them. The forensic lab has not yet determined the final cause of death yet. He buried them gently and tied a string between them. The first woman was buried a week ago, indicating that he didn't want her to be discovered yet. The second woman was left exposed so that we could find her, and the string connecting them was tied so that we would find the first woman, too, preventing her from being lost. But this grotesque connection between them appears so over the top that I can only think of one thing he might be trying to achieve."

"Which is?"

"He wants our attention to lead us in the opposite direction of his actual plan."

***

At 8 PM, every news broadcast led with the grim news of Dvora Goshen's murder and the discovery of the nameless woman. The processed image of the unidentified woman was published on all major news sites. The general officer appeared on two TV channels, vowing to bring the detestable killers to justice, and the police commissioner also sought the public's help in identifying the second woman.

Late that evening, at 11:04 PM, the minister of defense received a call in his office at the Kirya army base in Tel Aviv. On the other end of the line was the head of Egyptian intelligence.

"A week ago, a young woman named Malak Hamdan disappeared from Al-Mawasi town in Gaza," he explained in broken English. "Her son was found tied and unconscious. They've been searching for her ever since. The picture you published today—the husband claims that the woman you found bears a striking resemblance to Hamdan, and he wants to come and identify her."

The minister of defense glanced at Aharon Shaked, who stood before him. Shaked shook his head in disagreement, prompting the minister to cover the phone's mouthpiece with his hand. "This could be seen as a humanitarian gesture. It has significant international advantages," he suggested.

Since Hamas took control of Gaza in 2007, the connection between Israel and the strip had become severely disrupted. Gaza was declared an enemy, borders closed, and a state of war declared, restricting any movement in or out of Gaza without Israeli or Egyptian supervision. This measure aimed to prevent weapons and ammunition from reaching Hamas and subsequently being used in terrorist attacks or warfare. Even the Palestinian Authority of Judea and Samaria lost contact with Gaza. Despite the severed ties, communication with Gaza was occasionally facilitated by surrounding Arab countries, first and foremost Egypt, which acted as a mediator between Gaza and Israel. These requests from Egypt did not fall on deaf ears, as Israel understood the crucial role of Egypt as a mediator in negotiating with Hamas, which could potentially postpone the next armed confrontation. However, permitting people from Gaza to enter Israel was one gesture too much, especially in light of Dvora Goshen's murder. The minister of defense knew he would pay a heavy political price for this action.

"This woman is related to the heads of Hamas. She is the daughter of Aziz Shafiki," revealed the Egyptian.

The revelation raised a few eyebrows in the room. "This could be an opportunity. Ask them for something in return," Shaked whispered to the minister of defense. "If he inquires what we need, tell him we need to evaluate the situation first."

The minister of defense removed his hand from the phone's mouthpiece and responded, "Let me get back to you in a few hours."

"Thank you," said the Egyptian before hanging up.

At 5:06 AM, for the first time in several months, the Erez border, which separated the Gaza Strip and Israel, opened. A Palestinian man crossed the border on foot and entered a waiting military vehicle on the Israeli side. At 7:00 AM, Yazid Hamdan positively identified his wife, Malak Hamdan, at the Institute of Forensic Medicine in Tel Aviv. At that moment, the Israeli-Palestinian space underwent another profound shift, again.

4.
21.2.2015

*Judea and Samaria police district,
Judea and Samaria, Israel.*

"I spoke to Aharon Shaked. He asked how you are and wanted me to tell you how much he appreciates you," Chief Superintendent Uri Amit said as he placed the red phone back on its base. Yael Lavie returned to his office, holding a stack of binders in her hand.

She sat in front of him, opened the top binder, and said, "Thank you."

"You two have known each other for many years, haven't you?"

"Shaked was the commander of the territorial brigade when I served in the IUBP (Investigating Units of the Border Police) Lavi. We met then, and in a way, he adopted me. He supported my decision to study while in the army and appointed me as deputy unit commander and main interrogator. Yes, we share a lot of history, and he even knows my parents," Yael replied.

"So, I suppose you will need to turn your anger towards him."

"Anger? What do I have to be angry about?"

"Shaked demanded that I appoint you as the person in charge of the investigation in the Dvora Goshen and Malak Hamdan cases." Yael withdrew her hand from the binder and leaned back in her chair, biting her nails as she looked directly into Amit's eyes.

"Uri…"

"I know," Amit interjected before she could finish her sentence. "We talked about it..."

"Yael, I don't usually pass the responsibility around, but these commands came from above," Amit explained.

"Please tell him—"

"I don't intend to tell him anything."

"Why, if I may ask?"

"Because we both know he is right. It is time for you to get back to business. You are a senior investigator in the police, superintendent, not a sergeant taking her first steps. You have responsibilities; you have people under your command. This is a complicated case, and we need coordination with the Palestinians. We need you," Amit insisted.

"I don't think I can—"

"It will do you good," he interrupted her, and she fell silent. "Trust me, it will do you good."

Yael knew her commander well. He wouldn't back down. He would push her, and if necessary, he would order her to carry out her tasks against her will. She faced a dilemma: whether to leave the police or take on the case as Shaked wanted. These two men, Amit and Shaked, whom she had known for many years and considered an anchor, a source of sanity, and in a way, father figures, were now her exit door from the police or her path back to life, to routine. Amit had joined the Judea and Samaria district in 2009, a year after Yael had joined the unit. She arrived there with extensive experience as the deputy commander of the IUBP Lavi, a senior investigator in the IBP, and an Israeli General Defense Service employee. Not many people in the Israeli defense force possessed as much knowledge, experience, and connections within the complex zone of the Palestinian authorities. Yael was fluent in the local dialect, intimately familiar with the area's history, its people, inner conflicts within Palestinian society, tribes, headquarters, social classes, leaders, customs, and dynamics. She had skills that other investigators did not possess and was often an expert consultant for all defense groups when it came to creating tactics and building strategies for handling the embroiled zone of Judea and Samaria.

If she had continued on her predestined path, she would likely have replaced Chief Superintendent Uri Amit long ago and become the commander of the Judea and Samaria district. She desired the position, and he wanted to pass the command to her, so he could rise in the ranks. Neither of them had imagined that one morning in 2011, their lives would change forever, and all their dreams would shatter simultaneously in the face of harsh reality.

***

In 1999, Yael Lavie found herself embroiled in one of the most complex cases of her career. A string of criminal murders had sent shockwaves through the residents of the regional council in the north of the Dead Sea. After a painstaking investigation, Yael successfully apprehended Naif Badir, one of Israel's most dangerous criminals, involved in robberies, murder, and violent blackmails since his youth. He had been sentenced to life in prison, but in 2011, a prisoner exchange deal between Israel and the terrorist organization Hamas, led to Badir's release after serving only twelve years. Unbeknownst at the time, Badir had become further entangled with The Islamic Movement and Hamas during his incarceration, becoming an activist and nationalist.

Shortly after his release, Naif Badir carried out a terrorist attack in a mall in Natanya. Tragically, five Israelis lost their lives, and eleven others were injured before Badir was shot and killed by a security guard. Among the victims was Gidi Lavie, Yael's husband, who had been at the mall with their 9-year-old daughter, Keren. Shielding his daughter with his own body, Gidi was shot multiple times, and one of the bullets pierced Keren's young body, missing her heart by a bit. The girl, who had lost a significant amount of blood, came close to death on her way to the hospital. Despite the efforts to save her, they were in vain. She underwent multiple blood transfusions, but her body rejected them, causing her condition to deteriorate further. The doctors fighting for her life were perplexed, unable to comprehend why her body kept rejecting the transfusions.

At first glance, everything had appeared to be in order. Everyone followed the protocols accordingly. Yael felt helpless as she stood in the hospital's hallway, watching doctors coming in and out of her daughter's room with worried expressions. She kept herself occupied with funeral arrangements and comforting her six-year-old son, Ilan, who had just lost his father.

Ilan learned of it through the news. Answering numerous phone calls and a multitude of messages served as her means of diverting attention from the unfolding tragedy before her eyes: her daughter slowly slipping away into death.

Yael's worst fears were confirmed as the end drew near for Keren. She was aware that she would become both a widow and a grieving mother in an instant. She requested to enter the room, to bid farewell to her daughter, to plant one last kiss on her forehead, and to apologize for not doing everything in her power to save her. One of the nurses approached her, donning sterile clothes and washing her hands. Yael trembled, her feet rooted to the floor, rendering her unable to move. She broke down, collapsing under the weight of her emotions, crying aloud. There was no one around to offer comfort or a warm embrace. She lay crumpled on the hospital floor, and all she desired was death, to go with her daughter, to take her daughter's place. Yet, she knew she couldn't do that; she had to be there for Ilan. She desired to see Keren one last time, but could not. She was clutched with fear. After finally calming herself, she mustered the strength to stand up and entered the room.

Keren lay on her bed, appearing small and fragile. Life seemed to have drained from her, leaving her in a weakened state. Five empty infusion bags rested on a tin cart beside the bed. The monitor displayed weak signs of life as her heart grew weaker with each beat. In a moment, it would all be over. Yael mustered her strength and caressed Keren's hand, which was cold and dry. She put her hand down and caressed her forehead. "I love you," she whispered in her ear, saying goodbye. The room went quite as her eyes closed, and then a miracle unfolded.

"Bombay blood!" one of the doctors exclaimed as he rushed into the operating room. "She has Bombay blood; that's why her body rejected the IV."

"What?" yelled the other doctor.

"Bombay blood. We thought she had blood type O because we did not find antigens of A or B, but there is another blood type—Oh, also called Bombay blood. It's very similar to type O, but it's another kind, very rare and special. We cannot give her a blood transfusion, not even a type O one. We are lucky the transfusions we gave her did not kill her."

"So, what do you do in this state?" she asked, trying to retrieve her breath, praying for a miracle.

"We need a donor with the same blood type. I asked a plea to the blood bank to see if they have something that might help. It will probably take a few minutes before they reply." The doctor hurriedly left the room to pursue the urgent matter.

Kneeling above Keren's ear, Yael whispered, "I need you to fight for me, hold on just a little longer, just a few more minutes, we will save you." Though weak, Keren's breath tickled Yael's ear, it was very faint, but she knew her daughter was still holding on.

Tears streamed down Yael's face as she thought of Gidi, her husband. She needed him by her side. Her heart ached for him, but she pushed her grief aside, focusing solely on her daughter's life, as if nothing else around her existed. She had entrusted the arrangements for Gidi's funeral to his parents and left her son, Ilan, with her own parents.

Half an hour later, redemption came when the blood bank informed the hospital that they had one transfusion with Bombay blood. This rare blood portion belonged to Nitin Sharma, a foreign worker from India who came to Israel in 2003, and worked as a nurse to the elderly. Sharma contacted the authorities and asked to donate some of his unique blood—Bombay blood. He didn't do it out of the goodness of his heart or a desire to help others. He had donated it for his own potential need for a transfusion in case of an accident that would require him to get a blood transfusion. He did so in every country he moved to. Sharma had left Israel over a year and a half ago, leaving his blood portion behind.

As the precious pint of Sharma's blood made its way to the hospital and was infused into Keren's body, hope surged within Yael. It was the only transfusion of Bombay blood in Israel, and the doctors prayed that this sole supply would be enough to stabilize her daughter's frail condition, and so it was. Thankfully, the prayers were answered, and Keren regained consciousness in the early hours of the morning, just three hours before her father's funeral.

But even though she survived, Keren was forever changed by the tragedy. Consumed by grief, she withdrew from the world, seeking solace in computer games and severing ties with her friends. She created a bubble of loneliness and sadness around her.

The family was shattered by the loss of Gidi, and Yael struggled to hold herself together as she navigated in heaviness and blurriness between the funeral, the seven days of mourning—a Jewish tradition, and trying to return to some semblance of normalcy. Everything had collapsed around her. Her whole life. The sense of loss and lack of control was accompanied by feelings of failure and heavy guilt. She was the one who saved Badir's life, sending him to prison, preventing his assassination. And now, reality knocked on her door. She lost her ambition, her desire to succeed, to fight. She focused primarily on her role as a mother, but even there, she felt like a burning and ongoing failure.

Gidi's death tore the family apart. Yael's father, Yoram Nachmani, renowned as a professor of Middle Eastern studies at Bar Ilan University, filed for a divorce from her mother. He had raised both Yael and her brother Shai with an extensive knowledge and understanding of the complex processes in the Arab world, particularly the Palestinian nation, which was his expertise. But he detested the rising culture of violence and bloodshed. His heart longed to leave Israel and settle in the United States or Canada. Like many Israelis, he felt alienated as the radical opinions escalated, the intifadas, and constant military operations that became the daily life for the Palestinian-Israeli residents of the area.

Yoram remained due to his wife's pleas, and the fact that his children and grandchildren lived in Israel. However, after the brutal murder of Gidi and Keren's severe injury, he boarded a plane and left Israel, never to return. The divorce papers arrived in the mail from Ohio, and Dina, Yael's mother, received them from a local lawyer.

Dina, now left alone, sought solace and support in her daughter's home in Ariel. She became a second mother to Yael's children, offering love and care in the absence of their father. Half a year later, when she felt ready, Dina returned to her own house. Meanwhile, Yael knew she couldn't bear living in a house filled with memories of Gidi. She made a courageous decision to buy a new home next to her mother's place, seeking a fresh start and leaving the painful past behind.

However, even after four years, the weight of the tragedy was still palpable. Yael battled exhaustion, finding it hard to sleep at night, often plagued by anxiety attacks. Her career as an investigator had taken a backseat since the last case she took was when Gidi was still alive. Now, she preferred consulting and served as a deputy investigator. She still struggled to maintain focus, her dwindling self-confidence constantly gnawing at her.

***

"It will do you good," Chief Superintendent Uri Amit said as he got up from his chair. "I request, or rather demand, that you take the case and lead the investigation. I need you, and you need this. It's an opportunity for you to regain control, seize your passions, and take charge of your life and career. It's been many years, and it will never be enough. But you must move forward."

"Every cliché possible," Yael Lavie said while avoiding making eye contact. Amit's secretary entered the office, but Yael stayed sitting.

"Once you're back in the investigation routine, it'll pull you in. You will be back in a familiar and suitable environment for you. You're an expert in this field, the best we have. It can bring contentment back into your life. Seize this opportunity with both hands."

"Give me a day or two to think about it?"

"I want an answer this evening. Otherwise, I'll have to consider reassigning you to administrative work in another police district. I need investigators who are motivated, driven and want to succeed. We have people beyond the border seeking answers for their most devastating losses. I can't keep you here as a consultant. I need active investigators and officers. Pull yourself together."

She wanted to say something back, but everything was already said. Yael knew. **He was right**; Shaked had even discussed it with her. "Fine," she eventually said and got up from her chair "I'll try to give it my all. But if I can't dedicate one-hundred-percent of myself to it, I ask you to let me go."

"At this stage, even ninety percent would be enough—just get to work," Amit responded, gesturing toward the office door with his chin. He had urgent matters to attend to and couldn't continue with the motivational talk. He needed committed investigators, not wavering consultants. Only time would reveal the outcome of Yael's decision. This was her last chance, and they both knew it.

***

As Dina served the food, Ilan's usual energy was palpable, and Keren seemed engrossed in her phone. **Who is she talking to all day long?** Yael wondered. "I need to tell you something important," Yael began. Ilan's leg continued to fidget in agitation, and his curious squeaky 10-year-old voice chimed in.

"I've decided to return to a full-time job in the police. I feel like I need it, I owe it to myself," Yael shared, looking at Keren. She hoped the 14-year-old girl's response would lighten the weight on her mind.

"I'm happy to hear that," Dina said, taking a seat at the table.

"Keren?" Asked Yael.

"Mom, does this mean we are moving back to Ariel?" Asked Ilan.

"No. Keren? I need you to tell me what you think."

With an apparent indifference, Keren seemed to relish the momentary attention, but remained absorbed in her phone. Yael gently placed her hand on the screen and pulled it back to get her daughter's attention. Keren did not object. "It's important to me to know how you feel about it, whether you're okay with it," Yael said, nearly whispering.

"I don't really care," Keren responded, looking into Dina's eyes. "As I see it, since Dad died, I lost my mother, too."

5.
22.2.2015

Professor Yosef Arieli had been the manager of the Institute of Forensic Medicine in Abu Kabir, Tel Aviv, since 2012. A man of 61 years, he was lean and tall, adorned with a short white beard and multifocal glasses. Draped in a white robe, he moved slowly and heavily, bearing the air of someone carrying the weight of the entire world upon his shoulders. But perhaps it was the nature of his work that led to his peculiar gestures and behavior. He had a habit of tugging at his nose while speaking, often swallowing his words and constructing sentences with odd grammar. His coffee was always extra sweetened—three teaspoons of sugar—and he delighted in reading old Russian literature and indulging in French films. Professor Arieli led a solitary life, without any family ties, and his interactions with the bereaved were characterized by slight nods and a delicate hum. Nevertheless, his genius in forensic research was unparalleled, and his name was synonymous with many articles and breakthroughs in deciphering complex murder cases, earning him immense respect in the world of pathology.

Yael Lavie deposited her weapon and police ID, then proceeded to sign the guestbook before venturing inside the pathological institute. Professor Arieli was leaned over his desk made of tin and Formica, and meticulously filled out an autopsy report. It had been many years since Yael had set foot in this death-filled realm. The atmosphere was suffused with the powerful scent of disinfectant mingled with an underlying stench that even the air purifiers struggled to eliminate. As she stepped in, Yael could not help but wonder if this was the place she truly wished to be at that moment, yet the answer eluded her. Still, leaving was out of the question since Professor Arieli had already put the forms away and cast a glance her way, accompanied by a subtle nod of his head.

"Good to see you," he greeted, though the gravity of the situation weighed heavily on them both.

"Hello, Professor. I'm grateful for a familiar face," Yael responded.

"Come, let's head to the operation room, and I'll show you what I discovered during the autopsies," he said, gesturing her to follow. No offer of refreshments or seating was extended. Yael trailed him through the grey hallways with linoleum floors, passing refrigeration rooms and equipment storerooms. A few hospital attendants and representatives from the 'Kadisha' company, responsible for victim burials, crossed her path along the way. Upon reaching the third entrance to their right, the professor pushed the wooden door with his leg, inviting her into the room. Yael had been in this somber space countless times before, and the procedures were etched in her memory. She washed her hands, donned a pale blue paper robe and gloves, and placed a mask on her face. An ointment with a strong mint scent was applied to her nostrils to counter the pervasive smell of death. Once fully prepared, they entered the operation room, where two separate stretchers made of aluminum cradled the bodies of the victims, covered by white sheets. Professor Arieli pulled back the sheets, revealing the naked bodies that had undergone thorough examination and were now stitched up with thick black thread.

"These are two young women," the professor informed her without delay. "Malak Hamdan, 29 years old, and Dvora Goshen, 30. Their ages may hold significance in the killer's selection process." Yael jotted down notes in her small notepad, which she retrieved from her pocket. "Both women were in good health at the time of their deaths, showing no signs of sexual assault, illness, disability, or medication. They were not pregnant."

"And the cause of death?" Yael inquired.

"There is a strong likelihood that both died from strangulation, possibly with a robust rope used to constrict their necks."

"The cause of death isn't definitive, Professor Arieli?"

"Not yet. Malak Hamdan displays indications of severe head trauma at the base of her skull. I cannot determine with absolute confidence if this was the fatal blow or merely rendered her unconscious. It appears she didn't struggle against her attacker, given the absence of finger marks from attempted removal of the rope. However, as you can see here," Arieli pointed to a faint purple mark encircling Hamdan's neck, "there are signs of strangulation. I believe she was unconscious when strangled. As for Dvora Goshen, it's equally challenging to determine. Rope marks are evident around her neck and fingers, but it's inconclusive whether it caused her demise."

"What else could have killed her?" Yael probed.

"I don't know. The rope used to strangle them has not been found, making it difficult to speculate if it was the murder weapon."

"But they found them tied together with a rope; didn't they provide you with the rope?"

"No, and it's not the first time evidence has gone missing at a crime scene in the Judea and Samaria district. This is what occurs when irresponsible organizations handle crime scenes. The army, the ISA, and the IBP—none of them know how to collect, preserve, and file evidence correctly. Someone likely discarded the rope inadvertently, leaving it behind," Professor Arieli lamented. He then covered the two bodies once more in white sheets, instructing an attendant to take them to the refrigeration room. "I suggest you attempt to locate the rope. It could hold the key to identifying the killer."

Yael nodded thoughtfully and stated, "Besides their age, did you discover any other similarities between the two women?"

"Nothing. I examined everything I could. You'll find all my findings in the report. Perhaps you'll discern a connection between them."

"Thank you," Yael replied, heading towards the door. She removed her gloves and mask before proceeding to wash her hands.

"The only thing that strikes me as peculiar," Arieli mused aloud from behind her, seemingly talking to himself, "is that Malak Hamdan was likely in Gaza when she was murdered."

"I'm listening," Yael responded. "What does that signify to us?"

"To me, it's of no personal consequence, merely a professional curiosity. I was just wondering how her body wound up on the ground in an olive orchard in Judea and Samaria without anyone noticing at the Erez border crossing."

***

The olive orchard in the village of Sawia bore the marks of turmoil as if tanks had wreaked havoc on its once tranquil landscape. The furrows deepened under the weight of army jeeps, leaving some trees uprooted and leaning on their sides. The rage of the protesters had inflicted significant damage. Scattered trash lay around, remnants left behind by soldiers, Jewish settlers, and finally, the Palestinians from nearby villages, each group protesting against the threats they faced.

Parking the police car on the main road, Yael ventured into the forsaken orchard, sifting through the refuse piles in search of any overlooked evidence, particularly the rope that had bound the hands of the victims. **Did the killer intend to convey a nationalistic message, uniting Israeli and Palestinian hands in eternal connection? And if so, why murder them? To shock? To make the message clear? Or was the message a darker one, signifying that as long as their hands remained tied together, war and bloodshed would persist?** Numerous questions swirled in her mind. Did the rope, the most likely murder weapon, hold the clue she had been looking for?

The olive orchard covered several acres, and Yael attempted to follow the tracks of the ambulance that had transported the bodies. Perhaps the rope fell from one of the victim's hands while they were moving the bodies? Focusing on the heart of the crime scene, she methodically combed the area, meticulously turning clods of earth with her foot in expanding circles. The afternoon was waning, and the winter sun began its descent. Despite the encroaching darkness, she pressed on, unwavering in her search. Then, her phone rang, displaying Uri Amit's name on the screen. She answered the call.

"Where are you?" Amit inquired.

"I'm in the Sawia orchard."

"Are you alone?"

"Yes."

"Why?"

"Uri…"

"This is the last time you go to a crime scene alone. You know why."

"I'm armed."

"Yael!"

"Is there something you need?"

"I need you to get back to the station immediately."

"Has something happened?"

"We'll discuss it when you arrive. What were you doing there anyway?"

"Looking for the string you lost."

"What string?"

"The string that bound the victims together. It's gone." Suddenly, an explosion and shouts erupted from the road where she had parked her car. Adrenaline surged through her body as she drew her gun. "I need to go."

"Yael…" but she had already ended the call, moving swiftly along the detour to the source of the commotion. She stayed low, avoiding being seen from behind while maintaining vigilance over the area. As she pressed on, she discovered she was walking amidst the coulisse of a large truck—the ambulance. **Another path led to the crime scene.** With cautious steps, she kept her gaze fixed on her car in the distance. And there it was—a white string stained with blood, resting on a rock. Another explosion sounded from the road. She knelt, rolled up her sleeve, and secured the string in her pocket. Then she sprang to her feet, running toward her car, its silhouette still visible on the road. Leaping, she covered the ground, sometimes falling to the muddy earth, her eyes scanning the surroundings. She leaped again and reached her car, hugging its side. She circled it, keeping low and her gun drawn, ready for action. She was now standing by the trunk of the car gazing in all directions. **Where had the explosion come from?** She crouched by the driver's door, scouring the vicinity for any sign of danger. Then, she saw it—the front windshield shattered, and two large rocks occupied the driver and passenger seats.

6.

"He is 50 years old, a former major general in the Palestinian authority, who chose to remain in Gaza after it was conquered by Hamas. Presently, he holds a senior position in the security organizations there, maintaining a neutral stance in his political views, loyal to the government and a crime investigator. Although he is not aligned with Hamas, he works as an investigator for crimes in Gaza," Uri Amit read from the intelligence report supplied by the ISA. He cast a glance at Yael, who stood in the corner of the room by the locked door with her arms crossed. He felt furious with her, deeming her decision to venture alone into the crime scene in the midst of a hostile Palestinian village and amidst angry Israeli settlers as an unwise move, to say the least. This did not fit with Yael's character. His level of worry increased, and he questioned whether it was wise to assign her the investigation. He could not bear the weight of a guilty conscience if her children were orphaned due to her actions. He sought to assign someone to partner with her, someone who would keep a watchful eye on her. Until then, he insisted that she not take any action without his approval. Unfortunately, the damage had already been done, and after her car was attacked, Amit had to dispatch several police cars to rescue her and her vehicle. But the phone call he received from Shaked a few hours ago troubled him even more, leaving him unsure whether to be relieved or not. It seemed that this day was rife with bad news.

"I think this is a really bad idea."

Amit chose to ignore her, continuing to read the report. "He is a loner, residing alone in a small apartment in a respectable neighborhood at the heart of Gaza. He is regarded as a decent and upright individual. He had previously served in the joint patrols of Israelis and Palestinians in the West Bank after the Oslo Accords, and had personal connections with Israeli officers. He is considered trustworthy."

"And what do you think?"

"In any case, I believe we should talk to him. For now, it's only a phone call."

"Fine," she conceded. "I'll be in my office, waiting for your message." She opened the door and exited the room. Ten minutes earlier, when she had entered, she had no inkling of the dramatic news Amit would relay to her. After the identification of Malak Hamdan by her husband Yazid, the Egyptians contacted the Minister of Defense once more. The head of Egyptian intelligence conveyed a direct message from Hamas, the terrorist organization. They expressed their willingness to cooperate with Israelis in apprehending Malak's killer. Aziz Shafiki himself was open to discussing the matter with individuals in the Israeli defense system. Following a brief assessment at the Kirya army base in Tel Aviv, Israel decided to consider this offer. Collaborating with Hamas could, at least temporarily, help quell the violence between Gaza and Israel. The Minister of Defense agreed on the condition that the entire operation remained covert. Should any details leak, Israel would deny any involvement and immediately sever all ties. Israel could not risk exposing collaboration with an organization they publicly and internationally condemned, and imposed sanctions and a siege on. The message reached Hamas, and they accepted the conditions, designating General Ibrahim Azberga as their investigator and intermediary. The details were confidentially shared with Aharon Shaked and Uri Amit. Only four individuals from the Israeli side were privy to this information.

"No one else knows about this connection except for me, you, Shaked, and the Minister of Defense," Amit stressed before Yael closed the door behind her. "We must keep it that way."

Yael gave a thumbs up in approval before shutting the door.

***

Major General Ibrahim Azberga was far different from what Yael had imagined. Handsome and well-groomed, with a face characterized by symmetry and smooth skin, he possessed bright eyes, was fluent in Hebrew and English, and held an academic education from the Faculty of Business at the University of the Middle East in Amman, Jordan. Despite his impressive background, he exuded modesty, speaking in a deep baritone voice, almost in a hushed manner. Seated in the conference room were Yael, Amit, and Shaked, their door securely locked as they communicated with Ibrahim through a communication app, complete with pictures and sound. It was past 7 PM, and weariness permeated the room.

"Malak is the daughter of Aziz Shafiki," Ibrahim said. "He is the chief of preventive security for the *Murabitan*. This connection makes the case deeply personal, and Shafiki is demanding swift answers. It is apparent to everyone that this could be a direct threat to the heads of Hamas, and Malak is not the first to suffer."

"Were there more victims?" Yael inquired.

"Malak is the third woman to disappear in Gaza this past month, and the second connected to the leaders of Hamas, later found dead."

"Who were the other two?" Shaked asked, a tinge of relief was heard in his voice. Ibrahim noticed it and seemed to pause for a moment before responding.

"The first woman murdered was the wife of the Hamas spokesperson, Fatima Ashrawi. Fatima had diabetes and was hospitalized at Shifa Hospital, only to vanish from there. Despite extensive searches by soldiers and volunteers, her body was found only two days later on Gaza's beach."

"Were there any specific signs of violence or fingerprints? Was an autopsy conducted?" Yael inquired.

"An autopsy was performed, but the body was in an advanced state of decomposition, rendering it impossible to gather any useful evidence for the investigation. To this day, we remain uncertain of what caused her death, or whether it was indeed a murder. No one saw her leaving the hospital, and there was no CCTV footage of her. She simply disappeared without a trace from her hospital bed."

"You're right," Shaked concurred. "This does seem like an attempt to target Hamas leadership."

"I did not say that," Ibrahim interjected firmly. "I assume that if the killer wanted to target Hamas, they would have killed Hamas soldiers or politicians. Also, there's the fact that Malak was buried in Israel, tied to an Israeli. Furthermore, there is the third woman who disappeared. I believe she is also buried in Israel. That's why we requested your help."

"Who is she? Whom are we talking about?" Amit inquired.

"Anan Saeed. She is 28 years old and disappeared from her home a few days before Malak. We found no body or signs of struggle in her house. Among all of them, Anan worries me the most."

"Why?" Yael asked.

"Anan Saeed is the daughter of Sabri Saeed, a former senior member of Fatah. As you know, Fatah is Hamas's arch-nemesis. If there is even a hint that these murders are related to tensions between the organizations, it could trigger a civil war, and nobody here desires that."

The three Israeli investigators exchanged significant glances. Shaked finally spoke up, "Ibrahim, we have no interest in involving ourselves in the internal wars of terrorist organizations in Gaza. To be frank, as long as you are fighting amongst yourselves..."

"...We leave you guys alone," Ibrahim finished the thought.

"We are merely attempting to comprehend who murdered Dvora Goshen and what connection she and Malak Hamdan had," Shaked continued.

"If a war like this erupts in Gaza, it will quickly escalate to Judea and Samaria," Ibrahim warned. "This is something that should concern you. As the senior investigator appointed by Hamas, my responsibility is to safeguard personal welfare in the Gaza Strip. Internal conflicts could provoke vendettas and acts of revenge. Despite our differing stances, we have a mutual interest."

"I agree," Yael asserted after a moment of silence. "You will continue your investigation from your side, and I will pursue the Israeli side."

"What is your next move?" Ibrahim inquired.

"I intend to uncover how Malak Hamdan's body entered Israel. Whether she was still alive or already deceased, someone had to smuggle her in. If I can identify this person, we may begin piecing together the events in reverse until we get to the killer."

"And once you provide me with a possible name or face, I can help locate them in Gaza," Ibrahim offered.

"And then?" Amit queried.

"When that time comes, we will decide who will apprehend the killer," Ibrahim replied, his voice lowering almost to a whisper again.

"Very well," Shaked concluded. "We will keep you updated."

"Thank you," Ibrahim said before ending the call. Yael rose and stood before the two seated men.

"I don't know how you view this peculiar collaboration, but my gut feeling is that nothing good will come of it," she proclaimed, tossing her words into the air as she left the room. Shaked and Amit exchanged glances but remained silent.

7.
23.2.2015

Erez border crossing, known as the 'Erez checkpoint,' served as the primary border crossing between Gaza and Israel. Situated in the northern part of the Gaza Strip near Kibbutz Erez, it took its name from the kibbutz. This checkpoint bore a rich history, having been established during Israel's early years and used as a land crossing by Palestinians, Israelis, and Egyptians when Gaza was under Egyptian rule. After Israel's conquest of the Gaza Strip during the Six-Day War in 1967, the checkpoint was dismantled, and Israelis could move freely in and out of Gaza. since the 70's, many Palestinians sought work and education in Israel, while Israeli traders transported goods to and from Gaza. However, following the Oslo Accords and the establishment of the Palestinian Authority, the checkpoint once again became a border between Israel and the Palestinian Authority, which governed Gaza. Adjacent industrial areas were abandoned due to escalating terrorist attacks on the factories and checkpoint, resulting in numerous casualties. Subsequently, when Hamas assumed control of the Gaza Strip in 2006, the checkpoint experienced near-closure. Palestinian movement was restricted, and the border primarily served humanitarian aid and supplies for Gaza's citizens. Walls were erected around the strip, and all goods entering Gaza were supervised by the Israelis.

Yael Lavie recognized that if Malak Hamdan had been kidnapped or murdered in Gaza, the perpetrator must have taken her through the Erez checkpoint to bury her in Israel. Thus, Erez checkpoint offered a promising starting point to unravel the events and apprehend the killer. As she was leaving the police station the night before, she arranged a meeting with the checkpoint's manager, Yaakov Mizrachi, scheduled for 9 AM the next morning. Now, as she parked her car in the armored area in the southeast part of the border and approached the headquarters on foot, the strong smell of smoke and fires engulfed her. The pervasive scent bore witness to weeks of mutual firing between the two sides, causing wheat fields and the national park near Nativ Ha'asara and Kibbutz Erez to burn. Ashes had left their black-grey marks, contrasting with the lush green winter landscape. The cold sea wind played with her hair, prompting her to put on a coat and stuff her hands in her pockets as she pushed open the door with her leg.

The border crossing was nearly empty. Yael approached an IBP soldier, showing her police ID and the officer ID she still retained from her army days. The soldier saluted her and said, "He's waiting for you in the office. Follow me."

Yael followed the soldier through a maze of cement armored offices, protected from light weapon and mortar fire. Passing by a shelling-protected shelter, they reached an array of concrete-covered rooms with steel-shaded windows. In one of the rooms sat a man in his 60s, sporting thin hair and a thick mustache that concealed half his face. He was stout and tall, with an egg-shaped head and a hairy body. Extending his thick hand for a handshake, he gestured for her to take a seat on a plastic chair.

"Care for a drink?" he asked, making his way to the small coffee station equipped with an old electric kettle and a few glass jars of black coffee and sugar.

"I would love a cup of tea," replied Yael, following him. "I'll prepare one for myself." He boiled the water and poured it into a glass cup that had seen better days. Then, he made a coffee for himself and sat beside her.

"I need your help in understanding how it was possible to move her through the checkpoint without anyone noticing," Yael began.

"Are you certain she passed through here?" he inquired.

"Are there other ways to get out of Gaza?"

"I suppose if someone was determined enough, they could find a way to cross into Israel without using the checkpoint. However, based on our initial checks, there is no record of a woman named Malak Hamdan crossing the border. But it's plausible they took her through the checkpoint under a false name and entrance certificates."

"What do you mean by 'initial checks?'" asked Yael, placing her mug on the table.

"It takes time to sift through all the data. Around three hundred to four hundred people cross this border daily. Monitoring them closely is challenging because Hamas keeps changing their identities and certificates. A person might pass through multiple times a month under different names, making it difficult for us to keep track."

"How do you prevent terrorists from entering Israel then?"

"We rely heavily on intelligence and face recognition, checking if the certificates were issued by the Israeli Civil Administration, and physically examining everyone who crosses. However, this crossing is not completely sealed, and occasionally problematic individuals manage to slip through."

"Who are the people that pass through here, and why do you allow them to cross when we are at war with them?"

"There are various types of certificates. Some come to Israel for medical treatment or humanitarian reasons. We have truck drivers, merchants, and importers for trade. Then there are those with Israeli families or Israeli Arabs who have relatives in Gaza. We even have students attending universities in Judea and Samaria or East Jerusalem. Eight Gazans have work permits in Israel, seven of whom work for us here at Erez checkpoint. Additionally, over five-hundred-and-fifty Gazan businessmen have daily passes to Israel. These numbers are colossal. The checks are rigorous, but it's still possible to smuggle people through the border inside trucks or goods. There's always a way."

"Malak Hamdan disappeared from her house eleven days ago. If you could provide me with a list of everyone who passed through the checkpoint in the last two weeks, that would be greatly appreciated."

"No problem, but compiling that list will take some time."

"I understand," said Yael, finishing her tea. "Please prioritize it. I want to put an end to this list of victims once and for all."

8.
24.2.2015

The settlement of Einav, Samaria district

Tamar Avnun cherished these moments at the end of each day, where she found herself fully engrossed in caring for her children and preparing the house for the following day. Like every other evening, she skillfully managed her time between showering her two youngest sons, ages four and five, cooking dinner, assisting her 13-year-old son, Eitan, with his homework, tidying and organizing the rooms, and getting the school bags ready. Her eldest daughter, Abigail, who was 17 years old, had grown quite independent. An exceptional student and a true beauty, she possessed an endless drive to succeed. Normally, Abigail would lend a helping hand with her younger siblings, but today she was staying over at a friend's house, and Tamar had to adjust her routine to account for her daughter's absence. The dishes, laundry, and garbage bin emptying were tasks she left for her husband, Avner, who spent this time at the small synagogue in the settlement of Einav, beyond the green line, engaging in prayer and studying the Bible, a pursuit he deeply cherished. Avner was also the son of the settlement's rabbi and was destined to assume the position after his father's retirement.

Tamar Avnun moved around the house with the grace of a queen or the authority of an army commander, issuing commands in all directions. At her job as a food engineer in the industrial area of

Emek Hefer, she was like any other professional, but within the walls of her home, she felt like the conductor of a harmonious orchestra. From a young age, she had dreamed of a large house filled with children. She loved Einav, even though she always felt a sense of danger, particularly when traversing the roads to and from the settlement that passed through hostile Palestinian villages. A dedicated Zionist and settler, she spent most of her youth involved with the religious Zionist stream and the settlement of Judea and Samaria through her active participation in the 'Bnei Akiva' youth movement.

Tamar Avnun was a religious person. Each day, she adorned her head with a colorful kerchief and donned long dresses. Prayer was an essential part of her life, and she instilled Jewish values in her children. She considered herself blessed, a rightful heir to her grandparents who had survived the Holocaust and helped fulfill the prophecies of the Israeli prophets by settling in the Promised Land. At 40 years old, she showed no signs of slowing down in her endeavor to bring more children into the world, despite facing challenging pregnancies that sometimes endangered her life.

Standing in the heart of the house, she could hear the sounds of her boys in the bathtub mingling with the hum of the drying machine and the gentle rain falling on the small plastic canopy above the exit shutter to the backyard. The warmth of the oil fireplace filled the living room. One of her children passed by her naked, having forgotten his pajamas in his room, while another wore a tank top the wrong way around and stumbled over a ball that had been tossed into the middle of the living room. The dinner table bore the aftermath of a chaotic meal, and the sink was overflowing with dishes. Three boys and a girl, Avnun thought with a smile as she knocked on Eitan's door. The kid was busy on his phone, playing computer games, and not noticing it was already after 8 PM. She approached him and gently took the phone from his hands, prompting him to protest as he jumped onto the bed in an attempt to grab his phone back.

"Why didn't you go with your father?" she asked, sending her son to the shower. He resisted for a few more minutes, but eventually surrendered and entered the shower. Tamar took her phone out of her pocket and called Abigail, trying not to be too intrusive. Their relationship was more friendly than traditional mother-daughter, and Abigail would always keep Tamar updated on everything, including her intimate relationships with boys, which began budding this past year. With the current crisis, Abigail sought comfort from her friend on the other side of the settlement.

As darkness fell and the rain intensified, Tamar contemplated calling Abigail to offer her a ride home to keep her from getting wet and cold. **Should she disturb her or not?** Tamar knew she wouldn't feel at ease until she knew Abigail was safe. Eventually, she decided to send her daughter a text message: "Are you ok? Should I come to pick you up?" Putting the phone back in her pocket, Tamar picked up a few discarded clothes from the ground, finished clearing the table, feeling upset she did not ask the boys to do so, and turned off the TV. She checked her phone again after five minutes, but there was still no reply from Abigail.

Sending another message, this time just a question mark, Tamar proceeded with her nightly routine. Her two youngest sons were already in bed, and she sat on the carpet in their shared room, reading to them from a book. Minutes passed by, and Tamar glanced at the Mickey Mouse clock on the wall—it was already 8:30 PM. She got up from the carpet, kissed her boys on their foreheads, turned off the light, and left the room. Taking her phone out once more, she called Abigail, but it went straight to voicemail. **What happened?** she asked herself. Maybe her phone's battery had died. She opened her contact list and found Michal, Abigail's friend. She dialed the number and Michal answered after two rings.

"Michal, this is Tamar, Abigail's mother. I've been trying to reach her for half an hour, and she's not answering me. Could you ask her if she needs a ride home?" The rain continued to pour heavily, it did not appear it would stop anytime soon, and the house's windows rattled from the force of the storm.

"She's not here anymore," said Michal. "She left just before 7 PM. She was supposed to be home a long time ago." The blood faded from Tamar's face—something was definitely wrong. It made no sense that Abigail hadn't made it home from what was supposed to be just a few minutes' walk.

"Are you sure?" Tamar asked, hoping for reassurance.

"Yes," said Michal. "Maybe she slipped in the rain, and something happened to her."

"Thank you," Tamar said, hanging up without saying goodbye. Feeling helpless, she weighed her options. Should she leave the kids alone and search for Abigail in the rain? She tried calling Avner, her husband, but he did not pick up—he must have been praying or in a lesson. She called repeatedly and sent him five text messages, then called Abigail again but reached her voicemail straight away. **Even if something had happened to Abigail, her phone should still be on,** Tamar thought, growing increasingly frustrated with the lack of a solution.

Tamar stepped outside into the darkness, where the streetlights were off despite the houses having electricity. The rain battered everything in its path as she walked around the backyard, the road leading to the house, the parking area, and under the plastic canopy. She briefly considered heading toward Michal's house, but leaving the kids alone in such stormy weather worried her. Out in the darkness, she called out: "Abigail! Abigail!" But there was no reply. A light turned on in her neighbor's window, and the door opened. Her neighbor came out.

"Tamar? What happened?"

"Abigail is missing. She left Michal's house almost two hours ago and never made it home. She's not answering her phone."

"Where's Avner?"

"In the synagogue. His phone is on silent mode."

"Do you want me to keep an eye on your house while you go to the synagogue to get the boys?" Suddenly, Tamar's phone rang, cutting through the rain's noise. She answered the call.

"Avner?"

"Tamar! What happened?"

"Abigail is missing. Something happened to her. I can't go out looking for her because the children are home alone."

"Missing where?" her husband asked.

"Somewhere on the way between our house and Michal's house."

"I'm going out to look for her," he said, and she heard him shouting instructions to his friends before the call ended. Tamar Avnun stood alone in the pouring rain, staring into the darkness, her heart silently praying for Abigail's safety.

**

They split into four pairs, scattering around the settlement, each assigned to a specific zone. They set a meeting point in the synagogue half an hour later. Three other men rushed to the settlement gate to guard it and arm themselves, forming a preparedness squad in case it was a terrorist attack and other residents might be in danger. The settlement's rabbi, Avner's father, had already called the army and summoned search and protection units. In times like these, they couldn't afford to ignore a report of someone disappearing in the settlement. It was better to hope it was a prank than to risk finding out that a terrorist had infiltrated and was on a killing spree.

Three of the squads combed the settlement along the fence, searching for any sign of a break-in. The fourth squad checked the residents' houses to ensure everyone was safe. Concerns mounted, but eventually, all the residents of Einav were located and contacted, except Abigail. The hours passed, and the rain persisted, but there was no trace of Abigail's whereabouts. It was as if she had vanished from the face of the earth.

Tamar Avnun sat in her wet clothes on the living room floor, near the fireplace, staring at her phone, desperate for comforting news that never arrived. Her three children slept in their rooms, oblivious to the unfolding nightmare. Trembling from the cold and fear, she feared the worst and wondered what sin had led to the possibility of losing her firstborn. Thoughts of life without Abigail flooded her mind, and she chided herself for losing hope so quickly. Seeking solace, she approached the holy books cabinet, pulled out a Siddur, and began to pray. However, her thoughts wandered, and she could not concentrate. Finally, she collapsed on the carpet and broke into tears, unable to control her emotions.

At 5 AM, she drifted into a restless sleep on the cold floor. At 6:15 AM, as the sun began to rise and the rain ceased, Avner walked into the living room, his clothes drenched, his hair and beard disheveled. He sat beside her on the carpet, gently lifted her, and held her tightly to his chest.

"We lost her," he said, and they clung to each other, sharing their sorrow. They cried together until they heard a soft noise behind their shoulders. Their son, on the verge of celebrating his Bar Mitzvah that year, stood in the living room, observing them in silence. Tamar gestured for him to come closer, but he turned and fled to his room. Everything was about to change now.

***

Just an hour earlier, a squad of three soldiers had come across a small mound near the field's edges, not far from the surrounding fence. They had passed by the area a few times, but it was only when the rain eased that they noticed something unusual—a silhouette that seemed like a dry tree branch protruding from the ground. They cautiously approached with their weapons at the ready, scanning the space. One of the soldiers illuminated the object with his torch, and the horrifying truth was revealed—it was a human hand emerging from the mud-covered ground, initially camouflaged and difficult to identify. The preparedness squad and the resident's search units were immediately summoned to the scene. Kneeling on the muddy ground, they began to dig, slowly unearthing an amorphous, inhuman figure. The more they excavated, the more the horror intensified. Two deceased young women were buried there, bound together with a white, thick fabric resembling a dirty bandage. One of the bodies had reached an advanced state of decomposition, while the other still appeared to be almost alive. It was the body of Abigail Avnun.

***

At 8:14 AM, Yael Lavie parked her car on the road surrounding the Einav settlement, where military ambulances, police, and army cars were present. Soldiers stood on the other side of the road, savoring steaming coffee. She waved at them and put on waterproof walking shoes, a black raincoat, and a hat from her trunk. Carrying a forensic test kit and a small pocket camera, she approached the murder scene, where the bodies of the two women lay on a stretcher covered in a bright orange tarp. A sense of purpose filled her, knowing she was exactly where she needed to be, utilizing her abilities to the fullest.

Similar to the previous crime scene, chaos reigned, and Yael knew her options were limited. Fingerprint collection seemed futile with the rain having washed away any traces. The muddy ground was marred with footprints and jeep tire tracks. No remnants or evidence left by the killer were found. She focused on the bodies, ensuring she gathered any potential items that might have belonged to the perpetrator and fallen amidst the victims' belongings as he wrapped them in the white fabric. For nearly an hour, she worked alone, watched over by distant soldiers. Photographs were taken, a list of items was compiled, and she meticulously examined the bodies, fingernails, and remaining jewelry. Once she signaled the ambulance team to take the women, Yael returned to her car and drove to the police station.

Abigail Avnun was murdered last night within the protected, fenced settlement, buried by the killer right under the residents' noses without anyone noticing, she pondered. **The time of the crime fell between 7 PM and 8:30 PM. Could she retrieve CCTV footage?** She was doubtful due to the storm blurring the footage, as she gathered from the community's security coordinator. **Furthermore, the settlement was plunged into darkness from 6 PM onward, due to lightning striking the streetlights, complicating the investigation. No vehicles entered or exited the settlement during that time, indicating the killer that kidnapped her outside of the settlements' borders likely approached on foot. The strength required to forcefully**

carry or drag a 17-year-old girl over such a distance suggested the killer was likely a man or more than one killer.

Two unanswered questions plagued Yael. First, **Who was the second victim tied to Abigail Avnun?** Second, **Why did the killer choose to bind the bodies together once again?** The striking similarity between the two murder scenes led Yael to believe that they were dealing with the same killer. A serial killer.

***

At 11:30 AM, Yael sent the footage and details from the crime scene to Ibrahim. Among the materials were close-ups of the second victim's face, despite its advanced decomposition. She also provided images of her clothing, two bracelets, a necklace, a fingerprint retrieved from the victim's body, and a teeth photo for cross-referencing dental records. The bodies were sent to the Institute of Forensic Medicine in Abu Kabir.

By 1:46 PM, Ibrahim responded, confirming the identity of the second victim as the woman who had gone missing in Gaza on 8th February 2015. Anan Saeed, the daughter of a former senior in the Fatah organization, Sabri Saeed.

"We should investigate this case together," he told her, "I ask that you try to get me an entry pass to Israel. Everything would, of course, be done covertly."

Yael forwarded his request to Chief Superintendent Uri Amit and Aharon Shaked, and later that evening, received a direct response from the Israel's Minister of Defense. A temporary entry certificate for Ibrahim Azberga will be issued, allowing him to enter Israel from tomorrow for three days. During this period, he will be under the supervision of Yael and her superiors, prohibited from acting alone or without her permission. He will stay in a secure facility under guard during the night, unarmed, and restricted from freely using his phone.

"I will pick you up at ten AM tomorrow at the Erez border crossing," she told Ibrahim, to which he expressed his gratitude.

However, as Yael returned home that evening, she couldn't shake off her unease. She was about to collaborate with a representative from Hamas, the same organization that one of its members, Naif Badir, claimed her husband's life and nearly took her daughter's as well in a terrorist attack.

9.
25.2.2015
Erez border crossing

At 9:52 AM, Major General Ibrahim Azberga walked into Yaakov Mizrachi's office, the manager of the Erez border crossing. Superintendent Yael Lavie sat on one of the chairs, carefully examining the list of names and ID numbers that Mizrachi had provided earlier. Azberga approached the desk and shook his hand. Despite being aware of Azberga's impending arrival, Mizrachi could not help but feel uneasy. To him, the senior Hamas figure represented an adversary, one who might be using the checkpoint to harm the Israeli home front, the crossing, and indirectly also harm the Palestinians crossing through it. He could not shake the feeling that Azberga was more of a spy than a collaborator in the investigation of the heinous crime scenes. "Who gave him the certificate?" He asked Yael when she presented him with Azberga's entry certificates just half an hour earlier.

Yael responded, "The certificate was issued by the Minister of Defense, the General Officer of the Central Command, and the Commander of Judea and Samaria District in the police." She paused then continued with, "I'm just as concerned as you are, but we are dealing with four bodies of young women and no leads on the investigation."

"Do you trust him?"

"I'm the last person to trust him. But I'll keep an eye on him, and in the evenings he will be detained in the district station. I really hope we will not regret this in the future."

As Azberga entered the room, the tension seemed to ease. He greeted Mizrachi with humility and professionalism, bringing optimism to the small office. He sat on the chair and refused a cup of coffee or water, and immediately turned his attention to the extensive list of Palestinian names that had passed through the Erez checkpoint in the past two months. Many names on the list were similar with different ID numbers. A photo was attached to each name. But the names of the murder victims were not present on the list.

"Even if Saeed crossed the border into Israel, it was probably more than three months ago," said Mizrachi. "But in any case, I don't have this information available, and even if I did, I'm not sure it would have helped you."

"There is no need," Ibrahim stated confidently. He reached into a nylon folder, delicately retrieving a single page printed in Arabic."I did a little research on my side about the three victims." Adjusting his reading glasses, he proceeded to share his findings with the others.

"Malak Hamdan went to visit her family in the village of Ramin, in the north of Samaria, just two days before she met her tragic end. She received a pass and journeyed via a special transfer from the Erez checkpoint to the Qalandiya checkpoint, where her family awaited her arrival. As for Anan Saeed, four months prior to her death, she secretly drove to Birzeit University in Ramallah to explore her academic options. Fearful of being perceived as a runaway from Gaza due to her affiliation with the Fatah organization, she chose to keep her plans hidden, and her husband only learned of her excursion after the fact."

Mizrachi pondered, "So, it could be a family honor killing."

Yael chimed in, "But then why was she buried in Israel, tied to an Israeli?"

After a brief silence, Ibrahim continued, "Fatima Ashrawi, on the other hand, never left Gaza. Her ties to Hamas made it unlikely for her to escape the region. She had no family connections in Judea and Samaria or any reason to be in Israel."

"We are still missing crucial information," Yael remarked.

Ibrahim inquired, "Then what do you suggest?"

"I propose we visit the pathological institute to examine if there are any commonalities in the way all these women were murdered. Perhaps there's evidence pointing to the involvement of more than one killer."

***

Professor Yosef Arieli appeared visibly perturbed. It had been quite some time since he felt so utterly perplexed while attempting to solve a murder case. The results of his autopsy on the women's bodies were far from conclusive, and that is to say the least. The causes of death seemed to fluctuate with little significance. Comparing the two cases of women bound together presented a considerable challenge. It was conceivable that one victim was strangled with a special nylon or iron wire, while the other met her demise through the killer's bare hands. The bodies that remained intact showed no signs of struggle, and the causes of death for the more decomposed bodies remained unclear. In his office, the professor scrutinized the X-rays of two of the victims, and struggled to draw connections.

"The two elements that lead me to believe it's the same killer are the string used to bind the first victims and the fabric wrapped around the other two," the professor remarked, without looking at Yael or Ibrahim. "These particular details give us an insight to the killer's mind and motives. They indicate a significant amount of time and effort invested in the bindings, imbuing the murders with an entirely different meaning. There may be a nationalistic motive at play here. The question remains, what message is the killer attempting to convey?"

"Have you thoroughly examined these pieces of evidence?" Yael inquired.

"Not in depth. The fabric appears to be a type of bandage, but not one typically used in hospitals. As for the string used to bind the women, that's harder to ascertain. It may be a nylon string, possibly resembling fishing wire. Yet, it remains uncertain whether the string was the actual cause of death; the killer could have strangled them with an iron wire," Professor Arieli explained.

"Can you identify the specific wire used?" Ibrahim asked calmly.

"I will certainly do my best. Additionally, I have sent blood samples and tissues to the lab. Hopefully, we'll receive the results soon and determine if poison played a role in their deaths."

"Are there any signs of poisoning?" Yael inquired further.

"None thus far. However, given the differing times and locations of the murders and the uncertainty surrounding the cause of death through strangulation, it's plausible that poison may be the connecting factor linking all these cases together."

***

It was 1:14 PM when Ibrahim and Yael arrived at the scene where the bodies of Anan Saeed and Abigail Avnun were found. This was Yael's second time at the location, and she made a conscious effort to focus on the surroundings rather than the grave itself. Standing in the middle of the field, she looked around, while Ibrahim knelt to examine the findings on the ground.

"One needs an incredible amount of audacity to bury two women, wrapped together, in the middle of an open field during a rainy, stormy night," Yael remarked. "Anan was already buried, so the killer had to locate her burial place, dig through the mud, unearth the decomposed body, then place Abigail's body on top and bind them together."

"Do you comprehend the extremity of this act?"

"That's why I believe there is a message behind it, a message we have yet to decipher."

"How did he manage to bring them all the way here?" Ibrahim glanced around. The houses were quite far away, and he wondered how nobody had noticed him. And what about Abigail? After all, it would require a person of great strength to carry her such a long distance on a stormy and rainy night, even if the storm obscured his movements. "Perhaps he forced them to come here with him?"

"Are you suggesting he took them out of Gaza under threat or with consent, using false identities?" Yael questioned.

"It's a possibility. We'll have to scrutinize the list of names and pictures more thoroughly and see if we find any familiar faces under different identities."

"Add it to our task list," Yael instructed. She then glanced over at their car parked a few hundred meters away on the road. "Five women, three Palestinians from Gaza, two Jewish Israelis, all in their fertile ages, 20-30..."

"Fatima was 33..."

"...None of them were beaten or raped before the murder. It appears they were strangled to death, likely with a nylon or iron wire. Two pairs of women were buried bound together—one Israeli, the other Palestinian. What on earth is this perpetrator trying to convey?"

"I believe he's attempting to mislead us."

"What do you mean?" Yael inquired.

"I mean, there's a possibility this has nothing to do with their nationalities or religion. Our focus on the nationalistic motive might be misguided."

Yael's phone rang, and she took it out to see Chief Superintendent Uri Amit calling.

"I think a crucial clue to this mystery lies at the Erez checkpoint. This man must have crossed it once or twice and brought the women from Gaza with him. If we can figure out how he did it..." Yael contemplated, pressing the 'Accept' button to answer Amit's call.

"Where are you?" Amit asked.

"At the murder scene, looking for evidence," Yael responded.

"I suggest you return to the base promptly. We apprehended a group of young men affiliated with the extremist Jewish right-wing organization 'Shalhevet.' There's a good chance we may solve at least one of the murder cases."

"Which murder are you referring to?" Yael inquired.

"Dvora Goshen's murder."

10.

Samaria's territorial brigade, Horon camp, By Huwara checkpoint

Nablus area

The Samaria's territorial brigade found its home in an idyllic agricultural valley, nestled amid hills and mountains along the 60-highway leading to Nablus. If it were not for the contentious political situation, this picturesque scenery would likely have been a tourist attraction. The area boasted flowing springs, olive trees, streams, terraces flourishing with Mediterranean agriculture, and numerous hidden caves, preserving historical and archaeological secrets from ancient times. During winter, the valley turned lush and green, and in February, the first buds of leaves and flowers emerged on the trees. Silence permeated the region, becoming an integral part of the residents' lives. Occasionally, wisps of smoke from the coal stoves in the nearby Palestinian villages could be seen.

However, this corner of Samaria was a land of controversy, with Jewish Israeli settlements existing alongside Palestinian villages. Stuck together like Siamese twins in an inseparable position. Palestinian villages like Qallil, Rujeib, Awarta, and Izmut neighbored Israeli settlements such as Har Bracha, Mitzpe Yosef, Itamar, and Givat Sne. In the center of it all stood the Samaritan Mountain, Mount Gerizim. A mosaic of people and nations living side by side. Neighbors that were eternal enemies.

As Yael looked around at the scenery, she sensed the gravity of the killer's message in binding the murdered women side by side—a Palestinian next to an Israeli. Driving through the area, she allowed the beauty of the landscape to envelop her, trying to suppress the fact that a representative of Hamas sat by her side, adding to her unease, asking herself whether it was a smart move on her side to roam Judea and Samaria alone with him. Ibrahim, seemingly aware of her thoughts, remained silent throughout the journey, avoiding eye contact.

At 4:15 PM, Yael drove her car to the brigade's gate, passed the checkpoint, and parked in the visitor's lot. After exiting the car, the cold wind hit her face, causing her to zip up her coat. A robust man with a slight belly, wearing IDF fatigues and red army boots, approached her, the colonel rank on his shoulder indicating his seniority. His ginger hair and freckled face made him easily recognizable. His thick lips screamed, "Azberga," in a loud voice, while his right hand held a short M-16 rifle hanging from his shoulder, preventing it from moving.

Yael noticed that Ibrahim was about to exit the car but was interrupted by the man. "Wait inside," he ordered Ibrahim, whose motion was cut off in enmity as he complied and stayed in the car, leaving the door ajar. Yael stood her ground, waiting for him to come closer. She bent and quietly asked Ibrahim, "Do you know him?"

"Yes. Yonatan. We've known each other for many years," Ibrahim replied.

"Then do you know why he asked you to stay in the car?"

"He likes to be in control. He may give us trouble, but eventually, he'll let us go about our job. As per usual with him."

As he approached, Yael took a step forward, but he showed no signs of slowing down, seemingly about to run into her. "The fact that you got an approval from Shaked to come here doesn't mean you can do whatever you want in my brigade," he barked.

"I'm Yael Lavie, superintended—"

"I know who you are, and I know who he is. There is no need to introduce anyone here."

"I don't know you, and I have no intentions of doing whatever I want here."

"I'm Yonatan Uziel. I'm the commander of the territorial brigade. And the fact that you came here unescorted, without the protection of the army, is very rude. Did you even stop to think what might have happened if someone had kidnapped you? We've been on high alert for days now, with the entire territorial brigade dealing with unrest, rampaging, throwing rocks, and detonators. It's an extremely dangerous situation."

"I have a personal guard." She winked at him and nodded with her head towards the car where Ibrahim sat.

Uziel took a step closer, placing his thick hairy hands on his waist. Bending a little, almost whispering in her ear, he said, "I have a feeling you don't fully comprehend where you are and who you are hanging with. I suggest you keep your eyes open, or you might lead us all into a great disaster."

Despite Uziel's towering presence, Yael met his gaze without flinching. She spoke resolutely: "I've been serving in this place since I joined the army in 1993. I know every nook and cranny, every village. I've worked with the Palestinian Authority and police for as long as I can remember. There's no need for you to act like a peacock and preach to me. Every moment we waste here could cost more women their lives."

Silence lingered between them for what seemed like an eternity, and finally, Uziel broke it. "I need Azberga's pass before you take him to my base. Who knows what information he could take from here to Hamas."

Yael felt drained, fully aware that if Uri Amit had accompanied Azberga, none of this ordeal would have unfolded. Yet, the complexities of having a woman alone with a Hamas senior seemed beyond the army's understanding.

"Where are they?" Yael asked. "The group you found."

"They have nothing to do with the murders," replied Uziel.

Yael wanted to tell him: **I will be the one to determine that**, but she knew it would only escalate the situation. Instead, she asked calmly, "Why do you think that?"

"I know them. They are my neighbors, they come from good

families. Just kids who wanted to make some noise. They are not killers."

"Where do you live?" Uziel seemed less tense now. She managed to sway the conversation from an argument about areas of responsibility to cooperation.

"I live in Ofra."

"Listen, Colonel Uziel. I have no intention of interfering in your business. I just want to interrogate them and see if maybe I can get some information. As far as I understand, they belong to the extremist right-wing organization 'Shalhevet,' the hilltop youth that can create lots of chaos. I want to ensure this chaos didn't escalate to something much more sinister."

"You can interrogate them, but I doubt they will give you answers. Especially not if you go into the room with Ibrahim," Uziel responded, gesturing towards Ibrahim, who had stepped out of the car and was walking towards them. When Ibrahim extended his hand for a shake, Uziel refused, displaying clear animosity.

"I see we are no longer friends," Ibrahim remarked, slipping his hand into his pocket.

"You crossed the line. You are now serving the people I fight," Uziel stated firmly, not taking his eyes off Ibrahim.

Ibrahim remained silent, acknowledging the truth in Uziel's words. Yael wondered whether she should intervene or let the two men work out their differences. Finally, Ibrahim spoke with a cracked voice:

"He used to call me 'my neighbor.' We both have family roots in Judea and Samaria. We served together in mutual patrols over the years." Uziel snorted with contempt but maintained his gaze on Ibrahim. "And now?" Ibrahim asked, looking at Uziel expectantly.

"What exactly do you want?" Uziel asked in an accusatory tone. "What are you doing here? Why did they send you? Because you know me, they think that due to our acquaintance, you can do whatever you want here?"

"I assume it crossed their minds, yes! They know I might be serving Hamas now, but I oppose their ways. To tell the truth, I miss working alongside the Israelis. Alongside people like you. I miss this area," Ibrahim replied.

"Bullshit! Spare me your mumbo jumbo, Ibrahim. You could have stayed here after Hamas conquered Gaza. There was no reason for you to move there. You chose a side. You chose war instead of peace and cooperation. Don't expect me—"

"*Peace and cooperation*? What are you talking about, Yonatan? You say all these words about peace, but in reality, how did you help advance the peace between Israelis and Palestinians? True, it was a mistake moving there, but at that time, when the conquest happened, I thought Hamas would bring hope with it. Hope for something new, less corrupt, care for the citizens, democracy. Who thought this is how things were going to unravel? Now let's put it aside. Yael is right. We have a mutual goal here which we need to execute."

Uziel took one intimidating step towards Azberga, making his presence felt. "I want you to know," he said firmly, "that I don't trust a single word that comes out of your mouth. I have no idea why you came and what interrogations you plan to do, but keep this in mind: if I suspect for a moment you are using this situation to collect information about us or to commit hostile activities, I will throw you into administrative detention without hesitation."

"Deal," said Azberga, extending his arm for a handshake once more, but Uziel left it unanswered. "Now can you tell us who the guys in the group are and why they were detained?"

***

"We are dealing with three teenagers aged fifteen to sixteen from the 'Shalhevet' organization," Colonel Uziel explained, leading them towards one of the pavilions on the base. The structure was made of cement, its walls painted in white plaster. The windows were barred, and the area was surrounded by an internal fence and security cameras: the detention room of the base. To enter, they passed through a gate covered in a curling fence. Two armed guards were stationed in the outer area, and another guard, without a weapon, operated the gate for them. Inside the building's entrance, a secure room with an armored door awaited, manned by another guard and a clerk. After signing the guestbook and depositing their weapons, they were led into a broader secured space. In the center stood a steel table and two wooden benches bolted to the floor. The door closed behind them as they waited patiently.

"These teenagers were apprehended this early morning at our checkpoint on their way to Rujieb," Uziel continued. "We found iron poles, spray paint, a Canteen filled with flammable liquid, rags and various items in their car trunk. They were arrested and interrogated, and one of them, who happens to be my neighbor from the village, started talking."

"I assume your personal connection had something to do with him opening up," Yael said, her arms crossed, the tension palpable. It had been a while since she last interrogated someone. Uziel chose not to respond to her remark.

"It turns out that three days before Dvora Goshen was murdered," he continued, "they infiltrated Ramin village at night, vandalizing the place. They destroyed several olive trees, set a goat pen, two sheds, and a building on fire, and left 'Price Tag' graffiti on some houses. The consequences were devastating: three Palestinians were evacuated due to smoke inhalation, five goats died in the flames, and significant property damage occurred. Besides, this incident has the potential to escalate tensions."

"It could lead to further conflict," Ibrahim noted. "How are the affected family doing?"

"Two were released this morning, but a fourteen-year-old boy is still hospitalized in Ramallah."

"Yonatan, this sounds terrible, but I'm struggling to see the connection with our investigation," said Ibrahim.

Yael looked at him, crossing her legs, and added: "I can see some potential overlap. Ramin is where Malak Hamdan visited her family two days before she was killed. Dvora lived in Ma'ale Levona and was tied to Malak. We should investigate whether she was present in Ramin during that time. Perhaps Malak was murdered there, and Dvora witnessed it? Maybe that's why she lost her life?"

"But according to Hamas, Malak was killed in Gaza, and her body was found in Israel," Uziel mentioned. "Perhaps the information they provided is inaccurate?" The two looked at Ibrahim just as the door opened, and three teenagers entered the room.

"We should check Dvora's activities on the day Malak was in Ramin and see if their paths crossed. As for your friends," Yael addressed Uziel, "they don't come from good families. Burning a building with people inside—it shows they have no problem to kill."

***

The first person to enter the room was the tallest one. He wore a white woolen yamaka, a buttoned-up shirt with a tank top underneath, dark brown pants, and sports shoes. His face was adorned with a light brown beard and payot, and his hands were cuffed behind his back. His face bore a look of fury. He sat heavily on the bench, waiting for his two friends to join him. The second guy was very lean, with red cheeks and pale, watery skin. His unkempt beard and youthful appearance suggested he had yet to grow a full man's facial hair. He wore a striped woolen sweater and faded jeans, and his gaze was fixed on the cement floor, looking embarrassed and miserable. Yael assumed he was the one who broke during the interrogation and incriminated the other two. The third guy was skinny and hairy, with bright curls protruding from his shirt. He, too, had a beard, though it seemed recently trimmed. Dressed in a khaki fleece coat, cotton pants, and sandals, he had a distinct biblical figure appearance. His hands and legs were cuffed, and his bruised skin hinted he went wild during the interrogation.

"A masterpiece," Uziel muttered sarcastically.

"We are not..." the red-cheeked guy started to say, but Uziel barked at him: "Shut up! You will only talk when we ask you to. These two investigators came to ask you questions and you will answer them without playing around! Is that clear?"

"Just to be clear," Yael interjected, "this is a criminal investigation, and anything you say can be used against you in a court of law. You have the right to remain silent, and you have the right to hire an attorney. It's up to you." The three remained silent, prompting Yael to continue, "Where were you all day on the seventeenth of February? Were you together, or were each of you somewhere else?"

Silence.

"An Israeli woman was murdered that day, and there are signs tying you to the murder. If you can tell us where you were and we verify your alibi, you won't be suspected in her murder anymore."

"What about the Arab woman?" asked the red-faced guy.

"I told you to shut up," muttered the first guy who entered the room.

"The Arab woman," said Ibrahim, "was discovered alongside the Jewish woman but was murdered a few days prior." He couldn't finish his sentence before being spat on in the face by the third guy. The act left Ibrahim shocked, and everyone in the room watched his reaction. However, Ibrahim wiped his face with his sleeve, offering a smile. Uziel was the one to lose his cool now, prompting him to raise his hand as if to strike the young guy who spat, which had backed off and closed his eyes, awaiting the strike that was about to come, but just before he had managed to do so, Yael intervened, placing her hand on Uziel's thigh to stop him.

"I will not talk until that piece of garbage gets out of here," said the young guy, glaring at Ibrahim.

"You don't have to talk, but your silence only makes you look more suspicious," Yael said.

"No problem, Yael," said Ibrahim, getting up. "I will wait for you outside."

"No. I need you to stay here," Yael insisted. "If they don't want to answer, it's their problem." Ibrahim stepped back, leaning against one of the walls. Yael started pacing around the three guys. "I think Malak was not murdered in Gaza," she looked at Ibrahim, searching for any reaction. "Malak is the daughter of Hamas senior Aziz Shafiki. Shafiki didn't want the information publicized, so he claimed that Malak was murdered in Gaza. But you murdered Malak while you went wild in Ramin. I assume she stumbled upon you by accident, and you got scared and choked her. The next day, you buried her in Sawia. Only then, when Dvora Goshen drove on the road between Ma'ale Levona and Ramin, you got scared she saw you, so you took her down, too. Now, all that remains is to fill in the two missing pieces to complete the picture: did Dvora drive down that road, and where were you during those days." Yael stopped and looked at the three of them. It didn't appear that anyone was about to talk. She sat back on the bench.

"You can stay silent, but eventually, we'll thoroughly investigate and find all your traces, and you'll rot in jail for the rest of your lives. So, one of you better start talking now. The first one to do so will be rewarded with significant ease of sentence."

Silence.

"I think you don't understand the gravity of your situation," said Uziel. "This is the end, do you understand? Your last chance to sober up. You shall not kill—"

"We didn't kill anybody!" yelled the tall guy in fury.

"You burnt a building with people inside it," said Ibrahim in a near-whisper from the side of the room.

"We did not know there were people inside!" protested the red-faced guy.

"Nonsense!" Yelled Uziel, getting up. He went to the door and knocked on it until the guard came in. "Take them out of here. I don't want to see them until they decide to talk. I don't care if they rot in jail until the day they die!" He left the room just as the guy with the rosy cheeks began to whimper. The second guy attempted to headbutt him but was swiftly lifted off the bench and taken away, followed by the other two. Yael and Ibrahim were left alone in the room.

"I need to check what happened with Dvora Goshen on the day she was murdered. I suggest we start building an organized map of victims and suspects, timelines, and places they were. I will try to create a timeline for the murders, and we'll have to do the same, separately, for the three other women," Yael said. Ibrahim nodded, and as they left the room and headed to the parking lot, Yael searched for a phone number on her cellphone.

"...And Ibrahim," she said without looking at him.

"Yes?" he replied.

"If you are lying to me..."

Ibrahim held her hand and stopped her, looking into her eyes. "Yael, I'm not lying. Malak Hamdan did go to Ramin, but she returned to Gaza, where she was murdered. You can trust my word."

"We'll see about that," said Yael as she got into her car, started it, and pressed the gas pedal.

***

They proceeded towards the base's exit gate, but the guard didn't lift the barricade as they approached. Yael rolled down her window as he came over and said, "It's Uziel. He asked you to wait for him."

While waiting, Yael called Uri Amit, who finally answered on the fifth ring. "I need you to find out something for me," she said, catching a glimpse of Uziel's reflection in her car's mirror.

"What happened?" Amit inquired.

"I need to urgently talk with Dvora Goshen's husband. I'm heading straight to their place to interrogate him. Please send me his address."

"No problem. They're probably at home, sitting for the seven days of mourning. I will check for you," said Amit before hanging up, just as Uziel leaned on the car window.

"I have news for you," he said with purpose.

"Did any of them confess?" asked Ibrahim, a smile on his face.

"No. It's about something else. I received a message that a special Mista'arvim unit of the IBP in Judea and Samaria arrested a group affiliated with the Islamic Jihad an hour ago in Nablus. They attempted to kidnap a soldier from the Tapuach intersection a few hours ago. Their goal was to free a few of the organization members that were arrested in Israel. Five members in the group. I suggest you check them."

"I don't think everything happening in Judea and Samaria is related to our case," Yael countered. "It sounds like a waste of time and energy to me."

"I'm not sure," said Uziel. "The proximity of these events could indicate a failed kidnapping attempt, similar to Dvora's case. It's possible that this group tried to hide the Israeli women's bodies to blackmail Israel, but the discovery of the bodies thwarted their plans."

"So why murder Palestinian women?" Ibrahim asked.

"And why leave Dvora sitting on the ground exposed?"

"I don't know. You'll need to ask them that question," Uziel replied, standing up and properly slinging his weapon over his shoulder. "The five terrorists are jailed in Nafcha prison in the Negev. I'll talk to the prison's commander so you can go in to interrogate them."

"Thanks," said Yael. "But I'll drive to Dvora's house first."

"In that case, I'll meet you there later," said Uziel. "I owe this family a visit." He signaled the guard to open the barricade, and as the car slid up the dirt road onto the highway, they headed to Ma'ale Lavona.

"I suggest you drop me off at Huwara checkpoint. I'll go from there to Nablus," said Ibrahim.

"Excuse me?" Yael was taken aback. "Are you serious?"

"There's no logic in both of us going to interrogate Dvora's family or the Jihadists in Nafcha. Go by yourself, and I'll go to Nablus to conduct a thorough investigation on the group's members. I know the governor of Nablus and a few Hamas and Jihad leaders in town. I'll build their timeline, and then we can see if there's an alignment between their actions and the unfolding events. You extract information from them, and then we'll determine if there's a connection between the cases. I'll be back at the checkpoint tomorrow evening."

"Ibrahim, I can't approve such a thing."

"Yael, you're thinking with your heart instead of your head. There's no logic in us going together. It's a waste of time. There's information only I can gather from Nablus, and you can't enter there. This information is valuable because it'll minimize the time we spend investigating this group, which may have nothing to do with this case."

"I can't leave you. You can't move freely there."

"I'll only be on the Palestinian side, and tomorrow at 7 AM, I'll be at the checkpoint waiting for you."

The two investigators sat in the car in silence. Ibrahim didn't know what Yael would decide, and he felt tense, clasping his hands between his thighs. Yael drove fast on the highway, her mind racing. She tried to call Uri Amit, but there was no reception. When they reached the checkpoint, she knew what she was about to do. She pulled over to the road shoulder, stopped the car, and put it in park.

"If I catch you lying, I'll arrest you myself," she muttered in his direction.

He nodded, opened the door, and got out. Only after he disappeared beyond the curve did Yael realize how terrible her decision was to let him go.

11.

Ma'ale Levona

At 7:15 PM, Yael parked her car beside Dvora Goshen's house. The street was crowded with parked cars as people came to comfort the grieving family. Uri Amit awaited her in his vehicle. When she stepped out of her car and headed towards the door, he got out too and walked by her side.

"Where is Ibrahim?" was his first question.

"In Nablus," she replied, maintaining her pace.

He stopped and lightly held her hand, causing her to slow down and eventually come to a halt. Facing him, she said, "There are too many things happening all at once. I need him there. I will meet him tomorrow."

"You know this isn't part of the deal. There are protocols. You can't do whatever you feel like doing."

"Ibrahim is under my responsibility, you said so yourself..."

Yonatan Uziel, accompanied by another officer, approached them. Both were in uniform, their weapons on their shoulders. The three imposing figures surrounded Yael, making her seem small and frail in comparison.

"He is a Hamas man, did you *forget*? The same organization that fires missiles at our cities, a terrorist group that commits suicide attacks, kidnappings, and murders civilians! What the hell were you thinking?" Amit allowed himself to raise his tone of speech a bit.

"Ibrahim is not like that. He is a police investigator who came to investigate these horrific murders, not to kidnap soldiers," she retorted, feeling suffocated by the situation. An elderly couple came out of the widower's house and passed by them.

"Yael, you don't know him. Trust me, he is not who you think he is," said Uziel.

"What do you mean?"

"Ibrahim had the opportunity to stay in the West Bank and become a senior police officer in the Palestinian Authority. Instead, he got caught smuggling Hamas members and weapons from the West Bank to Gaza, using the entry permits Israel had given him. He was arrested and interrogated, then removed to Gaza. Who knows how many Israelis were killed by the same terrorists and weapons he smuggled."

"That was eight years ago. Much has changed since then," she tried to defend her choices, but as she spoke, she realized her words sounded like a feeble excuse.

"We need to keep an eye on him. That's why I asked you not to let him roam freely. That was our agreement with him," Amit explained, attempting to sound fatherly.

"Ibrahim will come to the Huwara checkpoint tomorrow at 7 AM. Uziel will pick him up, and I'll come as soon as I finish interrogating the group at Nafcha prison."

"And if he won't come?" Amit objected. Yael spread her hands wide in response.

"Yael..."

Now Yael was furious. "You need to let me do my job or replace me. I have no need for a close mentor." She maneuvered her way between the wall of men encircling her and climbed the stairs to the Goshen family's house. The three men exchanged glances and followed her inside.

***

Yael found Amiad Goshen, Dvora's husband, sitting in the living room, surrounded by many people who had come to comfort him. Some were praying, some were chatting with him, while others attended to the children. When he recognized Yael, he got up and approached her. She nodded, gesturing that she wanted to speak with him privately, and he obliged.

"Any news?" he asked anxiously.

"We're just at the beginning of the investigation. Most of the evidence was destroyed by the army and the weather, so we're relying heavily on forensic evidence from the autopsy. We're working in full cooperation with an investigator from Gaza who is examining the second body. I promise to update you as soon as we find out anything," she assured him.

"Thank you," he said, patting her shoulder lightly, as if she was the one in need of comforting. Chief Superintendent Uri Amit approached them, but Yael signaled for him to stay back.

"I need to ask you a few questions to rule out some suspicions that arose during today's interrogation," Yael began.

"Yes?"

"Could it be that Dvora passed by the village of Ramin on the day she was murdered or the day before?"

"Dvora drives... used to drive past Ramin every day. She worked in one of the factories at the 'Tnuvot' industrial area in Emek Hefer. Ramin is one her way to work."

"Did she ever mention anything weird or suspicious that she might have seen in or around Ramin during her commute to work?"

"What do you mean?"

"Did she tell you anything about it or not?" Yael insisted.

"Not that I can recall."

Yael pondered for a long moment and then said, "I need to understand her timeline on that day. The route she took and where she went missing from." Amiad sipped from his glass of water and leaned against one of the walls. A thought crossed her mind— **could Amiad be a suspect, and had they been investigating in the wrong direction?**

"I don't know her exact route on the day she disappeared, but usually, on weekdays, she leaves the house at 7:30 AM. I take care of the kids for school because Dvora takes a protected bus to work. She was afraid to drive her car to work."

"I see. Where is the bus stop located?"

"It's at the settlement entrance, by our grocery store."

"Do you know if she boarded the bus that morning, or did she disappear before that?"

"As I told the investigators earlier, she left the house in the morning as usual, but she didn't make it to work that day. I don't know if she got on the bus or not. You should check with the driver. It's the regular driver for our transports, so I assume he would know."

"Meaning she vanished between leaving the house and reaching her workplace. Did anyone else see her or hear from her that day?"

"Not that I know of," Amiad replied.

"And who was supposed to pick up..." Yael peaked in her notepad; "Tzofia from school?"

"Dvora usually comes back home around noon and picks up our daughter from school in her car."

"So, the car was parked at home, which means she didn't disappear on her way to pick up her daughter."

"That's correct. The car is here."

"I see. If you happen to remember anything else that could be relevant to our investigation, please contact me directly. Here's my phone number," Yael said, handing him her business card from her bag. "Call me anytime."

"Sure, thank you," he said, turning back to sit on the sofa. Amit and Uziel looked at Yael as she approached them. She stopped beside Uziel and whispered, causing both men to lean in and listen. "It's entirely possible that Dvora has some connection to the events in Ramin, and that might be the reason she was murdered. We need more details from the Institute of Forensic Medicine and further interrogation of the Shalhevet group. On the other hand, it could be circumstantial, and then we have no grounds for an indictment."

"I don't think they murdered four women," said Uziel. "I told you, these are just kids who got a little carried away."

"You'd be surprised how much evil can lurk in kids who got a little carried away," Yael replied before walking away.

"Where are you going?" Amit asked.

"Home," she replied, leaving her commander behind. "We're done for today."

***

When Yael returned to her home in Ra'anana, it was 8:05 PM. The living room was bathed in the glow of the television, but the night's headlines were not about the murder cases. Her mother, Dina, was busy in the kitchen, Keren's bedroom door was closed, while Ilan lay on his bed, engrossed in a book and chatting on the phone at the same time. Yael approached him, gently planting a kiss on his forehead. The 10-year-old didn't take his eyes off the book but responded with a beaming smile.

"I don't want to disturb you," she whispered, "but come to the kitchen later. I want to hear all about your math test today." He nodded, the memory of last Saturday studying together still fresh in their hearts. Yael cherished those moments, knowing they would have many more opportunities to share such times. Leaving his room, she made her way to the kitchen, where the aroma of simmering vegetable soup filled the air, the oven roasting chicken and potatoes. Dishes piled up in the sink, and without hesitation, Yael rolled up her sleeves and began to tackle them.

"How was your day with the kids?" she inquired of her mother.

"You know, eventually, you need to be present in your kids' lives."

"Amit gave me an assignment to investigate the murders of four women in Judea and Samaria."

"Yael, you're not young anymore. You're a widow and a mother of two. It's more important for you to sort your life out first. It's been four years..."

"Mother, this investigation might just be the thing that brings me back to sanity."

"Murders? I can't raise your kids instead of you. They need a mother, not a grandmother."

"I know. I've done everything I could to be there for them until now. But if I'm not valuable to Amit, he can't keep me there."

"Then leave. Leave the police, become a teacher at the academy, teach other policemen, or join intelligence, or the ISA. Shai can get you any job you desire," her mother suggested, referring to Yael's brother who headed the ISA cyber security array. He had extended numerous offers for her to work with him, away from the risks and tolls of her current job. Yet, Yael persisted in her role as a superintendent, as if her life depended on it. She turned off the tap, her hands pale from the cold water.

"If I can find myself again, realize the power I possess, I can be strong for Keren and Ilan. This is a great opportunity for me."

"And if you realize you're not strong enough, then what?"

"Then I'll know I'm halfway to recovery."

Ilan entered the kitchen, taking a seat at the table, intrigued by the 'old people' conversation between his mother and grandmother, and did not say a word.

"Are you hungry?" Dina asked him. "Do you want a soup?"

"Yes," he replied, and Yael resumed washing the dishes. Dina observed her daughter silently, her thoughts unspoken. She brought out a bowl and filled it with steaming soup for Ilan.

"Can you call Keren?" she requested instead of Yael, turning to Ilan. He left the kitchen briefly and returned empty-handed. "She doesn't want to eat," he reported, and Dina gently touched her daughter's hand. "Go call her," she urged. Yael made a dramatic gesture, plunging her hands back into the water-filled sink. Dealing with her introverted daughter felt overwhelming at the moment. Teenage dramas tested her patience, and what she truly longed for was some peace and quiet. But she couldn't avoid her mother's request. If Dina weren't there, she might have continued washing dishes and left a bowl of soup on the table for Keren to take or ignore as she pleased.

After drying her hands, she approached Keren's room and found the door locked. She knocked softly. No response. Knocking a little harder, she finally heard a yell from within: "I said not now!!"

Yael debated whether to persist or let it be. Eventually, she gave up and returned to the kitchen. Dina was already wearing her coat and had her purse on her shoulder. Ilan continued to enjoy his soup. Yael embraced her mother and kissed her forehead. "Thanks for everything," she said, walking her to the door.

***

At 11:35 PM, Keren's bedroom door creaked open, and the 14-year-old girl tiptoed to the bathroom for a shower. Yael had finished her shower and was now in the living room, engrossed watching the TV and folding laundry. Ilan, after recounting his glorious fail at the math test, was dozing off in his room, emitting soft snores. As Keren passed her, Yael greeted her with a warm "Hello."

"Hey, Mom," the girl responded, briefly pausing to pick up a piece of clothing she had dropped.

"How are you?" Yael inquired.

"I'm good." Keren continued on her way, ignoring the hand her mother offered.

"Can I talk to you?"

"Not now. I'm on a break, I need to continue soon," Keren replied.

"You didn't eat a thing; I left you soup on the table."

"I'm not hungry. I ate at lunch." Yael contemplated whether it was worth arguing with her daughter about eating habits but decided against it. Now was the time to draw closer, not push her away.

"Will you have some time to talk to me today?" she asked, but Keren had already closed the bathroom door. Yael reminisced about a time when Keren was a little girl, and Yael would sit on the toilet while she showered, sharing stories. How long ago that felt now—a different world, a world where all her dreams seemed within reach, just around the corner. A world Yael would give anything to return to, a world she would never experience again. Today, she needed to rebuild a new world for herself and her family.

When Gidi was killed in 2011, she left her home in Ariel and moved to Ra'anana near her parents. She abandoned everything, taking only what was necessary and leaving the rest behind. She bought new furniture, clothes, bedsheets, tools, and pictures, all in an attempt to forget, to leave the painful past behind. But the truth was, she had never truly recovered from the loss. The weight of grief bore down on her, drowning her in a sea of sorrow, struggling to breathe, struggling to find her way back to the surface, to sanity. And now, with this new case, she felt it might be her last chance—to save the next victim, to prevent the collapse into chaos, escalating tensions, and violence between the two nations, leading to the next altercation.

***

Keren emerged from the shower, clad in her pajamas, and made her way to her room. Yael followed, feeling a sense of determination. She entered the room before the teenager could lock the door again and settled on her bed. Keren stood there, gazing at her mother, waiting for her to speak. The computer screen flickered with characters engaged in a multiplayer game.

"They're waiting for me," Keren said. "Do you need anything?"

"Yes. I need you. I miss you. I miss spending time with you, just hanging out."

"Take me out for coffee tomorrow morning. I don't mind being late for school."

"Tomorrow? I can't. I'm in the middle of an investigation, and my boss—"

"—And I can't now. I'm in the middle of something," Keren interrupted, her response echoing with underlying accusations. She put on her headphones and sat in her father's executive chair, taking the keyboard into her hands to resume the game she had momentarily abandoned. Left to sit on her bed, Yael fell into silence, her mind momentarily empty of thoughts. After a while, she quietly fetched a chair from Ilan's room and placed it beside Keren.

Without uttering a word, Yael watched her daughter become thoroughly engrossed in the virtual world while also writing notes on a piece of paper. Keren looked surprised by her mother's move. She took off one side of her headphones and half-looked at Yael, inquiring, "What are you doing? I'm in the middle of a game."

"We're both very busy, but I want to be with you, even if it means watching you play. This is your world, and I want to be a part of it," Yael said, trying to bridge the gap.

Keren raised her hands in a gesture of surrender.

"Can you at least tell me who's against whom and how the game works? Maybe I can join you?"

Keren seemed unsure of how to escape the situation her mother had put her in. She played on for a few moments before finally relenting and explaining the rules of the game.

"It's a global multiplayer game where players interact both cooperatively and competitively. Each player has various goals, like acquiring resources and assets, while guarding against theft and harm. It's crucial to know how to trade virtual money, form alliances, and recognize potential enemies in time," Keren explained.

Intrigued, Yael was drawn into her daughter's virtual world. She couldn't help but notice the parallels between this digital realm and the real world she was in.

"And how can you tell in the game who's on your side and who's against you?"

"In the beginning, everyone plays against everyone, so it's hard to trust others. But there is a player or two that I've known for a long time, and we tend to play together. For example, this character," she pointed at one of the female characters on the screen, "belongs to one of the girls in my class. We're friends, and I know she won't betray me. Occasionally, we cooperate against other characters. But with the rest of the characters, you can't trust anyone."

"So, how do you determine if you can cooperate with another player?"

"Sometimes, two players may have a mutual enemy, and they team up to fight against that common adversary. It means even your biggest enemies can become your allies in certain situations, halting the war against you."

Yael recalled a course she took years ago at Tel Aviv University, where she learned that between countries or political entities, there was no intimate friendship. Supposed enemies were not necessarily enemies—it was all about interests. The love-hate relationships between countries were fictitious, driven by relationships between leaders, alliances, or shared enemies, just as Keren described.

"But how can you tell if you and another player have a mutual enemy? Is there a way to communicate with each other?"

"There's a chat function on the side of the screen, allowing players to talk to each other privately and form alliances. I'm talking to people from all over the world, and every time I ally with another group, it lasts until it breaks, and then we become enemies again. I'm keeping notes on this paper to track who's on my side now and who's my enemy. It changes often, so I'm always forming new alliances."

"And how's your progress in the game? Are you winning or losing? How do you know?"

"In this game, there are no losers. The one who manages to make the most alliances and gather the most resources is considered the 'winner.' They become stronger and richer, making it much harder for others to take them down."

They spent long minutes together, playing and talking. Yael asked questions and offered advice, while Keren shared her tactics and introduced her mother to the virtual world she inhabited. For a brief moment, they were a united front—a mother and her daughter against the world, that no one can outdo. Eventually, feeling exhausted, Yael got up, kissed her daughter goodnight, and advised her not to stay up too late. She left the room, closed the door, and settled into her own bed. Even half an hour later, as she was drifting off to sleep, she could still hear the clicks of the keyboard emanating from Keren's room, blending into her sense of weariness until she finally closed her eyes and succumbed to slumber.

12.
26.2.2015

The ringing phone next to her bed jolted Yael from her slumber. At first, she couldn't quite grasp the source of the annoying sound that yanked her out of her nightmares. Slowly, she got up and grabbed the phone by her. Chief Superintendent Uri Amit was on the line. She pressed the **Accept** button and answered the call.

"Do you know what time it is?" he demanded. Yael glanced at the clock on the screen but didn't bother to respond.

"It's 7:15."

"Alright, thank you for the information. My meeting in Nafcha is at 10 AM. I'll take the kids to school and head there," Yael replied, trying to keep her composure.

"Don't play games with me, Yael!" Amit barked. "Where is Ibrahim?"

"Ibrahim is in Nablus with his family—I told you..." she began.

"You told me he'd be at the Huwara checkpoint at seven AM. Uziel has been waiting for him for fifteen minutes," Amit interjected. Yael was torn; it was only 15 minutes, and she was well acquainted with "Mediterranean time." She contemplated whether to argue, but she eventually relented.

"I'll try to reach him. I'll keep you updated," she assured him.

"Yael... If he doesn't come back..."

"What then? What do you think will happen? Will he commit murder? Blow up the checkpoint? Eventually, he has to return to Gaza, and the only way is through Israel. Give him some time.

Let us do our job," Yael retorted. She wanted to hang up, but Amit wanted to be the one saying the final word.

"Hamas is our enemy. Despite that, we allowed him to come here. If it will be known that he's walking around freely, and Israel allowed it, it could ignite a war, and people will die. Their blood will be on your hands," he warned before abruptly ending the call.

Yael remained sitting on the bed, phone in hand. After a few long minutes, she finally stood up and dialed his number once more. He answered promptly.

"I need you to check something for me," she whispered into the phone. "What's the number of the driver who picked up Dvora Goshen." She hung up this time and tossed the phone onto the bed, preparing herself for another day of battle. The battle of existence.

***

The "Nafcha" prison stood as a formidable jailhouse for dangerous Palestinian prisoners, established in 1980 in the heart of the desert, far from any village, nestled between Mitzpe Ramon and Sde Boker on highway 40. Enclosed by towering cement walls, watchtowers, and sensor surveillance, the 700 inmates within were destined to serve long years for crimes of murder, dangerous criminal activity, often motivated by nationalism or ties to terror organizations and bomb attacks. The prison's layout strategically separated inmates based on their organizational affiliations, with the Hamas prisoners held in a secure and guarded section, distinct from the rest.

At precisely 9:55 AM, Yael approached the prison gates and parked her car near the main entrance. Though she presented her police ID, the guard recognized her from previous visits and was well aware of her arrival today. After depositing her weapon, she received a concise briefing on the protocols and procedures involved in interrogating individuals with high-security clearance inside the prison.

The designated interrogation room was designed with a physical partition, ensuring a safe distance between the interrogator and the subject. The room featured steel bars dividing the space, with the interrogatee handcuffed on one side and the interrogator positioned a few meters away, seated at a heavy metal table bolted to the floor. The prisoner's legs were restrained by a metal shackle embedded in the cement, preventing any sudden movements that might pose a threat to the interrogator. The entire session would be recorded on CCTV, while two armed guards remained outside the door, prepared to intervene swiftly should the inmate become uncontrollable. Yael was strictly prohibited from bringing her phone inside, and she was allowed only a plastic pen and a notebook for her investigation, and nothing else.

With a deep breath, she stepped into the interrogation room, facing Palestinian terrorists for the first time in many years. The last encounter had been when Gidi fell victim to the hands of Hamas. Despite the weight of her personal loss, she knew she had to remain strong and not let it distract her during this encounter, and what was about to unfold. Islamic Jihad prisoners were notorious for their verbal and physical aggression, seeking to plant seeds of doubt in her mind.

On that fateful day when news of the Natanya bombing surfaced, she had been tasked by her commander to interrogate the imprisoned Hamas leaders at Nafcha prison regarding the horrifying terrorist attack that had left many casualties. Unaware at that moment that Gidi had become one of the dead, and Keren was fighting for her life, she had yet to learn that Naif Badir—the man whose life she had saved during her junior officer days in 1999, was the killer. Badir had been associated with the 'Mah'mara' criminal organization in the northern part of the Dead Sea in the late '90s. He had been the right-hand man and executioner for the organization's leader until he became entangled in the murder of a young Israeli during a car break-in at Kibbutz Kalya. Captured and imprisoned, Badir eventually joined Hamas through his encounters in prison, adopting their nationalistic ideology. Upon his release, he orchestrated the horrifying terrorist attack.

On that particular day at Nafcha prison, Yael had interrogated Badir's cellmates. On the table were aggravation of the conditions of confinement in front of comprehensive information about the terrorist; Where did he acquire the weapon, how did he choose the target, how did he get there, and many other questions that remain open. Though Hamas soldiers were notorious for their silence when dealing with the Israeli army, preferring to be buried in a dungeon rather than cooperate, one man in the interrogation room had revealed a detail out of personal vendetta—

The name of the terrorist attacker.

Now, she found herself back at Nafcha prison, facing the same circumstances once more. Would she succeed where she had faltered before? Today, she had more tools at her disposal to handle such situations, more than she had in the past. Today, there were mutual interests between her and Hamas—a common enemy united them, despite being eternal foes.

***

One by one, they were brought into the interrogation room and bound. Yael sat across from them, beyond the metal table, gazing at them intently. She tried to see beyond the intimidating façade, to search for the person within the terrorist, the individual concealed inside the squad. She wanted to confront them, but believed that her fragile appearance and pragmatic approach would open them up for conversation. She pondered whether it was wise to interrogate each of them separately or all together. Each method had its advantages and disadvantages. Group dynamics could negatively affect their willingness to share information. Each one feared their comrades. On the other hand, unanimous consent to provide information to save themselves or thwart the next murder could set them free to speak openly. This approach had worked in cases where the suspects were truly innocent, as Yael had presumed. On the other hand, individual interrogation allowed her to use tools like the prisoner's dilemma, which could lead one of them to testify more easily against their comrades if the suspect was indeed guilty of murder. Yael opted for the first strategy.

"Three Palestinian women were murdered," she said in fluent

Arabic. "Two of them were affiliated with Hamas. Two more Israeli women. The killer linked them to one another."

The five of them stared at her, not uttering a word.

"I have two requests from you. First, I want to help clear your names. I don't believe you are guilty—you have no access to Gaza. On the other hand, Hamas is an enemy to both you and to Israelis."

Silence. Always silence. Could it be that her tactic was wrong?

"The second thing is if you know anyone who could have committed the murders..."

"Why do you think we would want to help you?" said one of the detainees, a young man in his early twenties, with a deep, hollow voice.

"To prevent the next murder, by someone from your own group."

"We have nothing to do with the killings."

Yael scanned the five and questioned her own presence there. She had no evidence linking the detainees to the murder cases. These were military detainees whose goal was to harm IDF soldiers, to capture them for prisoner exchange with the organization's security prisoners. And now, they had become security prisoners themselves.

"I want to believe you. In order to do that, I need to establish a timeline, to see where you were during the time of the murders, so I can match it with the evidence. If that's the case, I can remove the suspicions from you."

"You have no suspicions, no evidence, so why don't you just crawl back into the hole you came from before we deal with you too?" said the second guy, around 30 years old, spitting through the bars.

The other four burst into laughter. "I would do you a favor, sweetheart," sneered the third one, making an indecent gesture with his crotch. The young man who spoke first blew a teasing kiss into the air, and the fifth one started cursing. Yael got up, packed her belongings, and proceeded towards the iron door, with shouts and curses following her.

"Sweetheart! Where are you going?" one of them yelled. "We're not done with you yet!"

"Come here," the second one shouted. "We're looking for a new friend in the cell." They all burst into laughter again.

"Is that what you came all this way for?" asked the fourth guy, who had been silent until now.

"No," she said. "I came to look you in the eyes and make you an offer. Each one of you is facing between twenty to thirty years in prison. And after the failed prisoner exchange deal with Hamas, I doubt such a deal will happen again. Based on my familiarity with guys like you, there's a high chance you'll continue to get into trouble in prison, and every time, a few more years will be added to your sentence. So, in general, there's a good chance some of you will spend the rest of your lives here." She looked around to let her words sink in.

"I promise, to the first one among you who will provide me with useful information about the murder, your attempted abduction, and the person who sent you on the mission and supplied you with weapons, that you will go to a lower-security prison, with the possibility of meeting with your families, and early release after only three or four years. This deal will be on the table until tomorrow at the same time. Think carefully if you want to let your ego bury you in this hole for life."

A long silence followed, and then a barrage of curses was fired into the air. She took two more steps towards the door, stopped, turned back to face them, and watched as they fueled their enthusiasm while leaning against the bars. The scene was so surrealistic that for a moment, she felt an overwhelming power surging within her. Here she was, completely free, standing before them—five young men who would spend their lives in prison. And all they could do was sneer at her, annoy her. That was all the power they had. How pitiful, how pathetic the moment was. Suddenly, she realized she was smiling, a small smile, but noticeable to the eye. She waved goodbye and left the room, leaving the five without an audience, without an object for mockery. And that was her small, fleeting victory.

***

As she walked out of the interrogation room, a man approached her, appearing to be in his mid-40s. His hair was thick and dark, but with streaks of gray, his lips were full, and a thin mustache adorned his upper lip. A few gray whiskers graced his cheeks, although it was evident that he had recently shaved. He was dressed in a well-tailored gray suit with blue and white stripes, a blue tie adorned his white, buttoned-up shirt, and black leather shoes covered his woolen socks. He greeted her with a light nod and extended his hand towards her.

"I'm Attorney Jamal Jaroushi. I represent two of the suspects you were interrogating. Do you have a few minutes to talk with me?" Yael hesitated but eventually shook his hand, but nodded her head in reluctance.

"I'm not involved in the charges that were filed. I'm investigating a different angle—"

"I know," interrupted Jaroushi. "They informed me. Nevertheless, there are a few things…"

"Why are you representing only two out of the five and not all of them?"

"I am an Israeli citizen. I have no interest in Hamas or Islamic Jihad. I oppose their violence and the way they seek to advance their vision. The thing is, these two guys who were arrested are my family. They are my brother's sons, and he specifically asked me to step in and protect them."

"Alright. So how can I help you?"

He motioned with his hand towards a small wooden table with two chairs placed next to the concrete wall, shaded by a wooden canopy that provided some relief from the sun. She followed him and took a seat on one of the chairs.

"I just want to tell you that these five have no connection to the murder cases you are investigating. It's important for you to know; the arrest of these guys was made possible thanks to intelligence information provided by the father of one of the terrorists, my brother. He didn't want his son to be killed. Since the information was handed over three days ago, the group has been on the run, and it doesn't seem possible for them to have carried out such a significant act of violence at the appropriate time." He pulled out a box of Chicago-style cigarettes, Illinois, smooth blue. He took out a cigarette and placed it in his mouth. Yael observed him closely as he lit the cigarette and took a deep drag, filling his lungs with smoke. When their eyes met, he offered her a cigarette, but she politely declined.

"Do you understand?" he said. "These guys indeed committed a serious act, one that should never have happened. It could have ended in murder. But that's not what happened. The soldier managed to escape from them, and the father alerted the security forces, and from there, the way to Nafcha was short."

Yael looked away for a few moments, then looked back at the esteemed attorney and asked, "Have you recently been in the United States, Attorney Jaroushi?"

Jaroushi chuckled lightly and inquired, "Why is that important? I don't understand."

"One testimony is not enough to dismiss all the evidence from the scene. In other words, just because you have cigarettes from Chicago doesn't mean you were there. The same applies to the father's testimony. Just because the father vouched for his children doesn't mean they weren't involved in at least one of the murder cases."

Jaroushi put on his sunglasses, took another puff from the cigarette, and said, "The burden of proof is on you. If you don't have evidence linking them to the murder cases, it indicates they have no connection to the matter."

"I agree," she said, rising from the wooden bench. "I genuinely hope, for their sake, that they didn't get involved in something beyond their control. Good luck, Attorney Jaroushi." With those words, she walked away. He flicked the cigarette butt onto the asphalt and entered the prison building.

***

She needed a few seconds to gather her thoughts, start the car, and drive away. Yael got on Highway 40 heading north, maintaining the speed, even though her heart was pounding. She noticed two missed calls from the Institute of Forensic Medicine and decided to call them back. The receptionist answered, and Yael identified herself. She asked if anyone was looking for her, and the answer was affirmative.

"Professor Arieli has new findings to present to you."

"Can it be done over the phone?" Yael inquired.

"No. He specifically requested you to come here in person."

"I understand," she said. "I'll be there later today." She hung up and dialed Ibrahim's mobile number. The call was immediately forwarded to voicemail. Yael debated whether she should try to track Ibrahim's location but decided against it, for now. Instead, she called Uri Amit and updated him on the events in Nafcha, omitting the meeting with Attorney Jaroushi.

"What about Ibrahim? Have you heard from him?"

"Not yet, but I—"

"I insist, sorry, I'm instructing you: after the Institute, head straight to the territorial brigade of Samaria. Uziel is waiting for you there with two more teams. You'll enter Nablus, find him, and take him straight to custody in the district. This saga must end today." He disconnected before she could respond. Yael thought to herself: Too many disconnections and ruptures are affecting my relationship with my superiors.

***

The clock struck 1:00 PM as Yael stepped into Professor Yosef Arieli's office at the Institute of Forensic Medicine in Abu Kabir. The man, aged 61, appeared fatigued and unfocused. A disarray of disposable coffee cups were scattered across the table, and the air conditioner struggled to warm the room, emitting intermittent noises. Despite his invitation to sit, she remained standing.

"Anan was the first among them to be murdered," he began, as though the conversation had already commenced beforehand. "My estimation is that her death occurred on February eighth. Malak Hamdan was the second, on February twelfth, four days after

Anan. Dvora Goshen followed, on February seventeenth, and Abigail Avnon on February twenty-fourth. Assuming that Hamas' data is accurate and Fatima Ashrawi was murdered at the end of January, we can infer that the killer initiated his killing spree in Gaza before crossing into Israel with two of the bodies, which, for some reason, he chose to bury here."

"What about the killing method?"

"Several issues rose here. It is very challenging for us to pinpoint the exact cause of their deaths. However, I suggest you come with me. There are a few things I would like to show you. That's why I asked you to come to the Institute." They walked together through the hallways of the Institute, but this time, they entered another, smaller room. He switched on the light. At the center of the room lay two of the victims, on the sstainless steal surgeon table, covered in blue paper. Arieli circled the tables and stopped at one corner, turning on a powerful ceiling lamp. He signaled her to approach and put on a face mask.

"The last two women who were murdered, Dvora and Abigail, were likely strangled with a thin and strong cord, but not with an iron wire as I initially suspected. I took some iron wires and tried to see their effects on the bodies, but none of the results matched what we found on the victims. Therefore, it must be a different type of wire, perhaps nylon, like the one Malak and Dvora were tied with, or some other type. Either way, miraculously, no traces of the wire were left on any of the victims."

"What about the other murders?"

"That's what I wanted to show you." He gestured for her to approach Malak's body, and she complied. He pointed to a specific area on the woman's neck and said, "Both Palestinian women have a small puncture point, as you can see here, near the throat. This could indicate the injection of some substance into their bodies before death. It's extremely difficult to detect the substance in bodies so heavily decomposed, but I sent some samples to the lab for further analysis. We must consider that it could be a volatile or degradable substance, leaving no traces in the body."

"Did you find injection points in the Israeli victims as well?"

"No, but I didn't search the entire body; I focused only in the neck area." They both scanned Abigail's body, but found nothing. "If there are injection points, they must be very tiny, and it's possible we couldn't detect them if the women were alive for several hours after the injection."

"Is there another way to examine subcutaneous tissue damage?"

"Not really. I'll do what I can, and as soon as I have the results, I'll send them to you. But if, by any chance, there are more victims, try, first of all, to look for such injection points so we can link the killer to all the cases."

"Understood. And did you want to show me something else?"

"Yes. Regarding the cloth that wrapped both Abigail and Anan's bodies in the second murder, it's a special fabric used as shrouds for deceased bodies and is mainly found in mortuaries."

"I need a sample of that. I'll send it to the laboratory of forensic science in Jerusalem, and maybe we can trace the source of the mortuary room from which it was taken and find a lead to the culprit." Professor Arieli cut a small piece from the shroud and placed it in an evidence bag. He sealed the bag and handed it to Yael. Then he turned off the lights and led Yael out of the room.

They walked through the hallways again, heading towards the exit gate, as Yael asked: "Did you find any other evidence related to the killer? Fingerprints? Semen residues? Saliva? Fingernails? Anything that can be analyzed for DNA?"

"No," Arieli replied.

"I understand. In any case, if you find anything new, please update me immediately."

He sighed and then said, "Yael, this is a tough case. It could very well involve more than one murderer. I truly believe you should focus on the motive. Don't rely solely on the forensic evidence. Try to find contextual, patterned, social behavior. In my opinion, if we understand the motive, we can base the forensic analysis on it. If I were you, I'd go back to the crime scenes and try to pinpoint exactly where the women were murdered. There might be hidden answers there."

13.

*Samaria's territorial brigade, Horon camp,
By Huwara checkpoint*

At 16:12, Yael entered the Samaria's territorial brigade Base with her car and parked it near the officers' quarters. A cold breeze greeted her, and she wrapped herself in the blue army field coat, took her gun, shoved it in her belt, and put on a black wool hat. No rain fell, but the ground was soaked with water, and her black shoes sank lightly into the mud, dampening them. She could not recall the last time she had carried a weapon, but Uri Amit had requested it from her now, and she knew he was right. She noticed how the handling and loading of the gun felt natural in her hands, and she even felt a slight sense of power and strength, knowing she was armed. She concealed the gun as she wrapped it inside the coat, locked the car, and went inside to Yonatan Uziel's office.

"Ibrahim hasn't reached the checkpoint yet, and he hasn't made contact," he said as she approached the coffee station to prepare a drink for herself. He sat in his shabby chair, legs propped up on the table, and his hands clasped behind his head. When she settled in front of him, he remained in that position, gazing out the window.

"It will be dark soon. What do you suggest we do?"

"Do you know anyone in the Palestinian Authority or the Palestinian police who could help?"

"Help with what? I won't send forces to Nablus to rescue a Hamas operative."

"Help in locating him. Maybe something happened to him."

"If he wanted to, he would have made contact."

"Do you know anyone or not?"

"And if I do know someone? What do you expect to happen now? That the Palestinian police will go and search for a senior Hamas operative in Nablus after we brought him there, and then hand him over to us?"

"That's exactly what I expect to happen."

"Yael, it doesn't work like that."

"I have no patience for your 'politics on the side.' We have five murder cases to investigate. There are killers running amok in the area, and Ibrahim is a crucial contact to solve these cases. I cannot find myself every few hours engaged in discussions and negotiations over 'yes Ibrahim, no Ibrahim.'"

Uziel bent his legs, sat on the chair and leaned closer to Yael. "That is the situation. It is a complicated area. There are Jews and Arabs, settlers and Palestinians, Hamas, Jihad, and Fatah, and the Palestinian police, and tribes, half of the world walks around here, Americans and Saudis, Iranians and Turks, the European Union and the Israeli government. Each one has different interests, each one wants something else, and you, me, and Ibrahim need to find a way to manage this event amidst all the chaos. You know that, and I know that. This is what we have."

She stood up, pulled out her phone, and dialed a number.

"Who are you calling?"

She signaled him to wait as she listened to the ringing tone on her phone. After a few rings, a deep, Arabic-accented voice emerged from the device's speaker, he spoke Hebrew in a thick Arabic accent.

"It's been a very long time since I last saw this number."

"Yaser, my dear, how are you? It has been a while. How old are you, if I may ask?"

"I am eighty-one years old. Still alive and kicking, just as you can hear."

Yaser Fahamawi was a major in the Palestinian police, the deputy commander of the Jenin police station, one of the busiest and most challenging stations. Fahamawi was a people's person and excelled in navigating between Israelis and Palestinians, managing to serve for many years in the police without making enemies from either side. His connections with the Israelis were well known, and he managed to maintain them even during times of tension. He had worked closely with Yael in several cases, including an incident in the late '90's involving the rescue of Naif Badir, the same Hamas operative who later murdered Gidi.

To solve the case, the two of them had traveled together to the city of Madaba in Jordan, where they learned about the killer's methods of operation. However, their bond deepened after Fahamawi had already left his post and retired from the police in the early 2000s, becoming a covert adviser. The last time she saw him was at Gidi's funeral in 2011, and they lost contact since then. Fahamawi secluded himself in his home in Ramallah, maintaining a low profile regarding his former police work. Yet, Yael occasionally heard whispers about him being sought after by Palestinian authorities for mediating between them and Israeli security mechanisms. He was indeed a key figure and an important liaison.

"It's good to hear your voice again."

"Yours too. I would be happy to hear more about how you're feeling, but I'm guessing you didn't call for that. There must be a connection to the murders of the women, right?"

"Indirect connection," she said, catching the penetrating gaze she got from Uziel. She turned her back to him and continued the conversation. "I need to locate someone who crossed into the Palestinian territories yesterday with our approval, and he has disappeared."

"Is he a suspect?" Fahamawi asked.

"No. He..." Uziel waved his hands, but she ignored it again. "He is helping us solve the case."

"What is his name?"

"Ibrahim Azberga."

"Ibrahim Azberga, the Major General of Hamas from Gaza?"

"Yes."

"What is he doing here? Since when are you collaborating with Hamas?"

Silence.

"I understand," he said after a minute. Uziel looked desperate.

"I need your help. I can't just call the Palestinian police and inform them that we made a deal with their enemy. It has to be subtle, as you know."

"Alright. Give me some time to snoop around. I'll update you as soon as possible."

"Thank you," she said and ended the call. Uziel raised his hands in surrender.

"What?" she asked.

"You are like a train rushing at two-hundred kilometers per hour into a wall. You might..." he lit a cigarette and puffed on the smoke that escaped, "manage to break through the wall—who knows. But it's also very possible that you'll crash into it and take everyone in the compartments down with you."

***

Just a few moments passed until Yael's phone vibrated, and the name Fahamawi appeared on the screen. But during that brief time, Yael and Yonatan Uzial managed to exchange accusations. "You're lucky that behind you, there are two like Aharon Shaked and Uri Amit who appreciate you and allow you such freedom of action. I wouldn't have allowed it," he told her, and she deliberated on how to respond, eventually giving up on the confrontation again. Yonatan Uzial was a key figure in her investigation, and she might need to use him later. Opening a front against him seemed unnecessary at this stage. When she'll need to, she'll put him in his place.

"I appreciate your honesty," she said, answering the call while walking around the room.

"He's in our custody, in the Palestinian Authority," Fahamawi said.

"Who? Ibrahim?" Yael asked. "Are you sure?"

"Yes. Ibrahim Azberga, a resident of Gaza, crossed the Huwara checkpoint yesterday at 7:00 PM and entered Nablus. He was arrested at the city's entrance by a Palestinian policeman after failing to present any documents or permits for his visit to his family. He was taken to the police station in the city, where it was discovered that he is linked to the Hamas movement. He was detained, interrogated this morning, and is now awaiting trial."

"Did he explain to them that he's investigating the murders?"

"Not as far as I am aware."

"Yasser, you need to release him."

"I'm not the right person, Yael. I'm already out of the system. I'm sorry."

"No need to apologize. I don't know what I would do without you. Thank you."

"You're welcome," he said and hung up. He knew she wasn't alone, and this was not the time for small talk. Yael continued to move around the room uncomfortably, ignoring Yonatan Uzial's presence.

"What are you planning to do?" Uzial asked, but Yael had already raised her phone again and dialed a number. Aharon Shakad was on the line. From the moment she met him, she had never experienced a situation where he did not answer her call. The man, who was a general officer in the central command, followed superintended Yael Lavie's every move. Their joint service in the army made him believe she was destined to lead one of Israel's security systems with brilliance. He did not expect that Gidi's death would divert her from the path she had chosen for herself. He was also happy that she decided to return to serve and took on this complex and challenging investigation. In a sense, he was waiting for her to turn to him and activate him. And now, it was happening.

"Yael? What's going on?" He never asked about her well-being. It was always the mission at stake.

"The Palestinian police arrested Azberga, he is imprisoned in Nablus. I need to speak with someone who can release him—or at least understand why he was arrested."

"I'm on it," he said and hung up. Just like that, after three words only. Businesslike, purposeful, no warmth. That is how Aharon Shaked was. She placed the device in her bag and looked around. She did not want to stay in the same room with Uziel. She grabbed her coat and stepped out into the freezing wind, into the drizzling rain that had just begun to fall.

***

At 5:01 PM, Shaked called. "Ibrahim is at the detention station at the entrance to Nablus, after the refugee camp in Balata, on the city's main street, Al Shahid Mtawaa. The Palestinians refuse to cooperate with Israel and hand him back over at the checkpoint. There's no choice; the army will have to enter and get him out of there. Ibrahim will wait for them in the parking lot beneath the government offices, near the detention facility."

"Does Uziel know about this?"

"Yes. I spoke with him. He will brief the forces shortly. I suggest you wait until sunset, then enter the city under the cover of darkness, without causing any commotion."

"When you say 'you...'"

"That includes you. I think it is best if you are there to ensure they don't harm him."

After a long pause she said: "Okay. I'll go with them." Yael ended the call and returned to Uziel's office. He was sitting with two of his commanders near a map of the area, marking it with different symbols. She sat beside him, took out a notebook and pen from her pocket, and said, "I want to know exactly what your plan is and how I fit into it."

***

They worked for an entire hour on the operation plan. They would enter with two armored vehicles, using Road 5070 and then through Al Quds Street, which connects the rural area to the city of Nablus. They would bypass the Balata refugee camp from the west and blend in with the main entrance to the city until reaching the police compound where Ibrahim was held. There, they would split up. One car would wait hidden in the parking lot, in case of any confrontation. The second car would continue alone to the government building, pick up Ibrahim, and sneak away. The goal was to maintain a low profile. Each car would be manned by two armed soldiers, a driver, and a commander. Uziel would be in charge of the first car. Yael would accompany him along with another soldier and the driver. The travel time wouldn't exceed 10 minutes, and in case of roadblocks on the highway, they would escape through the dirt roads towards Mount Gerizim and Mitzpe Yosef, where they would connect with road 5072 and another force approaching from the checkpoint. In total, 11 soldiers were assigned to the mission, including three drivers, an observer, and a sniper who would wait on the Samaritan Hill.

Yael thought Uziel might raise objections and not allow her to join the rescue forces, but to her surprise, Uziel seemed resolute and receptive during the briefing of the operation, letting her speak her mind. When they finished, he sent her to the armory to get a bulletproof vest, a helmet, two additional magazines for her gun, and to change her shoes to military boots.

At 6:40 PM, the entire team was ready inside their vehicles, alerts were sent to all the checkpoints along the way, and Yael managed to speak with Aharon Shaked and Uri Amit to update them on the details. She hesitated about talking to her mother or Keren, but eventually decided against it. There was no need to open any more fronts, she reassured herself for the second time that afternoon.

Uziel got into the armored vehicle and sat beside the driver, covered in his bulletproof vest with five additional magazines, holding a Galil gun. A gun was holstered in his belt. He secured the heavy door, its window covered with steel grating, and locked it. "In case of a fire, we quickly dismount from the vehicle and assemble together on the opposite side of the attack, understood?" he shouted.

"Understood," Yael replied with a slightly jittery tone.

"The West Bank is burning," he said. "There's a good chance that if they see a military vehicle, they will attack us. I need you attentive and obedient. It's not the time to question orders." She nodded in compliance. The driver started the car, and it drove through the checkpoint towards the refugee camp.

***

They traveled for a few minutes and passed through the Balata refugee camp, heading north towards the access road to the city of Nablus. Throughout the day, the refugee camp was bustling with activity, children's voices blending with the prayers of the Muezzin, donkeys pulled carts next to luxury cars. The traffic congestion on the road slowed their progress, and they feared being targeted by stone-throwing and Molotov cocktails once it became apparent that the IDF had entered Palestinian territory. The camp, with a square shape and sides not exceeding 500 meters, housed around 30,000 Palestinian refugees who had settled there and erected shaky buildings. It was one of the most densely populated places on Earth. Its name was derived from a mispronunciation of the Platanus tree, as the Arabic pronunciation lacked the "p" sound and was replaced by a "b." But there were no trees there, and it had been considered one of the Palestinian terror strongholds since the 1960s. Despite being under the protection of the Palestinian Authority, its inhabitants failed to rehabilitate it, and poverty persisted.

Entering Nablus through the Balata camp was considered very dangerous for the Israeli forces, but entering from the north implied wasting precious time and traversing the city's territories until reaching the destination located in its southern part. Similarly, leaving through the northern part of the city would take more time and expose the forces to real danger. Uziel decided to seize the moment and bypass the camp without giving its inhabitants the opportunity to organize any action. Nobody in Balata expected to see IDF vehicles speeding along the road to Nablus, and even less did they expect them to return the same way. Uziel counted on the element of surprise, but it failed.

As the two vehicles reached the splitting point, the road seemed to clear as if on cue. A rain of stones started pelting toward them, but they continued driving along the road. The two drivers pressed on the gas pedal with determination, passing by mosques, grocery stores, and restaurants full of diners. Yet, throughout the entire journey, young Palestinians, some of them children, stood along the road and hurled everything they could find at them. The armored vehicle's front window, though protected by iron bars, cracked and split, allowing a cold breeze to penetrate. Yael could feel her heartbeat escalating, but she maintained her composure and alertness. She refused to let fear take over. More explosions and more stones followed, and then she saw it on the roadside—a Molotov cocktail held by a boy of about 16, waiting for them.

"Molotov cocktail incoming!" Uziel shouted through the communication system, but the Molotov cocktail was not aimed at them. Instead, it flew towards the trailing vehicle. Yael looked back and witnessed the Molotov cocktail landing on the military vehicle, setting its roof and driver's door on fire. The vehicle didn't slow down or stop but continued to race toward them at an alarming speed, almost colliding with their car.

"We need to get out of here!" the driver shouted to Uziel. "Where are you leading us?"

"Oleg," Uziel replied confidently. "Keep driving, don't get excited, everything is under control. We've done this a hundred times before."

"It's never been like this. We should have come with more forces. We should go back."

"We're not going back until we bring him, is that clear?" Uziel barked.

"Is it you?" Oleg shouted. "This is because of you, right?"

"Shut up," Uziel replied.

"If you hadn't let the terrorist go, this wouldn't be happening!"

"I said shut up!" Uziel turned his head towards a large rock that was hurled at them and landed on the car door.

"We're all going to die because of some wretched Hamas man? My blood is on your hands, do you hear me?"

"If you don't shut your mouth right now, I'll shoot you in the leg." *Boom.* Another rock exploded on the car roof. Yael looked back.

The trailing vehicle was entirely engulfed in flames. The communication device buzzed: "Commander, we're on fire. We need to stop and put it out, or we will all burn here."

"Two minutes," Uziel ordered through the communication device. "We will stop at the police compound, and extinguish the fire." But what happened a second later disrupted all his plans. They reached the intersection of Al-Shahid and Amman streets and discovered a makeshift roadblock made of rocks, garbage bins, and burning tires. They could not pass the intersection without colliding with the blockade. Dozens of Palestinians stood on the other side, throwing stones and Molotov cocktails at them. Going back was not an option, and they could not enter the Palestinian police compound, as its entrance was located behind the improvised roadblock.

"Prepare your gun," Uziel instructed Yael. "We might have to get out of the car and run into the compound."

"What do you plan on doing there?" Yael asked.

"To defend, fight, and wait for rescue," Uziel replied as a Molotov cocktail landed on the front window of the car, engulfing everything around them in flames. Oleg, who was very terrified, pressed hard on the gas pedal instead of stopping, plowing forcefully into one of the burning trash cans, acting as a makeshift ramp for the vehicle. The car took off into the air and landed on a young boy who had thrown Molotov cocktail towards them. The lower half of his body was crushed under the car, and he got covered in fuel from another Molotov cocktail he held in his hand. Only mere seconds later, the fire spread from the military vehicle to his clothes, turning him into a blazing inferno.

"Reverse!" Uziel shouted at Oleg. Oleg shifted into reverse and pressed the gas, but nothing happened except for the loud roar of the engine. A group of young Palestinians stormed towards them, but instead of attacking, they aimed to rescue the burning kid.

"Reverse!" Uziel yelled again.

"It's not moving!" Oleg cried out. He was sweating profusely, the intense heat inside the car becoming unbearable, and smoke seeped in through the cracks in the front window. One young Palestinian managed to climb onto the car's engine cover and began beating the iron with a wooden rod. One strike followed by another, and suddenly a spray of blood burst from his chest, staining the car's windshield. **The sniper**, Yael thought. This was a fantastic opportunity.

"Let's escape to the compound. They're busy rescuing him; the sniper will take care of anyone chasing us. It's the perfect opportunity." Uziel looked at her and nodded. "Unlock the doors and prepare your weapons. These are just young boys. If someone threatens you, fire a warning shot into the air first, then aim for the legs." he raised his communication device, pressed the button, and shouted into it, "One, this is Vertex, state your location. Over."

A few seconds passed before a voice came through the device, "We are under attack. Withdrawing to the rear."

"Copy that, head to defensive positions. We're entering the station. After regrouping, prepare for rescue."

"Understood," the voice replied and fell silent. Uziel quickly surveyed his surroundings. "Prepare your weapons," he directed.

Yael pulled out her pistol and loaded it. She gazed outside, waiting for the right moment to make a move. "On my command, we all scatter and run towards the station," Uziel announced. "Ready?"

"Yes," Yael said. "Yes," Oleg responded. Yael noticed that he held a shortened, loaded M-16 rifle. Uziel waited another minute as the young Palestinians moved the burning kid away from the car, then signaled for them to go. But just as they were about to act, an explosion erupted, launching the car into the air, landing forcefully underneath it. Yael was thrown backward, her head hitting the passenger seat. Oleg gripped his rifle and attempted to lift it towards the window, but the long barrel got stuck on the dashboard, discharging a round towards his own legs. A cry of terror escaped his lips as the engine roared back to life when Oleg instinctively pressed the gas pedal. The car lurched forward with Yael helplessly thrown into the back compartment. She tried to grasp onto something to steady herself, but failed. Through the smoke enveloping the car, she saw flickering flames surrounding her, and a suffocating feeling overcame her. Suddenly, the car door swung open, and a blast of fire burnt her face.

14.

Ibrahim Azberga waited at the entrance of the government building in Nablus. He was furious with himself for allowing the Palestinian police to apprehend him without a fight, wasting hours in custody as a result. If it were up to him, he would have walked out onto the street, hailed a Palestinian cab to the checkpoint, and crossed back into Israeli territory. However, the Palestinian Authority had already marked him and restricted his movement within their territories. The tension between the Palestinian Authority and the Hamas movement was escalating in the recent weeks, and the Authority was apprehensive that Azberga might have hidden motives, refusing to let him roam freely.

Azberga had no interest in getting involved in the internal conflicts between the Palestinian Authority and Hamas. He came to investigate the murder cases, not to wage war, and he had been trying to convey this message to his investigators all along. He directed them towards the Israelis, but the Palestinian dynamics had their own pace, and nobody bothered to come to his aid. Eventually, he simply lay down on his cot in the detention room, waiting for his trial or release.

When one of the guards entered and led him down the stairs towards the entrance of the police station, Azberga already sensed that Yael figured something had happened, and he did not just vanish before her. "They're coming to pick you up in half an hour," the guard informed him. Azberga was tired and hungry, his body drenched in sweat as he hadn't showered in two days, and his mouth tasted stale. He walked slowly, glancing around, looking for familiar faces from previous years. But the police station continued to operate slowly and indifferently, completely ignoring his presence.

Suddenly, an explosion echoed through the building. Policemen rushed out of their offices, running towards the source of the noise, some with guns drawn. Ibrahim ran alongside them. They burst through the main entrance of the station to the parking lot, and there they were faced with a horrifying sight.

An IDF vehicle engulfed in flames, had collided with a makeshift Palestinian barricade formed by dozens of young Palestinians who were acting wildly, hurling stones and Molotov cocktails. One of the boys lay on the asphalt, his body broken and engulfed in flames, screaming in agony. One of the Molotov cocktails exploded forcefully on the vehicle, which tried to maneuver and escape the scene but got trapped between a heap of rocks and a barrage of stones, unable to turn around. The vehicle began to skid, its tires and windows ablaze, and more Molotov cocktails hit it one after the other, igniting the trunk and driver's door. Inside the vehicle, Ibrahim managed to catch a glimpse of several figures moving, and amidst them, he thought he recognized Yael. Dozens more young Palestinians made their way to the scene, their cries echoing, the lynching seemed inevitable now. Ibrahim knew that if the soldiers were not rescued immediately, they would burn to death. Even worse, if the soldiers were forced to leave the vehicle, the law dictated they would have to shoot in all directions to extricate themselves, resulting in numerous dead and injured Palestinians.

"Come!" he shouted to several policemen, but at that moment, gunfire rang out above them, and a Palestinian boy who had climbed on the roof of the vehicle was thrown back and fell to the asphalt.

"There is a sniper!" someone yelled in Arabic, and some of the policemen rushed back into the police station.

The fire spread rapidly, and Ibrahim knew there was no other choice. He started running towards the scene. He was unarmed, and he knew it could cost him his life. Two Palestinian policemen ran with him. He thought that there could not be a more surreal sight than this: a high-ranking Hamas official running with two Palestinian policemen to rescue Israeli soldiers from a burning jeep under attack by enraged young Palestinian. Surely, God must be laughing. He wondered if his sprint would be interpreted as another attack on the jeep, and the Israeli sniper would also try to shoot him. In that moment another shot was heard, passing above his head. Another Palestinian boy, who had approached the jeep with a Molotov cocktail, was thrown back when his left leg was hit by a bullet, and he started bleeding. Some of his friends carried him across the road, disappearing into one of the houses. Chaos reigned all around.

Ibrahim rushed towards the burning vehicle, with no extinguisher or any way to put out the flames. As he approached the passenger door, a loud explosion was heard from the engine area. One of the tires exploded with force, lifting the vehicle into the air. Several boys standing nearby, watching the military vehicle go up in flames, panicked and retreated. Ibrahim stumbled a few meters backward and landed on a rock by the roadside. The two policemen who had arrived with him did their best to disperse the young Palestinians, but to no avail. Ibrahim struggled to get up and noticed that his leg was injured. A piece of flesh had been torn off his thigh and stuck out of his pants. Ignoring the pain, he took a deep breath, covered his face with his shirt, and darted through the wall of flames towards the passenger door. He stormed at the handle, pulling with all his might until he managed to break open the door. The pressure differences pumped the flame into the interior of the vehicle, then retreated at once. Yael's bruised face emerged from the car, and he immediately grabbed her by the arm that was holding the gun, and pulled her out. She staggered to the asphalt, struggling to breathe with heavy coughs and wheezing. Ibrahim feared she might eject a bullet from the gun in her hand. She tried to say something but choked repeatedly. Finally, she pointed towards the vehicle and managed to say, "They are still inside," as she struggled to rise.

He started running back towards the vehicle, but a hail of stones welcomed him. The two policemen who were with him began to retreat as well. The leg of another boy was pierced by a sniper's shot, and the young Palestinians backed off again. He approached the passenger door and opened it. Uziel lay in front of him, unconscious. Ibrahim grabbed his jacket and pulled him outside. Uziel showed no signs of awareness. Yael began crawling towards him as Ibrahim moved to rescue Oleg. She started attending to Uziel, trying to revive him, and wake him up. Uziel was alive, but his pulse was fast, and his breathing weak. Ibrahim struggled with the car door, but it was locked from the inside. It seemed that the young driver got overwhelmed by the chaotic scene and locked the door. The vehicle was already engulfed in flames, making it impossible to approach. Ibrahim circled the car, his leg throbbing, the pain taking its toll on his body. He entered the vehicle through the passenger door. The driver was in his seat, seatbelt holding him in place, flames engulfing his hair. Ibrahim took a deep breath, darted into the fire, and released the seatbelt and door latch. At that moment, the driver's door swung open, and the faces of Uziel and Yael appeared in front of him. They grabbed Oleg and pulled him out, then dragged him towards the police station. Ibrahim collapsed outside the car door. He lay on the asphalt dazed and struggling to breathe. One of the policemen approached, helped him up, and they made their way to the police station together. Glancing back, he saw the burning car, consumed slowly by the flames. Gunshots and explosions erupted from it, keeping the group of stone-throwing young Palestinians at a safe distance. Five minutes later, two Red Crescent ambulances arrived and began evacuating the injured boys from the scene. Only an hour later, a convoy of armored vehicles arrived at the station and took the four back to the checkpoint. But it was too late for the IDF driver. Oleg's fate was sealed right there. He died on the spot.

***

Aharon Shaked sat across from Uri Amit. The two brothers in arms had never clashed before; on the contrary, their friendship had lasted for many years. It seemed that the first disagreement between them had led to some distance.

"We need to stop this madness," said Amit. "It's getting out of control."

"Exactly the opposite," replied Shaked. "We should acknowledge that we are seeking engagement, that there is activity in the field. Let the killers and troublemakers know that we will not stop until we put our hands on them."

"We would not be having this conversation if she were dead."

"She's fine..."

"You have a dead soldier. How can you just carry on as if nothing happened?"

Shaked got up from his chair and walked to his office window. The stout man, barely reaching 165 centimeters in height, and with his head seemingly attached directly to his body, knew in his heart that if something had happened to Yael, he could not have forgiven himself for it. Despite that, he knew he had made the right decision.

He turned back to Amit and said: "We both know she is the right person in the right place. She is a level-headed and balanced woman, with deep thinking ability, and she will not go to war for no reason. I don't need another hothead in the equation. I need a manager."

Amit stayed silent for a long time, then finally raised his hands in surrender. "What should we do with Ibrahim?"

"Leave him at the station tonight; he'll sleep in the detention room. He's not under arrest, but he shouldn't wander freely. How is he doing?"

"He is injured, but had already received treatment. He has five stitches on his leg."

"And Uziel?"

"Hospitalized under supervision. He Inhaled a lot of smoke. I believe he will be released in a few days."

"And Yael? How is she holding up?" Now the two men stood face to face.

"I'm not so sure she will cope well with this adventure," said Amit. He patted Shaked's shoulder lightly, and left the office.

15.
27.2.2015

When Yael entered her office at the Judea and Samaria District Police Station, Ibrahim was already there, drinking coffee and reviewing documents. The whiteboard on the wall gradually filled with more and more information, yet many question marks still remained.

"How are you?" he asked, and it was a question she struggled to answer. When she got home last night after the long interrogation at the territorial brigade, the water in the boiler was already cold. She took a shower nonetheless, letting the low temperature freeze her body. Afterward, shivering, she got out, looked at herself in the mirror, her hair disheveled, too many gray hairs crowning it, and dark circles appearing around her eyes alongside wrinkles. She didn't recognize herself. Then she went to the kitchen and made herself a sandwich with butter and an omelet, trying to somewhat nourish her exhausted body. She drank tea, followed by a glass of wine, and then collapsed onto the bed, utterly fatigued, but still barely managed to fall asleep. Eventually, she gave in, got up at 5:30 in the morning, and decided to prepare breakfast treats for her children. She fried omelets and toasted bread with yellow cheese, squeezed fresh orange juice, and made dessert mousse. She laid some sausages on the table and cut vegetables abundantly. The two, who got up earlier than usual, sat down and enjoyed their meal. Then she drove them to school and said goodbye to them with a big hug. Now, as she arrived at the office, she felt somewhat better, but fatigue started to take its toll, and she promised herself that she would finish this day much earlier.

"I'm fine," she lied. "A bit tired. How about you?"

"I looked at the timeline you made and added a few more details. We still lack information about the two Israeli victims."

"I am waiting for the number for the bus driver who drove Devora Goshen to work on that day. Uri was supposed to give it to me."

"Do you mean this?" He picked up a note from her desk and handed it to her. She glanced at it.

"Yes," she said, taking out her phone.

"Amit and I already spoke with him this morning," Ibrahim said. Yael glanced at her watch; it was already past 10:00 AM. It was the first time in the last five years that she allowed herself to arrive so late for work.

"And what did he say?" she asked.

"Devora did not get on his bus that day."

"Meaning..." Yael said, and they both completed the sentence together: "She was kidnapped somewhere between her house and the bus stop."

They approached the map of the area hanging on the office wall and looked at it together.

"Both Israeli women left alone within their settlement's boundaries and went to their destination without anyone seeing them. Devora walked from her house to the bus stop," Ibrahim marked the two locations on the map, and then he also marked Abigail's route: "Abigail walked from her friend's house to her house."

"We need to go there and trace the routes they took. We will check all possible roads between the destinations; perhaps we can find clues to the motives or the actual murder scene," Yael said as she began to pack her bag.

"Perhaps," said Ibrahim.

He stood up and waited for her by the door.

***

Ramzi Abu-Shaqra stood over the bed of his 17-year-old younger brother, Saeed, at the Nablus University Hospital. For the past year, 20-year-old Abu Shaqra had spent his time in dorms at Bir-Zeit University near Ramallah, barely seeing his family. As a refugee coming from the Balata camp, Ramzi had set his goal to obtain an academic degree and become a Palestinian lawyer representing his people against the Israeli legal system, fighting for their freedom and rights. He worked tirelessly day in and day out, saving every penny, working construction, cleaning streets, as a porter, and herding sheep. When he returned exhausted to his crowded and grim home in the camp, he never gave up on himself, studied, and narrowed the gaps to be eligible for a degree. His impoverished parents, bitter and anguished, desperate against the apathy of their leaders, the apathy of the world, drawn into the daily chaos of the impossible life under the control of the Palestinian Authority—had given up. His father stopped working, his mother sank into depression, and the burden of providing fell on Ramzi and his five siblings. When he decided to break free, to depart and study and leave his family behind, it was the hardest decision of his life. But he knew that if he did not do it, he would never escape the refugee camp.

Saeed lay in a sedated slumber, his breathing shallow, a thin stream of air escaping his exposed mouth. Parts of his face were bandaged, as well as his neck and chest. The hospital blanket concealed the space that was torn underneath his lower body—both legs severed by the medical team after they crashed beyond repair. The young boy, full of life until yesterday, now lay mortally wounded, connected to monitors that were measuring the faint activity of his heart and breath, appearing like a lifeless body.

Ramzi Abu Shaqra felt the anger boiling inside him, not knowing whom he was angry at; himself, for not being there for his brother, his family; for being unable to protect and watch over him; his people, who had known many defeats but still kept pillaging his kids with the Zionist enemy, or the Zionist themselves. Abu Shaqra was not a staunch supporter of the Palestinian Authority. Like many of his relatives, he wanted to have an Israeli blue ID, be an Israeli citizen with equal rights. He dreamed of freedom, rights, and justice, tired of wars. He also knew that justice was a matter of perspective, and struggles for justice were often in vain.

But now, with his blood boiling, he realized he had to take action. Yesterday evening, a convoy of army vehicles had once again invaded the Palestinian territory in the heart of Nablus. Saeed, along with his friends, got caught up in the protest that erupted along the main access road to the city. They began throwing stones and then Molotov cocktails. The fight was hard. As planned in advance, a barricade was set up at the city entrance, and Saeed was among its founders. Like a true hero, he stood on the barricade facing the approaching armored vehicle and hurled rocks and Molotov cocktails at it. But the Israeli vehicle drove towards him, crushing him with force, and his lower body was tragically crushed. The Molotov cocktail he was holding, ignited, and Saeed caught fire. When his friends managed to put out the fire, the horrific truth emerged. Saeed's chest, neck, and face were severely burned, third and fourth-degree burns. The doctors did not think he would make it through the night, but Saeed survived. When he will wake up, he will no longer be the lively boy he used to be. And Ramzi knew he could never return to his life, either. His grand dream shattered on the harsh reality, and even though the perpetrator driver did not survive, the desire for revenge flared inside him. He kissed his brother gently and bid him farewell, left the hospital, and disappeared.

***

The settlement of Ma'ale Levona was nestled between boulders, in the hilly landscape with orchards, and fields, at an altitude of 750 meters above its surroundings. The only entrance to the settlement was from the east, through a road passing close to a wooded grove and then wound through various public facilities, recreational areas, and educational institutions of the settlement. Dvora Goshen, whose home was situated on the northern side of the settlement, would make her way each morning from its center to the bus station located in the southern part. The passage between the two parts of the settlement was possible through several streets and alleys, and Yael and Abraham mapped them all.

It was noon when they began walking along each of the marked routes, searching for evidence and signs of the woman's abduction.

"The only way to lead her from here to the field where she was found is by car. That means, at a certain point, the killer had to catch her and put her into his car," Yael said.

"If that was your mission, what would be the best way to do it?"

"Morning hours are problematic. The streets are crowded with people. So I would catch her close to her home and take her to the grove, where the chances of being noticed are lowest. If she passes through the center of the settlement, the story is lost as far as the murderer is concerned."

"I agree," said Ibrahim. "He could have parked his car in the dirt road in the grove's entrance, and leave it there without anyone noticing. After you," he gestured with his hand towards the route.

They walked along the perimeter fence of the settlement, turning over rocks and stones, examining the positioning of security cameras, and flipping through scattered trash the winds blew, until they reached the grove area. They left the road and took a dirt path leading through the trees, walking towards the outer perimeter road of the settlement. Among the trees, various types of grass grew, making their path difficult and easily hiding secrets and clues among them. They shuffled along, using a stick to clear the way, pressing aside grass here and there, trying to expose the ground, but it seemed futile. The shrubs were damp, the soil was marshy, and the search was in vain.

"Is there any point in bringing canines here?" Ibrahim asked.

"I doubt it," Yael replied. "It has been raining here for a few days. I don't believe any scent would be left behind." She stopped in the heart of the grove, looking around hopelessly. Everything was in place, nothing disturbed.

"Come," she said after a few moments. "We are done here. It is a waste of time."

"Where do you want to go from here?"

"To Einav settlement. Maybe we will find out what happened to Abigail."

***

The religious settlement of Einav was divided into three residential clusters. The older and larger southern neighborhood housed the administration building, the shopping center, and public facilities. The younger northern neighborhood was to the north of the older one, and the new neighborhood sat on the northwestern ridge of the settlement. The access road to the settlement cut through the three neighborhoods, connecting at its edge to a newly constructed trail that was recently dug and paved, aiming to establish a fourth neighborhood, west of the existing settlement. Abigail Avnun's house was on the southern street of the older neighborhood, as her parents were among the founders of the settlement and early settlers. Her friend's house, on the other hand, was in the northern cluster of the settlement, beyond the main access road. Therefore, when Abigail went to visit her friend on that evening, she had to walk a distance of nearly a kilometer in darkness and rain, crossing the main road to return home.

Yael and Ibrahim estimated that Abigail would likely choose the shortest and fastest route to cross the settlement, possibly risking passing close to the settlement's perimeter fence. They went to her friend's house and then began marching southward towards road 5570 and the main streets. They employed the same methods, scanning the paths lengthwise and crosswise, searching for debris, torn fabric, her lost phone—anything that might hint at what happened and where she might have been kidnapped or murdered. But they had no success.

"If not the short route, then maybe the long one?" Ibrahim suggested.

"Why would she do that?"

"I don't know. But right now, we have nothing."

They returned to their starting point. It was already after 4 PM, and there was not much time left until sunset. The air was cooling rapidly, and the skies were once again covered with clouds. It was a particularly cold and rainy winter, with the promise of snow on the mountain peaks of the Samaria region. Yael's fingers were freezing, and she tried not to take them out of her pockets. They crossed the access road again and continued straight towards an inner circular road surrounded by one-story buildings, a park and playgrounds. They circled the park on the road until they got to the other side, then turned and entered the park. There was a small lawn, a few playground structures, benches, and water drinking fountains. Two kids were playing and fooling around on the grass, used to the cold, their shoes filled with mud, their joy evident, unafraid. Yael wondered if they were aware of the lurking danger, that the killer had not been caught yet, and he might be observing them.

They scanned again, going back and forth, and then split up. She went towards the lawn, and he checked the playground structures. She searched between rosebushes, lavenders, and aloysias, in the public restroom facilities, and in the parking lot. He scanned the artificial grass surfaces, the recycling bins, and the trash cans. But the bins had been emptied long ago. He passed by one trash can after another until he reached the last one—still finding nothing.

Yael walked around the buildings that were on the southern end of the cluster, and then walked towards Ibrahim and stopped. "Did you find anything?"

"There is nothing here," he said. "I looked everywhere." He gazed at the surroundings once more, trying to find other possible routes. But they both knew that too much time had passed, and thanks to the rain and the wind, their chances of discovering any clue were slim.

In disappointment, Ibrahim kicked the metal trash can, shifting it a few centimeters. That is when they saw it. There, on the damp and sandy ground, beneath the overturned trash can, lay a small syringe, typically used for vaccination or insulin injections for diabetic patients, and gauze lay right next to it. The needle was still fixed at the end of the syringe, and the plunger was pressed down to the end. They exchanged glances, and Yael, who pulled out a pair of surgical gloves from her pocket, picked up the syringe and gauze, and began to walk quickly towards the car parked in the southern neighborhood. Ibrahim followed her steps. A faint smile gradually appeared on his face.

16.

The Laboratory for Forensic Science in Jerusalem stood on Ha'oman Street, situated in the southern region of the city. Knowing that the laboratory would shut its doors at 6:30 PM, Yael firmly pressed the gas pedal, fully aware that time was slipping away. She required a prompt analysis of the evidence to proceed with the investigation by the following morning. They stormed the gate at 6:02 PM and were taken by a clerk to one of the investigators who had stayed after hours especially for them.

"I apologize," Yael said, "but this must be done today. It's a matter of life and death."

The lab technician nodded her head and did not say a word. She took the syringe and gauze from Yael's hand. She began dissecting the gauze into pieces and placing them in various test tubes. The syringe went into an incubator for fingerprint analysis, while the needle was dipped into different substances to check the blood type. In the meantime, Yael filled out the required forms.

"Do you have any specific preference regarding the examination?" asked the lab technician.

"I have a feeling that Abigail's blood is on the needle. I would like to know what was injected into her. As for the gauze, I believe you might find traces of anesthesia," Yael replied.

"We won't be able to complete the examination today. Tomorrow morning, we will also conduct DNA tests and investigate the presence of toxins in the syringe. However, this process will be time-consuming due to the numerous varieties of poisons involved."

"Very well," said Yael, standing and waiting. After a while, the lab technician raised her head and said, "I suggest you go and grab something to eat. It will take a bit over an hour. I will wait here for you."

"Good idea," Ibrahim said. "We have not eaten anything since morning."

They left the laboratory and began walking towards the exit. As they passed the clerk, she stood behind the counter and called out, "Yael?"

"Yes?"

"You sent us samples of bandages and shrouds two days ago, right?"

"Yes. Any updates?"

"You wanted us to locate the company that made the bandage, or the origin of these specific ones."

"That is correct."

The clerk handed her a form inside a plastic cover and said: "I'm sorry, but we could not find anything. It is a regular bandage sold all over the country, including the Palestinian Authority. There's nothing that sets it apart. We can try and compare it to a similar bandage found in other crime scenes."

"Did you also search for other substances? Toxins? Disinfectants? DNA?"

"We always conduct a thorough review of what we receive. But in this case, it seems as if it was taken directly from a sealed plastic wrap and handled with gloves. We found nothing beyond the genetic materials of the victims."

"Understood," Yael replied. "Thank you."

"I apologize," the woman said once more. Yael and Ibrahim stepped out into the freezing Jerusalem air. Delicate snowflakes brushed against their faces as they stood by the roadside, surveying their surroundings, uncertain of their next destination.

***

When they returned to the laboratory an hour later, the lab technician had already departed, leaving the research findings in the care of the night guard. Indeed, the gauze contained traces of an anesthetic, confirming Yael's suspicion. The blood on the needle matched Abigail Avnun's type, but the comprehensive DNA test results would only be accessible the following day. Regarding the injected substance, no traces of narcotics, poison, or anesthesia were discovered in the syringe. Additional examinations were imperative. No fingerprints were detected anywhere—neither on the syringe, the plunger, nor the needle.

"What can we conclude from this?" Yael asked, examining the results.

"The killer drugged her, and then injected something that killed her. It's unclear what the substance is," Ibrahim replied.

"He lured her, drugged her, injected something, and then kidnaped her, either dead or alive. One thing is clear: he wanted something from her. If he planned to kill her from the start, he would not have drugged and sedated her. There was something she had that he needed..."

"She was not sexually assaulted, as far as I can tell."

"No evidence supports that."

"Then what the hell did he want from her? Why not just kill her and be done with it?"

"I have no idea," Yael said, falling into silence, pondering all that she had learned in the past few days. Finally, after a long pause, she said, "I suggest we go over the list of names we received from Yaakov Mizrahi, the manager of Erez Crossing. Perhaps we can link the faces and names with underlying motives and intentions."

"I agree. Take me back to the station; I will continue working from there."

"I would join you, but I have to spend some time with my kids. There is a limit to how much I can burden my mom with household responsibilities."

"I completely understand."

"Do you have a family, Ibrahim?"

"That is a complicated question," he said, shifting his gaze from her to the street. They stood there, in a long moment of silence, and then he began walking towards his car. She followed him. When they arrived, she opened the door, and before he got into the passenger seat, she said, "Maybe you could come to our home today? We will have dinner with the family and then sit for a few more hours with the lists. You can stay the night at my place."

"Are you sure it is okay, I mean... I'd much rather sleep in a proper place than in a prison cell."

"You're meant to be under my watch, so I suppose it's alright," she remarked, playfully winking at him. It was only in that moment that she fully comprehended her action. She had extended an invitation to her home to a senior member of Hamas, the very terrorist organization that had waged war against her people and her nation. The same group accountable for her husband's death and her daughter's severe injury. However, she realized that regret would serve no purpose now; the deed was done, and it was too late to turn back.

***

The dining table at the Lavie family's house was full of goods. Dina, Yael, and Ibrahim toiled in the kitchen, preparing a variety of dishes. On their way back home, the two of them had stopped to buy groceries, and Yael decided that she must prepare a royal feast for her children. Not the kind you get from a restaurant, but a homemade, warm and comforting meal, with tastes and aromas of home. One that would bring smiles to everyone's faces, and its leftovers would gladden the family for days. Ibrahim was delighted with the opportunity. Like Yael, he had not cooked for a while. The senior Gazan security official was a lonely man and tended to dine at Gaza's restaurants or coffee shops. He couldn't recall the last time he had prepared a meal for himself or his friends and enjoyed it at home.

They prepared aperitifs and salads, oven-baked meat, and fried meat. They bought a bottle of sparkling wine and freshly squeezed juices, and set the table as if it were a festive banquet. Dina reminded her daughter and grandchildren of the old days when the family used to have Friday dinners together, back when Gidi was still alive. But now the family was distant and estranged. Yoram, Yael's father living in the USA, did not bother coming to Israel, and it had been years since he had seen his children and grandchildren. The divorce from Dina was carried out remotely, and the connection between them was severed. Yael used to talk to him occasionally on the phone, but with time, naturally, the gaps between conversations grew, almost cutting off the bond.

Shai Nachmani, Yael's brother, who'd established the computer division in Israel's ISA, also distanced himself, became introverted, and entangled in his career and family. His children, who were born with a substantial age difference from Yael's children, were busy with their own worlds. After Gidi's death, Keren and Ilan distanced themselves even further from the family and refused to go out and meet them. Even today, when Yael had called and asked him to join the meal, he declined with curtesy. He had not finished his tasks at work yet, and in general, midweek did not work well for him and Ronia, his Norwegian wife.

Yael lit two candles and placed them on the marble, and music played softly in the background as the five of them sat to enjoy their meal. It was the first time in many weeks that Yael saw her children smiling. A serene harmony prevailed until the moment Keren began questioning Ibrahim about his life. Yael was more concerned about that than anything else. Keren was aware that Yael collaborated with a Palestinian partner, an investigator, in their pursuit of the case that had garnered media attention. What she did not know was that Ibrahim was associated with Hamas and hailed from Gaza. Keren had assumed he was an official from the Palestinian Authority, someone with whom Yael had maintained a long-standing connection. In fact, Keren had even met Yasser Fahamawi in the past, who had come to offer condolences to the family after Gidi's tragic death. However, with the possibility of the truth coming to light, Yael harbored concerns about how her daughter would react. She had refrained from briefing Ibrahim on the matter and was uncertain whether he would skillfully sidestep direct questions or choose to reveal the whole truth.

"How old are you, Ibrahim?" Was the first question her daughter asked.

"I am 50," Ibrahim replied. "In two months, I'll be 51."

"Are you married? Do you have children?"

"Keren," Dina said, "that is very impolite..."

"It's alright," Ibrahim interjected. "I don't mind talking about it." Yael and Dina exchanged looks with Ibrahim, who had set his fork aside on the plate. "I am divorced, and my ex-wife and I didn't have any children."

"I'm sorry to hear that," Yael said.

"What do you think about my mom? How do you manage to get along with her?"

"Keren! Enough!" her mother scolded.

"Your mom is wonderful. She is very wise. She reminds me of my wife," Ibrahim chuckled, pouring himself some wine.

"I thought you are not allowed to drink alcohol," Keren continued.

"I am not a religious person. I enjoy drinking wine, and it is a great opportunity for me because there is no place to buy wine in Gaza."

Silence followed, and then a puzzled look. "In Gaza? What are you doing in Gaza?" Keren asked.

Ibrahim scanned his surroundings, searching for a response to the question posed by the 14-year-old. Uncertainty clouded his judgment as he grappled with whether he should respond or remain silent. His expression subtly implored Yael for guidance, but a lengthy minute passed, and no one offered an answer. Yael had a sinking feeling, fully aware of what was impending, and her mind raced to find a solution to the impending dilemma, but her efforts proved futile. At last, after what felt like an eternity, Ibrahim spoke up, saying: "I live in the Gaza Strip, in the Al-Rimal neighborhood."

Yael was well aware of her teenage daughter's emotional turmoil. Ever since she lost her father and endured the injury, Keren's mood has oscillated between moments of elation and moments of despondency. For weeks, the young girl would isolate herself, bottling up her emotions until, suddenly, she would explode. And when that happened, the house would be turned upside down in an instant, as if a hurricane had passed through, leaving destruction in its wake. There were only a few things that could get Keren's emotions out of balance. She did not hate anyone and knew that the society around her consisted of both good and bad people. She comprehended the sense of guilt that Yael bore for rescuing Naif Badir, the man who had killed her husband.

She possessed very few boundaries that could not be breached. One of those boundaries, though, was Hamas; the other was Gaza. Keren struggled to comprehend how her mother continued her work beyond the Green Line, which separated Israel from the Palestinians. But she forgave her more than Yael forgave herself. But on this evening, it was evident that all the boundaries had been breached. From Keren's perspective, Yael brought the Devil's advocate into their home. And the implications were clear—Keren was losing control.

"Did you bring a killer into our home? Have you gone mad?" Those were the first words spoken. And from there, the descent was rapid and unrestrained. "My father was killed in cold blood because of people like him, and you are bringing him into our home?" Keren leaped from her chair, knocking her plate and cutlery off the table. Food scattered over the table and spilled Ibrahim's wine, soaking everything. Ibrahim stepped back and stood on his feet, his hands raised in defense.

"Keren," Yael simmered, but by now, Keren was also standing on her feet. "Are you from Hamas?" she yelled at Ibrahim.

"Ibrahim is a detective in the Gaza police. We are trying to save people—not to kill them!" Yael said.

"Is that what you tell yourself?"

"Keren, enough. If you don't want to sit with us, it's okay. You can leave. But don't attack Ibrahim. He's a good person. He didn't do—"

"You have no idea! How do you know what he did and with whom? And what if he slaughters us tonight? That's what they do!

You're bringing a Hamas man into your home, a senior police officer like you? And if he kills you, me? Ilan?"

"I think it would be for the best if you take me back to the station," said Ibrahim. "I'm sorry. I did not mean to cause such a commotion." He moved away from the table and went to pack his things.

"Why are you talking like this? Ibrahim is our guest. He is not the one who killed your father," Yael tried to approach her daughter and hold her hand, but Keren broke away, crying and storming towards her room, slamming the door behind her. Ilan and Dina were left sitting, stunned by what had just happened. Ibrahim was already standing by the door. Yael approached him.

"I'm sorry. I did not know this would happen. You can stay if you want. You don't have to leave."

"I want to leave. I understand her, really. It was a bad idea for both of us."

"Come on, let's, at least, complete our meal..."

"Yael, I'm asking to leave."

Yael looked around her helpless. This dinner was peaceful just a minute ago, a small piece of sanity that turned into a world war. "I will take a few things for us, and we will continue to work in the office," she said and walked to the kitchen to take food containers. Dina stood and started cleaning the table. Ilan got up to help as well, for a second everything seemed as if it was back to normal.

"I hate you!" Another cry came from behind Keren's door, followed by silence.

"This is a bereaved family house," Dina told Ibrahim, taking his hand. "Gidi, Yael's husband, was killed in a terrorist attack by a young Palestinian from Hamas."

"I understand," Ibrahim said. "This war is terrible. But not all of us are killers. I'm not a member of the organization, but I work with Hamas to help maintain order in the Gaza Strip. I don't support their ways, but I also need to survive." She gently patted the back of his hand and returned to clean the table.

"Let's go," Yael declared, her bag and keys clutched in her grasp. Her coat was fastened, and she held a cloth bag containing food, leftovers, and a wine bottle. "We have a lot of work ahead of us."

***

"On that same day, I almost lost her, too. The bullet went through Gidi's chest and lodged near her heart." Yael drove the car through a foggy mist and raindrops that enveloped them. The air was cold, and the front window was fogged up. Gusts of wind hit the car occasionally, and the roads were dark and empty. It was late at night, and Yael knew that this was the price she paid for her arrogance and insensitivity towards Keren.

"She had lost a substantial amount of blood, and by the time the ambulance arrived, she had already fallen into unconsciousness. Despite multiple blood transfusions, her condition didn't improve. No one knew that she had a rare blood disease. It took them several good hours until one of the doctors figured out that she could only receive a donation from people with the exact same blood type as hers, Oh. This blood type is exceptionally scarce on a global scale, and besides Keren, there is no other known Israeli with this blood type. Luckily, at the last moment, we managed to find one suitable blood transfusion. I had to ensure its swift transfer to the hospital while simultaneously dealing with the funeral arrangements for Gidi and preparing for her coming death. Looking back, I consider it one of the darkest moments of my life."

"But why is she blaming you? Her anger towards me is understandable. I represent her enemy, the one who killed her father. But why is she mad at you?"

"Because I saved the life of the person who carried out the bombing."

"You mean...?"

"Naif Badir, the killer, had not always been affiliated with Hamas. Prior to his association with them, he had been a criminal, functioning as a hired assassin for a Palestinian syndicate that held dominion over the region north of the Dead Sea. Badir became embroiled in the murder of a Jewish individual, and one of the victim's relatives took justice into their own hands, apprehending Badir and leaving him to perish in an abandoned monastery near Qasr al-Yahud. The case fell into my jurisdiction during my tenure as an investigator for the Border Police. In the eleventh hour, I managed to rescue Badir from certain demise and he was sentenced to several years in prison. While incarcerated, he formed bonds with Hamas members, eventually joining their ranks. Upon his release in a prisoner exchange agreement, he went out to kill again. Gidi was one of the victims."

Ibrahim glanced out the side window and said, "But she knows deep down that you are not guilty. I am sure of it."

"Maybe. But you have to remember that she is just a young girl, and has already been through so much. A huge part of it is because of me. So, there is a certain measure of justice in her words."

They drove in silence for a few moments until Ibrahim asked in a hushed voice, "How did you manage to get her a blood transfusion?"

"Sorry?"

"You said Keren's blood type is so rare, and it does not exist in the country at all. How did you finally manage to get her a blood transfusion?"

"There are a few cases in India of people with the same condition. It turned out that a foreign worker from India came to the country and, as a precaution, donated a unit of blood, in case something happened to him. He had already left the country, but the blood transfusion remained, and that's what saved Keren. Today we also store a few transfusions of Keren's blood for emergency cases."

"Meaning, Keren has Indian blood flowing in her veins?" Ibrahim smiled and Yael smiled back.

"Yes. That is why the doctors call it 'Bombay Blood.'"

17.
28.2.2015

Yael Levi, Aharon Shaked, and Uri Amit, stood upright facing the different media channels microphones. Shaked was the one speaking, with Yael and Uri standing behind him. Ibrahim remained in Yael's office, going over the lists sent by Yaakov Mizrahi from the Erez checkpoint. As she stood there, facing the cameras, a thought crossed Yael's mind— Why did she allow herself to leave Ibrahim alone without supervision in the heart of the resistance against Hamas in Judea and Samaria? What information could Ibrahim gather, and what would he relay to his superiors in the organization in Gaza. She wanted to trust Ibrahim; she owed him her life, but something weighed heavy on her heart. One of the reporters directed a question at her, which she had not heard, and she hoped Shaked would be the one to answer. But Shaked slightly lowered his body, revealing her face to the cameras and the reporters. She felt weak, her hair wild after a sleepless night of stressful exhausting office work.

"Sorry," she said, "I didn't hear the question."

A young reporter in his thirties fixed his blue eyes at her and asked with a sly smile, "Is Hamas collaborating with you in the investigation of the cases? I understand that some of the victims are related to the organization."

Where did he get this information from? Yael pondered for a moment, and eventually answered his question, "In this case,

Hamas and us have a common enemy," Keren's face shifted in front of Yael's eyes – "and interests also intersects with enemy entities."

"So, you are collaborating with Hamas..." Yael looked at her commanders helpless, waiting for redemption.

"I will answer that," said Shaked. "We are not collaborating with terrorist organizations, but we do share information with Hamas through various communication channels to neutralize threats and save lives." A young officer approached Uri Amit and whispered something in his ear. Uri's eyes widened in surprise.

"If Hamas will escalate their activity," Shaked continued, "we will halt the transmission of information."

Uri patted Shaked's shoulder lightly. Shaked turned his head back to receive the information from his colleague. After a moment of tension, he said firmly, "Friends, I have to stop the briefing. I apologize." He turned and walked away, Yael and Amit following him. Murmurs arose from the crowd of journalists.

"What happened?" Yael asked as they ascended the stairs towards the offices' floor. Uri Amit answered while quickening his pace, and his breathing became heavier. "A suicide bomber detonated himself at the Huwara checkpoint. Three casualties on-site."

"And Uzial? Did you hear anything from him? Is he okay?"

"We can't reach him," Uri said, storming into his office. "When I hear something, I will update you." He shut the door behind him, leaving Yael alone in the hallway.

***

A few minutes earlier, Ramzi Abu-Shaqra strode confidently towards the Huwara checkpoint. He wore jeans and a buttoned red flannel shirt adorned with blue stripes, and a branded international logo cap on his head. A black fleece scarf was tied around his neck. His canvas sneakers with white rubber soles had gotten soaked while passing through one of the puddles, but he did not seem to mind. He walked swiftly, carrying his computer bag, which had served him during his studies at Bir Zeit University, containing a small explosive charge made of metal tubing, a kilo and a half of nails, an accelerator, and an explosive. The charge was meant to be remotely activated by his phone, which he held in his hand. A short press on the **Send** button, followed by an immense blast, would surely kill him, and those around him. Anyone within a four-meter or more radius, would get hurt from the nails scattering in all directions.

Ramzi had no expectations. He was not a religious person, nor did he believe, even for a moment, that his death would lead him to heaven, granting him virgins. He sought revenge. A few hours ago, he was informed of his brother Saeed's death. The treatment had failed, and the Israeli army refused to transfer the wounded teenager, with his driver's blood already soaked in his hands, to an Israeli hospital, where his chances of recovery would have been higher. When Ramzi Abu-Shaqra left the hospital where his brother was hospitalized, he headed straight for the student dorms at the university. Upon arrival, he went directly to his friend's room, a member of Hamas. After closing the door behind him, he laid out his plan. He was willing to volunteer to carry out a revenge attack, but only if his family, which would lose two of its sons in the process, would receive full support, both communally and financially, from the terrorist organization. He needed means and a legitimate goal, and he was already committed to the rest. Half an hour later, he was dispatched to an apartment on the outskirts of Ramallah, in the refugee camp of Kalandia, where the pipe bomb was attached to him, and he received instructions on how to activate it using his mobile phone. He left the place and boarded a bus back to Nablus. He had not eaten for hours and did not bother to say goodbye to his parents, girlfriend, brothers, or sister.

The old bus plodded slowly through the rugged roads of Judea and Samaria, its wheels skimming potholes that were never fixed. The agricultural landscapes gave way to urban ones, and the desolation that was a part of his life was more apparent now than ever. He was determined and focused on his goal. He heard and saw nothing around him, his mind solely occupied with planning his course of action from the moment he will step off the bus and pass through the checkpoint. He would wait in line for security check, occasionally glance at his phone, completely composed, at peace with his decision. Once he approached the checkpoint, there would be no turning back. If the explosion failed, he would be immediately arrested, the device would be dismantled, and he would be sent to prison for the rest of his life. No. He made up his mind, and nothing would deter him. If necessary, he would envision Saeed's scornful face and fuel his anger to transform himself into a killing machine. He was prepared and ready for that.

The wind died down, when he stepped of the bus. It was 8:10 AM, and a line of Palestinians making their way to work in Israel stood before him at the checkpoint. Ramzi did not want to harm his own people. He positioned himself at the back of the line and waited for his turn. He wanted to allow the workers to cross the checkpoint safely before he activated the explosive charge against the soldiers, but another bus stopped behind him, unloading dozens more Palestinians, and another bus appeared on the horizon. He had no choice. He would have to leave the line and approach the group of soldiers standing in the posts on the sides of the road, keeping an eye on the secure passage. He waited for a few more moments, and when he felt confident enough, he left the line and started walking towards them calmly, a smile dancing on his face, his hands in a non-threatening posture, as if he was just approaching to ask a question.

At first, the five soldiers, engaged in conversation and sipping coffee from their IDF mugs, did not pay attention to his actions. But as he got closer, one of the soldiers raised his gaze and alerted his comrades. He had officer's insignia—Abu-Shaqra recognized them well—and his Galil rifle was loaded and ready. He immediately raised the rifle and aimed it at him.

"Halt there. What do you want?" the officer asked. He stood at a distance of 40 meters from Ramzi. The other soldiers turned their gazes towards the young man and assumed defensive positions in front of him. Ramzi knew. 40 meters was too far for an effective explosion. He needed to shorten the range. If he started running towards them, they would open fire, and he would not get close enough in time. If he moved slowly, he had a better chance. Now the distance was 30 meters, and the officer that noticed him first shouted again, "Stop!" and raised his weapon. The other four began to spread around, and one of them loaded the rifle that hung on his neck.

"*Wa'aquf, wallah b'tuhaq,*" the soldier yelled in Arabic—"Stop, or I'll shoot!" Ramzi did not stop. He only raised his hands in surrender and said, "I just need to ask something. I request. Please, sorry." He noticed the tremor in his own voice, but he did not retreat. He continued to advance, slightly increasing his pace. Now he stood 20 meters away, still too far. If he started running now, they would shoot him, but the same thing will happen if he keeps on walking. He stopped.

"I need help," he said.

"Lie on the ground!" the officer shouted towards him.

"It's alright," said Ramzi. "I don't want to lie in the mud. I'm just asking for your help."

"Get down on the ground." Now everyone was already tense. Ramzi was not prepared for this situation. What would he do? He turned his back to the soldiers and raised his hands in surrender. Surely, one of them would come forward and try to restrain him. He made himself look clueless and knelt down, waiting. Three soldiers approached him cautiously, their weapons loaded. The other two kept their distance, aiming their rifles at him. He reached for the button to activate the explosive on his phone when he noticed his lower lip trembling, as if whispering indistinct words. Could it be that he was praying? He heard footsteps approaching from behind, so he quickly got back on his feet and turned around. A blast sound echoed, and his left shoulder jerked backward. A spray of blood came out of his back and pain pierced through his entire body. He was shot. Blood gushed from his back, staining his shirt. His hands still remained in the air. It was the end. He let out a cry of agony but remained stable in his place. "Cease fire!" the officer shouted, and the three soldiers rushed towards him. He waited for another moment, braced himself, and then pressed the button. Yet, the resounding explosion that reverberated through the dawn at the Huwara checkpoint remained unheard by him.

***

Ibrahim found himself seated in the sanctum of Yael Lavie's office when whispers of the fatal attack stealthily reached his ears, drifting through the hallways of the Judea and Samaria police station. The conference table before him stood distinct from Yael's desk, which bore the weight of her numerous binders. The boundaries were crystal clear, and Ibrahim diligently fought against the clandestine urge to steal glances at the confidential documents or probe into the folders on her computer—an act that could be misconstrued as espionage. The fear of being caught and incarcerated gnawed at him, and he dreaded losing the trust of his ally, the person who had shown him kindness, inviting him into her home and offering him solace in the form of a bed. He reminded himself repeatedly that he had come there to address the murder case, a debt he owed to the powerful figures who reigned over Gaza. Nevertheless, as chaos and agitation captivated his senses, he could not resist the temptation to calculate how he will capitalize on the absence of his partner.

Initially, he was oblivious to the unfolding events, but when he unlocked his phone and browsed the news sites, the headlines revealed the truth, carrying with them a dire threat to both his existence and liberty. Yes, Ibrahim held a prominent position within Hamas, the very organization that claimed responsibility for Ramzi Al-Shaqra's terrorist attack. Now Judea and Samaria district morphed into a jail for him, far removed from its previous role as a conduit for reconciliation and cooperation. He was well aware that the Israelis would never tolerate his presence there, and as his mind grappled with the impending challenges, he pondered whether he should venture into the realm of calculated risk, collecting vital information about the aftermath of the terror strike.

At first, he received reports of two fatalities and five grievously wounded. However, the figures soon escalated to three deaths and then four, with an additional ten individuals suffering varying degrees of harm. He did not know of Yonatan Uziel's fate, whether he was among the deceased or the injured. Eventually, the identity of the terrorist was unveiled—the Abu-Shaqra family, a well-respected name in Nablus and the Balata refugee camp. He personally knew several members of the family, knowing them to be upstanding and dedicated to providing their children with quality education and a sense of openness.

Some of the family's sons had even pursued higher education, earning degrees from prestigious institutions like Bir Zeit University and Amman, like the terrorist's nephew. Now, tragedy had struck, and the family had to confront this disastrous reality. Two young lives, one day apart, entangled in such dire circumstances.

Ibrahim was burdened with a crucial piece of information. Knowing that Ramzi Abu-Shaqra was the terrorist behind the attack, he realized that the army would soon demolish his parents' house, leaving them with nothing. What else is left for him to do? He returned to his work, exchanging desperate text messages with those who had sent him to Israel. Feeling trapped and anxious, he walked toward the office window and flung it open, inviting the cold wind to sweep into the room and scatter the papers on his desk.

Abruptly, the door slammed shut with force, cutting him off from the bustling world outside, in the station's hallways. The commotion from beyond the door reached his ears, yet he remained seated, his eyes fixated on the closed entrance, as if his legs were rooted to the earth itself. There was an abandoned building right in the heart of the refugee camp. Hamas had occasionally used it as a hiding place for its members and weapons. Perhaps, after their house was destroyed, the Abu-Shaqra family could find shelter there. Ibrahim had already sent a message to Aziz Shafiki, requesting support from Hamas members in Nablus to aid the family in retrieving their belongings from their soon-to-be-destroyed home and relocate to the abandoned building. However, Shafiki remained silent. Minutes had passed. The TV screens flickered to life throughout the station. Yells and sirens echoed from the parking lot, and a military jeep made its way in, parking close to the entrance gate.

They are about to embark on a military operation, Ibrahim thought. **They cannot stay silent after so many casualties.** The question lingered— **How did they know the whereabouts of the terrorist's house? What was the source of this crucial information?** An idea began to gnaw at him, one he could not ignore. Perhaps he could manipulate the data and redirect the army to target the abandoned building instead of causing further distress to the already miserable Abu-Shaqra family.

He cast a cautious glance around the empty office. The door was firmly shut. He took out his phone, and he attempted to call Yael, but she did not answer after several rings. In that moment, he made a pivotal decision. He rose from his chair and positioned himself in front of her computer. The device was powered on and easily accessible, with no password to obstruct him. Yael must have left it unguarded while leaving in a haste to attend her press conference in a hall on the entrance floor. He placed the cursor on the search field and typed 'Ramzi Abu-Shaqra,' discovering a folder containing only a handful of documents. The system contained general information about the young student and the events surrounding him, including details about his studies at Bir Zeit University. A force had already been dispatched to search his room, hoping to unravel the mystery of how he obtained the explosives, and it also held information about his brother's death in Nablus. Ibrahim found the family's address in Balata and knew what he must do. He altered their address, substituting it with the address of the abandoned building owned by Hamas. He understood that upon his return to Gaza, he would have to confront those who had sent him on this mission, but at this moment, it felt like the right decision to make. He closed the folder and the program, stood up, and took one last lingering look at the computer screen. In the very next moment, the door swung open, and Chief Superintendent Uri Amit stood in the entrance.

***

The Erez checkpoint's various check posts were now tightly shut. Ibrahim's return to Gaza had been meticulously arranged, thanks to the connections of General Officer Aharon Shaked. Shaked was well aware that having Ibrahim's presence in Israel could become a media spectacle and it was far from desirable. He understood the impending confrontation and wanted to distance his 'burden' as far as he could, concerned about any potential scrutiny over the judgment involved in making this decision. Ibrahim was discreetly led to the car garages of the police station and ushered into a police car with tinted windows. Two policemen secured him in the back seat, searching his phone while a third officer drove the car. Another police car, carrying two additional policemen, formed a convoy with them. Time was of the essence, and they quickly activated their police sirens, rushing towards the Erez checkpoint. At precisely 6:43 PM, they reached their destination. Yaakov Mizrachi awaited them there, accompanied by a member of the IBP.

"We are on high alert, an attack could occur at any moment."

"Certainly," one of the policemen responded, leading Ibrahim to a dedicated post that had been opened solely for him. Swiftly, his entire information was meticulously recorded in a form, and a thorough body search ensured he had not smuggled anything. As he made his way through the search lines and emerged on the Gazan side, Ibrahim could not help but wonder about Yael's thoughts. He had been taken from her office, leaving behind all his work, without the opportunity to bid farewell. Would she discover what he had done? Could they ever collaborate again? Ibrahim did not know, but at that moment, when he had done what he had, he was certain he did the right thing. But now, uncertainty gnawed at his heart.

Amidst the clamor of people crowding around the separating wall that encircled the Gaza Strip, the distant sound of Israeli sniper fire echoed. They were trying to keep the crowd at bay from the fence. Ibrahim knew all too well that it would not be long before mortar bombs and Qassam missiles, crafted by Hamas over the years, would be launched towards southern Israeli cities. The inevitable Israeli response would lead to even stronger bombings, causing havoc in Gaza and inflicting casualties and injuries on the Palestinian side. Another vicious cycle of violence was on the horizon, with no clear end in sight. Only one thing remained certain:

after this round of fighting, things would return to normal, as if nothing had happened. Gaza and Israel were entwined with each other, and hope for any resolution seemed elusive. They were two enemies bound together like Siamese twins. He made his way to his car, which he'd parked there a few days ago, started it up, and began driving just as the first round of mortar bombs soared overhead, heading to burn Israeli fields in the towns surrounding Gaza. The Iron Dome missile defense system intercepted two of the missiles. They exploded a mere few meters in front of him, creating potholes on the road he was driving. Ibrahim hit the brakes hard and tried to maneuver around the gaping hole, but it was too late. The car plunged into it, colliding forcefully with a dirt mound.

***

"He was taken back to Gaza," Shaked informed Yael as she sat in his office. "Once this round of fighting ends, we will determine how to proceed from here." She met his gaze and nodded in approval. "Make the best of the new conditions for now."

"Alright," she replied and exited his office. Once the door was shut behind her, Shaked retrieved his phone and composed a text message in Arabic: Your guy is causing us problems. Unless you ensure he follows our instructions, we might have to withdraw from our agreements. He pressed **Send** and waited. Within thirty seconds, a response arrived: "I'll take care of it," the reply said. Shaked read it, then promptly deleted the message from his phone.

PART B

18.
1.3.2015

When Ibrahim arrived at the hospital at 10:50 AM, the scene that greeted him resembled a battlefield in its grim chaos. Scores of injured individuals sat huddled in the hallways, the operation rooms bursting at the seams with patients in need of urgent care. Doctors and nurses raced in all directions, their faces etched with exhaustion, attending to anyone they could reach. Bloodstains marred the floor, reminders of places left uncleaned due to the overwhelming circumstances. The hospital suffered a severe shortage of essential supplies—medicine, painkillers, and bandages were in scarce supply. From the inpatient rooms, agonizing screams of the injured pierced the air, and surgeries were performed with scarcely a moment to desensitize or prepare for the next critical case. Amidst the chaotic backdrop, armed Hamas soldiers moved through the throngs of people, gathering details from anyone they encountered, meticulously compiling lists of vital information. Prioritization was evident; those affiliated with Hamas received immediate attention, while others faced obstacles in gaining access to the hospital. Expectant mothers were relocated to shacks outside, individuals with less severe injuries were turned away, and regular patients found themselves relegated to a separate area in the facility. The tumultuous events unfolding at the fence had resulted in an alarming number of casualties, overwhelming the hospital's morgues to full capacity.

Ibrahim brought in his car two young injured, each facing a different level of severity. The first, a 20-year-old, had been struck by an Israeli sniper's bullet, wounding his leg and causing blood to flow from his thigh artery—a life-threatening situation. Ibrahim applied a tourniquet to stem the bleeding, knowing that immediate medical attention was essential to avoid the peril of blood poisoning and potential amputation. Yet, in the midst of this dire situation, priority had to be given to the second young man—a 16-year-old boy, shot in the stomach perilously close to his heart, experiencing heavy bleeding and the potential for lung damage. The young teen was unconscious and in severe condition. Inside the hospital, chaos reigned supreme, and they could not park the car by the hospital. The hospital was brimful, with full capacity. There was no management or control over who entered or departed. Ibrahim rushed to the hospital's entrance, spotting an available wheelchair, albeit one with a broken wheel. He dragged the chair all the way back to his car and made the 20-year-old injured man maneuver the younger boy on it. Together, they dragged the wheelchair with much difficulty back to the operation room, the injured boy supporting himself on the chair and limping. The entire journey took close to 20 agonizing minutes, but to their dismay, no one came forth to assist them. Upon reaching the entrance, the absence of help persisted. There were no medical personnel to attend to the two young cousins from Khan Yunis in the south of Gaza. As they were not related to Hamas, they were relegated to the back of the list for treatment. However, Ibrahim's ties to the organization allowed him entry, and he managed to place the severely injured boy on a hospital bed. The young boy's consciousness waned, and his breaths grew fainter by the minute. Ibrahim walked around the operation room, urgently summoning doctors to save the boy's life. The other guy, the 20-year-old shot in the leg—was tended to by a nurse and sent to wait in the hallway. Ibrahim lost eye contact with him.

In his despair, Ibrahim rushed to the 16-year-old boy's bedside, desperately attempting to stem the bleeding from his wounded lungs. His hands shook as he sought the bullet's exit wound on the boy's back, locating it nestled between two ribs. He applied a bandage to the wound, hoping to staunch the blood flow. He then took off the boy's shirt and placed his hand on his chest as an attempt to stop the bleeding. Despite his best efforts, the bleeding persisted, and the young boy's condition rapidly deteriorated. In a moment of determination, he seized a passing doctor and screamed at him: "I'm major general Ibrahim Azberga, and I command you to take care of this boy or he'll die."

The doctor, however, appeared unmoved by the distinguished title and status, yet he entered the inpatient room cordoned off with white curtains. The doctor swiftly assessed the critical condition of the young boy and spoke with unwavering resolve.

"I can't handle this alone, you'll need to assist me."

"Whatever you say."

"I need to operate immediately, but all our operation rooms are taken. We will have to attempt it here. Fetch me an operation trolley from the stand behind the reception desk, and the CPR kit." Ibrahim hurried outside, pushing his way through the crowded hospital hallways. "Operation trolley!" he yelled at a reception clerk, who pointed him in the right direction, a corner where a cluster of trolleys were stored behind a curtain. He seized one and rushed back to the doctor who was already preparing the young boy for the impromptu operation, administering anesthetics. He took a scalpel and bone saw from the trolley and started operating. "CPR kit." He muttered to Ibrahim, when a nurse came in to assist with the operation. Ibrahim raced out again, and spotted the CPR kit with another doctor attending to a patient who had been shot in the stomach, writhing in pain on the bed. Two hospital attendants were preparing to transfer the injured man to another department for further treatment.

As Ibrahim rushed with the CPR kit, the pandemonium around him caused him to lose his bearings. In the midst of the chaos, he accidentally entered the wrong room, then another, until he finally regained his composure and found the right room, five minutes had passed. When he finally arrived, he witnessed the desperate attempts of the doctor and nurse to resuscitate the 16-year-old boy. The boy had stopped breathing, and his heart had ceased to beat. The nurse swiftly grabbed the defibrillator from Ibrahim and placed it on the boy's chest, delivering an electric shock followed by resuscitation attempts, then another electric shock and another. They once more preformed ventilation attempts and heart massages, but their efforts proved futile. The boy had passed away. Ibrahim stood in stunned silence, his eyes fixated on the lifeless boy before him. The doctor turned away and leaned on the bed. He exchanged looks with Ibrahim and the nurse as he collapsed on the floor.

"I'm sorry," Ibrahim uttered softly as another nurse hurried into the inpatient room.

"I need the CPR kit." She said without pausing for a response. She took it and disappeared into the busy hospital hallway.

"Do you know who he is?"

"I don't know him," replied Ibrahim. "I picked them up on the street after they were injured." He left the inpatient room and went in search of the other young boy. Ascending to the hospital's second floor, he found him seated in the hallway, his injured leg carefully bandaged. Ibrahim sat down beside him on the floor, observing the sizable bandage wrapped around the young boy's thigh. "Are you in pain?"

"A bit less now," the young man replied.

"Did they give you any painkillers?"

"No."

"How are you doing, otherwise?"

"They took the bullet out and gave me antibiotics. I'll rest here for a few hours before going back home to rest. I think I'll be alright. How is Salim doing?"

"His name is Salim?"

"Yes."

"I'm not sure if he will make it," Ibrahim lied, and the young boy nodded solemnly. "Go and see him later, okay?" Another nod followed. Slowly, Ibrahim rose to his feet, only then realizing that his shirt and pants were stained with blood. He quickly checked his body for any injuries but found none. Fortunately, he seemed unscathed. He gently patted the young man's head, eliciting a faint smile in return, and then walked slowly towards the exit gate.

***

Three hours prior, Ibrahim was busy extracting his car from the gaping hole that marred the road. The seatbelt had been his shield against the full impact of the steering wheel hitting his head, saving his life. Still, his head throbbed with a relentless intensity. Guiding the vehicle, he weaved back and forth. Grains of earth were strategically wedged beneath the tires, offering a much-needed traction to the one tire suspended in the air. The worn-out vehicle coughed and grumbled, yet eventually drove out of the hole, just as a fresh volley of missiles soared overhead. Hamas's calculated decision to escalate the confrontation carried multifaceted motives, intricately entwined with the intricate fabric of Gaza's internal dynamics. As a complex interplay of terrorist organizations and tribal influences and as a calculated demonstration of power to the Palestinian Authority governing Judea and Samaria. Ibrahim's understanding of these intricate layers ran deep. He was well-acquainted with their mindset, the web of international forces entangled in the fray. He recognized that within a matter of days, this harrowing episode of conflict, a mere release valve for accumulated tension, would inevitably subside. Yet, as always, its aftermath would leave a grim trail of casualties and injured citizens, both from physical and psychological wounds.

As had been the pattern countless times before, Hamas orchestrated the gathering of young individuals from Gaza and Khan-Yunis, herding them onto organized buses bound for the border fence that encircled Gaza. Thousands surged forward, a fervent display of dissent against the Israeli military. Tires were set on fire, projectiles took flight—rocks and Molotov cocktails—while incendiary balloons floated overhead. Light weapons and the thud of mortar shells were being launched. Shoulder-fired missiles targeted armored military vehicles, while homemade ground missiles found their trajectory, streaking toward the southern Israeli towns. The Israeli defense apparatus worked relentlessly to thwart the onslaught, striving to minimize casualties and injuries. The Iron Dome, a testament to their technological prowess, intercepted and neutralized a portion of the incoming missiles. Despite the searing intensity of the battlefield, the situation remained somewhat contained, and the grim toll of casualties held in check. The localized damages inflicted were a mere blip, swiftly repaired with materials flowing in from the very nation at odds with the besieged Gaza—Israel—aided by funding from European and American sources. To him, this Kafkaesque act seemed absurd. Israel and Hamas were locked in a suffocating embrace that propelled them both down a steep slope, toward depreciation times. To the abyss.

He drove slowly towards his residence, allowing the frenzy to swirl around him, as if it was and yet was not, whatever will be, will be. Then, a young boy with a leg injury darted toward him, blocking his path, lunging at the flagellated vehicle with urgency, shouting at Ibrahim to stop. He pounded his fists on the engine hood and then on Ibrahim's door, attempting to open it. Ibrahim halted the car and stepped out, and that is when the boy had recognized who he was talking to, and the tone of his speech shifted dramatically.

"Mister, you must help us. He was hit by a bullet in the chest. He can hardly breathe. We need to get him to the hospital!" Ibrahim glanced down at the young boy's leg and the expanding stain of blood on his torn pants. The young man limped back and forth, then grabbed Ibrahim's hand, pulling him towards a heap of rubble and debris. There, a young boy lay, grunting, his mouth frothing with blood and saliva.

Ibrahim stood still for a moment, gazing at the boy, then commanded: "Come, help me."

They lifted the young boy and dragged him to the car. Ibrahim pulled the backseat flat, and gently laid the gurgling boy down. He retrieved a belt from his pants, quickly fashioning a makeshift tourniquet for the other boy's wounded leg. "Sit here," he instructed the young man, "and place your hand on his chest. He has a hole here, and if you don't clog it with your hand, he will not be able to breathe. Understand?"

"Yes," the young man replied, settling on the car floor next to the injured boy, placing his hands on his chest. A loud explosion echoed nearby, shattering the rear window of the car and showering them with fragments. Both of them jumped in alarm. Ibrahim quickly returned to his senses. "We must go. No time to lose," he ordered, pushing towards the driver's seat. He started the car again, this time a cloud of black smoke was billowing from beneath the hood. **Something had gone wrong**, he thought to himself, but he clenched the gas pedal and sped towards the Shifa hospital, which was half an hour away. He hoped the car would hold out until they reached their destination.

***

Salim's death had been anticipated. Ibrahim knew it from the moment he'd lifted the young boy into his car. The battered vehicle was parked on Ibn Sina Street, looking like a stolen wreck that had been forcibly brought back to the road against its will. Now he stood at the entrance of the emergency room, gazing into the distance, contemplating his next move. The stream of injured patients continued to pour into the hospital and showed no signs of abating. Ambulances arrived, packed with three or four wounded individuals. The dead were left behind on the field. They would be collected later, under the cover of night, and everything would return to normalcy. He looked at the emergency room, contemplating whether to stay and contribute to the war effort or return to his house and continue the investigation. Which was the wiser choice? He did not know. With a few steps forward, the automatic door of the emergency room opened before him, and he emerged onto the ambulance bay in front of the hospital. The Al-Rimal neighborhood, where he lived, was within walking distance, northeast of his current location. He considered making his way back home on foot. Then he caught a glimpse out of the corner of his eye of the doctor who had treated Salim. The doctor was leaning against the railing, his hand trembling and he was holding a cigarette, smoking it fervently. The doctor appeared weary, agitated, and confused. His eyes darted around, looking at the chaos surrounding him, and three cigarette butts were discarded at his feet. Ibrahim took a deep breath and approached him.

He extended his hand for a hand shake, and the doctor met his gaze, turning his attention toward the Major General who leaned toward him. The doctor flicked the burning cigarette to the ground and straightened up. He extended his hand back for the handshake and nodded. "Thank you," Ibrahim said. "For everything you have done."

"This is the fourth young boy today whose death I've pronounced since morning. The oldest was 25 years old."

"A tough day," Ibrahim commented, giving his shoulder a gentle pat before turning to leave.

"Aren't you all tired of these wars?"

"You all?" Ibrahim questioned, taken aback.

"Hamas. How many more dead children do we need to bury before you stop your senseless wars?" The doctor reached into his pocket, pulled out a pack of cigarettes, extracted one, and lit it. Ibrahim stared at the pack as it was offered to him like a tempting gift.

"I'm not a participant in your politics," the exhausted doctor said angrily. "I'm just putting out the fires you are igniting. But how much more blood will be spilled?" Ibrahim took a cigarette from the offered pack, lit it, and inhaled the toxic smoke deeply. He looked around suspiciously. It took a lot of courage for the doctor to say what he had to someone in Ibrahim's position, especially during times of conflict when the hospital was teeming with members of the Hamas movement. If Ibrahim let it slide without a response, he could be considered a traitor. On the other hand, Ibrahim knew that the doctor was right. There was little logic in Hamas' policies, and he himself felt drained, having lost faith in the righteousness of the struggle, in the path of terror, and in the organization's ideology.

"What's your name?" Ibrahim asked.

"If you want to arrest me, you are welcome to," the doctor replied. "I have no more fear. I'm tired."

"Why would I arrest you? You are speaking from the heart. I understand you."

"Doctor Mansour Al-Qasem," the doctor said, tears welling up in his eyes.

"You need to be strong, for everyone, for these children, for the homeland," Ibrahim said, hating what he was saying.

"Last year," the doctor took another drag from his cigarette, "my little brother was killed at the fence." Ibrahim felt a colossal hammer pounding him with force, shattering his bones. He staggered, feeling unable to stand on his feet any longer. He gripped the concrete railing, trying to steady himself.

"Hamas sent him along with two of his friends to place an explosive device on the fence. They were sixteen-year-olds. Three kids. Their heads were filled with empty ideology. Their thoughts were poisoned. I tried to dissuade him from carrying out the operation, but he refused to send his friends alone into the field. I knew exactly how it would end. I told him. But he didn't listen." Another ambulance rushed into the parking area in front of the building, unloading more wounded. The doctor took another drag from his cigarette and then flicked the burning end onto the pavement.

"They crawled in the darkness with the explosive device toward the fence, but an Israeli army surveillance detected them and opened fire. My brother was slightly behind, but the bullet hit the explosive device and detonated it. All three were killed on the spot."

"Do you have children?" Ibrahim asked.

"No. I'm not married, and, Major General, I must tell you, I'm tired. Tired of your wars, tired of the open-air prison you imposed on us, tired of death. I want to leave this place. I don't care if you arrest me, if you threaten my family. If you torture me. My soul is already dead, and every time another young boy dies in my hands, I feel like life is draining out of me. Do you understand?"

Ibrahim understood. Like the doctor, he too was imprisoned. He was imprisoned in the concept that Hamas built around Gaza, in the sense of victimhood, in loss. For Ibrahim had also lost so much in the role he had to take to survive. And like the doctor, he was tired and lonely. He sighed lightly and continued to gaze into the doctor's eyes, as if waiting for more. But no more words were spoken. The doctor extended his hands towards him, as if ready to be cuffed, and Ibrahim stood there, desperate, and did nothing.

The emergency room nurse sprinted out of the automatic door, followed by another doctor bearing a tag that Ibrahim managed to read only the "Dr." part. It was the shift supervisor of the emergency room. His hands were gloved in blue surgical gloves, and his uniform was stained with blood. "I've been looking for you for half an hour," the nurse said and tugged at Dr. Mansour's hand. The shift supervisor said impatiently, "We are in a mass casualty event, and you are taking a smoke break outside? Do you know how many lives we could have saved in the time you loafed around?"

Dr. Mansour al-Kasem lowered his outstretched hands that he presented to be handcuffed to his sides and winked with his left eye. "I'm going to save more of your victims," he muttered and walked inside with his colleagues. Ibrahim was left alone on the pavement, watching another ambulance, its doors flung open, carrying two more gunshot victims, young boys no older than 16, crying out in pain. Their parents held prayers for their well-being, prayers that will probably fall on deaf ears.

19.
2.3.2015

At first, Ibrahim heard it faintly, but gradually it seeped into his dream and pulled him out into the realm of reality. Loud knocks on the door. He opened one eye, and then the other. His bedroom was bathed in light despite the seemingly grey sky peeking from his window. The room felt chilly. The double bed, on which he lay alone, was positioned in the center on a Persian carpet that was worn and frayed. A wool curtain in shades of beige and brown hung by the window, and on the side, by the disheveled makeup table, was a wooden chair with his clothes from yesterday hanging on it. He lay there, dressed in a thin blue pajama, covered with a comforter. He extended his hand from under the covers and felt the sharp chill that made it harder for him to leave the warmth of the bed. As he reached for his fleece jacket, he remembered he had left it in the living room, far from where he now was. The knocking on the door grew louder, along with his fear of it being broken in. He threw off the comforter and walked to the door, reaching for his keys. A slight tremor passed through his body, and he pulled his fleece jacket off the couch and shouted, "Just a moment. I'm coming."

The house was enveloped in silence. He had been alone there for many years. The apartment, situated on the fifth floor of the building, offered a view of the sea, and beyond it, thoughts of the future. Should he continue living there? It came with its share of pros and cons. When the elevator was operational, it was one of the finest apartments in Al-Rimal. However, during power outages, he had to laboriously climb five flights of stairs, a challenging feat for a man of his age, 50, who had been a smoker for three decades. He donned his fleece jacket and headed towards the door. The pounding on the door reverberated through the house, and Ibrahim sensed it as an ominous sign of impending trouble. As he turned the lock for the second time, the door swung open towards him, and Aziz Shafiki forcefully entered the apartment without awaiting an invitation. Two soldiers from the Izz ad-Din al-Qassam Brigades, the military wing of the Hamas organization followed closely behind him. Shafiki strode to the worn-out sofa in the living room and took a seat. "Sit," he ordered Ibrahim, who was still standing near the door, flanked by the two soldiers. "Did you manage to get some sleep?" Shafiki inquired, leaving Ibrahim uncertain if he detected a hint of politeness in his tone.

"Yes. Would you like something to drink?"

"I don't have time. It's already 07:15, and we have a cabinet meeting soon. We need to decide where to go from here." Shafiki's reference was, of course, to the war that Hamas had waged against Israel and the looming question of how much more damage they could inflict on the Israeli side before the cost became too high and internal unrest might ensue.

"Alright," said Ibrahim. "I'll make myself some coffee, if you don't mind."

"Sit," Shafiki ordered, this time with a more assertive tone. Ibrahim settled into the chair opposite him.

"What happened? What's so urgent?" Ibrahim's breath was stinky, and the hairs on his chest peeked through the pajama and fleece jacket he wore, struggling to provide warmth to his body. He shivered slightly, unsure if it was from the cold.

"What is going on with the Malak case? Have you found anything?"

"Is that why you came here at seven in the morning?"

"Did you find something or not?"

"There is no breakthrough yet, if that is the question. When there will be, you'll be the first to know."

"I sent you on a specific task, I put a lot at risk. The results are particularly grim. I'm marking you as one of the factors fueling the escalation against Israel. The boss doesn't give you much credit. I need to know what is going on."

"It takes time, Aziz. I'm dealing with several fronts here, I don't have access to information. Malak was buried on the Israeli side, and I can't freely move around there, especially not when you're firing missiles at Tel Aviv."

"You need to act faster."

"I'm working alone."

"You know we can't provide you with manpower. It's important to keep this whole operation in the dark so no ideas will come to those who seek to hurt Hamas. We can't show weakness."

"I know," Ibrahim said. "Weakness invites all our competitors to come out of their holes. They investigated me about you in Nablus."

"And what did you do in Nablus?"

"I went to check if the murders are related to the Islamic Jihad's attacks. But the Authority stopped me shortly after the checkpoint..."

"I did not approve your entry into the Palestinian Authority territories."

Ibrahim fell silent. Both knew that it was not the murder investigation that motivated Ibrahim to go to Nablus.

"I went to see my family. My mother... I haven't seen her for years." Shafiki fixed his gaze on Ibrahim, then rose from the couch and approached him. He knelt down beside Ibrahim, grabbed his fleece jacket, and clenched it in his fist. "You," he said quietly, "will do what I tell you. Do you understand?"

Ibrahim's nodded his head like a beaten child.

"I know where your family lives in Nablus. We have people there. If something like this happens again..." He lightly slapped Ibrahim's cheek twice, and on the third time, Ibrahim grabbed his hand tightly and stared into the eyes of the senior organization member.

"I hate being threatened. Don't think you are immune. I have people too, in various places," Ibrahim said. Both men stood there for a long moment without moving or saying a word. Finally, Shafiki signaled for one of the soldiers to approach and hand him something. It was a thin green envelope. He took it and pulled out a photo of a young woman wearing a black hijab adorned with gold metal ornaments and red-yellow embroidery.

"This is Abir Adallah. She is 21 years old. Disappeared three days ago, same method as the other girls. She is the niece of the head of Hamas' diplomatic bureau. If her disappearance is linked to the other murders, then the threat has reached the highest levels of the organization."

"I understand," Ibrahim said.

"I don't think you understand well enough. In any case, he wants to talk to you, now."

"Who wants to?"

"The head of the bureau, Isma'il Bader. He is waiting for you in his office. Get dressed. You are coming with us."

Ibrahim was furious. Bitterness rose in his throat. He contemplated resisting, throwing Shafiki and his soldiers out of his house, consequences be damned. Shafiki stood up and forcefully thrust the photo of Abir into Ibrahim's hand. "Move. You are holding me up. I'm running late for a meeting."

"I'll get there by myself. You can leave." Shafiki scrutinized the Major General seated before him. From an imposing and accomplished figure, Ibrahim suddenly appeared fearful and ridiculous in his thin pajamas and his neglected, cold home.

"Don't make me come here again. Be here in half an hour, and don't discuss this with anyone," he whispered under his moustache and left the apartment. The two soldiers followed him, leaving the door open.

Ibrahim remained seated on the chair, but his frail body no longer trembled. Not from fear nor cold. In a peculiar way, he felt as if he was dead inside, and this sensation was oddly comforting and warm, much more so than the comforter waiting for him on the bed in his room.

20.
Erez checkpoint

Abed Kaboa was a diligent worker. Employed as a driver of a refrigerated truck, he was among the 550 Gazan Palestinians who held daily entry permits to Israel. With unwavering commitment, he showed up for work each day, following the strict regulations and maintaining a professional demeanor to uphold the trust he had fairly earned. He understood that even a minor misstep could jeopardize his entry permit to drive through Israel to the Palestinian Authority territories, thereby jeopardizing his livelihood. The dire financial circumstances in Gaza left him no room for error. His truck transported substantial quantities of poultry from Gaza's farms, traversing through Israel to reach the markets of Hebron and Ramallah. Kaboa meticulously ensured that only approved goods were loaded onto his truck, categorically rejecting any substandard or uninspected abominated meat by the veterinarians.

Kaboa's workday commenced at 4 AM. He would bring his pre-packed breakfast, prepared by his wife the previous evening, and accompany it with black coffee from his thermos, and wold then break his fast as workers at the slaughterhouse loaded chicken crates onto his truck and completed the necessary certificates and permits. The truck would be weighed upon entering and exiting the loading area, and another report would be added to the pile of reports: the goods' weight. By approximately 5:30 AM, the truck would be loaded, ready for his familiar routine. Setting out on his long journey, he would travel to the Erez checkpoint, then embark on highway 60 toward Hebron, the towns of East Jerusalem, and Ramallah—all within Palestinian Authority-controlled territories. The number of unloading sites would change daily, yet Kaboa would complete his deliveries by the noon hours. He would return to Hebron for lunch, refuel his truck, and then embark on the return trip to the Erez checkpoint and his home in Gaza. Kaboa maintained a strict schedule, never risking reaching the checkpoint after 6:00 PM, despite his entry permit being valid until 8 PM. He always allowed extra time in anticipation of unforeseen delays such as a flat tire, engine trouble, accidents, or any other hindrances that might arise along the way.

Yesterday, the tension in the region led to the closure of the Erez checkpoint. This unfortunate circumstance resulted in a significant setback, leaving numerous goods trapped within the confines of the slaughterhouse's refrigerated storage. The financial repercussions for the slaughterhouse owners were substantial. The residents of Gaza paid a steep price during the recent conflicts involving Hamas, enduring a staggering toll. Amid this upheaval, Kaboa, much like his fellow Gazans, opted to remain silent, and did not say a word. Today, Kaboa aimed to mitigate the losses incurred the previous day. He meticulously packed a larger quantity of goods, ensuring it remained within the permissible limit stipulated by both Israeli and Hamas agreements. Leaving a wide enough space at the center of the truck, intended for inspection purposes, he secured the cargo and embarked on Salah Al Deen street, en route to the Erez checkpoint. This checkpoint typically opened at 6 AM daily. Kaboa was well aware that punctuality was of the essence; a delay on his part could lead to an extensive queue of vehicles at the border crossing, squandering valuable time in the congestion. He delicately pressed the gas pedal and maintained a steady, law-abiding acceleration.

Arriving at the checkpoint around 6:10, Kaboa joined a line of 15 trucks, positioning his vehicle a few meters behind an empty truck likely laden with goods from Ashdod port destined for Gaza. He rolled down the window for a little, inviting a refreshing breeze to sweep through. Despite spending hours within the confines of the truck daily, Kaboa consistently maintained its cleanliness and never smoked inside. During the traffic-filled hours at the checkpoint, he refrained from engaging with the radio, concerned that it might hinder his ability to promptly respond to instructions or commands from the border police, ultimately heightening the already strained tensions between Palestinians and Israelis.

As Kaboa pulled up to the security checkpoint, it was 6:40 AM. The process of the truck inspection only took a few minutes. Finally, a sense of relief washed over him as he spotted the passageway he longed to reach, mere meters away from his current position. He rolled down the driver's window again. A gust of icy wind infiltrated the otherwise heated truck cabin. From the passenger seat, he gathered all the necessary approvals, neatly bound together in a single stack. Kaboa handed the papers to the border policewoman, and she swiftly passed the papers to a clerk who proceeded to hop from one truck to another. While the documents underwent scrutiny, the soldier directed Kaboa to step out of the truck and unlock the trunk for inspection. The border police meticulously inspected his truck from the outside. They used long poles, each adorned with a mirror at its tip, to search for any signs of suspicious objects or explosives attached beneath the vehicle. Specially trained dogs were sniffing the truck, smelling it, but not finding anything unusual.

Approaching the rear of the truck, Kaboa opened the trunk door. Before him, a neat arrangement of cardboard boxes awaited, forming orderly lines creating three quarters of a square, positioned against the walls of the truck. A soldier, accompanied by a dog, lit his torch inside the truck. Everything looked normal. The clerk returned the papers to Kaboa, who folded it and placed it in his pocket. Another soldier asked him to lower the loading ramp, Kaboa did as he was told. It was all part of the routine, he knew what was required of him and complied. Everyone understood the situation and did all they could in order to minimize the tension between the Israelis and Gazans at the checkpoint. The passage was a matter of necessity and the flow of people through it could not be stopped. This would mean exerting financial pressure on Gaza and imposing a siege, which is why even during periods of conflict, both parties endeavored to facilitate unhindered movement through the checkpoint. Hamas sought to avoid targeting or damaging the checkpoint to prevent its closure, while Israel implemented easier security measures to ensure smoother processes.

Everyone around was tired. The night shift was about to be relieved by the morning shift. Two weary soldiers ascended the ramp along with the search dog and Kaboa. The female soldier remained outside for security, while the two snipers stationed at fortified and distant observation posts slightly adjusted their weapons, ready for any scenario. The ramp halted at the cooling chamber entrance, and the soldiers entered together with the dog, which immediately began to growl. Something was wrong.

"Stay there," the soldier instructed Kaboa in a commanding tone. "Wait, please." Kaboa remained standing on the ramp. Throughout his career, he had never encountered such a situation. He was tense, the strain evident on his face. He knew that any misplaced action on his part could lead to his immediate arrest, or worse—after the events of yesterday, they could shoot him. Another soldier stood beside him, the female soldier positioned at a comfortable angle for reaction, and the third soldier entered deep into the cooling chamber, flashlight in hand, with the search dog snarling at his side.

"Search," the soldier commanded and released the dog from the leash. The dog began to scurry around the cooling chamber, while the female soldier who remained outside signaled to the rest of the soldiers to be prepared for any possible scenario, taking two or three steps backward. Kaboa stood in place, pale, peering over the soldier's shoulder as he approached, signaling for him to extend his hands forward. It seemed likely to him that Kaboa might trigger a detonation charge and blow up the truck at the checkpoint. Kaboa complied. Then the soldier asked Kaboa to turn around and face the cargo space of the truck. Kaboa felt as if his blood was draining from him, fearing he might faint. He signaled to the female soldier that he was feeling unwell and asked her to sit down. She refused. He heard the dog behind him pacing back and forth in the trunk, and then, suddenly, it started to bark. Kaboa knew exactly what was happening. The dog had found something. In an instant, everything could change. He began to think about what had occurred. Where was the mistake, and could it be that someone had loaded something they should not have? By now, the line of trucks at the entrance to the checkpoint had grown, and Kaboa felt the mounting tension.

The dog barked again, and Kaboa heard it snuffling at one of the cardboard crates filled with poultry. "You," he heard the soldier behind him say. "Come here." Kaboa turned and, his hands in the air in surrender motion, he began to step into the cooling chamber, passing by the soldier who remained guarding behind him. He saw the dog snuffling inside one of the cardboard crates, and the other soldier shining his torch towards one corner of the chamber. "Open this box," the soldier commanded. Kaboa complied. The cardboard boxes were never closed or sealed to allow for quick searches. Inside the box were several pieces of poultry wrapped in plastic bags. The dog quickly pawed at it and then pounced on the next box in line. Kaboa moved that one too, and then the next and the next, to give the dog access inside, into the pile of crates. As he finished moving and opening 13 cardboard crates, the beam of the torch fell on a wooden crate, without any marking. Kaboa had never seen a crate like this before.

"Here, this one," the soldier said. "I need you to take it out." Kaboa squeezed his way to the crate and uncovered its contents. The crate, made of thin cedar wood, was about a meter long, half a meter wide, and approximately 60 centimeters tall. Its parts were held together with screws, and thick wooden supports formed a sturdy frame that held it together and prevented its collapse.

"What's in there?" the soldier asked. A sergeant approached the truck now and peered inside to see what was happening and why there was a delay.

"I don't know," Kaboa said.

"Do you have a screwdriver to open it?" the soldier asked.

"There is a screwdriver in the cabin compartment," Kaboa answered, waiting for the command to retrieve it.

"No need," the second soldier said, pulling a multi-tool knife from his pocket. He opened it to reveal a screwdriver and handed it to Kaboa. "Don't think of doing anything foolish with this," he said. Kaboa approached the crate, then a horrible stench rose to his nose. A feeling of nausea rose in his throat, and he felt like he was about to vomit. The dog continued to growl, occasionally barking. "I can't," he said.

"Why? What's in there?" the soldier asked.

"I don't know. I did not load this. I'm scared," Kaboa replied. Tremors ran through him, tears welled up in his eyes. He was framed. Someone had done something terrible, he could feel it in his bones, and he could not move.

"Sir, I need you to be with me right now," the soldier said. "Open the crate, I'm not allowed to do it for you." Kaboa held his nose and approached the crate. He turned two screws using the multi-tool knife and then used the pliers to pull them out. The stench was awful, and Kaboa feared what he might find inside. He knew it would not be abominated poultry meat; it was something much more sinister. He loosened the fourth screw, and the wooden lid jumped from its place. Without looking, Kaboa took two steps back, leaving the soldier to uncover the cargo. But the soldier would not allow it. He took two steps back and repeated, "Open it."

He shone his torch towards the crate. Kaboa clenched his eyes shut and then opened the lid.

"I need a reinforcement here immediately!" the soldier shouted, and the dog started growling. Kaboa could not hold back any longer and opened his eyes. "Oh no," a cry escaped his lips. He lifted his head and saw before him a shotgun. "Step back," the soldier said. But Kaboa could not move. At his feet, inside the wooden crate, lay the body of a bound woman, cut in half. The upper half lay atop the lower, and she was in an advanced state of decomposition. "Step back," the soldier repeated, this time with a more forceful tone, but Kaboa no longer heard. He collapsed onto the cold floor of the cooling chamber, losing consciousness.

21.

The chairman of Hamas' political office was Ismail Bader, who usually resided outside the Gaza Strip, often in Syria or in the state of Qatar within the Persian Gulf. However, circumstances had led him to return for a visit via the Rafiah Crossing, connecting Gaza to Egypt. Bader was concerned about the internal disintegration of the organization he had helped bring to power in Gaza, an organization to which he had belonged to since the age of 10. Through years of perseverance, enduring numerous wars and immense bloodshed, Bader had risen to its top leadership position. And now, seemingly out of nowhere, someone had decided to undermine him, challenge his authority within the organization, and even threaten their families. Bader knew that if he were to relocate his children from the Gaza Strip, it could be interpreted as a sign of a terrorist organization's collapse under the force of Israel or another terrorist organization looking to conquer, without a certain cause or without knowing who was behind them. On the other hand, leaving his children behind might endanger their lives.

Bader, like Shafiki, Ashrawi, and Sabri Saeed, had become prey in a witch hunt, with an elusive enemy confronting him. He had already deployed forces to investigate throughout the Gaza Strip, exploring with necessary brutality representatives from Fatah, Islamic Jihad, and other groups, both past and present, collaborators with Israel. Yet, nothing concrete was found. No one knew what fate had befallen Abir Adallah, his sister's daughter.

Ismail Bader sat in the makeshift office he built for himself on

Omar Al Mukhtar Street. He read the newspaper 'Palestine' which lay open on his desk. The time was 7:50 AM. Ibrahim Azberga, appointed by Shafiki to investigate the murders and disappearances in the Gaza Strip, had not yet arrived. Bader knew time was running short. At 8:15 AM, a meeting of Hamas leaders would convene to discuss the current security state, and decisions would be made there regarding whether to continue the escalation against Israel or conclude the ongoing cycle of conflict. He understood the importance of his presence, not because someone would force him to come or criticize him in his absence, but because it would influence his status within the organization. If the organization leaned towards ceasefire, Bader would remain a few more days, hoping that Abir would be found, with a glimmer of hope for her survival. He cast a quick glance at his phone's screen. Another minute passed. He felt growing anger boiling within him, but knew he had to keep his composure. His reliance on Ibrahim was greater than Ibrahim's reliance on him. He intended to serve revenge to him like a cold dish once the killer was captured.

At 7:53 AM, Ibrahim Azberga entered the office. He did not appear agitated or confrontational, and he did not attempt to challenge Ismail. On the contrary, he seemed as if he had been thrown out of his sickbed, weak. Ismail chose to forgo any attempt at dominance and opted for a more cordial approach. He rose from his seat and extended his hand in greeting.

"I apologize," he said, "for making you get up so early for me. I understand you spent many hours at Shifa Hospital yesterday. I'm sure you witnessed horrible things."

"I'm fine," Ibrahim replied. "I heard something terrible happened, that your sister's daughter disappeared."

"Yes," Ismail said. "Sit down, I'll tell you a few details about her, in the hope that it might assist your investigation, and perhaps, if the Prophet wishes, she will be found alive." Ibrahim settled onto an unpadded wooden chair, and everyone left the room. The two men locked eyes, and there was no trace of suspicion in their gaze.

"Her name is Abir. Abir Adallah," Ibrahim retrieved a small notebook and a pencil and began jotting down notes. "She's 21 years old, a devout Muslim, from an observant and conservative household. Abir was set to be married in two weeks. She dreamt of becoming a nurse and began her studies three months ago. She's an only sister to two brothers, a good girl from a respectable family. I want to believe that nothing happened within the family or with her intended husband."

"How did you find out she disappeared? Who reported it?"

"I don't know how they found out, but yesterday I received a call from my sister, who told me that Abir had gone missing. I immediately returned to Gaza. I have a bad feeling. You understand, of course, that we are under attack."

"I am taking that under consideration," Ibrahim said. "But if there is indeed a connection to the murders of the Jewish women, I doubt this is an attack on the leadership of the organization as you describe."

"Did you discover anything when you were in Israel?"

"I did, but not enough to launch a search or take preventive measures."

"And what happened there? Why did you return?"

"A crisis erupted, a minor one," Ibrahim lied. "I hope the Israelis will let it be and move on. But the security tensions, along with the pressure from Shafiki to obtain more and more information—it puts me in a very precarious position with them, especially with my colleague, Yael Lavie. I need you get off my back and let me work, otherwise it will be very difficult for me to recruit them, and they are the ones that have all the intelligence I need to solve the case."

"I understand," said Ismail. "I'll talk to Shafiki. But from now on, I request that you report directly to me."

"That's a problem," Ibrahim said. "If they catch wind of the connection between us, they'll distance me."

"So find a way to do it without getting caught. I want to know what is happening all the time. Clear?"

Ibrahim stared deeply into Bader's eyes, finally nodding his head. "Clear," he said.

"Thank you," Ismail said, rising from his seat. Ibrahim got up after him. "Just know that we don't have much time. If there are more killings or kidnappings, the organization could collapse from within. It all rests on your shoulders."

"You just make sure to stop your wars. If there is anything that hinders my work more than anything, it is these battles."

"I'll do my best," Ismail said, shaking his hand.

"I would appreciate it if you could establish a connection between me and Abir's family. Just to create a timeline for her disappearance."

"Sure," said Bader. Ibrahim turned around and headed for the door. He opened it and stood about to leave, then heard Ismail's voice again.

"You know, Ibrahim, I've raised this girl since she was born. She is like my own daughter. I really ask that you bring her back to me alive."

"I'll do everything I can," Ibrahim said, but deep within him, he knew the chance of saving Abir's life was close to zero.

***

Ibrahim stepped out onto the street, his gaze sweeping the surroundings. Despite the late morning hour, a hushed tranquility lingered, with sporadic vehicles navigating the avenue while occasional figures strode purposefully along their paths. The specter of war, Ibrahim pondered, had woven its intricate threads into the fabric of Gaza's daily existence. Here, existence wasn't truly lived; it was a relentless endeavor to endure. He retraced his steps down the avenue, only to be interrupted by the muted chime of his pocketed phone. He cast an apprehensive glance around, his demeanor bespeaking a sense of guilt. Retrieving the device, he glanced at the illuminated screen, the name **Yael Lavie** emblazoned upon it. Ever since his covert departure from the confines of the Judea and Samaria district police station, Ibrahim had remained uncertain about the ongoing collaboration with the Israelis. The encounter with Uri Amit and his meddling with Yael's computer, had cast shadows of ambiguity over their shared inquiry. Yet, no word had come from Yael, signaling either the cessation or continuation of their joint endeavor. A text message he had sent had remained unanswered, leaving him uneasy, as though the fragile thread of connection they had painstakingly woven might have frayed, rupturing the essential trust that had been nurtured. And now, it was Yael Lavie on the line, her call beckoning him. A fleeting debate flickered within him, the idea of not answering now, returning her call from a more discreet vantage a tempting prospect, yet he recognized his inability to deny her summons. He pressed the button to accept the call.

"Where are you?" she inquired.

"In the northern expanse of Gaza, I just left one of the organization's offices" he replied, a trace of regret tainting his words. He was acutely aware that their conversations were under the watchful gaze of Israeli surveillance, harvested intelligence contributing to the mosaic of data regarding Hamas. The day would arrive when this information would coalesce into a repository of targets, earmarked for potential future strikes upon Gaza. But Yael ignored these words.

"I implore you to come urgently to the Erez checkpoint," she entreated. "I've secured entry permits for you."

"Why? What happened?"

"We have stumbled upon another woman's body. She was discovered within the cooling chamber of a meat refrigeration truck, trying to cross from Gaza into Israel. Your assistance is vital in identifying the deceased and initiating an investigation. Later, you will continue your investigation in Gaza. My fear is that another body might be concealed on the Israeli side."

"Where is she now?"

"We have dispatched her to the Institute of Forensic Medicine in Abu Kabir. However, the truck driver remains detained at the checkpoint. My intuition veers towards him being an unwitting pawn in this affair. This man has been crossing the border daily for over 15 years, his record unblemished by wrongdoing or suspicion. It is plausible that his innocence was manipulated, facilitating the unwitting transport of the body into Israel."

"I understand," Ibrahim acknowledged.

"I await you at the checkpoint. I will take you back there tonight."

"I need to get approval from my side, too."

"I know," she affirmed. "Have you heard of any recent disappearances or abductions?"

A moment's silence ensued, Ibrahim's thoughts mulling over the inquiry before he deliberately responded, "No. However, I will check around."

"Very well. Come here as fast as you can." She hung up. He stood there momentarily, his gaze fixated on the clock displayed on his phone's screen, before retracing his steps to the very building he had just vacated moments ago.

***

"Do you trust him?" Ismail asked Aziz Shafiki. They conversed on the phone, and Aziz sounded perturbed.

"I've learned not to trust anyone. But my gut feeling is that he won't cause us any trouble."

"We are in a precarious situation. We need to neutralize the threat to the organization immediately. We can't allow internal accusations to ignite. It usually leads to internal conflicts."

"With all due respect, she is my daughter..." Shafiki stated. Bader fell silent, and Shafiki continued, "I'll watch him closely."

"Don't let him disrupt our plans. I'll see you shortly," Bader said as Ibrahim's head reappeared at the office door. Bader hung the call and gestured Ibrahim to enter.

In his office, several buildings away from there, Shafiki held his phone tightly and looked at it. He ensured the call was disconnected, then dialed a number and waited a few seconds. A voice answered from the other end. Shafiki said, "We proceed as usual," and ended the call.

***

At 9:30 AM, Ibrahim Azberga strode into the Erez checkpoint. Quickly navigating the security procedures, he completed the required two approval paperwork and transitioned into Israeli territory. Yael Lavie's reception lacked the customary pleasantries. Not a single question arose regarding his covert departure from the police station, nor did she offer an explanation for her unresponsive stance to his messages. A mere gesture from her hand directed him towards the conference room adjacent to Yaakov Mizrahi's office. He followed her. Yet, Yael herself refrained from entering the room, she passed the glass doors and continued on. An imposing armored door marked the conclusion of the hallway, wide and heavy, leading to the fortified enclosure beyond, made from cement, with no windows—a makeshift interrogation room. A central wooden table was securely anchored to the floor, while leather-clad couches encircled it. Near the entrance, a modest coffee station stood, housing a water heater, assorted tea containers, and dark Arabic coffee. Seated upon one of the couches was a man draped in a faded brown corduroy jacket, a green shirt, and well-worn jeans. He got up as they entered.

"This is Abed Kaboa," Yael announced. "He is the driver of the truck in which we discovered the body." The conditions of Kaboa's detention struck Ibrahim with astonishment. Given his status as a suspected murderer or an accessory to such a crime, the favorable treatment afforded to Kaboa appeared remarkable. Observing Kaboa's form, it was evident that he had endured considerable distress, his clothing dampened with perspiration despite the room's chill. The telltale signs of agitation and tears were etched upon his face, and his trembling hand extended hesitantly for a handshake with Ibrahim. Accepting the gesture, Ibrahim introduced himself, "I am Major General Ibrahim Azberga."

"I know who you are," Kaboa replied, "I am sorry that our meeting takes place under such dire circumstances." Ibrahim nodded and they all took their places on the couches.

"Abed, I require you to recount your day with the truck step by step," Yael declared. She retrieved a pen and notebook, diligently transcribing Kaboa's words.

"I'm a meat refrigeration truck driver, transporting frozen poultry from Gaza to Judea and Samaria. This has been my business for many years. I possess a regular work permit in Israel, and I pass through the checkpoint every day."

"We are already aware of that. I want you to focus on the past couple of days."

"Today, I followed the exact same route. I woke up a little before four in the morning; the truck was already fueled. I fuel up in Israel before re-entering Gaza. I was inside the truck around 4:05 AM and set out on the road."

"Where do you live?" Ibrahim inquired.

"I reside on Mostafa Hafez Street, right next to Al-Aqsa University. My building is internal, with dirt parking in front, where I park the truck. From there, I head towards the chicken coops located in the agricultural areas to the southeast of the city."

"Who owns these chicken coops? I need precise details, otherwise I won't be able to let you go." Said Yael.

"The chicken coops belong to the organization. I don't believe they have individual owners."

"Alright, please continue," Yael prompted.

"I headed towards the eastern border with Israel, along Al-Montar Street, until the road's end, and then I turn into the agricultural area. There is a main road there, and at its center are the cooling facilities. That is where I load the cargo, usually around four-thirty in the morning, a quarter to five."

"And who loads cargo? Who do you work with?"

"Every time I arrive, there are new faces. Mostly young guys, but since they are not keen on rising early in the morning and engaging in this kind of work, especially not during winter, there is quite a high turnover of workers there. There are two managers who have overseen the facility for years. They're brothers, I believe."

"I'll need their names," Ibrahim stated.

"Write them down here," Yael said, extending her notebook. Kaboa jotted down the information.

"And do you conduct inspections after loading? Do you check what they have loaded onto your truck?"

"They weigh the truck upon entry and exit from the facility, and they sign off the forms indicating the correct weight. Typically, after loading, I perform a check inside the cooling chamber to ensure there is enough space for the soldiers to board with the dog. I dislike being detained at the checkpoint."

"And you did not notice anything suspicious this time either..." Yael remarked.

"No, everything seemed normal."

"Didn't you notice they added an extra crate to your truck? A crate that looked quite different from the rest?" Yael scribbled a few notes in her notebook.

"I think the crate was already in the cooling chamber when I arrived at the chicken coops, as there was nothing unusual during the weighing. I had entered the chicken coops with the added weight of the crate, so nothing seemed suspicious. They loaded the other crates on top and around it, concealing it. As I mentioned, these are young guys. They don't know me, and they didn't think there was anything problematic with the crate that was already loaded."

"Where did you go next?"

"Directly to Erez checkpoint."

"Any stops along the way?"

"No."

"Meaning," Yael inquired, "Do you find it unlikely that someone loaded the crate onto your truck between the time you were at the poultry coops to the time you were at the checkpoint, or even directly at the checkpoint?"

"The crate was locked, and the ramp blocks the entrance door. I don't think anyone could have done it along the route."

"So, the only place where they could have loaded the crate onto the truck was..."

"In the parking lot, by my home. Sometime between 6:30 PM yesterday evening and 4:00 AM today."

They exchanged gazes, and then Yael said, "Alright. Thank you. You are free to go."

"Are you releasing him?" Ibrahim asked.

"Yes. If his cargo remains here, it will spoil. I have all the necessary information, and the body is under examination. We have already scanned the truck; I have no reason to detain him."

"When I return to Gaza, I'll drive along the path he described and look for evidence," Ibrahim stated.

"Ok," Yael acknowledged. "But right now, people in Tel Aviv are waiting for us. This permit has been issued for 24 hours. The driver is waiting for us outside." She handed him a folded sheet of paper, stood up, and exited the room, with Ibrahim and Abed following behind. Upon reaching the designated crossing area, Kaboa was led back to the truck, and Ibrahim passed the border with the special permit he had been granted. When he encountered Yael again on the opposite side of the crossing, he began to say, "Yael..."

"Not now," she cut him off. "We will discuss it on the way back."

22.

Institute of Forensic Medicine, Abu Kabir

Tel Aviv

"This woman is Abir Adallah," Ibrahim said, "She is 21 years old, from Gaza, vanished three days ago." Placing the photograph Shafiki had provided on the steel surface beside the dismembered body of Abir, Ibrahim and Yael joined Professor Yosef Arieli to study the image and then compare it to the lifeless body before them. Despite the swelling and pallid-blue hue of her face, a resemblance still lingered between the two.

"Without a doubt, it's her," Yael said, "Is she also connected to the organization's leaders?"

"Yes," Ibrahim replied, but refrained from sharing more details. "I'll have to inform them. Her parents and relatives are probably going out of their minds. I hope this is acceptable."

"Yes," Yael assented, though a trace of uncertainty tinged her decision. Amidst the ongoing escalation between Hamas and Israel, she wondered whether her choice aligned with her superiors' intentions. The possibility lingered that the heads of the security apparatus had plans to exploit Abir's body as a bargaining chip. Ibrahim exited the room and retrieved his phone to dial Aziz Shafiki.

"...I'll convey the message," Shafiki replied after Ibrahim had recounted everything. "Just ensure they release her body as swiftly as possible."

"It's beyond my control," Ibrahim responded, ending the call before Shafiki could say more. Returning to the operation room, he exchanged a nod with Yael.

Professor Arieli was engrossed in a brief analysis, closely examining the upper part of the body with Yael. "I believe it's the same perpetrator," he opined, "The method of murder closely mirrors what we observed in the cases of the other women. There is a mark here where he likely injected her with a sedative through the neck vein. Once Abir was incapacitated, he employed this thin nylon string to strangle her." Displaying a white nylon string with bloodstains that matched the deep neck wounds, Arieli emphasized, "This is the same string used on Dvora Goshen and Malak Hamdan."

Yael held the string with gloved hands, scrutinizing it closely. "I doubt we'll find any fingerprints or DNA traces of the killer on this. It seems unlikely."

"Nevertheless, I'll check it," the professor stated firmly.

"It doesn't resemble a typical string," Ibrahim interjected. "It's remarkably thin yet incredibly strong. Crafted from nylon as it is, it doesn't resemble ordinary twine, clothesline, or sewing thread. Do you recognize its purpose?"

Holding the string before the bright neon light, Yael studied it closely. Arieli took it from her, reexamining it. "Sewing thread, you say?"

"I mean, it doesn't resemble the kind of thread used for textiles," Ibrahim clarified.

"You're likely correct," Arieli concurred. "This doesn't appear to be thread for sewing fabric. It reminds me more of suturing thread for cuts, as used in medical procedures. Allow me to demonstrate." Arieli walked over to a drawer on the side of the room, retrieving a roll of thread. Though black and of varying thickness, the texture resembled the string retrieved from Abir's neck.

"I use this for suturing bodies after surgical procedures. There are numerous types of medical-grade threads on the market. Some are composed of animal materials or other biological substances that dissolve after a few weeks. I believe the samples we're holding are a form of suturing thread."

"So, perhaps the killer didn't intend for the bodies to be discovered quickly, allowing the string to dissolve and eliminate evidence. An effective way to erase traces," Ibrahim said.

"I'm uncertain about its behavior on a deceased body, however, it's plausible that as the body decomposes, the thread dissolves."

"So, the killer's intent may not have been to link the bodies together," Ibrahim suggested.

"It's hard to say," Yael acknowledged, raising the string to the light once more. "He left Dvora exposed on the surface and didn't bind her."

"Where might one acquire such strings, Professor Arieli?" Ibrahim inquired.

"I'd presume hospitals, medical clinics, and morgues. Even veterinary clinics could possess them. It's possible he has direct access to medical instruments, though it's difficult to pinpoint. I recommend sending the string for examination."

Yael nodded in agreement, briefly lost in thought before adding, "In any case, this narrows down our focus to individuals with access to medical tools. Doctors, nurses, hospital staff, or perhaps even makers or suppliers of humanitarian medical kits. This information provides valuable direction."

"He could have also been a patient," Ibrahim added.

"I lean more towards operating rooms," Arieli contributed.

"Due to the sedative injection," Yael noted.

"Exactly. And there's the gauze as well." Professor Arieli covered Abir's body, gently pushing it in one of the fridges' directions.

"Operations don't always yield success," he said without looking at them, then placed the body in the fridge and locked the door.

***

"There are over seventy hospitals, clinics, and medical centers in the Gaza Strip, along with thirty medical equipment suppliers. There are five veterinarians and even private clinics for aesthetics, dental care that uses medical equipment, and several funeral homes that prepare bodies for burial," Ibrahim said, placing his phone by his thigh. Nearly an hour had passed since he had asked Aziz Shafiki for preliminary information about medical institutions with potential suspects. Initially, Shafiki hesitated to share so much information with the Israelis, but eventually acquiesced, realizing that the possibility of harming Gaza and Hamas was low. It was better to prevent further killings.

"Let's say we narrow down the search areas to the victims' and Abed Kaboa's residence area. How many medical centers are we talking about?" Yael asked. They were sitting on the other side of Ben Zvi Street, across from the Institute of Forensic Medicine, at a street restaurant. They ate a Middle Eastern meal of minced meat inside pita with tahini, salad, and hummus. A Mediterranean meal that Jews and Arabs could agree on, a delicacy that held a consensus. Yael sipped from a bottle of mineral water, and Ibrahim also sipped from a can of sugared drink. For a brief moment, they were a pair of colleagues spending a short time having lunch, not adversaries from two opposing national camps.

"The incidents occurred in the central part of Gaza City, spanning from the western seaside area to the chicken coops near the border fence, and from Al Shawa Al Khasa Street in the south of the city, where Fatima vanished near the beach, to the Erez checkpoint in the north. All within this range, except for Malak Hamdan who disappeared from her home in Al Mawasi village in the southern Gaza Strip. In the central area alone, there are at least forty medical centers, each with doctors, nurses, paramedics, cleaning staff, patients, and suppliers of medical equipment. This could potentially involve hundreds of suspects, maybe even thousands." Ibrahim drank another sip, leaned back in his chair, and exhaled.

"There aren't many options. We need to gather this information and cross-reference it with what we got from Yaakov Mizrahi. Perhaps we'll find matching names."

"Not entirely certain," Ibrahim said. "Think about the recent case of Abir. The killer smuggled her through the Erez checkpoint in a meat refrigeration truck. I believe we can presume that the other bodies were transported similarly."

"True, but all the trucks go through inspections. If the **soldiers** found nothing..." Yael began.

"There's a slim chance **we** would find..."

"This is a substantial number of trucks we are talking about," Yael gazed at the pathological institute across the road. "...This remains our primary lead for now," she continued. They fell silent for a few moments, each avoiding the other's gaze.

Finally, Ibrahim spoke up: "Hamas will want Abir's body back. We can't continue working together unless she is returned."

"I understand," Yael replied. "You know this is beyond my control, right?" He lightly brushed her hand, resting on the table beside his plate.

"Yael, Abir is the sister of Ismail Bader. If you hold onto her, they will have a legitimate cause for military escalation. I'm telling you, because I hope you can persuade your superiors not to go down that path."

Yael withdrew her hand from under Ibrahim's hand and folded a napkin between two fingers. "Hamas is holding the bodies of two Israeli soldiers from the recent military operation in Gaza. I believe they will use Abir's body as leverage to pressure Hamas into negotiating a 'prisoner exchange.'"

"Then what do you suggest we do?"

"Our job. You will continue your investigation, and I'll carry on with mine. We will leave politics and wars to others, hoping they won't intrude upon our work." With her statement, she rose from her seat and started toward her car before he had a chance to finish his drink. He rose as well, trailing behind her. She settled into the driver's seat, and he took the passenger side. The car ignited, and they began their journey back to the Erez checkpoint.

"I'm aware you're upset with me," he said as they merged onto southbound Highway 4, passing by the city of Ashkelon. Ibrahim often wondered why the Israeli Zionists retained the ancient Philistine name for the city, which had a history spanning over five millennia. To him, Ashkelon was a Palestinian city engaged in a centuries-old conflict with Jewish kingdoms. While many cities in

Israel underwent a name change to a Hebrew version, Ashkelon retained its historical Canaanite identity. "And you're undoubtedly right."

"Let it go. I'll get past it."

"I took action not to cause you harm, or your colleagues."

"What you did matters less to me than how you did it. Sneaking around like a thief, without asking for help or permission. It's shattered the trust between us. I entered this partnership with you in good faith. I tried to ignore the whispers from individuals like Yonatan Uziel and Uri Amit who cautioned me about you. I welcomed you into my home..." Ibrahim hadn't mentioned Yonatan Uziel since their initial encounter. He remained uncertain whether Uziel was alive or wounded, and preferred not to ask.

"Remember, I saved your lives..."

"One driver died."

"That's not what we are addressing."

"I concur. We knew the whispers were there. We anticipated that. And if you had only asked, I likely would have assisted you. Instead, you exploited my innocence and betrayed my trust."

"I understand. So, what now?"

"Now you return to Gaza and proceed with the investigation. We'll do all we can to resolve this case, apprehend the killer, and then..." Yael turned up the heat, sending warm air across the car's windshield, which had grown misty. Raindrops danced upon the glass, and the wipers struggled to sweep away the veil of water obstructing their view. "And then, I never want to hear from you or see you again!" she said. Silence prevailed until they reached the Erez checkpoint. The time was 6:43 PM, and her voyage back to Ra'anana would be lengthy. Nevertheless, she lingered in her car for a few additional moments, watching him, ensuring he entered the terminal, accompanied by guards. With a firm turn of the steering wheel and a press of the gas pedal, she drove away.

23.
3.3.2015

The streets of Gaza were damp, with mist emanating from the asphalt and the concrete covering the sidewalks. Sinkholes pockmarked the road, now concealed beneath murky water, causing drivers to slow down cautiously, to avoid falling into them. A light rain drizzled down, and as Ibrahim maneuvered his weathered car, he mused about this year's heavy winter showers, pondering Gaza's lack of readiness for the ensuing floods. The time was 6:55 AM, the darkness still cloaked the houses, as he mapped the various paths taken by the kidnapped and murdered women. Every time he stumbled upon a potential clue, he would pull over, step out of the car, mark the spot on his map, take photos, and collect evidence. Occasionally, he would enter buildings, comb through apartments and stores, meticulously organizing the data into spreadsheets within his notebook.

He opted not to revisit Malak Hamdan's residence in southern Gaza; he had already combed through the place and amassed evidence. Now, his focus shifted toward constructing a timeline and pinpointing locations to deduce the killer's modus operandi, thereby narrowing down the list of potential murder sites.

By 9:15 AM, he had arrived at the vicinity of the chicken coops, skirting the edges of the slaughterhouse. The pungent stench of death assailed his senses as piles of waste were discarded into deep pits, where the reek of decomposing flesh mingled heavily in the air. Despite his attempts to shield his nose, the odor managed to infiltrate his senses, inducing a sense of nausea. Ibrahim recognized the grim potential of this place—a perfect spot to conceal a decomposing body. Amidst the overpowering stench, the discovery of a human body would prove arduous and its identification nearly impossible. Pacing around, he expanded his search radius, tracing a path from the slaughterhouse center to the incubator fences, yet his efforts yielded nothing suspicious. There were no traces left behind. Standing amid the compound, he gazed around, envisioning the killer's trajectory that day, his mind mapping what he thought was the route the killer took until the meeting with Abed Kaboa, the truck driver. Ultimately, he conceded defeat; his pursuit seemed devoid of rationale. The crux of the killer's activities was rooted in the heart of Gaza, intertwined with Kaboa's residency and parking spot. That was the focal point to concentrate on.

An hour and fifteen minutes later, Ibrahim retraced his steps back to the city. He parked his car near Kaboa's home and embarked on a trail marked by the truck, meticulously scouring for any concealed spot where the box containing Abir's body could have been stashed in the truck without anyone noticing anything. The rain-soaked streets had likely long erased any traces of blood, washing them away to the sea. Continuing northeast along Mustafa Hafez Street, he reached the gates of the Islamic University and the University of Al-Azhar. Along the way, two pharmacies and a private clinic crossed his path, yet neither held the gauze shrouds or suturing thread.

He came to a halt by the university's faculty of medicine. The building was gray, and stood on the fringes of the campus. Ibrahim strode inside. The corridors echoed with silence, bereft of the usual bustling student activity. A handful of individuals, likely professors or administrators, drifted through the spacious halls. Approaching one man attired in a subdued blue robe, Ibrahim's gaze settled on the name tag that read 'Professor Ashraf Barik,' he addressed the man:

"Good day, Professor Barik. I am Ibrahim Azberga, a Major General of the security force. I would greatly appreciate your cooperation in answering a few inquiries."

The professor cast an apprehensive glance around, his concern palpable. Ibrahim recognized that look all too well. There was no corner of the world where a person felt at ease when under scrutiny by security forces, let alone a representative of a terrorist organization. Ibrahim was acutely aware of the fear he was instilling in his surroundings, prompting him to take a step back and speak in a soft tone, "This is not about you personally. Everything is okay." The man's demeanor remained unchanged, but he gestured with his hand toward a corridor leading to one of the rooms, prompting Ibrahim to follow.

"We do not need to sit. I'm only interested in knowing where you keep your medical supplies, if they exist."

"Certainly," Barik replied. "Follow me." They ascended to the second floor, finding themselves the only occupants of the corridor. "Where is everyone? Why is this department empty?" Ibrahim inquired.

"We barely have medical students. In the nursing department, it is slightly better, with around thirty students registered," Barik explained. "Those who wish to study medicine go to Jordan or the United Arab Emirates. Quite a few Palestinians travel to European countries like Romania and Lithuania, and they do not return to Gaza. We maintain a minimal staff, mainly for nursing and dentistry studies. Gaza's academia does not produce doctors."

"I understand," Ibrahim said as they entered a storeroom adjacent to a preoperative and study room. The storeroom was nearly empty of equipment. "But where are all the supplies?"

"What exactly are you looking for?" the professor asked.

"...Bandaging materials, medications, suturing equipment, and sterilization tools."

"Our storerooms are empty, and the same goes for schools that deal with nursing. Everything was taken by you to hospitals for treating the wounded and the deceased." The professor fixed his gaze on Ibrahim's eyes, who remained without an answer.

"Could it be that someone took equipment from here without authorization or supervision?" Ibrahim asked.

"There is no oversight here. Hamas officials come in and take whatever they please, without reporting anything and without accountability."

"Where does all this equipment come from?"

"Most of it comes from donations from various countries around the world. Some of it comes from Israel and Egypt, and some of it is produced here in Gaza with funds from the United States and Europe. It is hard to tell. There is fierce competition for every medication that enters Gaza, but as you can see, we are not well connected with the ruling authorities, so our storerooms are usually empty. When there is some equipment, we are the first to be raided," the professor explained. He paused for a moment and then added, "I apologize. I did not mean to use those words."

"That's alright," Ibrahim said. "Thank you." He exited and headed towards the campus gate. The winds had picked up again, and he debated whether to return to his car or continue striding on foot. He had a few more destinations he wanted to visit, but felt the information-gathering process he had chosen was not yielding results, and the prospect of finding any clues seemed futile. He returned to his car, and drove towards the home of Abir Adallah on Moneer Al Rayyes Street, adjacent to the Gaza Field Hospital of Jordan. He entered the building's courtyard and passed by the mourning tent. Two of the occupants in the tent directed him to the family's apartment. He climbed the stairs to the fourth floor of the building and knocked on the door. It was 11:00 AM when he entered the house.

A man stood up to greet him upon seeing him, approached, and shook his hand. "Thank you for coming, sir," he said. "My name is Amjad Adallah, I am Abir's father."

"Please accept my condolences," Ibrahim said. "Can we sit to discuss a few things?"

"Of course." Adallah gently pulled Ibrahim's hand, leading him towards the kitchen. They settled on two wooden chairs. A woman wearing a burqa approached them. She placed clay cups of coffee on the table and poured in them dark coffee from a Finjan made of copper.

"Abir was a student at the Islamic University," Amjad began

without being prompted, "about a fifteen-minute walk from our home. She completed her second year of nursing studies there. Three girls from her high school class, all studying together. She was an excelling student, a good girl."

"Did any of her friends know about her connection to Ismail?"

"I believe so. It's hard to hide something like that in Gaza. It's a small and closed place, and rumors spread quickly from ear to ear. But I don't think any of her friends tried to harm her because of it."

"So, to the best of your knowledge, Abir didn't have any other enemies..."

"Abir was sweet, funny, and beautiful. She never harmed anyone and was always happy to help. She dreamt of becoming a doctor, but it is extremely difficult to complete medical studies here. We suggested that she could go to Europe to study for a few years, we could gather some money from the family, and there was a chance she could get a scholarship. But then she met her boyfriend and decided to stay here. He proposed to her just a few weeks ago, and she said yes. I, obviously, gave my blessing."

"I did not know she had a partner," Ibrahim said. "I would appreciate it if you could give me his details."

"His name is Khalid Karkabi, he works as an ambulance driver. He traveled to Egypt two weeks ago to visit his parents and tell them about the upcoming wedding. His father and mother left Gaza shortly after Hamas took over. Khalid stayed with his grandmother in Gaza and planned to move to Cairo with Abir after she finished her studies. The wedding was supposed to take place there." Ibrahim wrote down everything that was said in his notebook and wondered how much of this information was known to Ismail Bader. Nevertheless, it was better to remain silent and not interfere.

"Did your family have any internal conflicts, blood feuds? Did you have any problems with the police, or perhaps with members of other organizations like Fatah or Islamic Jihad? Were you threatened due to your affiliation with Ismail?"

"We were never threatened. We are simple people, keeping a low profile. Nowadays, almost everyone in Gaza has a direct or indirect connection to someone in Hamas. I don't believe it is a reason for such a brutal murder." Adallah wiped a tear from his eye.

"I need you to tell me about the day of her disappearance. What was her schedule like, and did anything change?"

"Not as far as I am aware. Abir would leave the house around eight AM daily. Classes start at nine AM, and she likes to meet her friends at the bakery on Mustafa Hafez Street. They grab a bite together and continue to the university."

"What happened after they met?"

"Well, they did not meet. Abir never arrived at the bakery, which is just a three-minute walk from our house. Somewhere between our house and the bakery, someone abducted her in plain sight and murdered her."

"Do you know someone named Abed Kaboa?"

"No, why?"

"He is the owner of the truck in which we found Abir." Ibrahim took another sip of his coffee and continued, "He is your neighbor, he lives quite close by."

"What did you do to him? Did you arrest him?"

"No. He's a victim just like you. Someone used him to smuggle Abir's body into Israel." Ibrahim knew how weak this argument might sound to the father, so he added, "The killer had already moved a few bodies into Israel. We assume he uses different vehicles each time."

"I understand."

"What happened after Abir did not show up for the meeting? Did anyone try to contact her?" Ibrahim noticed Ismail Bader approaching them out of the corner of his eye.

"No. Only when Abir did not return home that evening, I contacted her friends, and then I found out she never arrived. They thought she was tired or sick, so they did not bother to call or ask. They sent her messages on her phone, but her phone was missing." Ismail settled down beside them, holding a cup of coffee. When silence lingered, he spoke with a thunderous voice:

"The Israelis are unwilling to return Abir's body to us." Amjad shifted his gaze to Ismail.

"I know," Ismail said. "I promised you we would bring her back for burial, but they want body swaps, which is something I can't arrange right now. We are negotiating for the release of some Hamas prisoners held in Israeli jails." Ibrahim thought about the organization members Yael met in Nafcha Prison.

"So, what are you planning to do?" Amjad asked.

Ismail shifted his gaze towards Ibrahim, as if the answer lay in his hands. "Ibrahim's Israeli contact has not been able to help in this case. We will remind them that there are other ways to exert pressure on them."

"Are you planning to embark on another round of escalation, Ismail?" Ibrahim asked. "Don't you think there was enough bloodshed this week?" Ismail was not surprised or deterred by Ibrahim's challenging words. He stood up from his chair, the small coffee cup still in his hand, and only after turning his back to the two, he said:

"That's the only language they understand, Ibrahim. Haven't you learned that yet?"

24.

Bureij refugee camp, Central Gaza strip

Hisham Samara exited the shop where he worked and stepped onto the frigid street. His attire, a thin shirt and a fabric coat, offered little defense against the biting wind and the cold. His body trembled slightly, and he thrust his hands into his pockets, walking briskly down the road, his gaze fixed on his feet the entire time. His shoes were old and damp from the rain, and his jeans bore holes through which the chill seeped, numbing his legs. He fished out a cigarette and ignited it, inhaling deep drags. Despite being only 19, he had been smoking for years, leaving his teeth yellowed and his breath foul. His slender figure matched his average height, and his brown eyes were slightly protruding. A hint of stubble dusted his youthful face. His determined pace held a purpose, his attention fixed ahead.

Upon reaching the sandbank that bordered the camp to the east, his gaze locked onto the tall wall the Israelis had constructed. Anger surged within him, almost immediately dispelling the cold as sweat began to form on his forehead. With one hand lifted above his eyes to shield them from the sun's glare, he scrutinized the fence, searching for signs of Israeli soldiers, watchers, or heavy machinery such as tanks and armored personnel carriers. Yet, his search revealed nothing.

The worn asphalt beneath his feet transitioned to soft sand, yielding beneath his light steps. He ascended a small dune and maneuvered toward a dirt road, casting furtive glances in all directions, ensuring no prying eyes were on him, no one shadowing his movements. He proceeded for several more minutes, the road bending northward, and continued for a few dozen meters before entering a dilapidated concrete building. Once an agricultural equipment shed, then a Hamas lookout post, the structure's history contrasted starkly with its present state. Two years prior, its windows had been sealed with tin and wood, an iron door instilled, emblazoned with bold red letters saying: 'Do not enter.'

Samara retrieved a small key from his pocket and inserted it into the lock. With a twist, the door creaked open. Before stepping inside, he cast a quick glance around, ensuring his surroundings were clear. The floor of the building was coated in dry sand that clung to his damp shoes. Propped against a wall rested a modest hoe, which he reached for. He began to gather the sand, accumulating it in one corner of the room. The task took only a matter of minutes, revealing a square wooden door set within the floor. The door was secured to an iron frame and sealed with a substantial lock. This concealed entrance led to an underground passage. Samara continued his efforts, freeing the door from its sandy cover. Extracting a second key from his pocket, he undid the second lock. Ensuring the main entrance door was securely locked, he squeezed into the hidden underground space.

Descending the steel ladder affixed to the wall, he ventured downward, five meters into the depths. A quick flick of a steel switch illuminated the underground space, unveiling an intricate network of electric switches and handles. Arrayed along the concrete wall, a series of numbered electric cords emerged. From a small wooden box placed on the damp floor of the structure, due to the rain dripping in, he retrieved a slightly moist notebook. He took out his old phone from his pocket and looked at the message he received half an hour prior. He powered it down and turned his focus back to the notebook. Marking down the numbers corresponding to four specific cables, he deftly connected three of them to a single switch and the fourth to another. Engaging both switches, he then pulled the handle.

An ominous explosion reverberated through the walls of the

structure, its force palpably shaking the structure. Without delay, a sustained whistle followed, signifying the launch of five Fajr-5 missiles streaking toward Israel's central cities. With a swift disconnection of cables, he erased the markings from the notebook of the cables used and extinguished the light. Ascending the ladder, he secured the door, locking it tightly, and covered the floor with a layer of dry sand. He waited for a few more seconds, and then exited the structure. He cast his gaze skyward, observing the trails left by the five missiles he had dispatched toward Gush Dan (Tel Aviv). Distant echoes reached his ears, the sounds of explosions resonating. Though Hisham Samara was uncertain whether they were the rumble of thunder, the response of Israeli missile interception systems, or the bombs the missiles had carried leaving destruction in their wake and claiming human lives.

25.

Jawazac, Palestinian police headquarters, Gaza

Three medical facilities seemed to hold potential as the site of the murder, Ibrahim thought. Their bustling activity presented an environment where the victims could be easily concealed among a substantial number of patients, and there was a surplus of medical supplies at hand. Positioned centrally within Gaza, near the heart of unfolding events, they fell within a radius encompassing Malak Hamdan's residence, the chicken coops, and Erez checkpoint. The first of these was Shifa Hospital, the largest and most prominent medical center in Gaza. The second was the Al-Shaba Medical Center, situated along a street sharing its name. Lastly, the Gaza Field Hospital of Jordan was adjacent to Abir's house. Though an additional eleven medical establishments existed within this radius, the dire circumstances in Gaza prompted Ibrahim to prioritize these three for his investigation. Operating in secrecy, he pursued his task independently, without the support of a team to assist in gathering and analyzing information. He would have to examine the lists of workers and patients, aiming to cross-reference them with the list of individuals who had passed through the Erez checkpoint. If he failed to uncover any corresponding information, only then would he consider broadening his investigation to encompass additional medical facilities within the vicinity.

Seated within his modest office at the Jawazac headquarters on Majdal Al-Majdal street, Ibrahim leaned back in his chair and surveyed his surroundings. His desk was constructed from Formica-coated plywood in a shade of brown. The drawers occasionally got stuck and their plastic handles broke. The room's walls had gone unpainted for years, the plaster crumbling in places, and patches of mold emerging with each passing winter. The chair in which he sat had traveled with him from Nablus, featuring metallic octopus-like legs mounted on silver wheels. The once-luxurious brown leather upholstery had faded over time. Adorning one wall hung a single photograph: a portrait of Layla, his former wife, from whom he had been divorced for eight years. The inexplicable presence of her image persisted as a mystery, both to himself and others. His home contained no remnants of their shared past. Following their divorce, Layla had departed Gaza, and their paths had not crossed since. Yet within his office, a small shrine of sorts was left for her.

On the opposite wall, two chalkboards were suspended. He utilized them for crafting mind maps to aid in solving hard cases. The tabletop was strewn with papers, notebooks, a computer screen, and another old laptop, both perpetually operational. He perused web pages aimlessly, grappling with a sense of mental impasse and heartache. Swiftly skimming headlines on various Arab websites, he then accessed the file Yael had sent him, containing a list of individuals who had crossed the Erez checkpoint. Exhausted and contemplative, he debated whether he should defy Shafiki's authority and enlist one of the officers to assist him. Ultimately, he opted against it, deeming a confrontation with Shafiki superfluous. Retrieving Malak Hamdan's files from the desk—Shafiki's daughter—he delved into the testimonies and evidence compiled for the case. He reviewed the interrogations conducted by Shafiki with his son-in-law, Yazid, and his grandson, Khalil, before looking at the files of Abir, Fatima, and Anan. A gentle knock on the office door announced the entry of his secretary, Nasrin.

"I'm heading home," she stated. "Is there anything else you need, Ibrahim?"

"No," he replied. "Actually, yes, I'd appreciate a teapot." Nasrin nodded and withdrew from the office, gently shutting the door. Ibrahim fixed a vacant gaze on the closed door. He was fond of the young woman, a daughter of one of Hamas's influential echelon, and chided himself for compelling her to invest extra hours at the office, extending beyond her designated shifts. Contemplating whether he sought her presence for a touch of feminine gentleness, he mused briefly, then rose from his seat and approached the map of Gaza adorning the wall, encased in protective plastic. He marked three red circles around each medical facility. An additional red circle encircled 'Shifa' hospital. This is where he should commence, he reasoned, before returning to the desk. Lifting the phone, he searched for a contact, then grasped the landline and dialed. A single ring resonated before a thunderous explosion rocked the air, propelling Ibrahim into the air and slamming him forcefully against a wall.

***

Upon reopening his eyes, the world around him remained a blurry haze. Enveloped in swirling clouds of dust, comprehension of his surroundings proved elusive. Above him sprawled an overcast sky, yet he was not out in the street—instead, he found himself still within his office. He ascertained this by his prone position, nestled between his desk and chair. Missing were two walls of the room, along with sections of the ceiling. Struggling to move his limbs, his attempts to rise and stand were thwarted by a heavy weight pinning him down. With a slight lift of his head, he observed a massive concrete beam resting atop his body. He was trapped. Endeavoring to map the sensations of pain coursing through his body, he sought to assess potential injuries to his organs and the odds of his survival, yet his tactile sense had seemingly deserted him. The disconcerting thought that his spinal cord might be injured, rendering him paralyzed, loomed ominously. He hoped this was not the case. In his search for his phone or any sign of impending rescuers, his gaze swept over his surroundings, yet no one came into view. Lying there, his mind grappled with the question of what had caused the building's collapse upon him. Trails of fighter jets streaked across the sky, offering a grim clue, and he pieced together the puzzle before him.

Moments later, the roar of fighter jet engines pierced the air once again. He squeezed his eyes shut and waited for a brief span of time. Then, a colossal blast resonated, not far from his location. Shock waves from the detonation reverberated through his immobilized body. He observed a plume of smoke billowing upward, originating from nearby ruins—the wreckage of a building. Whether it was the very structure Ismail Bader had been in or Gaza's municipality building, such details eluded him. Light droplets of rain descended upon his face, yet Ibrahim remained detached from any sensations of cold or warmth. With closed eyes, he made a concerted effort to calm himself. Aware that the arrival of rescuers might not be imminent, he grappled with the stark possibility of his impending demise within these confines. However, an internal tempest raged within him, despite the dire circumstances, he knew he would make it out alive. He would be fine. And so, he allowed sleep to claim him.

***

As his eyes opened again, the shroud of night had descended. He remained prone in the same spot, the chill of the air seeping through his clothes, causing his lips to quiver uncontrollably. Shivers wracked his entire frame, his body now drenched by the persistent rain that cascaded onto his face, intermittently causing him to choke. Within the rainwater, an unexpected taste emerged—a bitter metallic tang, the taste of blood. A growing awareness that he was injured, particularly in the head, settled over Ibrahim. Yet, the extent of the injury and whether the bleeding had persisted, remained unknown to him. He comprehended that his odds of survival dwindled as blood continued to escape his body. Then, a glimmer of hope materialized. He managed to shift his right leg. By withdrawing it slightly, his foot slipped free from his shoe. With his knee at an awkward angle, he manipulated it into the space wedged between the concrete beam and the steel legs of his office chair. He elevated his knee slightly and successfully liberated his right hand. Pain flared as he freed it, a harsh reminder of his injuries. Nonetheless, a sense of relief washed over him; the very ability to feel his hand and leg suggested the injuries might not be as dire as he'd feared. Efforts to dislodge the concrete beam proved futile—agonizing pangs erupted from his back. Many hours of lying on a crushed brick had resulted in the material penetrating his skin, pressing against his shoulder blades. His attempts to shift and remove the brick were thwarted. Recognizing that his only hope lay in the hands of rescuers, he relinquished his struggle, resigning himself to remain immobile. He lay there, motionless, until the sound of voices drifted closer. The dawning sun's soft glow painted the sky, or perhaps the illumination emanated from the ambulances stationed outside the wreckage—his perception had grown hazy. Yells reverberated, his breaths came with a newfound relief, and pain surged through his body as he was gingerly moved and lifted. Hands held an infusion tube before him, then he sensed his body being securely fastened and jostled onto a stretcher. Every so often, the heavens painted his thoughts with hues of red and orange. Howling dogs echoed in the background, and the image of one of his colleagues lying there, her body broken, rose before his eyes as he was ushered into the Red Crescent ambulance. He attempted to call out to her, yet his voice remained trapped, unable to escape his parched throat. His mouth felt arid, filled with gravel. An endeavor to extend his hand towards her proved futile, as his hand was tied to the stretcher. He laid there helpless, and then a slender, glistening object captured his attention—a syringe's needle. A brief, pricking sensation pierced his shoulder, and then darkness enveloped his consciousness.

26.

7.3.2015

'Shifa' hospital, Gaza

When he opened his eyes for the third time, he was on a bed, in a small private room with a window at the hospital. He lay still in bed, winter sunbeams piercing through the window and falling onto his face. Despite the glare, his eyes were fixed on the light and remained open. His hand was connected to an infusion, and his head was bandaged. He attempted moving his legs and arms, and felt a response from his limbs. His mouth was dry, and he longed for water. He tried to speak, a weak and raspy voice barely emerging from his throat, but it was enough to summon a nurse from the nurses' station to come and check on him.

"Good morning, Ibrahim," she said with a smile, retrieving a stethoscope from her pocket. She examined his body, checked for bruises and bandages, took his temperature and blood pressure, and felt his pulse. "How are you feeling today?"

"I'm very thirsty," he managed to say, attempting a smile.

"I'll bring you some water, and maybe you would like to try eating something? You must be hungry."

"I don't know," he replied, and she left the room. When she returned, she brought a bottle of mineral water and a straw. She opened the bottle, propped up the back of the bed a little to a sitting position, and brought the straw to his mouth. He sipped from the bottle and immediately felt relief.

"Here, try to hold it on your own," she said, pulling his hand from under the blanket. Ibrahim struggled to lift the bottle to his hand, but managed to grab it and drink. He felt a sense of accomplishment.

"Is there someone you would like me to call for you?" she asked.

"The doctor. I want to know how I'm doing."

"The doctor will get here in half an hour, you will be able to ask him then," she replied. "There is a urine bottle here if you require. I changed your diaper this morning so you are clean and tidy, but if you want, you may go to the restroom," she pointed to a small cubicle at the edge of the room. "I'll bring you some food, and I ask that you try to move a bit, to sit up, to stand up. It's very important. You have been lying here for a long time."

"How long have I been here?" he asked in a hoarse voice.

"You were brought in at 4:30 AM on the fourth of March, and today is the seventh of March, so three days. But I think you will be fine. You will be released to your house in a matter of a day or two." She placed the urine bottle on the bed, patted his head, and left the room. Ibrahim lay for a few more minutes, then slowly propped himself up and began feeling his body, counting his injuries. Half an hour later, the door opened, and a familiar man stood in the doorway. Ibrahim Azberga smiled at Dr. Mansour Al-Qasem.

"I see you have finally woken up. I lowered your dosage yesterday, yet it still took quite a few hours for you to wake up. I was getting worried."

"How am I, Doctor Al-Qasem?" Ibrahim asked.

"Let's see..." Dr. Mansour Al-Qasem took the medical chart hanging on the bed and examined it. "Your tests are good. You don't have any fractures in your bones except for a small crack in one of your ribs. It might hurt a bit, but there is not much we can do about it. I stitched up your left hand that was trapped under the concrete beam – you were very lucky, believe me. Your chair and desk saved your life. But your left hand was slightly crushed, and we had to remove some muscle tissue that won't regrow. You will have a scar for life. You also had a few frostbite burns on your legs and three deep cuts that required stitches, one along your crotch, the second on your abdomen, and the third on your shoulder. It's a jagged cut, probably from lying too long on a broken brick in waste water. The eardrum in your right ear is torn, likely due to the explosion, but it will heal, and your hearing will be back to normal. Until then, you might experience a slight sense of instability, perhaps mild vertigo. You are receiving antibiotics and pain relief medications, but I assume that within two or three days, you will be able to go home."

"Do you know what happened? Are there any casualties?"

"I do hold that information, but I ask that you not plead with me for updates. I'll inform Shafiki that you've awakened; he asked me to let him know. He will tell you everything."

"I'm feeling intense pain in my legs and back, and I find it very difficult to move."

"I understand," the doctor said and examined the bandages again. The nurse entered with a food cart, but Dr. Mansour had signaled her to take it away, as it was unneeded. He approached one corner of the room, retrieved a syringe from one of the drawers, and filled it with a substance. "I'm going to give you a bit more sedative. When you wake up, you will feel much better."

"Fine by me," Ibrahim said, struggling to endure the pain that enveloped his entire body. Dr. Mansour Al-Qasem raised his hands and carefully inserted the needle into Ibrahim's vein. He injected the substance, sterilized the area, and taped a bandage over it.

"You're a very kind person, Doctor Mansour," Ibrahim said.

"Thank you," the doctor replied and covered him. He drew the curtain over the window and dimmed the room slightly.

"I wonder..." Ibrahim whispered, his eyes narrowing, "what made him... so anxious about the doctor who treated him..."

"Who? What are you talking about?" Mansour asked.

"The boy... when he woke up... in the hospital... and saw the doctor... I ask myself, why was he so flustered? I mean, you are really... really... a kind person..."

27.
Makassed Islamic Charitable Society Hospital

Suha Al-Madhoun stood in the yard of the 'Al-Makassed' hospital, at the Abu Tor neighborhood in Jerusalem, and smoked. It was another day, a particularly hard one, in which she divided her time between clerks and nurses, doctors and hospital attendants, doing everything she could to advocate for her father, who had cancer and was hospitalized there. She knew this was the end. She understood that every additional minute he had to live might not necessarily be a joyful one. Yet, she wanted to believe that she was doing the right thing by fighting to prevent him from dying in agony. And now, worn out from the day's battles, she needed to grant herself a few moments of respite. She had waited for hours for the rain to stop; it was an unusually cold and rainy winter, a particularly challenging time for smokers like her. She retrieved a pack of cigarettes and stepped out into the yard, enclosed by a low wall of bricks covered with graffiti and concrete beams. The hospital's yard held no aesthetic charm, healing ambiance, or serenity. A few trees were scattered around, mostly cypress trees. Many cigarette butts littered the black soil ground, strewn among the nettles and wild weeds. She had thought of taking her father out in a wheelchair, so he could inhale the fresh mountain air, witness the world's continuous movement, and absorb some semblance of reality. However, she ultimately decided against it.

She walked slowly toward the rear of the building, which had been constructed with donations from the oil-producing principalities of Kuwait. She filled her lungs with the cold air and cigarette smoke, surveying her surroundings in search of some semblance of solace. Yet, there was no solace to be found in the dilapidated hospital—only a gray structure, partially clad in Jerusalem stone and adorned with shades of reddish-brown on its upper section. Several tall antennas protruded from its rooftop, presumably belonging to cellular companies. Suha mused to herself about the absurdity of placing antennas on a healthcare facility. The back of the building abutted a neglected orchard of ancient olive trees, amidst which trash was haphazardly strewn.

She treaded lightly until she arrived at the small Jerusalem gate, constructed from iron and painted in a metallic light blue hue. The gate stood open, leading into the orchard, and she made the decision to enter and take a brief stroll before returning to the inferno within the hospital. The ground was muddy, yet she carefully stepped on rocks and wild weeds to avoid soiling her shoes. Olive-laden trees surrounded her, their fruits unpicked. A scattering of raspberry and mellow bushes emerged among them, triggering memories of her childhood—the days when she and her friends would frolic about, gathering fruits alongside mustard and purslane leaves, brimming with iron, for her mother's evening salad. Rain clouds drifted from the west, and the impending sunset cast its golden rays. As she observed, a swarm of wasps buzzed above a pile of presumably molasses or some other discarded food, strewn across the orchard. However, the aroma in the air was not that of fresh produce; rather, it carried the stench of decay and death. Her mind wondered about the unfortunate victim who had become sustenance for the wasps. Could it be a stray dog carcass or a donkey? Donkey carcasses were not uncommon in this Arab neighborhood of Jerusalem, where the majority of residents were Arab Israelis. Drawing closer, she hesitated—the last thing she desired was an encounter with a swarm of wasps. Taking a few cautious steps forward, the dirt road before the orchard sloped downward toward a small wadi, then ascended toward the hospital, some 100 meters ahead. Unexpectedly, a glimmer caught her eye at the road's edge. She inhaled from her cigarette once more, extinguished it on the ground with her foot and, using the same gesture, brushed aside the weeds to unveil a phone—powered off—nestled between the shrubs. The element of surprise lay in the phone's pristine and new appearance. She picked it up and attempted to power it on, only to find it unresponsive. A sensation of something bad swept over her.

She turned her attention back to the malodorous heap of molasses. Forging a path through the tall grass, mud now coating her shoes and raindrops left on the leaves dampening her pants, an inexplicable force drew her toward that spot—something more potent than her will. The impending death of her father mingled with a sense of imminent danger, a somber shadow lurking amidst the forsaken orchard. Her pace quickened, coming to a halt mere meters from her destination. She need not advance any further. Her eyes fell upon it. There, sprawled across the ground, lay the dismembered body of a woman. It appeared that scavengers, perhaps wolves or jackals, had dragged her here, then abandoned her. Hovering above her was a swarm of wasps. A horrified scream escaped Suha Al-Madhoun's lips as she dropped the phone from her grasp and fled back to the hospital as fast as she could.

***

Yael Lavie was acutely aware of the significance that lay in the discovery of yet another Palestinian woman's body, particularly within an Arab-Israeli neighborhood. The ongoing tension between Hamas and Israel had been escalating, especially following recent exchanges of missiles. Yael harbored doubts about whether apprehending the perpetrator would effectively halt the military strikes and clashes between the two factions. Nevertheless, the mounting death toll under her watch was becoming increasingly concerning, adding to the pressure that weighed heavily upon her shoulders. Five hours had elapsed since the woman's body was unearthed at 'Al-Makassed' hospital before being transported to the Institute of Forensic Medicine. Yet, the hospital staff, who were acquainted with her, had already managed to identify her. It was, with a high degree of certainty, Aisha Aqil, a 30-year-old ambulance driver for the Red Crescent, single and devoid of children. Aisha had received nursing training and had arrived a mere two days prior, escorting two cancer patients from Gaza for their chemotherapy sessions. Her intended return to Gaza had been scheduled for that very day, yet all attempts to reach her by the hospital staff had proven futile. She had vanished. Initially, it was thought that Aisha might have seized the opportunity to visit family or friends in the Palestinian territories. However, as the hours ticked by, her phone remained inactive.

"Why didn't you inform us, or the IBP? You are aware that several women have gone missing in recent days," Yael questioned the hospital's deputy director.

"The ambulance left and things fell through the cracks. Someone assumed that Aisha had already arrived and left with the ambulance, and no one bothered to check if she had disappeared. She was living alone in the refugee camp of Shati in Gaza. Her mother passed away not long ago, so no one was looking for her or thought that anything might have happened to her."

"Do you have CCTV around the hospital? Maybe someone saw her entering or leaving? Maybe she was walking with another person?"

"We don't have CCTV around the hospital. We are struggling financially as it is. Most of our funds are allocated for the treatment of our critically ill patients."

No testimonies, no footage. Somehow, during the evening hours, someone had dragged Aisha Aqil to the orchard behind the hospital, a few minutes after she'd arrived in the ambulance, and murdered her there without anyone hearing or seeing anything. How is it possible? Did Aqil know her killer and willingly followed them without suspecting their intentions? Was she involved in the murders?

"Who drove the ambulance back to Gaza that evening?" Yael asked.

"I'll need to check that. The Red Crescent is not directly connected to us. They provide external ambulance services to the hospital, and we don't have access to the driver's information."

"Thank you," Yael said. It was late evening, and once more she was out in the field, far from her family—her children. She stepped into the chilly Jerusalem air and circled the hospital on foot. She debated whether to enter the olive orchard again but decided against it. The darkness, the cold, and the fact that she was alone, all these factors tipped the scale, and she strode toward her car, started it, and activated the strongest heating setting. She glanced at her phone; Ibrahim still had not replied. She had been trying to reach him for two whole days, to no avail. His phone was disconnected, and there was no response in his office. She had sent him over 10 text messages, but he had not answered, and she began to wonder if the things she had said to him in their last meeting had upset him and pushed him away. That was undoubtedly a mistake. She needed him now to crack this case—she knew that, and couldn't bear the thought that perhaps she had driven away with her own hands the only chance she had to stop the impending terrible murder of the next woman.

28.
8.3.2015
Shifa hospital, Gaza

When Ibrahim awoke in his hospital room, it was shortly after 8:00 AM. He lay alone in his bed with the door closed, and a faint stream of sunlight seeping through the curtains. He sat up, his stomach rumbling with hunger. With the infusion stand in tow, he made his way to the restroom. While seated on the toilet, he noticed the presence of a shower and decided to wash himself. His body was tainted with the scent of Savior disinfectant cream and sweat, his breath was overwhelmingly foul. Shedding his clothes, he stepped into the shower, turning on the hot water and relishing its warmth against his skin, enjoying every moment of it. Following his shower, he used a bottle of mouthwash from the sink to freshen his breath, then dressed himself. As he finished, he approached the window and peered outside. The view of the Gazan street was dimly lit, scarcely traversed by pedestrians. He walked to the door, but his strength waned, and he found himself leaning on the door handle for support. A nurse spotted him and hurried over. "You need nourishment," she advised. "You're still weak. Breakfast is being served in the dining room until nine AM. Come, let me take you there."

    He sat on a plastic chair next to a table covered in plastic wrap, and slowly ate some salad, yogurt, a slice of dark bread, and a hard-boiled egg. He also had tea with three spoons of sugar and a splash of lukewarm water. The nurse had already disconnected the infusion from his vein; he felt free, but still quite weak. Finishing his meal, he returned to his room, where he discovered his bed linens had been changed.

"I need new clothes," he told the nurse.

"Is there someone who can fetch clothes from your house?" she asked, and he shook his head in negation. "I'll see what I can do," she said.

"When will I be discharged?" he inquired.

"You need to ask the doctor."

"Could you call him? Call Doctor Mansour?"

"Doctor Mansour is not here today. Another doctor will come to the ward in the afternoon, and then we will see if you can be discharged or if you need to stay another night for observation," she said, then left the room. He settled back on the bed and gazed out the window, attempting to recollect the events of the past few days. His body ached, his head throbbed, and he leaned back and reclined. A few minutes later, he closed his eyes and drifted back to sleep.

***

When he awoke again, it was noon time. The nurse, entering with a food cart, roused him. Hunger commanded his attention, and he immediately straightened himself into a sitting position, drawing the cart closer. As he ate the piece of chicken and the little rice on the plate, the nurse remarked, "This is what I found for you." She held in her hand a pair of brown pants, a buttoned navy pale blue shirt with a high collar, and a knitted wool sweater.

"Thank you very much," he said. "Where did you get these clothes?"

"We have a storage room full of clothes in the hospital. Some are from deceased patients, and some are donations to the hospital. I took what seemed to be your size."

"And the doctor? Has he arrived yet?"

"He is here, but he is currently in an emergency surgery. He won't be available until the evening hours." Ibrahim stood up, took the pants, and headed back to the restroom. He put on the pants but kept the hospital shirt on with the patient tag attached to it. "Don't worry," he reassured the nurse. "I'm not going anywhere, just within the hospital."

"They requested that you remain in the room until the doctor..."

"Very well," he told her, and then exited the room.

***

He chose to utilize his time within the hospital to delve into the various wards and acquire an in-depth understanding of the hospital's operations. His focus was keenly set on Shifa, and it occupied a prominent place on his task list. Navigating through the wards, he introduced himself and posed probing inquiries. He traversed each floor, observing the operation rooms, laboratories, and storage facilities. He ventured into the sanitation areas, explored the kitchen and dining spaces, and engaged with both the operation room personnel and reception staff. He conducted interviews with doctors, nurses, hospital attendants, janitors, patients, and workers from the storage rooms. Descending to the hospital's basement, he encountered the bustling laundry and boiler rooms. In these steam-filled chambers, the din of machinery masked the conversations of the workers, and the potent scent of disinfectant permeated the air. His exploration led him to the morgue, yet he found himself halted by a guard stationed there. The guard, meticulously listing down the incomers, denied him entry without either a doctor's authorization or clearance from hospital management. Concealed behind a massive steel door that resembled an entrance to a nuclear shelter, the morgue remained out of reach, flanked by the guard's post behind a curved reception desk.

"I hold senior positions in both the police and Hamas," Ibrahim stated. "Kindly open the door for me."

"If you hold a senior position, you can request the necessary authorization from your superiors. I am not permitted to admit individuals I don't know without approval," the guard responded.

He was towering and stood at least 1.90 meters tall. His arms were muscular, and his head seemed directly attached to his shoulders. Ibrahim seethed.

"I am Major General Ibrahim Azberga, a senior figure in the Hamas organization. I can go wherever I please, whenever I please, and I can also immediately detain you for obstructing a murder investigation. Chances are, if that happens, you won't see daylight for many years. Do you understand?"

The guard stared at him, a mix of anger and submission in his gaze, and Ibrahim could not tell if he was about to be forcibly ejected with great force or granted entry to the morgue.

"What do you need from there?" he asked Ibrahim.

"Samples."

"Of what?"

"That is none of your concern. It is a murder investigation."

"I'll need a good reason to present to my superiors..."

"What's the deal? Why were you stationed here? This is a morgue. What the hell are you guarding?"

"I can't talk about it," the guard said, restraining himself from leaping at Ibrahim.

"Open this door, immediately!" Ibrahim ordered. "Who is your commanding officer?"

"Aziz Shafiki," the guard said.

"Shafiki is my colleague. We work together. He assigned me to this investigation. You can ask him. Now, open this door or I swear it's the end for you."

The guard opened the door.

***

Beyond the door, there was no morgue, no operation tables or refrigerators holding bodies. When Ibrahim stepped through the security door, he was met with an enormous array of concrete tunnels, underground chambers, and spacious halls. It was a colossal bunker, meticulously prepared for prolonged days of battle. Hidden beneath the hospital's surface, that will never be bombed by the enemy. As Ibrahim ventured forward, he navigated through the labyrinthine passageways, each leading to another hall. The first rightward hall was sealed off by imposing iron bars. Peering through, Ibrahim gazed upon 20 detention cells. He surmised that these cells were likely intended for those who opposed Hamas, or for captives subjected to interrogation and information gathering. Perhaps they were even meant for Israeli prisoners, destined to be held hostage by Hamas and used as leverage in negotiations for the exchange of captives. In the first leftward hall, a sprawling ammunition storage area came into view. Ibrahim estimated the space to cover several hundred square meters, with stacks reaching a staggering seven meters in height. The room was brimming with an assortment of weaponry—bombs, missiles, bullets, and firearms. Continuing his exploration, Ibrahim encountered living quarters that seemed designed for senior Hamas members during times of conflict. These spaces were likely designated in anticipation of Israel's potential strategy—targeted eliminations of Hamas leaders, an attempt to cut off the head of the proverbial snake. As this realization settled in, Ibrahim became acutely aware of his position in the command hierarchy. He had been kept in the dark about this facility, seemingly excluded from Hamas's comprehensive protection plan. Pressing onward, he discovered a war room fully equipped for times of strife. It contained a field phone, walkie-talkies, multimedia equipment, a news studio, and even a sand table. The walls were adorned with strategic maps, and computers hummed alongside a generator room—prepared to kick in should Gaza's electricity falter.

At the end of the corridor, Ibrahim discovered what he had been seeking. A hospital within a hospital, discreetly nestled within the sprawling bunker constructed by Hamas. The subterranean medical facility housed a handful of beds and an exceptionally well-equipped operating room, furnished with state-of-the-art equipment. An adjacent storage room held an array of sanitary supplies. However, in stark contrast to the other sections of the bunker, this operating room appeared neglected and grimy. Stains of uncleaned blood marred the linoleum flooring, and a pungent blend of urine and disinfectant hung heavy in the air. The floor was strewn with discarded bandages, tinged with blood and emanating the odors of decay. Surgery tools lay uncleaned. Ibrahim surveyed the room. It seemed this space had been frequently used, perhaps secretly, right under the nose of Hamas. He moved cautiously through the room, scrutinizing the steel surfaces, peering into closets, and examining the floor. Then, his gaze settled on something familiar—the remnants of suturing thread, an anesthetic vial, and a scalpel. Nestled beside them, beneath one of the closets, was a roll of specialized gauze, thick and elastic, the type often used for shrouds. Ibrahim found a bag within one of the closets and donned a surgical glove. He carefully gathered pieces of evidence, depositing them into the bag. His task completed, Ibrahim began to make his exit, only to feel a large hand clamp down on his shoulder, nearly crushing him to the ground. His heart skipped a beat as he pivoted to find himself face-to-face with Aziz Shafiki, who held a gun. Beside Shafiki stood the imposing guard. "What brings you here, Ibrahim?" Shafiki asked. The guard took the evidence bag from Ibrahim's hand and signaled for him to move toward the medical facility's exit.

29.

The two men sat on opposite sides of a metal table in one of the bunker's underground offices beneath Shifa Hospital. Shafiki gripped a Glock 17 handgun in his hand, though he did not point it directly at Ibrahim. The gun remained loaded and ready, yet holstered. He also had a cup of dark coffee before him, which he had prepared for himself. He rested his legs on the table and gazed deeply into his counterpart's eyes.

"I have no more patience for your theatrics," Ibrahim declared. "If you want to kill me, just get it over with now and spare me the unnecessary small talk."

"Why would I want to kill you?"

"Why are you pointing a loaded gun at me?"

"To prevent you from killing me. You are the threat, not me."

"And how did we arrive at this point?"

"Why are you wandering around in Hamas's basement?"

"I'm investigating the murders. Everything leads back to this hospital. I'm inclined to believe the killer spends a lot of hours here. I have scoured the entire hospital and questioned anyone I could. Eventually, I ended up here, in the morgue, and found a surprise. Endless Hamas bunkers."

"Up to this point, your story sounds fairly credible," Shafiki remarked.

"That's the truth. Now, can you tell me what is going on here? Why is there a guard with a weapon here? And why are you here?"

Ibrahim leaned back as well, placing his legs on the table. Shafiki did not react to his action.

"Because recently, we have discovered that someone has been walking around here without obtaining the necessary approvals from us. Someone is using our rooms. And as you know, very soon we will need to use them ourselves. Tensions with Israel are rising, and there is a good chance we will engage in another military operation, and the entire leadership will need to descend here."

"Are you talking about the missile that injured me and brought me here?"

"I'm talking about the three Israelis killed in our missile attack on the cities of Rishon LeZion and Bat Yam, and their response in which you were also injured."

"What was the damage, if I may ask..."

Shafiki paused for a moment, lowered his gaze, and then said, "The Israelis hit two of our training bases, your police station, and four observation towers along the fence that we managed to evacuate moments before the strike. In total, eight casualties and twenty-one injuries of varying degrees. We will have to respond to that."

"Anyone I know?"

"Yes, unfortunately. One of the casualties is your personal secretary at the station."

"Nasrin? Is she dead?" Shafiki nodded without elaborating.

"What do you have in the bag?" he asked Ibrahim.

"Evidence. I need to investigate here. I saw that someone used the operating rooms, and I have a feeling it is related to the murders. It is very likely they dismembered Abir's body here. I need to collect samples and pass them to the Israelis. Do you have CCTV down here?"

"CCTV? The last thing we need is to provide direct access to our bunkers to the Israelis. What evidence do you have in the bag?"

"Guazes, like the ones we found on Anan Saeed, and also a suture thread. We tend to think that was how the women were murdered. They were strangled."

"I'll instruct the guard to hand you the items."

"I also need some time to gather evidence from the rooms."

"You have ten minutes," Shafiki said, rising from his chair. "And Ibrahim..." Ibrahim lifted his gaze and removed his legs from the table also. "Do not dare to say a word to the Israelis about this place, clear?"

"Understood," Ibrahim said, as he stood up and began looking for more evidence. He asked Shafiki to take some photos and send them to his e-mail. "We need to figure out who is the medical staff that comes to the bunker and uses it. This person could be the killer."

"Let's go ask the manager a few questions," Shafiki suggested, signaling to Ibrahim they need to go. They exited the compound, and the imposing guard closed the giant steel door and locked it. He put the key back in his pocket and pulled the bag he had taken from Ibrahim from under the makeshift reception desk and handed it to him. Ibrahim peered inside, lightly tapped Shafiki's shoulder, and headed towards the staircase.

"Take care of the place," Shafiki told the guard. "Bring it back to a competent level, and then make sure no one comes in or out of it, clear?"

The guard nodded, and Aziz Shafiki unloaded his weapon and placed it back in its holster. "No more problems," he muttered, then followed Ibrahim. The guard stared at the disappearing men at the bend of the staircase, then took out his phone out of his pocket and sent a text message to an unknown number: **We have a problem**.

***

Professor Massoud Taha, the manager of Shifa Hospital, leaned against his office window, gazing outside through the white curtains. His eyes were unfocused, lost in thought, seemingly detached from his surroundings. The two men who had entered his private sanctuary now occupied an armchair with a worn fabric seat in shades of brown and black, a piece that seemed as though it had stood there since ancient times. Half an hour had elapsed since they had taken control of his daily routine and commenced their interrogation. An interminable half-hour, stretching like eternity. Professor Taha had nothing to conceal. First and foremost, he was a doctor, then a politician, and finally a Palestinian driven by ideology. He had often proclaimed that if an Israeli soldier were to fall into his care, he would treat him as if he were his own son. This declaration had provoked opposition from many within Hamas's leadership, some of whom called for his replacement. However, Hamas recognized that without Professor Taha, there was no suitable successor to manage a big and complex institution like Shifa Hospital. As years passed, doctors migrated out of Gaza in search of a refuge in quieter locales, leaving the hospital as a bargaining chip that Professor Taha adeptly employed to secure his own position. Yet, beneath his outward facade, Massoud Taha was keenly aware of the clandestine activities transpiring in the hospital's basements. He understood that Hamas was exploiting the hospital to shield its senior members from Israeli attacks, confident the Israelis would not bombard the hospital. With this knowledge, Taha chose to avert his gaze, allowing these events to unfold. He, too, had utilized the bunkers on occasion for personal ends, like his affair with a nurse and concealing illicit funds extracted from affluent patients seeking better treatment or protection for their families during times of conflict. But now, as the two senior Hamas men occupied his office, pressing him to reveal those who misused their facilities without authorization, Professor Taha found himself at a loss for words.

"I have heard rumors more than once about a doctor performing illegal surgeries in the underground operating rooms," Taha stated, his expression unwavering.

"And what did you do with this information?" Shafiki inquired.

"The bunkers are not under my jurisdiction, you made that clear on multiple occasions." His eyes burned with anger, yet he restrained himself from saying more. He knew that getting entangled in this conversation might lead to complications, and silence seemed the wiser choice.

"Doesn't it concern you to know that perhaps one of your doctors is a murderer, preying on women within the hospital's confines?" Ibrahim posed.

"How do you assume that it is one of my doctors?"

"Let's wait and see." They had requested a meticulously organized list of all the hospital staff. Ibrahim intended to cross-reference this list with those received from Yael and the checkpoint. He also wanted to investigate whether the murdered women had spent time between the hospital's corridors during the recent period. Now, the three men sat in anticipation, awaiting the materials that were to arrive from the hospital's secretariat.

"Do you have a name in mind, someone you find suspicious?" Taha asked Ibrahim, who nodded in affirmation. "There is one doctor, one individual, who has been unsettling my gut feeling."

"Who?" the professor inquired.

"At the moment, you," Shafiki replied, standing up. He began pacing back and forth in the room, allowing himself to pry through the manager's documents. The secretary walked in, unannounced, and spoke as if no time had passed since she left to retrieve the files:

"Here you can find the names of the staff members." She placed a folder on the table, containing a stack of printed papers with a list of names. "As for the women you asked me to check on, I found two medical records for two of the women on the list. Both of them were hospitalized at Shifa in the last six months." She placed the folders on the table, and the three men exchanged glances.

"Who are they?" Ibrahim finally asked, without touching the folders.

"Fatima Ashawi, a diabetic patient, was admitted here three months ago after high levels of creatinine were found in her urine."

"What does that mean?" Ibrahim inquired.

"She has diabetes. Elevated creatinine levels could indicate kidney disease, common among patients with her profile," Taha explained. "What was done to her, and who treated her?"

"She underwent treatment with a nephrologist who admitted her for observation. His details are in the file."

"And who is the second woman?" Shafiki asked.

"Abir Adallah. She broke her hand a few months ago and was treated here. Her hand was casted, and she was discharged on the same day."

"Who treated her?" Shafiki asked after a moment of tense silence, anticipation filling the air.

"Doctor Mansour al-Qasem," the secretary answered, and Ibrahim swallowed hard.

30.

"We need to meet urgently. When can you get to the checkpoint?" Yael Lavie asked.

"What happened?" Ibrahim inquired.

"We found another body," she replied. The tension was palpable in their conversation. Ibrahim debated how much to share with Yael over the phone about what had transpired in the past few days since he was hospitalized at Shifa Hospital. He decided to mainly convey the information he had gathered and received clearance from Shafiki to share. When they met, Ibrahim would fill in the necessary gaps to advance the investigation.

When he was connected to her through the operator of the Judea and Samaria district, Yael was deeply engrossed in the investigation at 'Al-Makassed' hospital in Jerusalem. Prior to that, he had gathered his belongings at Shifa Hospital, collected the evidence he had amassed, and secured the files of the two women who had been admitted, as well as the personal records of Dr. Mansour Al-Qasem. Together with Aziz Shafiki, he then made his way to his own house. The ruined police building, demolished by the Israelis, held no purpose for him. Shafiki dropped him off at the entrance to his building and drove away. Ibrahim was fortunate to find the elevator functioning on that day. Upon reaching his fifth-floor apartment, he sensed that Hamas had paid a visit during his absence. The door remained locked, but the arrangement of his belongings hinted at a thorough search. The possibility of listening devices being installed weighed on his mind. Due to being deprived of a phone—which he had lost in the rubble of the police station—he dialed multiple numbers using his landline, eventually managing to connect with Yael.

It was clear that Yael wrestled with whether to trust him and believe his accounts. The man had vanished amidst heightened security tensions between Israel and Hamas. Complicating matters were their past interactions and the words said in Abu Kabir. Yet, the mounting pressure on Ibrahim was undeniable, and he understood that he could not bring the investigation to completion without her involvement.

"Was she Israeli or Palestinian?" he inquired.

"Palestinian. An ambulance driver named Aisha Aqil. Come to the checkpoint in two hours, and we will talk." Ibrahim looked for his watch, but without his phone, he was clueless about the time.

"Do you know how she was murdered?"

"Yes. Professor Arieli says the method is the same. Injection to the neck, though he has not yet identified the substance, followed by strangulation using the same wire."

"It is all connected to Shifa Hospital, and I suspect someone from the staff might be the killer. We will discuss it when we meet. I'll bring some samples of bandages and suture thread."

"Do you have a list of suspects?"

"Yes. We will need to cross-reference our lists," he said, casting a glance at the stack of papers on his desk.

"Alright, see you at the checkpoint," she said.

"Keep in mind, I'm without a phone."

"Got it." She disconnected, leaving him holding the receiver, listening to the disconnected tone for a little while longer. Then, he took his clothes off and entered the shower, washing off the remnants of the hospital. Once dressed, he called a taxi, gathered his belongings in a bag, and descended to the street, well aware of the pairs of eyes scrutinizing his every move.

***

It was 7:07 PM when Ibrahim arrived at the Erez checkpoint. Yael awaited him in the secure facility within the conference rooms provided by Yaakov Mizrahi. A few papers were scattered across the table, and the faint clicking sounds of the laptop she was working on, filled the room. Ibrahim entered and took a seat, refraining from shaking hands or exchanging any courtesies. The absence of these gestures unsettled him, but he decided to overlook it for the time being. Rebuilding the trust they once shared would take time, and Ibrahim was acutely aware that as he drew closer to Yael, it increased the risk associated with dealing with Hamas, and vice versa. With this in mind, he maintained a stoic expression and aimed to conduct himself with the utmost professionalism. Placing the bag of evidence on the desk, he began:

"This is what I found at Shifa. There are bandaging materials, shrouds, and samples of suture threads for incisions. I suggest you compare these with what we found on the bodies of the victims."

Yael peered into the bag, folded it, and placed it inside her own bag. "Excellent," she said. "What else did you find at Shifa?"

"These are the files of Abir and Fatima. Both were hospitalized at Shifa. And there's Khalil Hamdan—something about his behavior was odd after arriving at the hospital. When one of the doctors attended to him, he seemed agitated and struggled with us. We also have the route taken by the truck Abir was found in; she lived pretty close to the hospital as well."

"Doctors can almost freely enter Israel for humanitarian purposes, especially if they are in an ambulance..."

"Like the one driven by Aisha Aqil," Ibrahim pulled out a file with her name on it and flipped through it.

"We need to check who was in the ambulance with her when she drove to Jerusalem."

"I have a feeling I already know, but we can call to verify with the hospital."

"Doctor Mansour Al-Qasem," Yael said. "I checked. He is on the checkpoint lists. He was the doctor, she was the driver, and they transferred a cancer patient from Shifa to East Jerusalem. But in recent months, they have crossed the Erez checkpoint together at least nine times with additional patients who were taken out and returned to Gaza. Some were transported to East Jerusalem, others to Amman, Jordan. Doctor Mansour accompanied them on behalf of Shifa, under the sponsorship of human rights organizations. And I found something else. There is a partial match between the murders and abductions, and the entry and exit times of Aqil and Mansour's ambulance to Gaza. Here." She placed a table before him, featuring the names of the victims, abduction and murder dates, and the travel dates of Mansour and Aqil.

"There is a connection, but it's not conclusive," Ibrahim said.

"The evidence won't stand alone in court. We need more than this."

"And what about the Israeli victims?"

"I'm still not entirely clear about that," Yael said. "From what I had checked, Dvora Goshen was also hospitalized. She gave birth six months ago through a cesarean section. As for the others, I still don't have answers."

"I suggest that tomorrow I will return to the hospital and interrogate Doctor Mansour again. If I suspect anything, I'll detain him and bring him to the checkpoint, then we would be able to interrogate him here together."

"I will try to find out in the meantime who drove Mansour's ambulance back to Gaza on the evening Aisha Aqil was murdered." They sat in silence for a moment, going over the scattered materials on the table, then Yael spoke up. "There is one thing that troubles me about Aisha Aqil's murder."

"What?" Ibrahim asked.

"He simply left her in the field, as if he did not even bother to make a statement, unlike all his previous murders. He did not bury her or wrap her up in bandages, he did not tie her. He just left her there, casually."

"Perhaps he ran out of time? Perhaps this was not a planned murder? Maybe she was his accomplice in his other criminal activities, and they had a falling out?"

"And there is the possibility, as we initially thought, that we have more than one killer," Yael said, closing her laptop. "Either way, we might have a starting point, but the road to solving this entire story is still long."

31.
9.3.2015

When Ibrahim eventually woke up in the morning, he still felt utterly exhausted from the long and sleepless night. Sleep had eluded him, causing him to toss and turn in bed. He had gotten up repeatedly to drink water and visit the bathroom, and he had wandered around his house, tormented and in pain. His body had yet to recover from the ordeal he had experienced; his bones ached, and he shivered from the cold and hunger that gnawed at him. The food in his home either lacked flavor or had gone bad, the milk in the fridge had soured, and the cupboards were nearly bare. Sitting on his bed, Ibrahim found himself updating the data on his new phone, purchased with his own money on the way back after his meeting with Yael the previous day. Whenever he attempted to fall back asleep, restlessness overtook him, and he found himself drenched in cold sweat. The wind howled outside, whistling forcefully through his open windows. He wanted to take a shower but the water was freezing, so he settled for washing his hands and face. His coil heater struggled to provide warmth, and even the television failed to captivate his attention—his mind was consumed by the relentless string of murders. He contemplated whether he should have detained Dr. Mansour for questioning the previous evening, but Yael had advised waiting for a more consolidated approach and additional evidence. Finally, at 5 AM, sleep had mercifully claimed him, only to abandon him two hours later. By 7 AM, he had risen, restlessness still gripping him. He dressed, grabbed his notebook, gun, and wallet, and ventured into the rain-dampened street. Entering a nearby coffee shop, he ordered a breakfast spread: a small salad, pita bread, tahini, eggplant spread, a hard-boiled egg, dark coffee, and a glass of lukewarm water. He ate and paid, ignoring the free morning newspaper offered to patrons.

Leaving the cafe, Ibrahim headed down Ezz Eldine Al-Qassam street toward Shifa Hospital. He arrived at 8:05 AM and made his way to the administrative and staff areas, seeking out Dr. Mansour Al-Qasem's office. Upon locating it, he knocked on the door, receiving no response. An attempt to open the door proved futile as it was locked. With a glance around, Ibrahim headed to the hospital director's office. The secretary informed him that he had not yet arrived and suggested that it would be a good idea for him to inquire about Mansour's upcoming shift in the doctors' lounge.

Ibrahim walked the hospital's corridors, scrutinizing his surroundings. Upon reaching the doctors' conference room, he entered to find four doctors engrossed in their daily matters.

"Who are you looking for?" inquired one of the doctors, wearing a name tag reading 'Dr. Kamal Sharif.'

"Doctor Mansour Al-Qasem," Ibrahim replied, introducing himself.

"Doctor Al-Qasem won't be at the hospital today. He returned to Gaza fatigued after accompanying a patient to East Jerusalem and went home to rest. He will be back at the hospital tomorrow."

"I understand," Ibrahim replied, his gaze shifting from person to person in the room. Could any of them be aware of the ongoing situation in the hospital? He pondered.

"Do you need anything? Perhaps we can assist you?"

"How is it decided who escorts patients to Israel? I have noticed Doctor Al-Qasem does it frequently."

"It depends on a few factors," Dr. Sharif replied. "Some doctors have personal permits to enter Israel, and that is a significant consideration. Additionally, the decision can hinge on the doctors' expertise and their connection to the patient's condition. Shifa Hospital has only a small number of specialized physicians, such as myself and Doctor Mansour, who possess permits to travel to Israel. So, we occasionally accompany patients referred to other doctors."

Ibrahim observed Dr. Sharif closely. The man appeared to be 50 years old, his expression marked by fatigue and impatience. Working as a doctor in Gaza was a relentless struggle, a near-impossible feat. The scarcity of medical professionals juxtaposed with a rising influx of patients created a daily challenge. Many doctors had contemplated leaving their posts and Gaza behind, but those who remained did so fueled by an unwavering determination to aid and contribute in one of the world's most difficult, impoverished, and isolated regions. Dr. Sharif was evidently among these dedicated few. Yet, in Gaza, ideals were not the sole driving force; tribal and organizational affiliations also held significant sway. Ibrahim wondered how Dr. Sharif perceived the role and work of an investigator affiliated with Hamas.

"What exactly are you investigating, Ibrahim?" inquired Dr. Sharif.

"I apologize," Ibrahim responded, "but I'm unable to discuss it at this time. I hope you understand."

Dr. Sharif nodded. In that instant, Ibrahim recognized that he was likely seen as an enemy of the people by Sharif an and his colleagues. He was not viewed as a bearer of relief or agent of justice, but rather as harbinger of chaos, much like his senders—Hamas. This realization brought forth another revelation for Ibrahim. Once this investigation concluded, he intended to resign from the police force and depart Gaza permanently, vowing never to return to this desolate and forsaken place again.

***

Ibrahim stood at the entrance of the hospital, his gaze sweeping across the surroundings. Everything appeared as it should. A woman pushed an elderly individual in a wheelchair, children with limbs encased in casts moved along, and people went about their business as usual. He made his way towards the spot where he had seen Dr. Mansour smoke what felt like ages ago, pondering his next steps. Should he head to Mansour's residence? Should he seek reinforcements? Should he report to Shafiki or Ismail Bader? Rain began to fall, and his car was still in the garage after being damaged during the Israeli bombing. He turned around and re-entered the hospital. Ibrahim traversed the ground floor, then approached a staircase and descended to the basement level. He was well aware that his investigation remained unfinished and that the bunkers were likely secured, but he was taken aback when he reached the basement and found it eerily deserted, devoid of Shafiki's guard's watchful presence. His attention was drawn to a heavy steel door, painted white, and a troubling realization set in: the door was unlocked.

Was Shafiki currently within the hospital? Could there be an activity in the bunker? Was Hamas preparing for escalation? His hand rested on the doorknob, fingers tightly gripping as he listened for any signs of movement nearby. The thought crossed his mind that the secrets concealed within this place might hold the key to solving his case, if only he dared to venture inside. Shafiki heard about Hamas's ongoing struggles to prevent unauthorized access to this restricted area, and a notion took root: capturing an infiltrator could potentially earn him favor with the seniors in Hamas. And perhaps, just perhaps, the elusive murderer was concealed within the bunker at this very moment, engaged in his gruesome dismembering. Ibrahim mulled over the idea of seeking reinforcements or contacting Shafiki for approval, but recognized the potential complications it could introduce. Ultimately, he resolved to abandon the idea of entering the bunker all by himself, intending to return to the ground floor and summon Shafiki and his team to the basement. However, his plan was abruptly interrupted by a piercing, horrifying scream that emanated from behind the closed door. A scream of a woman. The sound jolted him, causing a momentary recoil. Without hesitation, he drew his gun. Another scream, louder and even more chilling than the last, pierced the air. Ibrahim disengaged the safety, positioning the gun defensively in front of him, ready to shoot, while his left hand tightened around the door's iron handle. The door opened and a labyrinthine of tunnels was revealed before his eyes.

The entire space was dark and empty. Ibrahim was aware that underground was an extensive networks of tunnels, chambers, and halls designed to safeguard the leaders of Hamas and their families. The space encompassed everything from food storage areas to offices, media studios, a small well-equipped hospital, generators, living quarters, and even jail cells—all meticulously prepared for the inevitable clash with Israel. Another anguished scream pierced the air, and Ibrahim's eyes, slowly adjusting to the obscurity, caught a faint glimmer emanating from beneath the entrance to the bunker's operating room. A fleeting thought crossed Ibrahim's mind: Should he seal the steel door behind him? Yet, he chose to leave it ajar. Pulling out his new phone, he activated its flashlight feature to illuminate his path, not wanting to run into something which might cause a turmoil and make him face the killer directly. He treaded cautiously, his gun raised to align with the beam of light, and steadily advanced towards the operation room. Another scream filled the air, a terrible scream. The urgency of the situation compelled him to hasten his pace; he needed to save the woman before it was too late. **Does the killer torment his victims? And what was the nature of the substance he injected into his victims?** A masculine voice reverberated faintly—a voice all too familiar. Dr. Mansour's voice. There was no doubt. The doctor seemed to be hushing and scolding the woman. With measured steps, Ibrahim closed the gap, nearing the closed door of the operation room. He contemplated peering through a crack in the door to gain insight into the situation, but no such opening presented itself from his vantage point. He extinguished his flashlight, stowed his phone away, and adjusted his grip on the gun, his right hand on the weapon, and his left resting on the doorknob.

Exerting gentle pressure, he pushed the door, and a shiver raced down his spine. A large, formidable hand descended upon his shoulder, a vice-like grip seizing his gun hand, thwarting any attempt to fire.

The large man wrapped his hand around Ibrahim's neck. Struggling against the grip, Ibrahim fought to break free, but his resistance only seemed to weaken him further.

"Hush," a voice whispered close to his ear. "Release the gun if you value your life." The assailant wrested the gun from his grasp and subjected it to a merciless twist, nearly breaking Ibrahim's finger. Recoiling, Ibrahim withdrew his hand from the trigger area. The firearm was now in the possession of his attacker.

"Turn around slowly to face me," the man commanded. Ibrahim complied, his body swiveling to confront the stranger. As he turned, his expression morphed from shock to disbelief, his mouth agape. Standing before him was Aziz Shafiki's imposing guard—the tall, burly guardian. The guard pocketed the gun and directed his colossal hand to Ibrahim's neck.

"Come with me," he ordered, pushing open the door to the operation room.

***

What unfolded before Ibrahim's eyes was far removed from his expectations. Spread out on the operating table was a laboring woman, the baby's head already emerging between her legs. Dr. Mansour Al-Qasem, fully engrossed in the delivery, provided guidance and reassurance in equal measure, attempting to soothe the woman's distress even as she let out anguished cries. Her grip on the mattress tightened as she summoned every ounce of strength to push the baby into the world. Amid the whirlwind of labor, neither Dr. Mansour nor the laboring woman noticed the arrival of Ibrahim and the guard. The guard herded Ibrahim to a corner of the room, directing him to remain silent. Positioned with his back to the birthing mother, the guard effectively concealed her from Ibrahim's view. Just as Dr. Mansour glanced back and acknowledged their presence.

"I need assistance," he declared. "One of you, go to the sink, disinfect your hands, put on gloves, and come help me."

The guard, shaking his head said in surrender: "I can't do this." Without uttering a word, Ibrahim rose from his seat and made his way to the sink, diligently scrubbing his hands with soap before donning a pair of gloves. Then, without hesitation, he approached the birthing bed.

"Maintain a firm hold on her," Dr. Mansour instructed Ibrahim. "She hasn't received any anesthesia, and I need to perform an episiotomy. The baby's progress is impeded, and we must facilitate his passage." Ibrahim positioned his hand beneath the laboring woman's back, who was wearing regular clothes. He grabbed her hands and rested her head on his chest. Dr. Mansour went to the tool trolly and got a scalpel, disinfectant, bandage, needle, and suturing thread.

"Hold her securely," Dr. Mansour directed as he initiated a precise incision. The woman twisted and cried in pain. In a fleeting moment, the baby's body was freed, and Dr. Mansour cradled the newborn in his capable hands. With practiced care, he placed the baby on a cloth diaper, severing the umbilical cord before proceeding to cleanse and swaddle the infant.

"We're not quite finished yet," Dr. Mansour announced, passing the newborn into the large guard's waiting hands. The guard's massive palms gently cradled the baby, drawing him close to the woman's face. "Just one more gentle push, and we'll deliver the placenta. After that, I'll stitch you up." The woman, her fatigue palpable but her anxiety now tempered, summoned the remnants of her strength. A few minutes later, the placenta was delivered, and Dr. Mansour placed it carefully within a nylon bag before turning his attention to the stitching. The guard handed the baby over to the woman who concealed him, then took a seat in one of the room's corners. The doctor, meticulously thorough, disinfected the area and applied a substantial bandage to staunch any post-birth bleeding. Swiftly, he tidied the room, sanitizing surfaces and efficiently packing away the tools, directing the guard to discreetly dispose of the evidence. Throughout the entire process, Ibrahim stood faithfully by the woman's side, offering solace, hydration, and assistance in caring for the newborn, ensuring they were well-prepared for the task of breastfeeding. Ibrahim found himself growing increasingly fatigued, a realization that only dawned upon him once he glanced at the time. Two hours had silently slipped by since the guard had led him into the room. With a sense of weariness settling upon him, Ibrahim sank into one of the chairs surrounding the operating table, indulging in a cup of tap water from a single-use cup. The guard retrieved the gun to Ibrahim's possession. Afterward, he carefully lifted the woman, gently positioning her and the newborn onto a waiting wheelchair. The pair, enveloped in the shadowy embrace of the Hamas bunker's labyrinthine tunnels, began to fade from view. Ibrahim and Dr. Mansour remained, the doctor diligently tidying the room as he spoke. "Join me at my house this evening," he proposed, as he was cleaning, "and I'll provide you with an explanation." Ibrahim nodded his agreement. Leaving the subterranean bunker behind, Ibrahim ascended to the entrance floor of the hospital. The ebb and flow of daily life continued as usual. Exiting the hospital's doors, he set his course along the main street, putting distance between himself and the hospital, unable to stop his tears.

***

Only when he reached the entrance of the garage where his car had been repaired on Al-Jala Street, he noticed that his phone was vibrating in his hand. Glancing at the screen, he saw eight missed calls from Yael. He pressed the **Call** button and answered.

"Mansour returned to Gaza in a different ambulance," she began without preamble. Something about her words caught him off guard, unbalancing him. They were still pursuing Mansour, he remembered. "He arrived in an ambulance with Aisha Aqil. She stayed there to await another patient who was supposed to return later. Mansour returned with a Red Crescent ambulance about an hour and a half after arriving at the hospital."

"But Aqil did not report for duty," Ibrahim interjected, without extraditing what he had just witnessed in Shifa's basements.

"The patient she was meant to accompany passed away that same evening, that is the reason she remained there. She was supposed to stay and wait for instructions from the ambulance company, but they asked her to remain until morning to accompany another doctor and patient back to Gaza. She was infuriated by this and ended the call. When she did not show up for her shift the next morning, they assumed she had already returned to Gaza and sent another driver. No one knew she had been murdered that evening."

"Seems like we are at a dead end yet again," Ibrahim stated.

"This man we are looking for has some unique qualities, I believe the reason he did not place Aqil's body in the same manner as the other murders is because her murder was spontaneous. He did not plan to kill her initially, and when he did, he tried to dispose of her as quickly as possible. His ability to kill and leave no traces behind in any situation is astounding. He moves freely between three authorities—Gaza, Israel, and the Palestinian Authority. Everywhere he goes, he leaves victims behind without a hint, without evidence."

"I have never encountered a killer quite like this," Ibrahim entered the garage and signaled the owner that he was there to pick up his car.

"What about you? Any updates?"

"There is, but I can't discuss it right now. I'll update you tomorrow."

"Very well," she said and hung up. Ibrahim sat in the garage's office to settle his bill, his gaze falling on the list detailing the repairs made to his car. The damage seemed to be mostly superficial. The starter components were untouched, the frame and electrical systems intact. However, one particular repair entry caught his attention: the restoration of the dented metal and repainting of the area where the vehicle had been struck by a human body. It was then that Ibrahim comprehended the implication. The impact of the explosion had hurled someone through the shattered wall, propelling them into the rear window of his car. It was Nasrin, his secretary, who had met her tragic end this way during the bombing. She had been en route to deliver him a pot of tea. Had he not assigned her that final task, she might still be alive, he reflected, as he settled his bill. Starting the car's engine, he began his drive home, his mind heavy with contemplations.

32.

Like Ibrahim, Dr. Mansour also resided alone. His modest apartment on Al-Rebat Street exuded an air of cleanliness and orderliness. The floors were adorned with Arabic carpets stretching from wall to wall, while antique furniture crafted from teak and oak graced the rooms. A glass display cabinet in the living room showcased delicate porcelain pieces and clay cooking and coffee pots. The walls of the living room were adorned with oil portraits, and fabric curtains in shades of brown, red, and gold veiled the view of the unattractive street beyond the windows. Although the sea remained out of sight, its briny fragrance wafted in through the open windows. Black leather couches were strategically placed in front of an extensive wooden library shelf that spanned the length of a wall; he had no TV in the living room. The library was stocked with an array of books on science, medicine, biology, chemistry, different types of medicines, and alternative remedies, interspersed with texts of holiness and religion. Adjacent to an Italian-style armchair, two coffee tables stood sentinel—one cluttered with papers, and the other holding a cup of recently consumed dark roasted coffee and an ashtray brimming with cigarette remnants. Tucked into a corner of the room, by the entrance door to the kitchen, was a desk and an executive chair. The desk was strewn with an old computer, scattered papers, and an aluminum table lamp that emitted a soft, gentle glow.

As Ibrahim stepped into the apartment, he hung his coat on the executive chair's armrest and sank into one of the sofas. His gaze roamed the living space, and a sense of envy for the doctor swept over him. He could not help but wonder about Dr. Mansour's solitary lifestyle— Did he truly live alone, or perhaps he had an undisclosed partner, maybe even Aisha Aqil? An idea sprang to Ibrahim's mind: what if Mansour was unaware of Aisha's demise? The prospect of delivering such grim news weighed heavily on him, yet he contemplated how this revelation might unveil Mansour's true reactions.

"Care for a drink?" inquired the doctor.

"I'd appreciate a glass of water," replied Ibrahim. The doctor handed him a large glass brimming with tap water, then settled onto a couch across from him, and lit a cigarette.

"You smoke quite a bit for someone entrusted with healthcare," Ibrahim remarked, gesturing to Mansour to offer him a cigarette. Mansour obliged.

"I owe you an explanation, Ibrahim," Mansour began.

"Why didn't you return to Gaza with Aisha Aqil?" Ibrahim questioned. Mansour's eyebrows shot up in surprise. What could be the connection between Ibrahim and Aisha? How could he possibly be aware that they had departed together but returned separately?

"Aisha? She returned with another patient. We don't always go there and come back at the same time," Mansour suppressed the myriad of questions that nagged at him.

"Aisha didn't come back to Gaza," Ibrahim stated, keenly observing Mansour's reaction. "She was murdered in the courtyard of the hospital in Abu Tor." The doctor bent his legs, and a sudden realization swept over him.

"You suspect me. Now it all makes sense. That is why you came to the underground chambers this morning. I have been fearing all along that you were pursuing me due to our covert, illegal activities."

"Explain," demanded Ibrahim, shaken by the fact that Aisha's story had seemingly left Mansour unruffled. It was as if he was already aware of her death.

"Ever since Hamas came to power, their so-called enemies do not receive any medical treatment in Gaza. There aren't enough doctors or medications, and those affiliated with organizations like Fatah or the Palestinian Authority often go untreated. Hamas also withholds treatment from those who violate Islamic religious laws or harm their families or tribes."

"So, you are utilizing the underground hospital to provide such treatments covertly under Hamas's nose? Why didn't you tell me about this?"

"You are closely connected to the authorities, what did you expect?"

"And the guard? He is Shafiki's soldier."

"He is indeed Shafiki's soldier, but he is also a close relative of mine. We work together, and he helps when needed."

"And the woman in labor from this morning?"

"She was sexually assaulted by a family member and became pregnant. She concealed the pregnancy and came to give birth secretly, fearing blood revenge. The baby and her are now in one of our safe houses, and soon we will attempt to move her to Jordan or Egypt."

"Is anyone else involved in this? The hospital?"

"We are a group of three doctors who studied medicine together and specialized in different areas within the Gaza area. We decided to collaborate, but no one at the hospital knows about it. I beg you, keep this story confidential; otherwise, many Gazans will lose access to medical care. I believe you are a good person, despite working for Hamas. Your motives are pure. I'm sharing all of this because I need someone within the system to keep an open eye and alert us if anything goes wrong."

Ibrahim felt weakness in his body. "Do you have any idea who could have harmed Aisha?"

Mansour maintained a solemn silence, drawing from his cigarette before extinguishing it in the ashtray. Rising from the sofa, he paced back and forth in his living room, and said: "Ibrahim, we are on a journey of survival. Pursued and hounded. Me, the cadre of doctors, along with Aisha and fellow volunteers, are acutely aware that any moment might usher someone akin to you into our homes, terminating our lives. This grim prospect has not been lost on us as we choose to do the things we do. Yet, the doctor's oath, our faith—my unwavering devotion to Islam—compels us to embrace this risk. I knew all too well that the day of reckoning for one of us was drawing near, and now that day has dawned. If you bear any respect for us, Ibrahim, I implore you to catch the killer behind Aisha's demise and mete out the justice that is rightfully due. This is all I ask for."

Ibrahim rose from his seat and mirrored the doctor's pacing. A question loomed within him: Should he disclose the truth about the other women to Mansour? However, he chose to keep this information quiet. "I will do my best," he affirmed, before proceeding to the desk area to retrieve his coat. Amidst this, a printed line from a discarded medical document on the desk caught his discerning gaze.

"I extend my gratitude to you," acknowledged the doctor, igniting another cigarette as Ibrahim adroitly sifted through the scattered papers, unveiling the document's headline. While the title was lengthy and predominantly in English, two specific words seized Ibrahim's attention: 'Bombay blood—OH.' As he pulled the paper, he simultaneously presented it to Mansour, while grabbing his coat from the chair.

"Bombay. Can you believe that this is the second time I have heard about this within the span of a few days? What does 'Bombay blood' signify in your context?" Ibrahim inquired, his intrigue deepening.

"It pertains to a research article I am currently perusing. A colleague of mine is grappling with his daughter's affliction of the rare blood disease. We are engaged in covert efforts to assist him. May I inquire as to how you came across knowledge of this?"

"Our narratives bear a striking resemblance. A colleague of mine faces a dire situation as her daughter also contends with this same rare blood type. She nearly died when given the wrong blood transfusion."

"I would greatly value the opportunity to converse with her, to learn how she had solved this problem," he said, approaching Ibrahim.

"I don't think I can help you with that. She is Israeli, we are working together to investigate the deaths of... the death of Aisha Aqil."

"I understand," said Mansour. "We are an underground movement, you know. If your assistance materializes, it will indeed be a welcome blessing."

"You have my word," said Ibrahim. Donning his coat, he extended his hand for a handshake with Mansour before departing the apartment. As he settled into his car, Ibrahim glanced upwards at Mansour's living room, his gaze capturing the silhouette of the doctor's figure through the curtain, his face peering at him from above.

33.

10.3.2015

*Judea and Samaria police district,
Judea and Samaria, Israel*

When Yael pulled her car into the parking lot, the clock showed 11:00 AM. She lingered inside the vehicle, enveloped in silence. The radio remained off, and the rhythmic motion of the wipers brushed away raindrops from the windshield. Everything around her unfolded in its accustomed manner. Policemen bustled in and out of the station, police cars glided past her—just another routine day. Her hand ventured to the glove compartment, retrieving a gun which she secured in her belt beneath her pants. She zipped up her police-issue blue coat, its collar lined with fur, and took a deep breath before stepping out of the car. Entering the station's main building, Yael received a signal from one of the clerks, prompting her to approach.

"Amit is waiting for you in his office," the clerk informed her. Yael acknowledged the words with a nod, yet she made a detour to the kitchenette on the second floor. There, she busied herself brewing a cup of coffee. One policeman was busy in a conversation, and had not noticed her. Sipping her coffee thoughtfully, she then opted for a glass of water before leaving the room.

Proceeding down the hallway, Yael navigated her way to the very end, where Amit's office was located. His door stood ajar, revealing him engrossed in reading papers and scouring his laptop.

"It will take some time," Yael began tentatively, an instant pang of regret washing over her for saying that.

"I'm aware," he responded, his gaze remaining fixed on his work.

"...And I'm not entirely certain I have enough energy to bring it to a close, Uri," she confessed.

He paused, setting aside his work and reclining in his chair. His gaze met hers squarely. "If you fail to crack this case, your tenure here will be at an end. I trust you comprehend the gravity of that."

She understood very well. Yet, as yesterday's noon hours found her returning home, her drive had been tinged with confusion and simmering anger. Her thoughts had wondered between the complexities of the ongoing investigation and the absence of Gidi. Perhaps it was not solely Gidi's presence that she yearned for—perhaps it was the resonance of human connection, the embrace of romantic love, a partnership. Many had advised her to seek new love, especially her brother Shai, who always cared for his elder sibling, even extending a handful of potential suitors her way. However, Yael was not yet prepared for that venture. In her own way, she found solace in solitude. Time itself seemed to slip through her grasp, leaving her with scant moments for familial engagement. Yet, the prior day had ushered in a poignant sense of loneliness, igniting an insatiable yearning for an embrace, a tender touch. She had driven slowly, her gaze meandering across the landscape that enveloped her. Unbeknownst to her, the traffic light shifted to red, compelling the vehicle ahead to halt. A momentary lapse led to her pressing the brake pedal just a tad too late. The impact, though not substantial, bore semblance more to a gentle graze, slightly crumpling her hood and causing a modicum of damage to the other car's plastic shields. The engine endured, and following the requisite exchange of insurance details and a report to the police, she drove homeward as if nothing had happened.

Stepping over her threshold, an overwhelming sensation, as though burdened by a weighty boulder, draped her shoulders. Collapsing onto the living room couch, she'd surrendered to a torrent of uncontrollable tears. She was exhausted. She lacked many hours of sleep, and her nutritional habits bore signs of neglect over the past fortnight. She traversed to the kitchen, where she poured herself a glass of white wine, and looked around the house.

Ilan was gone, a note was left on the refrigerator—Dina had taken him for a sleepover at a friend's house. Yael knocked gently upon Keren's door, which yielded the faint chorus of key presses and thrust sounds. Yael gently swung the door ajar. The girl was seated, her back to Yael, engrossed in the luminous glow of the computer screen before her, headphone on her ears. A moment of contemplation coursed through Yael—should she intrude or bide her time, awaiting a more opportune moment? In the end, she concluded that this was the ideal time to engage in conversation, as they were alone.

"Keren," she said, but the girl did not respond. "Keren!" Her tone grew more assertive and forceful. The girl startled from her place in agitation and then flung one of her nearby bed pillows in Yael's direction, annoyed by her mother's disturbance.

"Are you hungry?"

"No."

Yael entered and settled herself on the bed, gently brushing the girl's hair. Karen had quickly noticed the traces of tears in her mother's eyes. Only then did Keren remove her headphones.

"What happened?"

"Nothing," Yael replied, her throat choked up from tears. "I just need a hug, are you willing to give me one?" Keren emitted a small snore, but then rose and embraced Yael. Yael began to cry once again.

"Mom? Are you okay?"

"I'm okay," she said, wiping her nose. "It's just been a tough period, lots of decisions to make." The girl did not quite know how to respond to that, and suddenly it dawned on Yael that she was conversing with a 14-year-old orphaned of a father, and with a part-time mother who was hardly ever present at home.

"I'm sorry about what happened with Ibrahim," the girl said, and Yael gently brushed her hair once more.

"Do you want to go out with me to a café for dinner? Just the two of us?"

Keren nodded with approval. She'd minimized her game window on the computer screen, turned off the monitor, draped a light coat over her bare shoulders, donned sneakers, and signaled to her mother that she was ready.

***

They strolled by foot for two blocks, heading toward the café named 'Emilia,' which had become a refuge for Yael after Gidi's passing. They ordered starters of focaccia with assorted spreads, followed by Israeli salad—minus the onions (as Yael discovered about her daughter's culinary preference: "**I hate onions.**") Sipping their coffees like two old friends, Yael made an effort to engage her daughter in conversation, firing off numerous inquiries that went unanswered. **How's school going? How are your tests? Any boyfriends on the horizon, or perhaps even on your mind? And what's new in your computer game—the virtual world where you spend so much time?** However, Keren did her utmost to evade these questions, prompting Yael to eventually shift her approach. Instead of prying into her daughter's life, Yael chose to open up about her own experiences—what's happening in her world, how much she misses Gidi, her musings about a potential new relationship, and her contemplation of possibly stepping away from her demanding work at the police force.

In a heartbeat, the girl's expression transformed. A faint smile graced her lips, and her curiosity about her mother's realm of investigation surged. She delved into a flurry of inquiries, completely engrossed in the tales her mother was sharing, with Yael finding it nearly impossible to hold back. Story led to story, and Yael had become entranced by the captivated gaze of her daughter, her words flowing unbidden. Before Gidi's tragic demise, he was the one Yael would confide in. They would sit on their porch in Modi'in, and she would pour her heart out to him. Gidi always provided a fresh perspective, a distant vantage point on matters, and in some way, those insights had often enabled her to crack even the most challenging cases. But now, there was a significant void, a void left by his absence. And for a brief span of time, she had a new partner, right here. Yael momentarily forgot she was conversing with a 14-year-old girl.

"Perhaps you could assist me?" Yael found herself asking Keren as they'd finished their meal and requested the check.

"Of course, with what?" Her daughter was already fully committed to the task.

"Keep your eyes and ears open on social media, especially anything related to the Arab world. Any piece of information could be valuable. Someone bragging about acts of violence. Someone who heard something. Threats being made. Even seemingly insignificant details might be crucial."

"Understood," the girl replied, rising from the table. "I'll do my best to help."

They walked side by side, arms linked, the conversation between them flowing naturally. Yael found herself daring to ask more personal questions, only to realize that, as she suspected, much of Keren's world—despite her status as an exemplary student—revolved around her computer game, the realm of gaming. In that virtual space, she lacked for neither friends nor challenges.

***

They returned home close to 10 PM. Keren bid her goodnight with an air kiss before retreating to her room. Yael stepped into the shower, then settled at her living room table, notebook and pen at the ready. With a determined hand, she'd penned her letter of resignation. Uncertainty loomed over when she would choose to step away—immediately or once this investigation reached its conclusion, assuming it ever did. Yet one thing remained unequivocal. Tomorrow morning, upon her return to the office, she would place the letter in Uri's hands. Together, they would chart the course of her departure. Aharon Shaked also needed to be informed of her decision—relieving herself of this heavy burden would be a welcome relief. A new chapter awaited, a fresh start. Her brother Shai had already extended an offer for her to join the ranks of analysts at the ISA or Mossad. Shai's connections, much like Aharon Shaked's, would be instrumental in facilitating this transition. She was steadfast in her determination to leave behind her role in the police force and, by extension, her association with Uri Amit.

The following morning, upon entering Amit's office, the resignation letter remained concealed within her pocket. Yael knew she would not be departing the precinct until she had handed him the letter. After all, Amit had been a constant pillar of support throughout her career, backing her decisions and overseeing her well-being. It was only fitting that he be made aware of her intentions prior to her exit. However, when she disclosed her understanding that this marked the end of her journey, she was not prepared for him to place before her an extensive list of names, containing two that would jolt her heart. There, etched onto the paper, were the identities of the Hamas terrorists responsible for guiding Naif Badir to the site of the attack, providing him with the weapon and the knowledge that led to Gidi's tragic murder, and Keren's nearly fatal injury.

"What is this list?" Yael inquired, feeling a surge of pressure constricting her throat. Her fingers brushed against the resignation letter in her pocket. Superintendent Uri Amit swiveled the computer screen towards her, and in an instant, the color drained from Yael's face.

On the computer screen, an image materialized—a woman, bound and shackled, seated on a wooden chair within what appeared to be a graffiti-strewn cave. Adorning her leg was a conspicuous yellow sign with Arabic script. Beneath the image, a chilling message proclaimed her as an Israeli doctor hailing from East Jerusalem, identified as Nur Zarubi. The words below conveyed a grim ultimatum: Nur Zarubi's life was set to extinguish within 48 hours, unless Israel released 75 Hamas and Islamic Jihad prisoners currently incarcerated. Yael lowered herself onto a chair, burying her face in her hands.

"Doctor Nur Zarubi. She is an intern in the emergency room at Hadassah Ein Kerem hospital and is also active in the organization 'Physicians for Human Rights.'"

"Does anyone know where and when she was abducted?"

"No. We are still in the early stages of the event."

"Do you think it is connected to the murders of the other women?"

"It is possible. We are dealing with a professional woman from the medical field again. And once again, the backdrop is Jerusalem, with the delicate relations between Jews and Arabs."

"Jews and Arabs?"

"Zarubi's mother is Jewish, and she was married to a Palestinian researcher from Bir Zeit University. They divorced when Zarubi was twelve, and her mother now lives in Ma'ale Adumim. Zarubi occasionally volunteers at the 'El-Makassed' Hospital in East Jerusalem."

"Where Aisha Aqil was murdered."

"Yes. The doctor left her mother's house in Ma'ale Adumim yesterday after a brief visit, driving alone towards the hospital. However, security camera footage from the settlement's entrance shows that she stopped her car at the gate, and an unidentified individual entered her vehicle. His face was concealed, and we have not been able to identify him. They seemed to know each other, hugging before he got into the car, and they drove away together."

"Had no one that passed by seen him before?"

"No. It seems he disembarked from another vehicle, stood at the gate for a few moments, and then she arrived. By the way, her car was found abandoned on Highway 1 near Khan al-Ahmar. The passenger himself had disappeared, leaving no traces behind in the car. The vehicle is currently at the police lab, but I doubt we will find anything there."

"If our killer is from Gaza, how could Zarubi know him?"

"We will need to check with Ibrahim if Mansour knows Zarubi. It is possible that everything is connected, but it is also quite possible that it is not."

"Where were these images published?" Yael inquired.

"It's a video released on social media networks, from which we took a few screenshots to identify the captive's face and the text."

"And what do you intend to do?"

"The captor has presented a list of seventy-five Palestinian prisoners. Many of whom have blood on their hands. As you understand, it is highly unlikely that the Prime Minister and the Defense Minister will authorize their release."

"And I assume there is no room for negotiation here."

"We need to wrap up this situation as quickly as possible, because it is escalating by the minute. My question is whether I can count on you to be part of this team fully, giving a hundred percent of yourself, until the event concludes."

Yael fidgeted with the resignation letter in her pocket and said, "Yes. I'll do my best."

"Perfect. We will hold a briefing in half an hour in the conference room. Try to get Ibrahim in on the conversation as well. We need someone on the other side, and more importantly, we need to ensure that Hamas is not behind the threat. It could be all part of a hoax."

"Hamas would never admit to it, even if the prisoners' release is not their decision."

"True. But right now, we don't have many options." Yael stood up, ready to leave the office. Uri Amit also stood and lightly touched her arm. "Yael," he said, "there is something else."

He pointed to the computer screen once more. "Did you see what is written on the yellow sign on her leg?"

"No," Yael said and leaned closer to the screen. The image was taken from a distance, and the writing was slightly blurred. She enlarged the picture until the red letters on the yellow background became clearer. She read the Arabic letters again and again: عدو مشترك. It took her a moment to comprehend, but eventually the letters formed words, and the words took on meaning. On the yellow sign were the same words she had used at the press conference she held, the words she first heard from her daughter Keren: 'Common Enemy.'

***

When Keren had returned home last night from the outing with her mother, she turned on her computer screen once more. Her mother had entered the shower, and the sound of running water, along with the rustling of the shower curtain, could be clearly heard through the door. Keren placed the headphones on her ears, opened the homepage of the game, and the chat screen that appeared on the right side. As expected, a waiting message greeted her, and a red heart emoji throbbed at the top.

'**It is me and you against everyone else**' the message read. '**But we will prevail. I'm from Tel Aviv. Do you want to take this game to the real world?**'

Keren stared at the computer screen for a while, then typed without hesitation: '**Where and when?**'

34.

"I don't think it is our killer," Yael said. "There are too many things that don't add up in the overall picture."

"Like what?" Ibrahim asked. They were sitting around a wide table in the conference room. Aharon Shaked, Uri Amit, Yael Lavie, and four other security personnel were present, two from the military and two from the police. Ibrahim's figure loomed over everyone from the large screen hanging on the wall.

"The kidnapping aspect. This is the first time he has kidnapped and not killed. Also, the social media publicity is a new twist, and the nationalist demand for prisoner release. Until now, ransom was not being asked, and the nationalist motive was our interpretation," Yael concluded.

"And what about the 'Common Enemy' that is written?" Ibrahim asked.

"Maybe it is a response to our miscalculation, and the killer wants to send us a message that we are off track. Otherwise, I have trouble understanding the meaning of it. The writing contradicts the motivation for the kidnapping as presented by the perpetrator. He wants to release Hamas prisoners. What 'common enemy' is he talking about?"

"It is not clear," Aharon Shaked said. "Maybe it is pointing at you." Silence settled in the room. Yael paced from side to side, her thoughts troubling her, and her hands constantly fiddled with the resignation letter she had written and was still in her pocket. Finally, she said: "The question is whether we need to allocate resources to both scenarios now or treat them as one case. I believe it would not make sense if I go looking for Zarubi now, while the real killer might strike again and target another woman. On the other hand, if it is the same person..."

"It could be the only way to catch him," one of the police officers interjected.

"I feel like we are drifting further from a solution. The common denominator in all of this is the medical field, and that is where we need to focus our efforts. We need to draw the lines between..." said Yael.

"At the moment, the priority is locating the captive and securing her release," Shaked said. "I doubt the Minister of Defense will approve releasing Hamas prisoners."

"We will upload the image to all social media platforms in Arabic and won't specify that it is an Israeli woman. Ibrahim, you should do the same," Amit said. "In hopes that someone in Judea and Samaria will recognize the cave and point us in the right direction."

"How do you know the cave is in the Judea and Samaria?" Yael inquired.

"Because she was kidnapped near Ma'ale Adumim. There are no such caves in Gaza."

"We don't have much time," Shaked said. "It has been eight hours since the news of the kidnapping was released."

"I think I can help with that," Ibrahim said. "But I'll need something in return."

"Ibrahim," Shaked said. "You have to understand how this looks and sounds from our side. If you ask me to release two or three prisoners at most, there will be no escaping the fact that you are behind the kidnapping and exploiting our cooperation to secure the release..."

"That is not what I'm asking for," Ibrahim said. "I need a permit to enter into Israel, freedom of movement within Israel, and unrestricted passage to the West Bank. These checkpoints you impose make our work very difficult." Shaked glanced at Yael, who raised her hands in resignation.

"What do you think about it?" he asked, completely ignoring the fact that Ibrahim was still listening to the conversation.

"I think he is right."

***

Yael arrived at the Erez checkpoint to pick up Ibrahim at 12:30 PM. His eyes were tired, and he looked haggard. "The Palestinian people are feeling a great sense of despair," he said. "I hope your prime minister considers releasing some prisoners to provide us with more time. The doctor is respected and cherished within the Palestinian Authority's territory and also in the Gaza Strip. The killer targeted her because she is a national symbol. Harming her is like striking at the heart of Palestinian society. We must ensure her safety."

"We are committed to doing everything within our power. What is your suggestion?"

"I recommend that we make our way quickly to the Palestinian police offices in Nablus. That is where they gather and analyze all the available information, from social media and general information that flows there. They could use more assisting eyes and expertise to interpret the data, and I believe we can be of significant assistance there."

"They can share the information with Israel, our analytical capabilities are significantly greater."

"It is mainly phone-based information, and we don't have a digital collection system. We need to be on the ground, managing the war room. Going through the data from social media, answering phone calls—everyone is recruited for that. We don't have the time to process everything and send it to you for analysis. I can go alone."

"No, you're right. I'll come with you."

"Are you sure? I don't want you to risk yourself needlessly. The tension on the West Bank is high, and it could escalate towards you."

"I don't plan on announcing my arrival with fireworks. We will enter discreetly, do the job, and leave."

"I'll make sure that the Palestinian police will pick us up at the Huwara checkpoint..." Ibrahim fell silent. He wanted to ask Yael if Uziel had been at the deadly attack at the checkpoint, but he didn't want to disrupt the delicate atmosphere between them. Eventually, he decided to glean the information about Uziel through indirect means. After all, he had known Uziel for years.

"...if Yonatan allows you to cross again." Yael fell silent. Ibrahim's attempts at prying had ignited her anger, and she felt it was part of a manipulative cycle surrounding the Palestinian's figure, who had betrayed her trust repeatedly, and for what purpose? Was Ibrahim secretly involved in a scheme intended to eventually force Israel to kneel and release Hamas prisoners? Was that the narrative?

"Yonatan won't make things difficult for us," she finally said, and he sighed in relief and smiled. For the first time in a long while, she found herself smiling as well.

"Still, it is wise to ensure everyone from your side is aware—"

"Everyone is aware. We agreed on that before I came to pick you up," she stated. "I'm protected."

They parked close to the checkpoint at 2:30 PM and crossed it smoothly. Uziel was not waiting for them, and no unnecessary questions were asked by the checkpoint personnel. Yael covered her head and followed Ibrahim in silence, avoiding speaking Hebrew or drawing any attention. A secure Palestinian police vehicle awaited them by the side of the road, and they got in. A driver and two armed officers were inside the vehicle. Arabic songs played on the radio. The car's windows were tinted, and several antennas adorned the roof.

They drove down Al-Quds Road towards the Balata refugee camp, skirting its northern edge, merging onto the main road leading to Nablus. They passed by the parking lot where the driver who had taken Yael there the previous time had been killed. Finally, they parked at the secure compound of the Palestinian police on Al-Shahid Mtawaa Street. Entering the six-story building constructed from Jerusalem stone, they found themselves in the government offices on the sixth floor. An intelligence room had been set up to gather information from social media about Dr. Nur

Zarubi's abduction. Her image was displayed on the wall, adjacent to a whiteboard with a table containing a long list of suspected areas where she might be located, names and phone numbers of the information sources.

A woman sat at the edge of an old Formica-covered desk, typing on a computer from the 90s, processing the constant influx of information. The desk was cluttered with notes, papers, and aged maps. Two weary police officers sat on the other end of the desk. Exhaustion and helplessness were palpable in the room. The phone incessantly rang, adding to the chaos. Yael pondered how challenging it was to conduct a comprehensive search for someone abducted amidst such a bustling backdrop. She was well aware that the Palestinian authority lacked the manpower to comb through all possible hiding places for Zarubi. She yearned to take control of the investigation, to make it more efficient, but the glances she received as she stepped out of the elevator and into the war room made it clear she was not welcome there at all, let alone as a leading force of the operation. She settled into a corner of the room, studying the information and attempting to integrate. Ibrahim sat by her, to the disdain of those present in the room. When the phone rang again, Yael answered and engaged in conversation. All heads turned towards her with anticipation. Her fluent Arabic seemed to soothe the tension, and a routine gradually formed. Yael's presence became absorbed into the room's grim atmosphere.

At 7:30 PM, the Israeli government convened to discuss Hamas' demand for the release of prisoners. Tension escalated within the war room. Every individual present was acutely aware that time was dwindling, and the Israeli government's decision could become a formidable obstacle. The cooperation between the Palestinian Authority's police, Ibrahim—a representative of Hamas, and the Israeli Yael was delicate, a fragile alliance in which any misstep could lead to catastrophe.

Ibrahim and Yael comprehended the gravity of their situation being in the heart of Nablus, entrusting their safety to the secrecy of their presence. By 8:05 PM, Israel's Prime Minister was en route to a prepared conference. Media outlets across the country eagerly anticipated his words. While his supporters opposed releasing prisoners with blood on their hands, a few voices advocated for compromise, suggesting the release of certain prisoners in exchange for the life of an Israeli-Arabic doctor, an embodiment of coexistence and humanity. However, the Prime Minister meticulously elucidated the government's considerations and the underlying reasoning for their decision. He ultimately declared that Israel would not capitulate to terrorism, and no prisoners would be set free. As shouts reverberated through the streets surrounding the police offices in Nablus, Ibrahim and Yael exchanged glances. Moments later, one of the officers in the room directed their attention to an open TV screen broadcasting Middle Eastern news in Arabic. On the screen, the doctor's figure was visible, sitting in restraints, her breath heavy, eyes welled up with tears, and trembling as she attempted to free herself from the binding ropes. The distressing scene was broadcasted simultaneously on social media platforms. Suddenly, text appeared at the bottom of the screen: **Her blood is on your hands.** In the following instant, a gunshot resounded, causing the doctor's head to jerk backward. The force of the shot sent her chair toppling, and her lifeless body crashed onto the floor of the cave. A collective cry of horror erupted from those in the room as the broadcast abruptly cut off, leaving the news anchor's visage frozen. Echoes of anguish reverberated from outside, marking a moment that had never before been witnessed on live television across the globe. Yael sat in stunned silence, gripping her head in disbelief. Every gaze in the room turned toward her. After a brief moment, she rose, took hold of Ibrahim's hand, and spoke in a resolute tone, her words delivered in Hebrew: "Come. We must leave now, before it's too late."

***

But it was already too late. Thousands of Palestinians surged into the streets, their anger unleashed in a frenzy of activity—erecting barricades and setting government facilities ablaze. Many confronted Israeli forces at checkpoints and along the fences of the

Gaza Strip. Arabic social media erupted with fervor, the event disrupting the country's daily life on a grand scale. The military braced for an entire day of riots, commencing the recruitment of reserves. Zarubi's parents appeared in interviews on numerous TV stations, their voices pleading to retrieve their daughter's lifeless body. They implored for peace in the streets, an act that, in their eyes, honored their daughter's final wishes. The head of the Palestinian Authority called for calm and even suggested cooperation with Israel to capture the killer. However, his sentiment was tinged with the assertion that, had the Israeli Prime Minister released the prisoners, "We would not be in this situation." These words acted as a rallying cry, galvanizing thousands more protesters to surge through the streets of West Bank cities, chanting "Death to Israel." Some protesters even began to march toward Israeli settlements in Judea and Samaria.

The Israeli side was not without its own upheaval. Many Israelis pointed fingers at the Palestinians, accusing them of aiding terror and committing the cold-blooded murder of an innocent doctor whose only crime was her dedication to Palestinian wellbeing. How, they asked, could peace be pursued with a nation seemingly so extreme and ungrateful for the aid it received? Demonstrators clamored for the Prime Minister and the army to ensure Zarubi's return to Israel for a proper burial. Yael's phone incessantly rang. First it was Yonatan Uziel asking for her location so he could rescue her, then Uri Amit, and Aharon Shaked asking her to use every second she was in there to locate the doctor's body. And last was Keren, inquiring about her mother's safety. "I'm okay," Yael reassured her daughter and recounted her day's events.

"Would you like me to keep on searching on social media? Perhaps I can find something?" After a brief moment of contemplation, Yael replied with determination, "Sure. I would appreciate any help."

Leaders on both sides struggled to quell the escalating turmoil, but their efforts proved futile. Before long, the Palestinian police lost control over the West Bank cities, prompting the Israeli army to mobilize in massive numbers to prevent further escalation.

Within a matter of hours, chaos engulfed the entire region. The police station that housed Yael and Ibrahim emptied as officers, fearing an inferno, abandoned their post, leaving behind only the two individuals, an Israeli and a member of Hamas, standing alone to face the upcoming storm.

35.

"My family lives close by, on Al-Haras Street. It is a ten-minute walk. We could hide at their place until things calm down," Ibrahim suggested. He peered out of the window on the upper floor. "The street still looks calm. We can dress you in local attire and slip under their radar."

"Don't you think it is safer here?" Yael asked, her gaze returning to her phone screen.

"It is hard to say. They could redirect their anger towards authority's facilities, and then we might find ourselves under attack, trapped in this building."

"Do they have weapons here that we could take?" Yael inquired.

"I suppose so, but they are likely secured and locked," he replied. They stood for a few minutes, stealing glances through the window at the unfolding scene on the street below. Young protesters were gathering near the building, chanting anti-Israel slogans, igniting tires, and organizing piles of stones. Passersby still moved down the street without much interruption. Yael approached a map that hung on the wall. She located Al-Haras Street and traced the shortest route to it. "What is the house number?" she asked Ibrahim.

"31, it is roughly in the middle of the street," he pointed to a specific area on the map.

"Alright," she said. "Let's gather what we can and leave. I'll update Amit."

Ibrahim moved toward a closet near the entrance, retrieving a black dress adorned with tassels on the edges, a headscarf, and a face covering, which he handed to Yael. They collected the documents they did not managed to look at yet, the laptops and notebooks, and hurriedly snapped photos of the flowcharts and timelines on the erasable boards that lined the wall. They then stashed everything into two bags, and discreetly concealed them beneath their clothing.

Yael donned the dress and headed to the restroom to adjust. However, shortly after she left, her phone, placed near her bag, began to ring. Ibrahim hesitated but eventually gave in to his curiosity and glanced at the screen. It was General Officer Aharon Shaked on the line. Ibrahim took the phone and answered the call.

"She is getting dressed. We are leaving here," he said without waiting.

"Ibrahim..." Shaked's voice sounded surprise.

"I will tell her to call you back."

"Thank you."

"And Shaked..." Ibrahim waited to hear if the call had ended, but Shaked was still on the line.

"Yes?"

"I'm taking a big risk here, you know... my family."

An extended silence followed, and then: "I'll watch over you, if needed."

"Needed," Ibrahim confirmed.

"You have my word. Just make sure she returns in one piece."

Yael returned, and Ibrahim handed her the phone. "It's Shaked," he said, and she thanked him. They spoke for three minutes as Shaked briefed her on his plan. Then she ended the call, packed her clothes into one of the bags, and used the dress to cover her face and body as much as possible, even though her white sports shoes stood out in mismatch to her attire. They hurriedly descended the stairs on foot and stepped out onto the darkening street. A few tires and bonfires illuminated the surroundings, and a short distance away, up the street, several young Palestinians were constructing a barricade from furniture, barrels, and tires. There was no sign of soldiers or police officers. Yael's phone vibrated in her hand, and she retrieved it to read the message on the screen. It was a message from Uri Amit: **Send me your exact location, and I will come to rescue you as soon as possible**. She signaled her acknowledgment, intending to send him the location once they reached Ibrahim's family house. The phone vibrated again. Another message from Amit: **But it will take some time. All roads to Nablus are blocked now. There are intense riots. Hold on.**

In an instant, the figures of Ilan and Keren flashed before Yael's eyes. She was more afraid than ever of leaving her children motherless and fatherless. The same dilemma resurfaced: work or family? Life or life-threatening danger? How long could she keep juggling these responsibilities? She held Ibrahim's hand as she walked, slightly hunched, along the side of the street. The sidewalk was cracked and filthy. She walked with a haste. Ahead of them, a throng of young Palestinians marched towards the city's main entrance. Some of them carried sticks and rocks, their faces concealed, anger evident in their eyes. Ibrahim crossed the now-empty road, leading Yael between houses and through yards filled with trash, avoiding the chaos as much as possible. They passed by building entrances one after another, then turned west onto Al-Haras street, passed another building, and suddenly found themselves facing a group of four young Palestinians heading toward the highway. Ibrahim slowed his pace slightly, holding onto Yael's hand as they approached the group. Yael buried her face in the folds of Ibrahim's coat. She felt cold, but she was not sure if her shivers were from the chill in the air. Her left hand unconsciously brushed against the grip of the gun secured in her pants' belt, concealed beneath the dress. If she needed it, she knew drawing the gun would be slow and cumbersome, yet she was mentally prepared for whatever lay ahead. As they passed by, one of the young Palestinians lightly touched Ibrahim's hand.

"*Jish?*" he asked in Arabic. **The army?**

"What?" Ibrahim seemed surprised by the question.

"Did the army arrive?" The young man inquired. Ibrahim's throat tightened, rendering him speechless. The young man took a step back, his hand resting on Ibrahim's shoulder, who looked weary and old beyond his years.

"Where are you coming from?" he asked. Ibrahim remained silent. "Why aren't you talking?" The silence continued, and Yael's fingers grazed her gun in agitation. The other three guys turned back as well and approached them.

"How would we know if the army arrived?" Yael shouted in Arabic. "Just leave us." The young man hesitated, recoiling slightly. "Okay," he conceded. "I was just asking." Ibrahim straightened up, turned toward the young man, and looked into his eyes. "My brother," he said. "Be cautious. Don't do anything reckless. I implore you."

A chuckle rippled through the group, and one of them patted Ibrahim's shoulder, saying, "Allah is waiting for us in the sky with open arms." With that, they walked away, leaving Yael and Ibrahim alone. Ibrahim stood there, watching them disappear down the street. Yael tugged at his hand. "Come on. We need to keep moving," she urged.

They quickened their pace, passing through another alley where young men were busily assembling Molotov cocktails. Finally, they reached a five-story building with no elevator. Ibrahim bounded up the stairs two steps at a time, and Yael hurried after him. Arriving at a weathered wooden door, Ibrahim knocked lightly on it. A woman in her mid-40s, her eyes weary, her figure slender, and her coal-black hair cascading in shades of darkness, opened the door. Her eyebrows shot up in surprise as she saw Ibrahim and the woman standing behind him. "Ibrahim," she said. "What are you doing here?"

"We need to hide here for a few hours. Until tomorrow morning. Where is mother?" The woman stepped back and gestured for them to enter. Ibrahim led the way, and Yael followed closely. In the center of the living room, perched on a large leather couch, sat a large woman in her 70s, her head covered with a kerchief. Her ample frame dominated the couch. She looked at Ibrahim and extended her hands, signaling for him to come closer. He approached, embracing her and planting a gentle kiss on her forehead. "Mother," he began, then gestured toward Yael. "This is..."

"I know who she is," she said and looked at Yael. With a gentle tap on the vacant wooden chair beside her, she spoke again. "Come, child. Sit here. Are you hungry?"

***

"Mom, I'm scared," Ilan's trembling voice echoed through Yael's phone. The time read 8:13 PM, and Yael found herself perched on the edge of a metal-framed bed, its thick mattress bearing the marks of time, adorned with an embroidered red sheet and a dusty, coarse wool blanket. The room was cramped, dominated by a weathered wooden window and a cracked plastic shutter that peered into a narrow alley, far removed from the bustling main street. A faint, grayish curtain hung over the window, doing little to muffle the cacophony of chaos outside and the acrid scent of smoke and burnt tires that permeated the cold night air. An Arabic carpet stretched across the floor, its texture brushing gently against Yael's bare feet. A wooden dresser stood against one of the walls, and it served as a resting place for her black dress and work bag. A scattering of papers lay across the bed, and Yael's gaze shifted between them during the conversation. A lukewarm glass of mint tea sat on a folding wooden chair nearby. Soft murmurs in Arabic drifted in from the living room, diverting Yael's attention.

"Why are you scared?" she asked.

"When are you coming home?"

"I'll be back tomorrow at noon. I'll come to pick you up from school." The voice of the 10-year-old boy was laced with uncertainty. After he had experienced many disappointments, he knew his mother would not fulfill her promise, so he fell silent. Yael placed the paper she held in her hand on one corner of the bed and let out a sigh.

"Ilan.." she uttered his name, finding herself struggling to speak. "I love you," she whispered finally. "I need this time to focus on some things, you understand? If not, I won't be able to continue with this work anymore."

"But... that is a good thing," he said.

She remained silent for a long moment and finally said, "Where is Grandma? I need to talk to her."

"Grandma is busy. She will talk to you later." Yael knew exactly what was going through Dina's mind. She was tired too. '**I've already raised my kids. You chose to be a mom, take some responsibility**,' she had told her in one of the thousands of conversations they had after Gidi was killed.

I don't think I'm capable, Yael replied. **I need to find myself first, gather my strength to move forward.**

You don't have time to embark on a journey of self-discovery right now. You have two children who need you, who have just lost their father. You need to be here for them. Dina always knew how to confront Yael with harsh reality.

"Okay, sweety," she said. "What about Keren? Where is she?"

"She wanted to talk to you," the boy said, and Yael raised an eyebrow. **A refreshing development**, she thought. Keren wanted to have a conversation with her. Did their shared outing to the café change something? A sound of a kiss came through the line, and the phone was passed to her daughter. Yael took a deep breath and waited to hear her voice.

"Mom, I found something," Keren said without waiting. Yael got up from bed. She had almost forgotten that she had enlisted her daughter for the search efforts, and now she would have to carefully consider everything Keren would send her. If she stumbled over her words, she would lose the girl's trust.

"I'm listening," she said, her voice quivering.

"I searched every possible social network, famous bloggers' sites, and even global Arabic bloggers who write in English."

"And..."

"There is one blogger, a Palestinian, very famous. He writes a blog on the American site called Blog-Buster. He lives in a village called... one second..." typing sounds were heard in the background. Yael remained silent and waited. "...Rujeib something. Not far from Nablus, where you are."

"Yes, I know the place."

"This guy uploaded to his blog, around two months ago, an edited photo of a hand of a woman peeking out of the ground and wrote in English: 'This is how my plans for the future look like.' Do you understand? Isn't it like the case you are investigating of the woman buried with her hand tied out of the ground?"

"...Yes," said Yael. She was in complete shock. She did not know if she did the right thing by recruiting Keren to this horrible case, but on the other hand, she was really surprised to find out how much Keren was completely dedicated to the mission. Suddenly, a childhood memory resurfaced in her mind. A somber time—the 80s. They lived then in Ra'anana in an old apartment building, fourth floor with no elevator. The apartment was simple, much like Ibrahim's mother's apartment. The home was warm and full of love, with children's toys scattered everywhere. But there was one place in the house that was sacred. Yael and her brother Shai were never allowed to play there. Their father's office. As a researcher in the academy, her father, a professor of Middle Eastern studies, studied the Arab world and the development of terror organizations that claimed many victims. The office walls and carpets were sometimes covered with horrendous testimonies that Dina tried to shield from her children.

One time, Yael's mother asked her to call her father for dinner, and Yael playfully knocked on his office door. But Professor Yoram Nachmani did not respond. She gently touched the handle, and the door swung open. She must have been 11 or 12 years old when she decided to enter her father's room. Her father was not there, but she was captivated by what she saw. A library full of books, a desk made of plywood and green Formica, papers and lists strewn everywhere. The professor was working on his new book about Islamic terror. Clippings, photos, and drawings were scattered everywhere—on the walls, chairs, carpet, and table. Some were truly horrifying, depicting dismembered bodies, headless figures, blood and death. She stood in the center of the room, unable to look away. Yael could not recall her exact emotions back then, but she definitely knew she was not scared. On the contrary, what she saw fascinated her, drew her in like a moth to a flame. Eventually, she left the room and went to the dining room, never telling her father what she had seen. And now, she felt like she had opened the same door for her daughter. Where would this lead her? She had no idea, but it was already too late to turn back.

"Mom? Are you listening?"

"Yes, I'm here. I'm taking notes."

"I'm sending you a message with a link to his blog and all the details I gathered. Do you think it would help?"

"Keren, this is incredible! I think you've done research that's on par with some of the ISA and police analysts."

"You are kidding, right?"

"Not at all. I believe this is a very promising lead for the case. I'm sending the information to Amit." Keren's voice carried a note of mischief. Yael could sense her daughter's joy and did not want to miss the moment. "Thank you," Yael eventually said.

"No problem. I'll keep looking for more stuff."

"Don't stay up too late."

"Mom!" Keren said with purpose this time, but there was a smile in her voice. When she hung up, Yael stood there holding the phone for another moment. Then she set the device down and made her way to the living room.

**

"We might have a lead," she mentioned upon entering the living room. Seated around a generously-sized, round dining table were Ibrahim, his mother, and another woman. She had already met her. The table had been set for a late dinner, adorned with an assortment of baked goods, dark bread, spices, white cheese, goat yogurt, dried tomato spread, tabbouleh salad, hard-boiled eggs, and olives. A prominent tin teapot and mosaic-colored glass teacups took center stage. Uninvited but undeterred, she took a seat at the table.

"Please, help yourself," Ibrahim offered, extending a gesture of hospitality as he presented the food. Hunger gripped Yael; it had been hours since her last meal. It was not until she settled at the table that she felt hunger pangs in her stomach. She poured herself a cup of tea, sliced a piece of bread, and layered it with cheese. The trio observed her actions with a distant gaze.

Ibrahim said: "This is my older sister, Neri. I hadn't gotten around to introducing you."

"Nice to meet you," said Yael. "I would have never made the connection between you two—brother and sister."

"Neri moved back in with my mother after our father's passing. How long has it been?"

"Five years," Neri stated. "The kids have grown, my husband works mostly in Jordan. I thought it made no sense to stay alone at home, so I moved here to be with Mom. She lives by herself. Ibrahim can barely manage to visit." Yael detected a trace of reproach in her words, a hint of frustration.

"Ibrahim does what he can," the mother interjected, tenderly touching her son's head.

"The favored son," Neri chuckled. "Always will be."

"Keep an eye on him for me, will you?" The mother's gaze turned piercingly towards Yael.

"Mom, Yael has two children. Her husband was killed... in an attack. I think it is best for me to watch over her, not the other way around. She needs this."

"You two better be careful. There are many issues now, with Hamas and the Jews," the three of them exchanged glances. The tension around the table growing palpable. The underlying political discord loomed, but Yael opted to stay focused on the purpose that had brought her here. "We will do everything we can to apprehend the killers. Our goal is to bring peace to the field," she said.

"You're a good woman," the mother acknowledged. "It's a shame Ibrahim is not..."

"Mom!" Neri was the one who halted the mother. **He is lonely,** Yael thought to herself. **There is no woman in Ibrahim's life.** Suddenly, Yael ceased to view him as a colleague, an adversary, a Hamas member, or a Gazan. She realized that she actually knew so little about his personal life. **Why does he still live in Gaza? Why does he live on his own? Where is his wife? Why did she leave? And does he have someone else in his life?** She felt helpless. She had been so absorbed in her own thoughts, focused on cracking the case, that she had overlooked the human, the intimate aspect behind Ibrahim's enigmatic persona. Curiosity welled within her.

"Ibrahim," she said, "you never told me…"

"I'm divorced. My wife and I… parted ways many years ago," he cast a quick glance at his mother, who was sipping from her tea cup, and nodded.

"You can tell her."

"We got married in Nablus. We lived not far from here. I was in joint patrols, and she was a chemistry lecturer at Bir Zeit University. It was a time of peace, of optimism. Mid-nineties, the Oslo Accords between Israel and the Palestinians, the establishment of the Authority… We thought things were going to be good, that the wars were over. I was asked to move to Gaza, to oversee one of the police units. I agreed. I convinced her it was the right thing to do. In Gaza, there are several universities, and they need researchers and professors like her. I explained to her that it was time to bring progress and education to the young Gazans, to redirect their energy from terrorism and wars toward learning and advancement. She agreed, and we moved together. But when the civil war started between Hamas and Fatah, she asked me to flee. She said Gaza would become a field of death, poverty, and violence, that everything we built will crumble. She was right. But I did not agree to leave. I wanted to fight, to bring a better future to the Palestinians. I was wrong. She crossed the border to Egypt, caught a plane to Europe, and cut all ties. I have not seen or heard from her since. There were a few times I tried to contact her, to send e-mails, but she never responded."

"The fortunate thing is that they did not have children," Neri said, and the mother hit the table with her hand.

"That is not a nice thing to say!"

"It's okay, Mom," Ibrahim said. "She is right."

"You should have gone with her," Yael said. "Think about yourself a little. Our lives are fleeting under our noses."

"There are other important things in life," Ibrahim replied. His mother snorted at him.

"It is not too late for you to give me grandchildren," she said and nudged another piece of bread and egg toward Yael. Yael smiled, and Ibrahim looked embarrassed.

"We need to work," he said. "You mentioned there might be a lead?"

"Yes. Keren found a Palestinian guy with a blog. There are some pictures in it that suggest he knew what was about to happen. We need to locate him and investigate."

"Give me the details. I'll pass them to the Palestinian police." Yael placed a handwritten note with one line in his hand.

"I suggest both of you get some rest. You both look terrible. A shower won't hurt either. Go to sleep; tomorrow morning we will assess the situation and decide how to proceed from there," Neri said.

"I have updated Amit. If the turmoil settles, he will come to rescue us tomorrow morning. We need to be prepared."

"Go get some sleep," the mother repeated her daughter's words.

"I don't think I can fall asleep now. I'll review the new information for a bit longer."

"I'll rest my head for a few hours, if you don't mind," Ibrahim responded.

"I'll wake you up at four AM, and we will get ready to leave."

"Alright." Ibrahim rose from the table and began clearing it. Yael followed him. When they were done, he kissed his mother and headed for the shower, leaving Yael with the two women at the table. They sipped the remaining tea.

"You know Arabic fluently," the mother remarked.

"My father taught me. We spoke Arabic at home from the day I was born. He believed that in Israel, with over twenty percent Arab population, there should not be a situation where Jews can't speak the language."

"Your father was a wise man," the mother said.

"Thank you. It seems you have done a good job raising your children, too."

"Now things are better. But there were difficult times in our family. Ibrahim was not always calm and composed."

"What do you mean?" The three women exchanged glances, but Neri fell silent and nodded at her mother. It was okay to tell. Much time had passed.

"Before Ibrahim enlisted in the joint patrols with the Israelis, he was an active member of Fatah in Nablus," the mother recounted. "He believed he was a freedom fighter, not a terrorist. He thought his actions would bring freedom to his people, bring prosperity. When he took part in a terror attack with three of his childhood friends, he didn't even imagine in his wildest dreams that he would be involved in the murder of two Jewish children in a settlement." Yael stretched in her chair.

"The harsh memories haunt him to this day. Even today, he refuses to fight," Neri added.

"It was a retaliation for the Israelis' constant bombings in Gaza. Many were killed then, some of them children. They went out one night from Nablus and climbed into one of the settlements. Back then, there were no fences around the settlements, and they broke into one of the houses. The goal was a revenge attack. Blood for blood. But there were three children in the house, the parents were at the neighboring house, with friends. His two friends pulled out knives and stabbed the children. Two died on the spot. One survived. The parents, who heard the screams, rushed in and shot two of Ibrahim's friends to death. Ibrahim and the other friend managed to escape. A few years later, the third friend was killed in an action against the Israelis. Ibrahim was the only one left."

"How did he manage to escape without the army catching him?" Yael asked. The mother ignored the question.

"You can arrest him if you want. Ibrahim is willing to face the consequences for what he did. He did not commit the murder himself, but he was part of the planning and execution, and I believe he is willing to take responsibility for it."

"I have no interest in arresting him. Both of us have moved on in life. But I would like to know why his mother is telling this story to an Israeli police officer."

"I think Ibrahim has never forgiven himself for what happened. That is why he moved to Gaza, that is why he did not follow his wife to Europe, that is why he did not have children. Maybe now, especially after meeting you, he can forgive himself and move on with his life. Until he knows that he has paid for his actions, he will remain trapped in the past."

"Ibrahim is a policeman who came to arrest human scum like he used to be. A terrible killer in his past. That is his secret. That is his burden. His friends in Gaza tell others about his 'act of heroism.' When he walks among them, he is a hero against his will. We believe it is time for that to end," Neri added.

"Thank you for sharing this story with me," Yael said and could not quite put her feelings into words. Distress? Relief? Fear? She just wanted to go back and hug her children, but they felt so far away. She stood up, kissed the mother's forehead, then entered the room and continued reviewing the notes. But the letters danced before her eyes, and she struggled to concentrate. When Ibrahim lightly knocked on her door half an hour later, fatigue had already engulfed her mind. A chasm gaped between her and him. She lay on the bed with her eyes open, staring at the ceiling.

"The Palestinian police are now searching for the blogger that Keren identified. They will update us the moment they catch him," he said, gazing at her for a while. "What about you? How are you feeling?"

She straightened up to a sitting position, placed her hand on his shoulder, and pulled him gently towards her. He embraced her softly, and slowly lay down beside her. Entwined, they gazed at each other in silence until they drifted into a deep, dreamless sleep.

36.

11.3.2015

Nablus

The entire night was accompanied by riots and disturbances that swept through the streets of the Palestinian city of Nablus. At the stroke of 4:00 AM, Yael's phone, resting by the bed, rang. She found herself still enveloped in Ibrahim's embrace, shielded by his secure hold. They both stirred awake simultaneously and disentangled themselves. Yael answered the call, Amit was on the other line.

"We are on our way to rescue you," he declared. "Where do you want us to pick you up from?" Yael glanced at Ibrahim, a hint of inquiry in her eyes.

"I'd rather they did not come to my mother's residence, to avoid exposing the location," he voiced his concern. "Towards the southeast end of the street, there is a path leading up to a lookout spot, the Yosef Lookout. We will reach there on foot. An hour's trek. They should meet us there." Yael nodded, conveying the instructions to Amit. "We will be there by five-fifteen AM," she whispered and concluded the call. Swiftly, they gathered their belongings. Yael donned her dress, layered with a coat, secured a kerchief around her head, and discretely held her handbag close. For now, the gun remained tucked away in the bag, accessible at need. Ibrahim got dressed and prepared as well. They proceeded to the living room. There, by the door, stood his mother, awaiting their departure, clasping two sandwiches. She hugged them and opened the door.

"You should set your phone to silent, my dear," she advised Yael, who promptly obliged.

They descended the dark staircase, their steps muted to preserve secrecy. Upon reaching ground level, Ibrahim crossed the road and entered a barren, muddy and rocky field. Yael followed suit. He remained in the shadows, sticking to the roadside pavement until the path veered eastward. There, he veered off the sidewalk, leading the way into the field. Overhead, to the south, a towering round hill emerged, casting a veil over the winter night sky adorned with stars. A faint light glimmered at the hill's summit, coming out of a structure of some sort. "That is our destination," he murmured.

"Do you know the way in the dark?" she inquired.

"I spent most of my childhood around here," he responded with a faint smile. She trailed behind him. They began their ascent, with the city lights twinkling beneath them. Occasional sounds of passing cars reached their ears, yet the streets mostly remained tranquil and deserted. A sense of serenity enveloped the misty town, cocooned by mountains and valleys. Only the rhythmic sound of their footsteps on the gravel was heard. The air was icy, yet crisp and clear. They continued to ascend until they reached a circular road. The clock read 5:05 AM. Staying to the shadows at the roadside, they avoided the light's glare. The subtle hues of sunrise painted the skies beyond the mountains. Upon reaching the southern edge of the hill, where the circular road intersected with a driveway, they caught a slight rustling. Yael halted, her hand reaching for her gun as she unholstered it. They both crouched and surveyed their surroundings, but nothing was seen. A minute elapsed before they straightened up, resuming their cautious journey. No jeeps or armored vehicles stood in wait. They walked a few steps further, and suddenly, in an instant, five soldiers lunged out from the obscurity, their camouflaged forms converging upon Yael and Ibrahim, forcefully pinning them to the ground. Yael found herself beneath one of the soldiers, motionless. Her gun was taken from her hand, then she was turned to face the soldier, who silenced her with a finger pressed to his lips. "Yael?" he murmured.

"Yes," she replied.
"Follow me."

***

By 5:45 AM, Yael and Ibrahim found themselves within the bounds of the Samaria territorial brigade. By 7:05 AM, Yael had already stepped back into her dwelling in Ra'anana. She took a refreshing shower, changed her attire, and then prepared breakfast for Ilan and Keren. At 8:30 AM, after she took her kids to school with heartfelt goodbyes, Ibrahim's call came through. Yonatan Uziel and Uri Amit were also on the line. The Palestinian blogger had been apprehended. However, it was revealed that he was a 14-year-old boy, seemingly drawn to stirring up commotion, rather than a dangerous terrorist capable of maneuvering freely between Gaza and the West Bank. Nonetheless, he had been detained and subjected to questioning, dissuading any recurrence of his mischievous acts.

"Yet, what takes precedence," said Ibrahim, "is that I believe I may have a lead regarding the location of the cave where Doctor Nur Zarubi met her end. After you departed, I delved deeper into the information acquired by the Palestinian police. I stumbled upon something noteworthy. A young individual from the village of As-Samu, nestled in the southern reaches of the Hebron mountains, left a message two days ago. He mentioned that the cave seemed familiar due to the graffiti adorning its walls. It is a gathering spot for local shepherds, not far from the village, situated within one of the wadis. I think we should go there. This is a safe area under the jurisdiction of the Palestinian police. We could get there easily and relatively safely. They have dispatched two police cars already."

"I need you to pick me up, I'm uncertain if I can manage the drive."

"We will pick you up in an hour," assured Uri Amit. "And Yael, there is something else."

"I'm listening" she said.

"The lab results are in for the evidence Ibrahim secured from Shifa's bunkers."

"And what's the verdict?"

"There is a complete match between the gauzes and the thread discovered at the crime scene, and the evidence Ibrahim obtained from the hospital. Our perpetrator obtained his murder weapons from Shifa hospital with high certainty. It is the same manufacturer, same year of production, and identical raw material."

"If that is the case, there is no evading the conclusion. Ibrahim, we must uncover who else frequents these bunkers right under Hamas's noses. It is highly probable that our killer is either a member of the medical staff or someone closely intertwined with Hamas's security apparatus, with access to those bunkers. One way or another, we are dealing with a Gazan killer."

"And while he remains at large..."

"The tally of victims will continue grow."

37.
Adjacent to As-Samu village, Hebron district, south Hebron Mountain

The Palestinian Authority

The flat white roofs of As-Samu village stood out like massive boulders in the expanse of the desert, now cloaked in a lush carpet of thick greenery typical of every winter. The houses were scattered, leaving narrow streets woven with crumbling asphalt meandering between them. These roadways seemed to harmonize with the contours of the hilly terrain, as though they had been assembled only temporarily. Fields and orchards of olives and fruit trees lay between the neighborhoods, while slender watercourses meandered across the land, serving as conduits for the rainwater that had graced the earth in the preceding days. The village was nestled at the edge of the desert, affording it scant rainfall. Nevertheless, its soil was resistant to infiltration, and the terraces and canals constructed by the locals ensured that rainwater could be harnessed and sustained, nurturing the plants long after the showers had ceased.

They traveled in a convoy of fortified vehicles. The first car accommodated Colonel Yonatan Uziel, who grasped a shortened M-16 rifle loaded and cocked, its barrel protruding from the window, visible for miles around. Beside him were a driver and two soldiers. In the second vehicle, Chief Superintendent Uri Amit occupied a seat next to an army driver, while Yael and Ibrahim sat in the back seats. The third car carried an officer of the rank of first lieutenant, a non-commissioned officer, and two additional soldiers. Every soldier was armed, garbed in bulletproof vests and helmets, poised for any potential combat. The convoy navigated along Road 31, directing itself towards the northern Negev town of Hura, before veering onto Road 60, skirting the Yatir forest from the northern side. They cleared the Kramim checkpoint, entering the region of Judea and Samaria from the south. Continuing northward on Road 60, they reached the Meitarim industrial area, from where they merged onto Road 317, subsequently veering east until they reached the Asael settlement. Here, a Palestinian Authority vehicle awaited them, occupied by three policemen. Uziel alighted from his car alone, signaling the others to remain within their vehicles. Two of the Palestinian police officers disembarked, and Yael recognized one of them, a general ranking policeman. It took a full minute for the memory to fully resurface in her mind, prompting her to open the car door and step out, much to Uziel's dismay.

"General Fahamawi," she pronounced, conjuring a casual smile. She drew nearer to them, and the Palestinian officer reciprocated with a smile, extending his hand towards her.

"Superintendent Yael Lavie," he replied in broken Hebrew. "Haven't seen you in many years."

She shook his hand.

"How are you, Zohir?" she inquired.

"Are you asking about me or my uncle?"

"You are no less important," she quipped.

"I'm doing well, but unfortunately, my cousin is no longer among the living. He passed away two days ago, in good health."

"I chatted with him just a few days ago. I'm very sad to hear that. He always knew how to help me."

"Sounds like my uncle. He really appreciated you, after the incident in 1999."

In 1999 they had worked together on a complex investigation involving a serial Israeli killer named Dov Schwartz. This man had embarked on a private assassination mission as part of a Palestinian criminal syndicate's vendetta, resulting in numerous casualties among both Jews and Arabs. Yaser Fahamawi retired a couple of years later, after managing to see his relative, Zohir, appointed as a police officer, and after completing his officer's course, even rising to the rank of a station commander in the station he served at.

"It's mutual. I also appreciated him very much."

"I know. And it appears that now it is my turn to take up his position. But I assume you did not come all the way here just to inquire about my well-being. So we better take you to the cave."

"Where is it located?" Yael asked.

"We will drive our vehicles into the area. There is a path leading to the foot of the hoof cliff, at its center is where the Goat Cave is situated. We suspect that is where the doctor's body is."

"Have you not gone in to see yet?"

"No. We have been instructed clearly to wait for you, so as not to disturb any potential evidence. We stationed a guard at the entrance. It is about a five-minute drive from here."

"We will follow you," Uziel said, signaling the drivers to start their engines. Fahamawi returned to his vehicle, as did Yael and Uri. When Yael returned to the car, she turned to Ibrahim. "We might have a problem. Do these officers know you are here?"

"The Palestinian police kept my arrival in the area confidential. Only the Nablus station knows I'm here."

"Then maybe you should tell them you are coming from Nablus. It is better if they don't know you are associated with Hamas Gaza."

"Very well," Ibrahim said, turning his gaze back to the window. They traveled for another minute on the road before veering onto a dirt path that ran alongside a stream. Roughly 200 meters north from there, a tall cliff, about 40 meters in height, rose majestically, in the shape of a hoof. The stream flowed at its base. A narrow goat trail clung to the rocky surface of the cliff, and a small rocky platform appeared just before its peak. A narrow opening into the cave was discernible behind it. One officer stood at the entrance, his figure silhouetted against the backdrop, surveying the convoy that had come to a halt at the base of the cliff. A few Palestinian youths stood on the opposite side of the stream, observing the unfolding scene. The worst thing that could happen now, Yael thought, is for rumors to spread rapidly, attracting a large number of young people to the area. They might start acting out, and the entire event could quickly spiral out of control once again.

***

They ascended the goat trail, winding their way toward the entrance of the cave. As they reached their destination, the sight of bloodstains on the rocks immediately caught their attention.

"This secluded enclave is a retreat for shepherds," Fahamawi remarked. "The traces of blood are most likely from the sheep or goats they tend. These shepherds, seeking refuge from both heat and rain, occasionally resort to slaughtering one of their animals for sustenance."

The cave's interior presented a scene of disarray: remnants of past bonfires, weathered mattresses, charred cookware, and a lingering odor of decaying animal remains tainted the air. A strewn mess of refuse added to the chaos. With careful consideration, Yael and Ibrahim outfitted themselves with gloves before proceeding. "Remain here. Avoid further contamination of the area," Yael directed. "We shall permit one armed police officer to accompany us, for precaution's sake. Nonetheless, maintaining a certain distance from us is advisable."

"I'll accompany you," Fahamawi volunteered.

They meticulously scoured the space, collecting their discoveries in a plastic bag, while documenting their findings in notebooks and taking photos. Progressing ten meters into the cave, a more intense wave of putrid death assaulted their senses. Yet, this time it carried a weightier, more stale air. Picking up a makeshift staff from the ground, Yael navigated around discarded debris. Illuminated by daylight filtering through the cave's mouth, she found the need for a torch unnecessary. The walls bore Arabic graffiti and paintings, while plastic bottles, more mattresses, remnants of furniture, and animal excrement were scattered about. Traces of bonfires marked their presence, accompanied by the distant echo of bats. As they ventured another five meters, the darkness was all-encompassing.

Yael withdrew her gun, steadying it in her right hand, while Ibrahim produced a torch to light their way. At the cave's edge, a chair stood, and slumped upon it, head drooping, was the lifeless form of Dr. Nur Zarubi—the body already displaying signs of decomposition and bloating. Likely by the work of the murderer, she had been repositioned to sit upright. The graffiti seen on television had now taken on a more palpable and ominous dimension.

Having ensured no immediate danger, they transitioned from scanning for suspects to meticulously combing through the cave for evidence. "Search for any medical equipment—sutures, gauze, syringes—anything linking this murder to the prior ones," Yael instructed. Fahamawi and Ibrahim dispersed throughout the cave, diligently collecting potential clues. Yael, meanwhile, drew closer to Zarubi's body, subjecting it to examination. The woman was fastened to the chair, her attire intact. Her limbs were bound: legs secured to the chair's legs, hands tied behind the backrest. A sizable cavity marked the center of her skull, yet no exit wound was evident at the rear of her neck. Yael conjectured that she had been shot from a distance, likely by a small-caliber firearm. A positive detail, for it suggested the bullet might be lodged within her skull—a possible means to identify the weapon. She sealed the cavity with a bandage from her homicide investigation kit. Probing the restraints on Zarubi's hands and feet, Yael noticed that she was secured with an iron rope, causing the skin to tear and the right hand to take on a bluish hue, as blood could not flow to it. After photographing the knots, she proceeded to untie one, placing the iron rope into an evidence bag. Further examination of the body revealed no signs of injection. "I hold doubts that this is the same perpetrator," Yael mused. "All indicators suggest a differing narrative. It could be an imitator, someone exploiting the prior murders to advance a distinct agenda. The threads of the story do not align—kidnapping, threats, televised murder, the demand for prisoner release, the binding, the locale, the method of execution, diverging from strangulation to a gunshot wound. A disparate tale altogether. This murder seems a deliberate diversion."

"I concur with you," Ibrahim said. "I'm not finding any evidence here. Nevertheless, since we are already here, it is best that we explore this case as thoroughly as possible."

"We don't have much time to delve into this," she said, surveying the heaps of garbage around. She picked up the staff once again. "If I could, I would gather everything into bags and meticulously analyze the waste back at the lab. But we lack the tools for that; we must work with the evidence we have found."

"Have you managed to trace the IP address from which the videos were broadcast?" Ibrahim queried Fahamawi.

"We are under Palestinian authority here. We lack advanced intelligence units. I apologize."

Yael straightened up and cast a gaze around. "We are done here. Zohir, I suggest your team retrieves her body and transfers it to the Institute of Forensic Medicine in Tel Aviv. If we leave with the body, it could provoke anger."

"I agree. I'll ensure it is done when we leave."

Yael folded up her forensics toolbox, hoisting it in the air. Igniting a torch to avoid stumbling, she cautiously traversed through the mounds of debris, retracing her steps toward the cave's entrance. "It is unbelievable how much rubbish is here," she muttered, casting light upon remnants of plastic tarps, a water tank, cigarette boxes, and a plethora of nylon straws. "How do the shepherds endure amidst all this mess?"

Advancing three steps, with Ibrahim and Fahamawi trailing behind her, Yael halted suddenly. The two Palestinians also came to a stop. She pivoted on the spot, then doubled back, scouring the ground with her torch for an object that had caught her attention.

"What happened?" Ibrahim asked.

"I saw something... I think..." she mumbled, retracing her path, illuminating her surroundings for any clue. Finally, her torch's beam settled on a piece of litter nestled within a tall pile of garbage: a cigarette box.

"Yael?" Fahamawi inquired. "What did you find?"

Yael adjusted her glove, set her toolbox aside, and approached the cigarette box. She raised it, bringing it closer to her eyes, the torch revealing English lettering printed on the box's surface:

`Chicago Cigarettes, Smooth Blue`.
"I think we found Doctor Zarubi's killer," she said.

38.

Judea and Samaria police district, Judea and Samaria, Israel

As Yael entered the interrogation room at the Judea and Samaria District Police Station, the clock had struck 5:30 PM. Attorney Jamal Jaroushi sat in a chair, gazing at his phone often. Ibrahim followed her inside, and trailing behind them was another attorney, whose name Yael did not recognize, representing the public defender's office. He took a seat beside Jaroushi and whispered something in his ear. Jaroushi's expression shifted.

"Attorney Jaroushi," Yael began. "Do you happen to have any more of the Chicago cigarettes you brought from Chicago?"

"Yes, why?" Jaroushi inquired. "Am I being accused of something?"

"If you would agree to let me see the box, it would signify your willingness to collaborate with us in the murder investigation, nothing more than that."

"You don't have to show them anything," the attorney representing the public defender's office interjected.

"He actually should. We have a court order, but I wanted to see if he would do so willingly."

Jaroushi pulled the cigarette box out of his inner pocket. The very same box Yael had seen when they last met at Nafcha Prison. She took out an evidence bag, within which was a similar cigarette box.

"I want you to know that we found your cigarette box in the cave where Doctor Nur Zarubi's body was discovered. We also found your fingerprints on the box. I wanted to ask, what is a respected attorney like yourself doing in a goat cave in the South Hebron Hills? Precisely the same cave where Zarubi was murdered and where her body was found?"

Jaroushi remained silent. His attorney interjected, "These are circumstantial pieces of evidence. Maybe Jaroushi inadvertently handed the box to one of the killers, who then discarded it in the cave?"

"Perhaps," Yael acknowledged. "But I revisited the list of demands from the killer, right when negotiations were ongoing with the police for the release of seventy-five Palestinian prisoners. Guess what I found?"

"What?"

"The names of the five Jihad Islami prisoners, two of whom you represent. Your family members, if I remember correctly." Jaroushi tensed. "I assume they are not the ones responsible for the doctor's murder, as they are still incarcerated in Nafcha."

"I understand," Jaroushi muttered, despondent. She reached for the evidence bag and placed it before him.

"Your phone, please, and the cigarette box." He shoved them in a bag.

"You will be charged with multiple counts, including nationalistically motivated murder, kidnapping, and extortion. The investigation is not concluded yet, but I have a feeling that you will finally be able to join your family in Nafcha." She rose from her seat, followed by Ibrahim. They approached the door and signaled the officer to enter and apprehend the Palestinian attorney. Jaroushi stood up.

"You know, Ibrahim," he spoke in Arabic. "We will remember the time you cooperated with them."

Ibrahim stopped. Yael halted after him and lightly touched his arm. He turned toward Jaroushi.

"You know who appointed me for this, Attorney Jaroushi? Perhaps you should talk to him before you threaten me. I have a feeling he won't appreciate hearing that." Ibrahim exited the room. Jaruoshi remained behind, donning his representative robe, luxury watch, and stylish leather shoes. "Ibrahim!" he shouted. "I'm talking to you! I'm not the one who killed those women!"

For the second time, Ibrahim and Yael paused and turned back. Yael said, "We know. But Zarubi's blood—that's on your hands."

**

As Yael and Ibrahim stepped out into the main corridor, they exchanged smiles. One episode was behind them. She wanted to hug him. A feeling of relief swept over her. But then, she felt a faint vibration from her pocket—the phone. She reached for it and saw that it was her mother, Dina. She pressed the **Dismiss** button and then noticed her screen showed 20 missed calls and there were numerous unanswered messages, all from her mother. Something had happened. Pressing the **Dial** button, she called her mother back. Dina answered on the first ring.

"I saw you were trying to reach me. What happened?" Yael asked.

"I haven't seen Keren since yesterday evening," Dina said.

"I saw her this morning. I dropped her off at school."

"Well, she didn't make it to school. I got a call from her teacher an hour and a half ago, asking if she was sick."

"I don't understand. Where is she? Isn't she in her room? On the computer?"

"No. She didn't come home in the afternoon. She is not answering my calls. I have tried calling everyone I know, but no one has seen her today. The girl has disappeared."

"Why didn't you call me—"

"I did, dozens of times! And I sent messages. But you were busy and not answering." Yael was taken aback. It took her a moment to regain her composure, then she said:

"What about Ilan? Didn't he see her at school?" Ilan and Keren both studied at the same complex, though in different programs. Occasionally, he would tell Yael that he saw Keren alone in various corners of the school campus.

"No. He is here, next to me. He didn't see her at school or on the bus home. He thought she was finishing school later, but then we realized she was supposed to be with him on the ride back."

"I'm checking," Yael said. She ended the call and dialed Keren's number, but it went straight to voicemail. She tried again and then sent a message, although she knew she would not get any response. She started walking quickly toward Uri Amit's office, Ibrahim trailing behind her. Without knocking, she walked in. He was on the phone, so she signaled him to hang up. He disconnected the call.

"It is Keren. She is missing. We haven't been able to locate her since this morning."

"What do you need me to do?"

"I want you to try and locate her number," she said, typing the number on a note. "I'm heading home. Talk to me as soon as you have something."

"What about Ibrahim?"

Yael glanced back at Ibrahim. "I need him with me."

They left the office and made their way to the main entrance and parking area. Suddenly, they came face to face with Attorney Jaroushi, flanked by police officers, his hands cuffed for an extended remand. His attorney was by his side. In one swift motion, Yael covered the distance and grabbed his suit, pulling his face close to hers. "If you have anything to do with this, this will be the end of you," she said, gripping his shirt as Ibrahim pulled her by the hand away from there.

***

When they arrived at the house in Ra'anana, Dina was standing at the door in tears. They embraced, and Yael headed towards Keren's room. "Where's Ilan?" she asked as she walked.

"He's at Shai's house. Ronia will take him to school tomorrow." Yael's brother was a very busy man, and so was his wife, Ronia. Despite that, the family held a significant place in both their hearts. Their eldest son was three years younger than Ilan, but they had a strong bond when they met, and Ilan enjoyed spending time with them, even though this rarely happened. In any case, if something related to Yael and Ibrahim's investigation happened to Keren, it would be better for Ilan to be kept away from home and shielded from what was going on.

"Thanks," Yael said when she entered the room. "I request that only Ibrahim and I enter for now. From my perspective, this is a crime scene that needs to be investigated." She put on gloves again and began to scan the room but found nothing. She gently moved the computer mouse, but the computer remained unresponsive. Keren had never turned off her computer. At any given moment, there were ongoing actions in the games she participated in. Why was the computer off? She pressed the power button and turned on the computer. Her phone rang. Amit was on the line. She answered the call.

"We managed to locate Keren's phone," he said. Her heart raced.

"Where is it?" she asked, standing upright.

"At your building. It might even be inside the apartment, but it is hard to pinpoint exactly."

"Ibrahim!" Yael exclaimed. "Come quickly." Ibrahim surveyed the house with Dina, searching for clues or signs of where the girl might have disappeared to. But when he heard Yael's call, he rushed to the room.

"Yael, I'm sending you a team of three officers with a patrol car. They will expand the search and trace her steps from the moment she arrived at school until she vanished," Amit said. Yael glanced at the clock. It was close to 7:00 PM. Late. But there was no choice. "Alright," she replied. "Keep me updated on everything you find."

"Copy that," Amit said. She heard a few more commands from him before the call disconnected. Ibrahim and Dina entered the room.

"Her phone is here. I need you to turn the house upside down until you find it. Every drawer, every bag, under the beds, everything. If it is not in the apartment, maybe it is somewhere in the building." Suddenly, the thought crossed her mind that the phone might be with one of the neighbors. Who among them had a connection to Keren?

"Mom, I need you to go to all the neighbors, knock on doors, see if Keren left anything with them, a bag, a phone. Maybe she is spending time in one of the apartments in the building, and her battery ran out—who knows?" Yael knew it was not likely. Keren was isolated, disconnected, she had no real-world social connections. And worse, she had turned off her computer. Something was happening, and Yael had no idea what.

She accessed the computer and opened all the programs the girl had used recently. Social networks, various websites, gaming sites, and blogs. Eventually, she accessed the computer game that Keren had told her about. It took a while to load. She found the chat and started going through the messages. Everything seemed completely normal until suddenly she found what she was looking for, what she feared more than anything. A message from another player, dated March 10, 2015. '**It is me and you against everyone else**' the message read. '**But we will prevail. I'm from Tel Aviv. Do you want to take this game to the real world?**'

Her heart raced.

"I found it. I found the phone," Ibrahim's voice came from the living room. Yael jumped to her feet and rushed to the living room. Dina, who was already on her way to the staircase, stopped when she heard Ibrahim. She had already activated the device by the time Yael snatched it from her hand.

"Where was it?" Yael asked, her hands trembling.

"In the fridge," Ibrahim said. "In the vegetable drawer."

"Why on earth would she leave it there?" The phone lit up, but a password was required to access it.

She thought for a long moment, but did not know the password. She tried Keren's birthdate. The phone remained locked. Then she tried Gidi's birthdate. That did not work either. She tried the day of the attack, Naif Badir's name. Nothing worked. On the fifth attempt, the phone was locked.

Yael pounded it in frustration. She pulled out her own phone and dialed Amit's number. When he answered, she reported what she had found and said with determination, "I urgently need two things. First, someone to crack her phone as quickly as possible. Second—I need you to trace an IP address. Someone who corresponded with her on her computer, in an international computer game. I will also check if Shai can help with this." She disconnected the call without waiting for a response and rushed to the room, ready to delve into her daughter's virtual world.

***

At 1:00 AM, they sat in Yael's living room. Ibrahim, Dina, Amit, who arrived accompanied with three officers, Aharon Shaked, and Shai Nachmani. The living room looked like a war room. Maps were scattered around, phones kept ringing incessantly, laptops were loaded with databases. Everyone was prepared for action.

"When she left the house in the morning, she had her phone with her, I'm almost sure of it," Yael said.

"Meaning, she spent a short time at school and then came back home, turned off the computer, left her phone, and walked out," Amit said.

"We checked with all the neighbors. No one saw her," Dina said, casting a glance toward Ibrahim.

"What about friends? Youth organization? The route she took?" Shaked asked, looking at one of the officers.

"We talked to her classmates. She did not show up for the first lesson. That is why the teacher called to find out what happened. She does not have friends, nor does she go to any youth organization. There are several routes she could have taken. I don't see how we can extract relevant information from this. We walked the three main routes between the school and home, entered shops, checked security camera footage, but it is a shot in the dark. I assume she came straight here."

"There is one camera positioned at the end of the street, an ATM's security camera. We contacted the bank, but at this hour, there is no one to talk to. The branch was closed this afternoon and will only open tomorrow morning. The security footage is stored there for 24 hours, so tomorrow, a little after opening, they will send us the images. Maybe we will be able to gather more information about the person who abducted her," another officer added.

"You are assuming someone kidnapped her? Maybe she left willingly..." Amit said.

"Or she took a bus or a taxi..." Ibrahim chimed in.

"I assume she left willingly. Otherwise, someone would have seen a girl struggling with an abductor, and someone would have remembered, maybe even reported it."

"If she was kidnapped, why hasn't the kidnapper made any demands?" Shaked asked.

"Maybe he doesn't plan on returning her, like the rest of the women..." Yael said.

"Why did she agree to get into a car with someone she doesn't know, and leave her phone at home, in the fridge? That is very odd behavior for a smart and responsible girl like Keren. Especially after her past experience with terror," Dina said.

"I don't know, but I can think of two possible reasons based on what he wrote to her. The first one, they both share something very intimate, very deep, that created a broad foundation of trust for her. She relies on him. Or her. The second reason—perhaps it's some kind of declaration of intent. Against us, against the world... She is angry. She is alone. Her connection to the world is through these devices, where she lives. Maybe this temporary disconnection is her rebellion. The fact that she put the device in the fridge, that is her shouting out her defiance. In the end, we are dealing with an adolescent."

"Did you manage to crack the phone?" Aharon Shaked asked, directing his gaze at Shai.

"It is not that simple," Shai replied. "We are working on it."

Yael stood up and went to the kitchen. She muttered to herself, "There is something else I'm missing here."

She took out the vegetable drawer where Dina and Ibrahim had found the phone and pulled out its entire contents. Shai entered the kitchen and stood beside her.

"What are you looking for?" he asked.

"I know my daughter. She is a rebellious teenager, but the likelihood of her leaving her phone in the vegetable drawer is very low."

"What are you thinking?"

"I don't know, but I'm sure she is trying to convey some..."

"Yael?"

"Go fetch her phone." Shai dashed out to Keren's room, where he had left the phone on the table while working on the computer. Half a minute later, the mobile phone was in Yael's hand. She activated the device, and the demand for a password appeared again on the screen.

'**I hate onions**,' she whispered to herself, and pressed the letters of the word. **O-N-I-O-N**. The device sprang to life. The two siblings hugged.

"A clever girl," Shay said. "She left herself an insurance policy."

***

They connected the phone to Shai's laptop and scanned all the emails, messages, call logs, and various notes. Eventually, they found a conversation from a few days ago that seemed unusual. It appeared alone without any follow-up messages. **We can meet on Wednesday, 11.3.2015. I'll be in your area in the morning. Nadin.**

"Nadin? Who is Nadin?" Shai asked, but neither Dina nor Yael could answer the question.

"Can you try to retrieve previous messages?"

"Not sure, but I can try and check the number it was sent from."

***

At 3:07 AM, Shai Nachmani's phone rang. He answered the call while moving away from the others. Shai, who headed the operational cyber unit in the ISA, was the only person Yael knew who would be able to give her what she needed. When she dialed him after talking to Amit, he immediately arrived with a black plastic bag containing advanced computing equipment. He connected to the computer on Keren's computer and started working. When he found what he was looking for, he transferred all the information for scanning at his work place. All that was left to do was wait.

Now, Yael noticed that Shay's eyes widened as the conversation continued. The reports he received through his earpiece troubled him and occupied his thoughts. She stood up, moved by his side, and tried to listen to what was being said. But the buzz in the living room was loud, and she could not make out anything. When he finished talking, the human circle that had formed around him stood in silent expectation. His face was somber. Everyone fell silent.

"The results have arrived. We managed to locate the IP address from which the messages were sent to Keren's chat. I have some bad news. We will need to think about what to do next and how to proceed from here," he said, casting a glance at Ibrahim.

"Why? Where is the computer that sent this message?"

"It us in the Gaza Strip, Abo Baker Al-Arazi Street."

"What exactly is at that address?" Amit asked, standing up from his chair and taking out his phone.

"Shifa Hospital," Ibrahim said.

"And what about the mobile phone number from which they sent the message about the meeting?"

"That will take some time," Shai said. "I'll update you as soon as I have the information, and then we can also find the phone's location."

"I'm going to Gaza," Yael said, making her way to her work room to organize things. None of the people in the room dared to say a word, and each one of them set about attending to their task.

But a few moments later, Aziz Shafiki received a message on his mobile phone: **Erez checkpoint is about to close due to a kidnapping incident. Be prepared for executing the mission.**

PART C

39.

12.3.2015

Erez checkpoint, the border of Gaza strip

The time was 6:30 AM. Yael, Ibrahim, Aharon Shaked, and Yaakov Mizrahi were sitting in the conference room of Erez Checkpoint. The flow of movement through the checkpoint had been completely halted since 3:30 AM, at all crossings between Israel and the Palestinian territories in Gaza and Judea and Samaria. However, they all knew it was too little and too late, and there was a high likelihood that Keren had already been transferred to Gaza during yesterday's noon hours. Yaakov Mizrahi scanned again and again the names of people who passed through the checkpoint, looking despondent.

"Over four-hundred people," he said. "Just yesterday. The calm of the past few days allowed us to open all the crossings, and the supply to Gaza was renewed. Today, we passed seventy-one trucks, fifteen ambulances, one-hundred-and-thirteen private vehicles, and UNRWA vehicles. The rest are pedestrians and workers who crossed the checkpoint, and someone was waiting for them on the other side. These are record numbers."

"We need to focus on the ambulances," Yael said. "There is a very high chance he smuggled her that way."

"How do we proceed from here?" Shaked asked.

"I'll cross the checkpoint with Ibrahim, using fake IDs. I'll take weapons with me. I'll dress in traditional clothing. Ibrahim will accompany me the whole way. I have no other choice."

"Yael, if you get caught..."

"I have no choice. We are not entering with the military, and we are not going in with Gazan police. Hamas won't cooperate with that, that is clear. They also won't do anything to save her if she is still alive. I have to trust Ibrahim, trust myself."

"Consider that this whole story is meant to force Israel to make concessions for their prisoners. They need Israeli captives."

"I know."

"Ibrahim is a Hamas operative, you have to—"

"If you were in my shoes?"

Shaked fell silent. Ibrahim stared at the Central Command General Officer for a while then turned his glance to Yael.

"I trust him," she finally said, got up, and left the room. She walked towards Mizrahi's office, where clothes and additional gear awaited her.

"I know what you are going to say," Ibrahim said when left alone with Mizrahi and Shaked. "You can spare me the words. I'll take care of her. I'll bring her back safely."

Shaked nodded and said, "No one should know Keren is in Gaza."

"I understand."

"We need to extract them secretly, no matter what the circumstances."

"Understood."

"When you are done, I'll stand by my word. I promise."

"Thank you," Ibrahim said.

Yaakov Mizrahi nodded too, as if was a witness to a dark deal.

"I suggest," Ibrahim said, "that you prepare for another day of attacks on the checkpoint. Hamas does not like the crossings being closed, and they might be gearing up for a flare-up."

"I know," Shaked said. "But for now, we don't have too many options."

***

"Is everything ready?" Ismail Bader asked Aziz Shafiki over the phone. Bader detested being in the Gaza Strip during battle days against the Israelis. He knew well that there were countless rockets and mortars aimed at him, and the bunkers that Hamas had built under hospitals would not always provide sufficient protection. Bader also knew that there were undoubtedly many Hamas members who would like to see him dead, and quite a few Palestinians affiliated with other organizations that would do everything to advance the implementation of that vision. He drove his car towards Shifa Hospital, where he knew he would find safety, at least for now.

"Yes," Shafiki said. "Under my jurisdiction, everyone is prepared for an escalation." The phone call between them was intermittent, filled with noise, and Bader was inclined to blame the fragile infrastructure in the Strip, particularly in times of crisis.

"Did you call me for this reason?" Bader asked Shafiki.

"After this round with Israel, I want to take on a different role in the organization. Maybe even retire. Malak's death tore my family apart."

"We are your family," Bader said.

"You know what I mean."

"It is not a good time to discuss this. Let's meet in Dubai in two weeks and talk, okay?"

"Ismail," Shafiki said, "I'm asking you."

"We will talk," Ismail replied and hung up.

***

When Yael returned to the conference room, the three of them were engrossed in watching Yaakov Mizrahi's computer screen. She walked over and stood behind Shaked. On the screen was footage from a security camera. Yael's street was visible, and in the distance, they could see the entrance gate to her building's yard. A digital clock in the top right corner of the screen displayed 10:32 AM. A girl was standing on the sidewalk, her gaze shifting in all directions as she awaited someone's arrival. Despite the camera's distance from the girl, it was unmistakably Keren Lavie. At 10:35 AM, three minutes later, a Red Crescent ambulance pulled up in front of the building. A side door opened, and Keren glanced around before climbing inside and disappearing behind its doors. The doors closed, and the ambulance drove away. Due to the video's distance and the parked cars on the street, they could not make out the vehicle's license plate number.

"This footage is from the bank's security ATM's camera," Shaked explained. "I received it a few moments ago."

Mizrahi placed a paper on the table in front of them. "Here is the list of ambulances that crossed from Israel to Gaza today," he said. "Out of the fifteen vehicles that passed through the checkpoint, ten entered Gaza."

Yael studied the brief list and quickly pinpointed one entry. "They went to Shifa Hospital," she said. "Ibrahim, we are running out of time. They crossed the border yesterday at 12:00 PM."

Ibrahim scrutinized the list. One of the lines detailed the patient transferred at the checkpoint from medical care in Judea and Samaria to Shifa Hospital in Gaza. The patient's name was **Nadin Sharif**. The details of the doctor and the medical team in the ambulance were not provided—only the name of the ambulance driver, a Gazan Palestinian named **Aisha Aqil**.

***

At 7:30 AM, two Palestinians crossed the border into Gaza—siblings, a brother and a sister. The brother, Ibrahim Azberga, was a well-known figure in Gaza, a Hamas operative with close ties to the ruling authority. The sister, Neri Azberga-Talia'a, hailed from Nablus and was married to a worker who spent most of his time in Jordan. Both carried valid Palestinian IDs and passing permits. However, only a handful of people were privy to the secret that Neri's permit and ID contained a forged photo—a picture of a woman with a similar build, but she happened to be a superintendent in the Israeli police.

In the parking lot adjacent to the checkpoint, they got into Ibrahim's car as a light rain began to fall. When Yael glanced back, she saw the checkpoint closing behind them. All vehicles were being turned away back to Gaza or Israel—no one was entering or leaving. Soon, she thought, the barrage of rockets and gunfire would commence, followed by Israeli counterattacks. The unending, futile cycle of violence. Despite the tension, Yael was not afraid of being caught. Her disguise was impeccable. She bore no Israeli markings, spoke fluent Arabic, and shared a resemblance with Neri. No one would suspect her true identity.

They drove down Salah Al-Deen Road, passing through the towns of Beit Hanoun and Jabalya, ultimately arriving at the Sheikh Radwan and Rimal neighborhoods where Ibrahim resided. As they passed his house, he gestured and said, "This is my home. I hope that one day I can welcome you here as a friend."

Yael nodded, and they were already navigating Al-Nasar Street, heading west toward Shifa Hospital. The streets were crowded with armed youths—some masked, some in uniform—each poised for the impending escalation. Hamas had dispatched troops to confront the IDF soldiers at the wall, while rocket squads were positioned, ready for action. Ibrahim knew that many of them would not return home that night. They hastened toward the hospital, parking a block away from the entrance.

"It is going to be difficult to enter the hospital," Ibrahim remarked. "Even harder to reach the basements. I assume the Hamas leadership is already seeking refuge down there. The security guards won't let us through unless we can make it in before the battles commence."

They moved swiftly up the street toward the hospital, but upon reaching the entrance of the parking lot, they were halted by two uniformed Hamas soldiers. "I'm Major General Ibrahim Azberga, and this is my sister," Ibrahim asserted. "I need to see Aziz Shafiki, Chief of Preventive Security for the Murabitat." He pulled out an ID from his shirt, and Yael covered her face with the veil's fabric. One of the soldiers examined the ID in silence, then signaled with his weapon that they could enter the compound. They took a couple of steps before a splitting sound caught their attention, followed by several sharp whistles tearing through the air. Yael glanced upward. A handful of missiles were launched from a nearby street, passing overhead on their way to Israel. Moments later, they heard the echoes of the Israeli counter-missiles intercepting the threat mid-air, before they could land on Israeli soil.

"We are running out of time," Yael informed Ibrahim urgently. "The bombings and attacks will start any moment now. We need to locate her." Ibrahim nodded, though a sense of foreboding lingered. He grappled with his stance in the ongoing existential struggle of the Palestinian people, as well as the dilemma of defending an Israeli police officer against the desperate search for her abducted daughter in Gaza. How far should he risk himself? Would Shaked uphold his promise, or would he be left with nothing?

They sprinted to the hospital's entrance as quickly as they could, just as another volley of missiles shot skyward from Gaza. Making it to the lobby level staircase, Ibrahim gasped for breath and declared, "We need to get down to the basement. That is where I found the evidence. I doubt they will allow you down there, so you should wait here." Yael nodded, having no alternative. She sat on one of the benches and fought the impulse to check her phone. If anyone caught her reading messages in Hebrew, her cover could be blown. Opting for discretion, she picked up an advertising pamphlet from a nearby counter and feigned interest.

Ibrahim dashed down the stairs to the basement floor. The area was crowded with people—doors to the bunkers stood open, and guards were stationed at all checkpoints. Shifa Hospital had become the hub of Palestinian operations against Israel, with key Hamas figures already situated in the basements. Shifa was bracing for the influx of wounded following the expected Israeli counterattacks.

He maneuvered through the dense crowd, searching for a familiar face—perhaps Shafiki or Dr. Mansour. Someone who could provide access. With time slipping away, the disheartening realization crept in that it was highly unlikely Keren was brought to Shifa's basements, especially during wartime. Suddenly, a recognizable face appeared before him—the guard appointed by Shafiki for the bunker. Though Ibrahim did not know his name, he hurried forward and tapped the guard's shoulder. The burly guard immediately recognized him and inquired, "What are you doing here?"

"Where is Shafiki?"

"Inside, with everyone."

"And Ismail Bader?"

"He is on his way here, or another bunker. I don't know." Ibrahim looked at all directions.

"What do you need?" asked the guard. Ibrahim paused, pondering his course of action. What did he truly need? Should he approach Shafiki now? Given Shafiki's familiarity with Yael, it could end up badly. "Where is Doctor Mansour?" he inquired instead. The guard's expression turned fearful. Placing his large hand on Ibrahim's shoulder, he uttered, "What business do you have with him? I hope you are not hatching any schemes..."

"I need to speak with him urgently!" Ibrahim insisted. The guard hesitated, scanning the chaos around them before stating, "Follow me, but time is short. In ten minutes, they will seal the doors, and I need to secure the entrance." Ibrahim nodded. The guard pivoted on the spot, charging forward through the crowd, his imposing frame navigating the throng with urgency. Ibrahim clung to his retreating form, running as swiftly as he could manage. Upon reaching the lobby, Ibrahim spotted Yael and shot her a quick signal to follow, motioning with his hand to maintain a safe distance.

They sprinted up the stairs to the third floor. The staircase was a hub of activity, with emergency-mode elevators operational, no one was allowed to use them. Amidst the ascending crowd, Yael blended inconspicuously, keeping pace behind Ibrahim and the guard. Upon reaching the third floor, the guard gestured toward the operation rooms down the hallway. "He is in room number four," the guard conveyed, patting Ibrahim's back before swiftly descending the stairs. He nearly collided with Yael, who had just reached the third floor. "Best of luck!" he called from a distance, his words lost in the roar of two low-flying warplanes that rumbled overhead at a low altitude, shaking the windows. An explosion resounded from several blocks away. Yael and Ibrahim exchanged glances. Ibrahim nodded subtly, signaling her to follow him.

They arrived at operation room 4. The door was open, and the hallway was devoid of people. Peering through the glass window in the door, they glimpsed Dr. Mansour tending to an elderly patient who was semi-conscious. A nurse stood beside him, assisting in the procedure. The adjacent operating rooms were empty. Dr. Mansour spotted Ibrahim through the glass and gestured for him to wait. Ibrahim raised his hand in agreement. Three minutes later, the doctor instructed the nurse to finish dressing the patient's wounds and emerged from the room.

"I'm the sole one who remained here. Everyone else has fled," he remarked while washing his hands. "What brings you here?"

"This is my sister, Neri," Ibrahim introduced, and Yael nodded in acknowledgment, refraining from extending her hand for a handshake. "I did not want her to be alone at home during the bombardment."

"You can't wait until tomorrow or a couple more days to investigate? Why the urgency?"

"I'm concerned that the killer I'm pursuing might have abducted another woman, and he could potentially kill her tonight. I must get more information from you."

"Alright, I'm listening," the doctor replied and started walking towards the operating room where the nurse had just finished treating a patient.

"We conducted an analysis with the Israelis. The materials used for bandaging and suturing that I collected from your operating room in the bunker, the same materials used to treat your patients, are similar within a margin of one hundred percent to the samples found on all the victims. I need to know where this medical equipment comes from."

The doctor paused to think, and then said, "I assume this equipment is in all hospitals. But in the case of the bunker's operating and treatment rooms, the story is slightly different." He glanced at Yael, as if to ensure that what he was about to reveal would be acceptable to her.

"As you know, we perform secretive surgeries in the basement. The supplies run out quickly, and we need external sources for the hospital. In this case, one of my colleagues, Doctor Kamal Sharif, arranges for the supply equipment from other hospitals. Sharif works as a professional surgeon in several hospitals. With everything happening in the bunker, he, as a signatory like me on the Hippocratic Oath, does everything he can to assist the patients. He always comes to Shifa during major crisis, like now, but I have not seen him here in recent days."

Ibrahim and Yael exchanged glances. The threads started to connect rapidly.

"I met Sharif; I know him. Does he have a daughter named Nadin?" Ibrahim asked.

"He does have a daughter, but I'm not sure I remember her name," Mansour replied as he guided the patient's bed out of the operating room. More missile whistles sounded from outside.

"I understand that you both have exit permits to Israel for medical escort purposes..."

"Yes. Sharif and I accompany many patients to East Jerusalem and Jordan."

"Where can we find him?" Yael asked in Arabic.

"I have no idea. You could try calling him, but he could be in any hospital in the city now. Maybe even outside Gaza."

"Try to get hold of him on the phone, and I would appreciate it if you could provide me with his home address," Ibrahim instructed Mansour. Mansour paused for a moment, pulled his phone out of his pocket, and dialed a number, but immediately reached the voicemail. He then motioned to Yael to give him her phone. He would write Sharif's address there. Yael hesitated for a moment, but he already extended his hand and took the device. When the screen lit up, Mansour's countenance changed.

"It is in Hebrew," he said. Yael and Ibrahim exchanged glances.

"I need you to remain quiet, Doctor Mansour," Ibrahim said, placing a large hand on his shoulder. "If you dare to utter a word, you will be bidding farewell to your role in Hamas' basements rescue operation, understood?"

Dr. Mansour appeared lost for a moment but quickly complied, saying, "Understood."

"Now, please instruct your nurse to continue treating the patient while you come with us."

"But there are more..."

"It is a matter of life and death," Yael interjected.

"Especially your life or death," Ibrahim added, then pulled Dr. Mansour from his shoulders, guiding him toward the staircase.

***

They hurriedly left the hospital and dashed to the parking lot. Mansour momentarily lost his orientation, standing there and scanning all directions. A convoy of three armored vehicles sped down the road toward the hospital's parking area. Another senior figure from Hamas was en route to the bunker. Mansour quickly composed himself, gestured to Ibrahim and Yael, and they hastened to catch up with him. Their goal was to exit the parking lot before the convoy reached there.

"Give me the keys," Ibrahim demanded. Mansour hesitated for a moment, then threw his keys to Ibrahim. Ibrahim slid into the driver's seat, with Mansour and Yael following suit. He started the car, pushed down on the gas pedal with determination, and maneuvered onto the road. The convoy of vehicles raced past them and turned toward the parking lot entrance gate. They continued driving for a few more seconds, when suddenly an immense explosion rocked them violently. Yael glanced back—one of the three cars from the convoy had vanished, as though it had never existed. In its place lay a small crater in the middle of the road, where their car had been only moments ago. A colossal plume of smoke and fireball ascended into the sky. The signal to commence the military operation had been given. The countdown had begun.

***

"This man murdered seven women and kidnapped my daughter," Yael exclaimed as they drove fast in Mansour's car towards Dr. Kamal Sharif's house.

"Dr. Mansour, you are a physician, a good person. Every day you risk your life to help people in need. I need you to be with us now and help us put an end to this catastrophe," Ibrahim implored.

"Unless he is involved," Yael mocked. Dr. Mansour sat in the passenger seat, Ibrahim drove, and Yael occupied the backseat, her gun aimed at the doctor. She remained composed, confident that she would not need to use it. In any case, this was her last refuge.

"Doctor Sharif is a good man, who has faced many tragedies in his life. I find it hard to believe that he is the one who abducted and murdered so many women. There must be a justifiable reason for it..." Mansour said.

"To find out, it is crucial that we capture him as soon as possible. If it is not him, we will have to keep searching," Yael said.

"If someone stops us, I'll say that I'm taking you to another hospital in the city, that is suffering from a shortage in doctors due to the Israeli attacks." Ibrahim directed his gaze at Mansour. "Can I count on your agreement?" Mansour nodded hesitantly as Yael's phone began to ring. She retrieved it from her pocket and glanced at the screen.

"It's Professor Arieli on the line," she informed Ibrahim.

"Then you should answer it." Ibrahim suggested, and Yael answered the call on speaker so that both Ibrahim and Mansour could hear. "Professor Arieli?"

"Yael, I believe I'm onto of something important. When can you come to Abu Kabir?"

"It can't happen right now. I need you to guide me through it on the phone. Ibrahim is with me, and he can hear you as well."

"Remember that we could not figure out the substance the killer had injected into his victims? I mean, I had doubts whether it was a sedative or perhaps some kind of gas or air bubble that entered their bloodstream and caused death. I even considered water or some poison, but all the results were negative, or at least inconclusive."

"I remember."

"So, as part of my investigation, I conducted several blood tests on the victims to try and identify any poisonous substances. In one of the tests, I received peculiar results. I repeated the test multiple times, and the results were consistent each time."

"What are you talking about?" Ibrahim asked.

"I'm referring to the body of the girl, Abigail Avnun. It appears that the blood sample I took from her was composed of two distinct types of blood."

"Excuse me?" The three of them exclaimed simultaneously.

"I found that Abigail had two different blood types. One was O+ and the other was O, but I could not identify further details about it, whether it was O+ or O-. Since the two types are very similar to each other, one of them seemed to have slipped under the radar. However, after rechecking multiple times, including the blood on the syringe you found, I'm confident with a high degree of certainty. Abigail Avnun was injected with a different blood type, and that is what killed her."

Silence filled the car. Nobody spoke. Even Professor Arieli remained quiet. It seemed he understood that his words were causing shockwaves within the vehicle. After a while, he finally spoke, "If you inject someone with the wrong blood type, it can kill them." Dr. Mansour nodded in agreement.

"And what about the other women?" Yael inquired.

"I don't have further access to that information. Some of them were returned for burial in Gaza, while others were in an advanced state of decomposition. I'm working with what I have. I'll also conduct tests on tissue samples from Devora Goshen, whose body hasn't been buried yet. But I'm almost entirely sure. The killer injected these women with blood. That is why we could not find any traces of sedatives, poisons, signs of stroke. I'm telling you: the different blood type he injected into their necks—with very high certainty—is what killed them."

***

They knocked forcefully on the door of Dr. Kamal Sharif's apartment in the Rimal neighborhood, on Ameen Al-Ahusaini Street, just a few blocks away from Ibrahim's house, but no response echoed from within. The apartment was dark, and the building's residents had come out to the stairwell to see who was causing all the commotion. Compared to most buildings in Gaza, this was a luxurious apartment complex, inhabited by what seemed to be affluent individuals who were unaccustomed to street disturbances reaching their doorstep, especially not from such an odd group of people: a pretty and slender Palestinian woman, a senior member of the Hamas security apparatus, and a doctor in his work attire. Ibrahim sent them a menacing glare, and their doors closed in fear. Another knock, then another. Still, no answer.

The 50-year-old security man took a couple of steps back and delivered a forceful kick to the door. However, despite Ibrahim's athletic build, his body was not as formidable as it once was. The door resisted. He exchanged a glance with Dr. Mansour, and they both understood. Standing in front of the door, Yael positioned herself further back and began kicking it with all her strength, over and over. After numerous attempts, a creaking sound emerged from the doorframe. Ibrahim decided to employ his shoulder. He retreated to gather momentum and then lunged at the door, his right shoulder leading the way, crashing into it with determination. The door gave way and tumbled into the living room.

They stepped inside and began to explore the apartment. The place was deserted. The living room exhibited tasteful decor of Arabic furnishings and wall-to-wall carpets. The kitchen boasted solid wood fixtures, curtains adorned the windows, and there were lampshades, bookshelves, tokens of appreciation, and numerous diplomas. It was evident that the home was meticulously maintained, and its inhabitant was a prosperous individual. Everything was neatly in place, clean, and organized. A desk occupied the space by the narrow, elongated hallway, its walls adorned with oil paintings depicting Arabic landscapes and Islamic religious sites. Ibrahim approached the desk and began meticulously examining the numerous documents scattered atop it. He was not quite sure what he was searching for, perhaps a list of women's names, potential properties owned by the doctor, details about operation rooms and hospitals where he worked. If Sharif was indeed Keren's abductor and the elusive killer they were seeking, and if he had brought her to Gaza, he must have arranged a hiding place for her. If his intention was to kill her, he likely would have done so in Israel, reducing the risk of detection at a checkpoint.

"Did you find anything?" Yael inquired as she conducted an intense search in the kitchen.

"There are old family photos here," Mansour remarked, scanning a row of family pictures hung on one of the walls near the dining area, like a memorial. A low shelf with extinguished candles stood adjacent to the dining table. Yael approached it and gazed at the photographs.

"They seem like a happy family," she commented.

"They were, but the situation has changed," Mansour responded.

"What do you mean?"

"As far as I know, Kamal's wife was murdered by Hamas during the events of 2006. She was suspected of collaborating with the Fatah organization." Mansour glanced at Ibrahim, who kept on examining Sharif's documents. "Kamal's son, Rafiq," Mansour continued, "did everything he could to join Hamas but was rejected. Eventually, he managed to integrate into the Islamic Jihad movement and was killed in one of the operations against the Israeli army." This time, it was Yael who received a penetrating gaze.

"And this is Nadin?" Yael pointed to an image of a girl captured alongside her father in a different photo.

"Yes, that is his daughter," Mansour confirmed. He turned around, fixing a purposeful stare on the other two. "I really hope we are in the right place and have not barged into the home of a prominent Gaza doctor who has saved countless lives for nothing," he said, and then walked toward the bedroom hallway.

"We did not have a choice," Ibrahim replied. "Time is running out, and this is the only lead left. Plus, the man was not at home..."

"He was not at home because he is busy treating the victims you and your comrades cause every week in the fights with Israel. Someone has to clean up the mess of all the dead and wounded." Mansour walked into the bedroom hallway, leaving Yael and Ibrahim in the living room.

Ibrahim paused for a moment, took a deep breath, and tried to remind himself why he was doing what he was doing. He wanted to grab Mansour by the collar of his clothes and prove him wrong, but that could wait. Not now. He asked Yael, "What if it's not Sharif? Where do we go from here?"

"I found something," Dr. Mansour's voice echoed from one of the rooms. "Come here."

Ibrahim and Yael dropped everything they were holding and rushed toward the room. What they saw as they entered left them utterly stunned. But in that very moment, a cloud was lifted from Yael's mind, and now she was certain that Dr. Kamal Sharif was involved in the kidnapping and murders.

***

The room they entered was a meticulously equipped inpatient room. Dominating the space was a spacious operating bed designed to minimize bodily stress. Monitors were scattered about, tracking body temperature and pulse, with alert systems standing ready. An infusion pole with an automated system capable of distinguishing between various solutions stood nearby. A fridge housing medicines and infusion bags, a compact lab equipped with an array of testing kits, medical apparatus, surgical instruments, bandages, and sterilizing solutions—the room contained all the tools of a highly functional medical environment. The room was painted in stark white and illuminated by powerful LED lights. The air-conditioning hummed gently, maintaining a comfortable warmth. On one side of the room sat a small laptop, its screen black, surrounded by binders filled with documents detailing checkups, monitoring records, potential donors, and various diagnoses, all under a single name: Nadin Sharif, 21 years old.

Yael tenderly touched the bed, sensing the lingering warmth of Nadin's body. "They haven't been gone for long," she remarked, peeling back the thin blanket. Small bloodstains marred the bedsheets, as if the tubes connecting Nadin had been hurriedly disconnected. Mansour approached the bed, inspecting the infusion bag and the ongoing beeping of the monitoring system. A heavy binder was placed onto the bed next to him. "I need you to tell me what she has. I want to know where he might have taken her, them. Keren might be with them, too," Ibrahim's voice demanded. Mansour took the binder and began perusing its contents, while Yael joined him, poring over the documents in her hands.

"She has cancer," he announced after a prolonged pause. "There is a problem with her liver, she needs a transplant. This binder contains nearly 50 requests to have her treated outside Gaza. Submissions were made to Jordan, Israel, Egypt, the European Union, Doctors Without Borders, and the World Health Organization."

"Did he manage to take her out of Gaza for treatment?"

"Apparently not. Kamal faces opposition within Hamas, obstructing his efforts to secure treatment abroad for Nadin. Both Israeli and Egyptian security view her as a potential threat, refusing entry permits at the checkpoint."

"Nadin? A security threat? In her condition?" Yael voiced her surprise.

"Yes. According to the numerous requests being denied, Nadin's brother orchestrated several terrorist attacks, resulting in the deaths of Palestinians and Israelis. He was complicit in missile attacks on Israel and planted a bomb that resulted in the severe injury of an Israeli officer who lost both his legs. The Israelis fear that in her compromised state, Nadin could be manipulated into becoming a suicide bomber, detonating herself at the checkpoint. Take a look at this." Mansour handed Yael a request document, signed by Kamal Sharif, bearing a negative response with the signature of Yaakov Mizrahi. Three words in Arabic, jumped out at Yael: **Ticking time bomb.**

"So why hasn't he treated her in Gaza? I assume there are good hospitals here, potential donors, doctors coming from all over the world. And you also have your secret operation," Yael said.

"Because she has a medical condition that can't be treated within Gaza," Dr. Mansour replied.

"What does she have?"

"She has a rare blood type. Bombay blood," this time it was Ibrahim answering the question. "Isn't that right, Mansour? Sharif is the 'colleague' who left the documents I saw at your place."

Mansour fell silent and nodded slightly. "When you have Bombay blood, every simple medical procedure becomes problematic. Especially when dealing with diseases like liver cancer. She needs a transplant, but the chances of finding a matching blood type donor within Gaza are close to zero."

"Her situation is dire. He is trying to save her. That is why he was abducting them, the women. He was looking for a donor," Ibrahim stated.

"But why them?" Yael asked.

"They are young women, all of them were recently hospitalized in hospitals where he worked over the past few months. He had their profiles, knew their blood types. O. All he had to do was check which of them had Bombay blood type," Mansour explained.

"But why kill them all? I don't understand," Ibrahim interjected.

"I don't think he planned to kill them. It was an experiment, as Professor Arieli said. He found two types of blood in Abigail's body. I assume he immobilized them, then injected them with Nadin's blood and waited to see what happened. If the injection did not affect them, that was a sign he could take what he needed from them: blood units, perhaps bone marrow, maybe even organs. But for all these women, Nadin's blood was poisonous, and they died." Yael sat on the bed, scanning the scattered documents. "That is why he kidnapped Keren. He knew she had Bombay blood." She shot a significant glance at Ibrahim, who stood there, struggling to breathe.

"You conveyed this message to him, right?"

Ibrahim swallowed hard before replying, "I saw the research on that type of blood at Mansour's place. I told him I had a colleague whose daughter faced the same problem." This time it was Mansour who raised his hands in resignation. "I had no idea he would use it this way."

"He is planning to harm Keren to save his daughter. I assume she is still alive, if he is outpacing us by an hour or two. But time is running out. Doctor Mansour, where could he be?" Yael queried.

"He could be in any hospital in the city. I have already told you. Sharif works in many places."

"But not in Shifa, right?" Ibrahim asserted. "Every branch of Hamas is there. No one will allow him to enter with an Israeli girl and perform surgery on her."

"So where on earth is he?" Yael pressed.

"I have no idea," both men answered in unison.

40.

"What about tracing the phone from which they sent the message to Keren?" Yael inquired. She walked around the living room of Dr. Sharif's house, Shai on the other end of the line. "Every passing moment increases the chances that he will harm Keren. I need that information right now."

"I understand," Shai replied, and left it at that. He had no answers yet, and there was no point in explaining to Yael that it took time. She knew. This conversation was intended to relieve tension. He remained attentive, listening to the steady breaths of his sister, knowing that with each moment that passed, the risk of losing his niece grew. Skilled analysts worked around him, deciphering the code of the phone from which the message was sent. By now, he held additional vital information. The names of the owners of the suspected devices. Kamal Sharif and Nadin Sharif. One of them, apparently, was the one who sent the message to Keren's phone.

"How much longer will this take?" Yael questioned. She signaled to Ibrahim and Mansour that it was time to hit the streets and wait in the car for a message from Shai. No time could be wasted. She gathered her things, photographed every piece of information on previous hospitalizations in Gaza with her phone, and hurried down the staircase towards the street. Distant explosion sounds echoed in the background. **Couldn't Shaked grant her a few minutes of grace?** Dr. Mansour and Ibrahim followed in her footsteps. They got into the car, sat, and waited. Groups of armed youths stormed the streets, heading towards the Gaza border fence, that same old story of going to confront the Israeli army.

"At some point, I'll need to return to the hospital and support the staff," Mansour stated.

"I know," Ibrahim glanced at Yael with a questioning expression. **What do we do?**

Yael ran through every conceivable scenario in her mind. What if the situation escalated? What if she was caught? What if one of the youths stormed the car? How much could she trust Ibrahim, and how reliable was he? And what if Shai could not locate Sharif's phone?

"You are right. We need to devise an alternative strategy," she finally said. She sat on the back seat, Mansour in the driver's seat, and Ibrahim in the passenger seat. Both men turned their gaze backwards. "If we don't receive information from Shai within the next half hour, we will head towards Shifa. We will leave Mansour there, and you will drive me back to the border," she stated.

"What about Keren? This move could be a death sentence for her," Ibrahim stated.

"I can't help her in this current condition. All the cards are against me. I'll have to pressure Sharif in a way so he will be forced to release her, or he will pay a very high a price."

"Sharif has nothing to lose," Mansour said.

"But he has something to gain. If Nadin undergoes treatment in Israel, her survival chances will increase, and that is something I can vouch for him." Yael looked out. Three youths, around 15 years old, passed by the car and glanced inside. She hid her face under the veil.

"It is a shame you did not think of this earlier, before dismissing all of his requests for help," Mansour remarked.

"See for yourself. A 'ticking time bomb.' I think his actions are quite consistent with that definition, considering the fact that he has murdered quite a few women."

"What would you have done if you were in his place?" This time, Ibrahim posed the question. Yael fell silent. Nadin was the last remaining person in Sharif's family. As a woman who had lost her husband and nearly lost her daughter, what would she have done if she were in his position? Would she kill to save her daughter? There must be an alternative solution, but Sharif had exhausted all options. She realized she was biting her nails. The anticipation was agonizing. **What is happening with Shai? Why is it taking him so long?** Gunshots echoed not too far from their location. It was not a safe time to be wandering the streets of Gaza. Then, a more intense explosion resonated, also in close proximity to where they were parked. Yael cracked the car window open slightly, letting the cold air stream in. She glanced at her phone's clock once more. Time seemed to crawl, minute by minute. They had been in the car for 25 minutes. Mansour started the engine and turned on the heater. Yael had not realized how cold she had become. Her lips were tinged blue, and her hands trembled. She wrapped herself tighter in her thin black dress, blowing warm air onto her palms.

"Go," she instructed Mansour.

"Where?" he asked in surprise.

"To Shifa. We are finished here."

"Yael," Ibrahim interjected.

"I know. It's alright," she replied.

Mansour shifted into first gear and started driving toward Shifa Hospital. "I'll leave you my car," he offered. "Thank you." The warmth from the heater spread through the car, causing Yael's heart to race. Three more missiles streaked overhead, en route to Israel. The counterattack would be coming soon. **Time had run out**, she thought in her heart, and tears welled up in her eyes. She slowly realized that she might never see her daughter again. The circle had closed. Naif Badir, who could not end Keren's life, had merely postponed her grim fate by a few years. She had been granted a few years of reprieve, and she had foolishly spent them grieving her husband instead of focusing on her living children. She would never forgive herself for that. But then her phone rang, jolting her from her thoughts. On the other end of the line was Shai Nachmani.

***

"They are at the Indonesian Hospital in Jabalya," Shai said. "General Beit Lahiya Street in the northeastern part of the neighborhood, less than twenty minutes' drive from Erez Checkpoint."

"That is the closest hospital to the combat zone between Hamas and Israel along the border. All the wounded and killed from the Beit Hanoun area are taken there directly. It is right on the front lines," Mansour explained.

"Head there," Yael commanded.

"It is life-threatening to go to that location. Missiles are flying, gunfire. We are in an unprotected vehicle, not even an ambulance. They might shoot us down by mistake," Mansour warned.

"You are a doctor. You can do your job with greater..." Ibrahim tried to soothe, but Mansour interrupted him:

"What good would it do if I die?"

"Shai, I need you to talk to Shaked. We need ten minutes of peace to get there."

"I'll do what I can," Nachmani replied.

"Thank you."

"Take care of yourself." He disconnected before she could respond.

"I'm getting out in Shifa. Take the car and continue without me," Mansour declared. "You don't need me."

"If something happens to Keren, I'll need your help. I don't know what state she is in."

"I'm sorry, I can't assist you." Mansour slowed the car, turning onto Ibn Sina Street. Yael placed her hand on his shoulder. "Doctor Mansour, I'm begging you. I can't lose her too." He halted the car. Ibrahim and Yael stared at him. He rested his head against the steering wheel and clenched his eyes shut. More shots were heard. He pounded his hands against the wheel repeatedly. He cursed in Arabic, baring his teeth. Finally, he started the engine again and pressed on the gas. The car lurched back onto the road and headed east. A few kilometers later, he turned left, northward, onto Salah Al-Deen Street until he reached the Jabalya neighborhood. He veered west onto General Beit Lahiya Street. The sounds of explosions were now distinct. Israeli fighter jets repeatedly flew overhead at low altitudes. Occasionally, a plume of black smoke rose from one of the nearby streets. Salvo after salvo of gunfire erupted from the east, and the thick black smoke of burning tires filled the evening air. The cacophony of battle echoed, punctuated by the cries of the wounded and the wailing of ambulance sirens. Increasing numbers of armed young Palestinians from various terrorist organizations within Gaza advanced toward the border, firing at whatever was in their path. From slings to missiles, mortar shells to light weapons, the confrontation escalated and intensified.

***

The hospital's architecture was an octagon shape with its Jerusalem stone façade. Arched gates and triangular embellishments adorned the windows, creating an appearance more akin to a mosque than a hospital. The roads and parking lots encircling the structure teemed with rescue vehicles and ambulances, providing visible testament to the unfolding events within its walls. As they parked on the crowded main street, Yael, Ibrahim, and Mansour were faced with grim scenes that were all too familiar to the latter two. However, for Yael, this was her first exposure to such distressing sights. She shrouded her face with a veil and clutched onto Ibrahim's hand for reassurance. Mansour hurried ahead, and they followed his lead. Dressed in a white robe, he approached the hospital's entrance, brandishing his doctor's ID. Two armed guards halted their progress. Mansour spoke firmly:

"I'm Doctor Mansour El-Qasem from Shifa Hospital. I have come to offer assistance." He looked to Ibrahim and continued, "This is Major General Ibrahim Azberga, a high-ranking member of Hamas' defense network," Ibrahim interjected, "And a messenger of Aziz Shafiki."

"And this is Neri Azberga-Talia'a, Ibrahim's sister, who is a nurse in the hospital in Rafah. I asked her to help me." Ibrahim presented his police ID. The armed men scrutinized their identification documents and motioned for them to proceed.

Rushing inside, Mansour turned to Yael and spoke in Arabic,

"We need to get you into a nurse's uniform. It'll make you less conspicuous." Yael concurred, and in moments, Mansour had borrowed a nurse's uniform from the nurses and passed it to Yael so she could wear them. Concurrently, he inquired, "I'm looking for Doctor Kamal Sharif. I was informed he is here. He is a colleague and requested my assistance for an urgent surgery." The nurses exchanged glances as if harboring a secret. "I'll call him," one of them stated.

"No need to disturb him. Just guide us to the operating rooms," Ibrahim intervened.

"There are two rooms on the third floor, and another in the basement reserved for emergency cases. I'm not sure where he took the injured women," one nurse explained.

"Injured women?" Ibrahim asked.

"Doctor Sharif arrived with two injured women who were hurt by a Grad missile explosion nearby." Yael had joined the conversation, veiled and now dressed in a nurse's attire, she handed her bag to Ibrahim.

"The basement!" Ibrahim exclaimed. "How do we get to the basement?" The nurse pointed to the elevators near the staircase. The trio began sprinting towards the stairs, unaware of the commotion they were causing or the attention they drew from the two armed guards stationed at the entrance. One of them slightly adjusted his AK-47 Kalashnikova rifle, pulled out his phone, and dialed a number. A few seconds later, as he received a response, he moved his head to the side, covered his face with his hands, and whispered a few words. By the time he hung up, Yael, Ibrahim, and Mansour had already vanished from sight, and their place was taken by three young, injured Palestinians entering the emergency room, occupying his thoughts.

***

Having ascended the staircase, they entered a hallway illuminated by fluorescent lights. At its end, a glass door beckoned, leading to another corridor that led to a small operating room. They rushed forward, bursting into the room. What lay before Yael was chilling. In the room's center were two operating beds, each occupied by a girl draped in a green sheet, connected to monitors tracking heart rate, blood pressure, and infusion tubes. Two individuals stood present. The first was Dr. Kamal Sharif, garbed in surgical attire with a mask covering his face and glasses on his eyes. Gloved and wielding surgical instruments, he was bent over one of the beds, meticulously making incisions into a girl anesthetized and intubated. It was Keren Lavie. Beside the other bed knelt a nurse from the hospital, preparing the second patient for surgery. Like the first, she was under anesthesia and intubated, her abdomen exposed from beneath the green sheet.

"Stop!" Yael screamed. "What are you doing?"

The doctor glanced at her, and though she moved closer rapidly, he managed to set aside his surgical tools and extract an M1911 pistol from his belt. Loading it, he trained it on her. Dr. Mansour swiftly placed himself between Yael and the doctor's firearm, while Ibrahim approached the bed where Nadin lay, waiting.

"Doctor Sharif," Mansour began, "You must lower that gun. You are a doctor, not a killer."

"That is not an option," Sharif retorted. "Get out of here if you want to live, and let me finish my work."

"I can't stand by while you kill an innocent girl, even to save Nadin," Ibrahim intervened, now the gun aimed at him.

"Spare me your clichés. This is not an American movie. There are no clear-cut heroes and villains here. I don't care what you think. Nadin is the last thread keeping me alive, so leave now. I promise to do everything in my power to keep Keren alive. I don't want to kill her."

"Keren is all I have left of my family. My husband was killed in a terrorist attack," Yael declared. Sharif regarded her and swiftly aimed his gun at Keren's shoulder, firing a single shot. The nurse recoiled and crumpled to the floor from the explosion's impact. Everyone presents in the room held their ears. The bullet had grazed Keren's shoulder. Utilizing the shock's diversion, Ibrahim retrieved his own gun, aiming it at Dr. Sharif, and commanded him, "Drop the g—" Ibrahim's words were cut off abruptly as Sharif turned his gun towards him, discharging a bullet that struck him squarely in the chest. Ibrahim fought to react, squeezing the trigger repeatedly, but his gun was not cocked and the safety latch locked. Clutching his chest, he struggled for breath and began coughing up blood. Moments later, he collapsed to the floor, writhing and convulsing, as the gun he was holding fell from his hands and slid beneath Nadin's bed.

"Stay put!" Sharif roared upon seeing Yael and Mansour moving toward Ibrahim. "The next shot will be in the girl's head." Helpless, Yael and Mansour raised their hands in surrender.

"I must complete what I started. If you are unwilling to help me, then take her mother and Ibrahim and leave before I'm forced to neutralize you too." His gun was now pointed at Mansour's forehead.

"Are you going to kill me as well?"

"Understand this, Mansour," Sharif began. "I know my life ends here. I won't leave this room. But I need to hold onto hope for my daughter. Do you grasp that? I have nothing to lose."

"There must be another way," Mansour pleaded.

"I don't have time for this debate now. There are no other ways. We are trapped in Gaza. We don't have the luxuries they enjoy there," he gestured to Yael with his gun. "This is her last chance to win her life back. If I don't complete this surgery, she will die. There is a certain level of fairness in this." Another garbled sound escaped Ibrahim. Dr. Mansour cast his gaze downward.

"If you wish to help him, you are welcome to do so. Just leave the operating room. Take him away and tend to him. Let me finish my work." Slowly, Yael and Mansour lowered their hands and carefully approached Ibrahim, who lay on the ground with a growing pool of blood around him. "Grab him here," Mansour said, indicating Yael to the spot where the bullet had struck. As he gathered surgical tools—scissors, scalpel, and bandages—he positioned Yael to put her hand under Ibrahim's chest. "We need to stop his bleeding," he said, rolling Ibrahim onto his side.

"Take him out!" Sharif screamed.

"If we move him, he will die!" Mansour yelled back.

"I don't care. If you don't get him out of here now, you are next. Is that clear?" Dr. Mansour ignored Sharif's threats and attempted to staunch the wound gaping in Ibrahim's chest.

"We have no choice," he stated. "I must operate on him. Help me." Shoving his finger to stem the blood flow, he placed surgical instruments on Ibrahim's body and began pulling him from the operating room. Yael gripped Ibrahim's legs and pushed him forward. As they passed Keren and Nadin's beds, the nurse was back on her feet, looking bewildered. Yael winked at her, then seized the scalpel Mansour had placed on Ibrahim's body. Springing to her feet, she positioned the scalpel by Nadin's neck, while she remained crouched behind her bed, her head peering at Sharif, near his daughter's head. Mansour sat on the floor, recognizing that every passing second diminished Ibrahim's chances of survival. He started working frantically to stop the bleeding. If he were to tally the number of young lives he had saved from gunshot wounds on the battlefield, it would likely exceed a few dozen. But many had not survived under his care, and Ibrahim's condition was dire. The bullet had passed dangerously adjacent to his heart. Had it nicked the aorta? Punctured a lung? It seemed likely. Ibrahim continued to cough up blood and struggled to breathe. **We must operate** Mansour thought, but he was limited by his position on the floor. He glanced toward the unfolding confrontation between Yael and Sharif. Sharif's gun was aimed at Yael, but realizing he could not shoot without endangering hitting his own daughter's head, he redirected his aim to Keren's head.

"If you harm her, Nadin dies," Yael warned. "I have nothing left to lose either."

Yael noticed Keren's monitor weakening. The girl lay with her abdomen open. Yael knew she could not remove her from this room without treatment. "If you release her, I promise to take Nadin with me to Israel for treatment. I give you my word."

"This is not a real threat. You are not a killer," Sharif retorted, desperation evident in his tone. Yael grasped the gravity of his desperation. A doctor had transformed into a killer to save his daughter's life, indicating he would not easily back down. This was a zero-sum game. Time was rapidly dwindling, and Keren's condition was deteriorating as well. Meanwhile, Ibrahim needed urgent attention, and there was a significant chance that Hamas had already discovered Yael's presence in Gaza. What would she do?

"If you lay a finger on her, I won't let Nadin survive—this I promise. The only way out of this impasse is if you lower your gun, and both these girls come with me to Israel for treatment. You stay here and save Ibrahim." A tense minute passed, followed by another. The barrel of the gun wavered between Yael's head, Keren's head, and Mansour's head. The nurse had approached Keren and begun stabilizing her. Sharif remained silent. Another minute ticked by, and the sound of gunfire echoed from outside.

Sharif lowered his gun, locked it, and placed it in the nurse's hands. "Hand it over to her," he said. Yael rose cautiously, observing every move Sharif made, ensuring he did not reach for another weapon. Sharif, however, retreated, sinking into a chair, clutching his head in his hands. "How is Ibrahim holding up?" Yael inquired, keeping the knife poised at Nadin's throat.

"I can't stabilize him," Mansour exclaimed, struggling over Ibrahim's body.

"Sharif, stand up, attend to the girls, and prepare them for transport. We will transfer them in an ambulance to Israel," Yael commanded, but Sharif remained unresponsive.

"Why did you tie them?" Yael inquired as she removed the gun from the nurse's hand and aimed it at Sharif. She advanced toward Keren's bed and glanced at her, while the nurse passed by her and knelt beside Mansour, trying to assist him.

"Tie who together?" Sharif questioned.

"The Palestinian and Israeli women. Why bury them together?"

"I wanted them to appear as victims of a nationalist assassination, to distance the killings as far from me as possible."

"And Aisha? Why did you kill her?"

"Aisha was my lover. She helped me try to save Nadin. But in the end, she threatened to expose me and the entire story. I could not let that happen."

"And Keren? How did you get her through the checkpoint?"

"I had all of Aisha's documentation. I sedated her and covered her face with bandages, hooked up to a medical ventilator. Her face was concealed. No one bothered to check who was really lying in the ambulance." Nadin's monitor started beeping, her heart rate weakening and fading. Sharif leaped to his feet but halted before the barrel of the gun now aimed at him.

"Look at me now. Do you want me to save Nadin?"

He hesitated.

"Go to her," Yael ordered. He stood motionless.

"Go to her!"

"You don't understand. It's over. She won't survive another trip; she's too weak." Nadin's monitor fell silent. A straight line appeared on the device's screen. Sharif lunged toward the bed. The nurse had already begun the resuscitation process, but Sharif stopped her and pushed her aside. He knelt beside Nadin's bed and embraced his daughter. The monitor continued beeping, a prolonged tone. Sharif broke into tears, Nadin's lifeless body slipping from his desperate grasp. He kissed her forehead and gently placed the dead body on the bed. He gazed around desperately, then lunged toward Yael, who was taken by surprise and could not prepare in time. He grabbed the gun from her hand with force, and though she struggled, he was a thousand times stronger. With one hand, he seized the gun's barrel and pushed into his mouth. With the other hand, he grasped Yael's finger, which was pressed against the trigger guard. He opened the latch and pulled Yael's finger twice. Two shots rang out, both directed straight into his head. His body collapsed onto the operating room floor, lifeless, amidst the echoes of the nurse's screams. Yael recoiled from the gun. Her face was splattered with blood. It took her a few seconds, but when she noticed Keren, she immediately took action.

"Nurse," she called urgently. "Come quickly, help me. I need you to treat Keren."

"She needs stitches," Mansour explained, still engrossed in his efforts to save Ibrahim.

"I'll take care of that," the nurse assured, immediately tending to Keren. She began stitching up Sharif's incisions, disinfecting and skillfully bandaging the wounds. Afterward, she disconnected Keren's monitor and left the infusion bag in place. Taking measures to prevent shock, she covered Keren's body and administered steroids and stimulants to sustain her heartbeat. Yael, fatigued but determined, collapsed by Ibrahim and Mansour. While Mansour focused on stemming the bleeding from Ibrahim's blood vessels in this makeshift operation, Yael set up an infusion of anesthetics through Ibrahim's hand and meticulously wiped away his blood. Ibrahim had lost a significant amount of blood, and Yael was acutely aware that sourcing the appropriate fluids in this situation was challenging. She tenderly stroked his head, her touch a blend of comfort and care.

***

"Yael, you must escape from here," Ibrahim whispered. His breaths came laboriously, blood trickling from his lips and nose, dried blood staining his cheeks. His head rested on Yael's thigh, her hand pressed against the wound that gaped in his chest.

"It is okay," she soothed him and cast a glance toward Mansour, who was busy preparing her daughter for the journey ahead.

"Shafiki is probably on his way here," Ibrahim rasped. "He will use you out as a bargaining chip."

"Shh, don't worry. It will be okay," she reassured him and pressed her finger against the spot on his chest that Mansour had directed for her. Ibrahim's blood-stained body convulsed in pain. He was about to go into shock. "Mansour will take care of you once we leave. You will be okay."

"The armed men downstairs... at the entrance. They must have contacted him. He is on his way here, I'm sure of it." Yael fell silent now.

"Take Keren on the bed, wait by the elevator. Give me the gun. When they arrive, I'll delay them, and you'll be able to..."

"...There's no need," Yael cut him off. The nurse was now finishing up the last stitches and bandaging on Keren. "Mansour," Yael said. "I need you to finish."

"You must escape," Ibrahim now gripped Yael's hand, fighting through the pain. She leaned back slightly, her lips close to his ear.

"He is with us," she whispered in a voice swallowed by the hum of the hospital room and the echoes of gunfire outside.

"Who?" Ibrahim asked.

"Shafiki. He is with us. He is our agent. It is okay."

"I don't understand," Ibrahim whispered. His lips trembled, his eyes opened wide, his grip loosened slightly.

"We recruited him a year ago. He wants us to get him out of the organization. We waited for the right opportunity, and now it is here. The tragic circumstances aligned—Malak's murder. She visited Ramin to lay the groundwork for the family's transition there. But her murder set everything in motion. Shafiki recruited you to help us stitch up the murder and not raise suspicion from Hamas. But we asked something big from him. We asked for the head of Ismail Bader."

"I don't understand," Ibrahim's breath grew weaker.

"The explosion at the entrance to Shifa, just a few hours ago? Israel took down Bader. A few minutes before that, Shafiki had a phone call with him. It helped us locate and confirm that it was indeed Bader. Shafiki is coming back with me to Israel today. The whole story is over." Ibrahim closed his eyes. A single tear escaped from his eye.

"I'm done," the nurse said.

"Will you manage from here on your own?" Yael asked Mansour. Mansour nodded. Yael stood up, signaled to the nurse, and the two of them began pushing Keren's bed toward the hallway by the elevators. Yael tucked the gun into the waistband of her pants, hidden beneath her nurse's uniform. She wiped her face from the blood spray. A soft beep announced the arrival of the elevator, and its doors slid open. Aziz Shafiki appeared before them, accompanied by the two armed men who had been waiting at the hospital entrance. His gaze first fell on Keren's bed, then on Yael, and finally, he gestured with his head to the armed men. They lunged at Yael and the nurse, knocking them to the hospital floor, and wrested the gun from Yael's waistband. Aziz Shafiki put his knee on Yael's back and forced her down onto the floor, in front of Ibrahim's fading gaze. Desperately, Ibrahim struggled to find his gun that had slipped away from him in the commotion.

41.

"Where is Ibrahim?" Shafiki asked. Yael lay on her back, her hands tied, as Shafiki loomed over her.

"He is in the operating room. Sharif shot him near the heart. There is still a chance to save him."

"And Sharif? What happened to him?"

"He committed suicide," Yael said, swallowing hard. "Mansour will update you."

"And Nadine?" Yael shook her head in a negative gesture.

"You left me a room full of bodies."

"The question is whether that is enough for you or if you need a longer list of accomplishments."

Shafiki raised an eyebrow in response to Yael's question.

"Does Ibrahim know?" Shafiki asked.

"Yes," she whispered. He got up, entered the operating room, and looked at Ibrahim lying on the floor, breathing weakly. Mansour was still working on him. Shafiki placed his foot on the doctor and pushed him gently aside. He drew his gun and aimed it at Ibrahim's head.

"Aziz, I'm asking you. Don't do this," Yael said. Mansour stepped back a step. Shafiki glanced at Yael, then at the two armed guards, and then fired a single shot directly into Ibrahim's forehead. Yael turned her head away. She seethed with anger but understood in her heart. She had not left Shafiki any other choice.

***

At 9:06 PM, the Red Crescent ambulance pulled up at the Erez checkpoint. The checkpoint stood closed for both Israelis and Palestinians, and all were on heightened alert. A few soldiers were present along with the checkpoint's manager, Yaakov Mizrahi, and Aharon Shaked. Within three minutes, the ambulance transitioned to the Israeli side. Aziz Shafiki entered Shaked's car and disappeared. Yael never saw him again. Keren was shifted to an Israeli ambulance and taken to 'Sourasky Medical Center' in Tel Aviv. She was in a severe condition, but stable. When she arrived at the hospital she was immediately taken to the operating room. Yael remained outside. It wasn't until 1:00 AM that the doctors emerged to relay the news to Yael: Keren would recover. Yet, she would be placed in an induced coma for several days to stabilize her condition. At 5:00 AM, Shai Nachmani arrived to take Yael back to her home.

42.
Epilogue

Yael Lavie laid her resignation letter upon Uri Amit's desk a few days following her return from Gaza. Nevertheless, she lingered in doubt, unsure if her commitment to resign was steadfast. In a surprising twist of fate, the harrowing ordeal of Keren's abduction, the audacious rescue operation, and the profound blow inflicted upon the core of the Hamas terrorist organization had reignited her inner fortitude and determination. She now stood impervious to any challenge that might cross her path. She had decided that she wanted to avoid being exposed to violence. After persistent persuasions, she agreed to remain in her unit as an analyst, instead of working directly with terrorism. In 2016, Yael's brother, Shai Nachmani, received an invitation from the Minister of Defense to establish the `Israeli National Cyber Directorate`. His subsequent resignation from the ISA created an opportunity for Yael to join the organization. Two years later, she commenced her work with the ISA, in the Arab unit. Aharon Shaked, the head of the ISA, was instrumental in encouraging her to take up this role, though Dina and Keren did not share the same enthusiasm. But, neither mother nor daughter understood the true reason Yael chose to continue her service, following in her brother's footsteps within the realm of security and defense.

Three months after Keren returned home, Colonel Yonatan Uziel contacted Yael, summoning her to the territorial brigade of Samaria. When she inquired about the purpose, he offered no explanation. She deliberated for a while before setting a date.

On June 10th, 2015, she passed through the gates of the base. At the entrance, he welcomed her and led her to his office. As she opened the door, Yael's face illuminated with surprise. Seated in modest army chairs were two women and a man. One was Ibrahim's mother, the second was Neri—his sister. The third, a man holding Neri's hand, introduced himself as her husband. Yael's arrival prompted Ibrahim's mother to rise from her seat. Yael braced herself for the worst. Neri and her husband also stood. The mother approached Yael, locked eyes with her, and enveloped her in a warm embrace, her ample frame encircling Yael's slender form. Yael found herself unable to restrain her tears.

"Thank you," the mother said. "Thank you for giving him a reason to live."

"Ibrahim had lost his way. Haunted by the choices he had made, he lived for years feeling like a complete failure. When he learned he would be working alongside you, a true hero who endured the loss of her husband in a terrorist attack, and yet steadfastly believed in coexistence, he found hope. Just as you wished to bridge the gap between us, he saw you as a symbol. We wanted you to know this." Neri stepped forward and embraced Yael as well.

"You are an exceptional woman, kind and intelligent. People like you are our ray of hope—always remember that, dear," the mother spoke with warmth.

They sat there a while longer, exchanging parting words and promising to keep in touch.

"Ma'am," Yael said. Ibrahim's mother turned back, a smile gracing her face. "I apologize, but I don't know your name."

"Miriam," the woman replied. In due course, Yael learned that this name held significance in both the Quran and the Bible, representing one of the righteous women in heaven.

The End